Marked

A NOVEL BY

JEANNE HARDT

Gina –
Thank you for
sharing Cora's journey!
So glad we met!

Jean Hardt

Prologue

"I'm keeping her." The words fell from her lips with an icy edge he'd heard before.

Though he never told her *no*, he had to speak his mind. "She's not yours. She's bound to be missed."

Her head turned sharply, her dark eyes pierced him. "No one will miss her. He hasn't even bothered to see her."

The coldness in her eyes melted as she gazed at the tiny infant cradled in her arms. Displaying the love of a genuine mother, she took her finger and stroked the child's cheek. "My baby," she rasped, then kissed her sweetly.

He shook his head. They were playing a dangerous game, but his wife always won. As he watched her with the little girl, his heart softened. Perhaps she was right; no one would miss her.

Another babe cried from the corner of the room. With compassion, he lifted her into his arms, trying to soothe her. *Such a sweet little face ...*

"How did you choose?" He had to know.

She laughed. "It wasn't difficult. I chose the unmarked one, of course."

A shiver ran down his spine. There was something about her laughter that unnerved him. "Of course," he repeated, then carried the tiny baby out the door and into the cold night.

Chapter 1

"Mrs. Moss!" Cora cried out, running bare-foot across the muddy shore. The rain had finally let up and she couldn't wait to share the news. Her long, dusty-blond hair was plastered to her head; wet and dirty. Strands of her straight locks stuck to her cheeks.

Her dress looked even worse than her hair. Though she'd tried to hold it up with one hand as she ran, it drooped in the back and drug through the mud. Even her bloomers underneath were covered, having been spattered as her heels kicked back.

"Mrs. Moss!" she cried out again and opened the door to the tiny one-room cabin. The hinges creaked as she pushed it wide.

"What is it, child?"

Mrs. Moss was where she always was—at her pot-bellied stove making tea. How was she able to keep herself so neat and clean? Her blue cotton dress was pressed and crisp, the white apron covering it didn't have a single stain, and her hair never had even one strand out of place. Always atop her head in a neat little bun. Even though she was elderly, she stood upright. More so than Cora.

She looked down at her own filthy garment and prepared for a scolding. But even when Mrs. Moss fussed, it sounded like a poem. Her English ancestry hung on every word. Cora tried to imitate her, but the attempt was useless. Her pa was a much stronger influence on her vocabulary.

"Steamboat's aground," Cora said, while remaining in the doorway. The last thing she wanted to do was tromp across the clean-swept wood floor.

Mrs. Moss finally looked at her and shook her head. "You need a bath."

Cora pushed a strand of hair from her face and a trickle of water ran down her arm. "I got one." She grinned, but it did no good.

Mrs. Moss was not amused. She pursed her lips, then frowned. "Dirtiest bath I've ever seen."

"Dang, Mrs. Moss! Don't you wanna see the steamboat?" Cora's hand immediately covered her mouth. This was worse than mud.

"Cora Craighead!" Mrs. Moss shook her finger, scolding as she'd done for as long as she could remember. "I'll not have you cursing. You're seventeen years old and you should be acting like a lady. Ladies do not curse."

Before she could apologize, Mrs. Moss's yellow tabby, Muffin, darted through her legs and hopped onto a chair at the small wooden table near the stove. Muddy paw prints followed her.

Mrs. Moss placed her hands on her hips. "Well, Cora, you might as well come in. Perhaps you'll help me clean my floors after."

She'd gladly help Mrs. Moss do anything. Though the woman fussed, she was the only ma she'd ever known. Her own had died birthing her.

She took a seat at the table and Mrs. Moss set a cup of hot tea in front of her, then nodded for her to drink. For years, Mrs. Moss had instructed her on the proper way to hold the cup and sip like a lady. Some of her lessons had stuck.

"Sorry for cursin', Mrs. Moss. But when I get all excited, I can't help myself."

"Then don't become quite so excited. Ladies remain calm in all circumstances."

"I don't know why you think you hafta make me into a lady." She sipped her tea, then looked down at her bedraggled dress. She wasn't anything like Mrs. Moss, but why should it matter? "I like the way I am."

"I like the way you are as well, but I can polish you. One day, I hope to see you married. Under all that mud is a beautiful young woman." Mrs. Moss winked at her, then filled her own teacup.

"Married?" She let out a laugh. "I'm too young. I don't wanna get married."

"Nonsense. Every girl wants to get married. It will be a way for you to leave here. Much better than traveling on one of those steamboats. I don't know what you see in them. Blasting their plumes of black smoke into the sky. And the noise! I can scarcely tolerate them from here."

Cora rolled her eyes. She loved the steamboats. And the one she saw today was spectacular; white and pristine with a paddle wheel that spun and beat the water, pushing it miraculously upstream. The smoke didn't bother her. It was the boat's life-blood pouring from its pillared stacks.

"I see 'em different." She set down her teacup and rested her chin in her hand, leaning on the table. "One day I aim to go on one. I wanna know what's upriver."

"More water. Trees. And more people making a fuss about the boats. You'll be disappointed. And besides ..." Mrs. Moss took a seat and sighed. "Your father squanders what little money he has whenever one of them docks. Money he should be spending on you."

Yes, her pa gambled, but at least he was good at it. Most of the time. He was a capable cheat. "He says he's gonna make enough money so we can go to California and find gold. Then we'll be rich."

"Money isn't everything, Cora. Your father should realize that *you* are his finest gem."

She smiled at the sweet old woman, who one minute could be a hard disciplinarian and the next, a loving ma. "But goin' on them boats is all I dream about."

Cora stroked Muffin's head, then noticed that even her arms were mud-covered. "I reckon you don't want me to read today, bein' I'm so dirty." She nodded to the enormous Bible sitting at the center of the table. Mrs. Moss used it to teach her to read. It was the only book remaining in her possession and one she cherished, claiming it was the only book needed in life.

"No, not today. But come back tomorrow. My eyesight is getting worse and I enjoy hearing my favorite passages."

"I will. But I best be gettin' home now so I can have me a bath before Pa comes in."

"That's a fine idea, my dear." She cradled her hand against Cora's cheek. "I may be harsh with you, but you know I love you. You're like my own child."

"I love you, too. And I'll try to do better. Need me to help you with the floors?"

"No, you go on. And if your father comes home smelling of whiskey, you take care. I worry about you."

Cora stood, then approached Mrs. Moss to give her a hug, but stopped when she remembered she was wet and dirty. Mrs. Moss chuckled and patted her hand.

The rain came down even harder than before as Cora stepped off Mrs. Moss's front porch stoop. She didn't even try to lift her dress this time. There was no sense in it. Once she got home, she'd have a good bath, then wait for her pa. Maybe with luck—and a little sleight of hands —he'd bring home enough money to buy her a new dress.

* * *

Cora knelt down in the old wood shed and used her hand to sweep away the cobwebs from the metal bathing tub. She grunted as she drug it to the house. Since hauling and heating water was such an unwelcome chore, most of their bathing was done in the river.

Their tiny cabin was similar to Mrs. Moss's, with the exception of two beds instead of one. Most of the cabins on the river were alike. Occupied by poor folks just trying to get by. Since they had few possessions, there was plenty of room for the tub.

Bucket by bucket, she pumped water from the well behind their house. Part of it was heated in pots on the stove; the rest was poured directly into the tub. Once the water on the stove began to boil, she added it to the tub and created a desirable, temperate bath.

From a small shelf next to her bed, she removed a little box filled with crushed, dried flowers. Sprinkling them into the steaming water, she smiled. The sweet aroma was far better than that of the muddy Mississippi.

Though she didn't expect her pa before sundown, she bolted the front door of their little cabin before removing her clothes. Then, she slid into the water. Her eyes closed as she basked in the warmth.

Using lye soap, she scrubbed her body clean. As her hands moved across her skin, she thought about everything Mrs. Moss had said.

No man would wanna marry me.

She'd never been happy with her appearance. Having little to eat, it was difficult to gain weight. Though her body had transformed into a woman, she had very small breasts. She had a curved waist, and a very pronounced bottom, but from the waist up she could easily be mistaken for a boy. So, she intentionally let her hair fly freely, to avoid misconceptions.

Then of course, there was that *other* thing ...

The water began to cool, so she washed her hair as fast as she could and got out of the tub. Her stomach grumbled. Maybe one of the hens had laid and she could at least fry an egg or two.

She dried off and put on her only other dress. It was blue—simple cotton—nothing fancy. Her pa claimed it was all she needed.

"Cora!"

She jumped at the pounding on the door. "Comin', Pa!"

As quick as she could, she lifted the wooden slat and unbolted the door. The moment she opened it, she caught a whiff of whiskey and sighed. Though she'd become used to his drinking, she didn't like it. When he was sober, Clyde Craighead was kind and giving. Alcohol turned him into a stranger.

"We're rich, Cora!" From behind his back, he produced a chicken, dangling by its feet. In his other hand was a bottle of whiskey. A loud belch wafted the nasty scent of alcohol across her face as he teetered and nearly fell.

"Pa, you better sit down." She grabbed the bird from his hand and guided him to a chair.

His eyebrows danced and he stared at her as though trying to focus. He pointed at the chicken. "Fix me some supper!" His words were slurred, but stern, and he followed them with a scowl, making him ugly. She'd been told that when he was young, he wasn't bad looking. But after her ma died, he'd aged quickly and looked much older than his thirty-seven years. What little hair he had left was gray and he had deep wrinkles around his eyes. His wide nostrils were hidden by a thick mustache and his beard was unkempt and rough.

She dutifully took the bird outside to pluck and clean. When she returned, he was laying on his bed with the bottle of whiskey still clutched in his fist. He looked in her direction, then sat up and tipped the bottle in the air, taking another swig.

"It won't take me long to cook this," she said, trying to hide her disapproval. "You need to eat, Pa."

She set the chicken on a large cutting board and cut it into pieces while the lard in her heavy skillet heated. She seasoned the meat with salt and pepper and placed it into the sizzling fat.

Her pa raised the bottle, saluting her. "You're a good girl, Cora. A might fine cook!" Again, he belched, this time even louder than before.

"Where'd you get the chicken, Pa? I know it ain't one a ours."

"Bought it. With real money." He grinned, obviously proud of himself. At least it was better than the scowl.

She poked a fork into a large breast and flipped it over. "So, you won, huh, Pa?"

"I took 'em for all I could." He pushed himself upright on the bed. His eyes were half-shut as his head bobbed from side-to-side. "I showed *Captain* O'Brien who has more sense."

"Captain *O'Brien*?"

"Yep. Steamboat's the *Bonny Lass*," he grumbled. "Damn Irish are pilotin' boats now."

She ground her foot into the floor, building up courage. "Pa, Mrs. Moss said that Scots and Irish ended their warrin' long time 'go. Most folks 'round here can't tell the difference 'tween us."

He shook his finger at her. "Never forget you're a Scot! A full-blooded Scot! Your ma ..."

"Pa, I won't forget." She kissed his cheek, then returned to the stove.

Wavering, he stood and pulled a chair up to their kitchen table. After setting the whiskey bottle within reach, he laid his head down, resting it against his bent arms, and closed his eyes. "I shouldn't a had so much to drink."

She held back the words she wanted to say. Chastising him would do no good. She'd tried it before and it only seemed to make matters worse. "Coffee will help, Pa."

How different would their lives be, had her ma lived? Her pa told her that she favored her ma, and that she was beautiful. Of course, she wondered how she could be anything like her; she saw no beauty in the mirror.

She set a cup of coffee in front of him. He lifted his head to take a drink. When she attempted to remove the alcohol from the table, his scowl returned, so she let it be.

"You said we got money now, Pa?" Her heart fluttered at the thought.

"Yep! We got money. And t'morra we'll have even more." He tried to stand, but wobbled and plopped back down again.

"You're goin' back?" This wasn't a good idea. Money made at gambling was just as easily lost.

"Course I am. O'Brien has more to lose. I'll drain 'im dry. Win my own war against the Irish."

"Why don't you settle for what you got? I—I don't want you to lose it, Pa."

"I ain't gonna lose it. I know what I'm doin'." He tilted the bottle and emptied it. Then he grunted and cast it aside, letting it shatter on the floor. He paid it no mind. Muttering about money, he laid his head once more against the table.

She left the stove to sweep up the broken glass. Her pa ignored her and in no time at all was snoring.

The only good thing that came out of the evening was a satisfying meal. Her pa was right; she was a very good cook.

Chapter 2

When Cora rose the next morning, her pa was already gone. She'd hoped that if he slept off his drunkenness, his common sense would return and he wouldn't make a costly mistake. Though he never indicated how much money he'd won, she'd never seen him so happy about his winnings.

Holding fast to her dreams of a new dress, she threw on her old one and went outside to tend nature's call.

The rain had finally moved out and the sky was bright blue. She smiled, relieved that the clear skies meant the *Bonny Lass* would soon be on its way upriver. If she was lucky, her pa would still have money in his pocket.

Returning inside, she straightened the house and swept the floor again, fearing she might have missed a few shards of glass. Then she made the beds, neatly folding the top quilts at the bottom of each.

Her pa had never woken to eat any of the chicken, but she'd had no problem finishing it herself. Even so, she was hungry again and decided to check the hens for eggs.

When she went to the coop, she glanced in the direction of far-off laughter. Two young colored boys were chasing each other up the shore. She hoped they'd not run away from their masters—maybe they'd been allowed time to play. Some masters could be brutal when crossed. Slavery was taken for granted in the south, but the thought of being owned by someone else disturbed her.

It just ain't right ...

Sometimes she wished there were other girls close by. She longed for a friend. Most girls her age were already married and lived nowhere near the shore. It was a place reserved for poor fisherman, widows, and her pa—a gambling woodcarver.

Before she was born, her folks had moved to Plum Point because of the plentiful wood. Her pa could carve anything. Carving calmed him, but when he drank, he wouldn't touch a knife. She saw that as a good thing.

She made up her mind that once she finished her chores, she'd pay Mrs. Moss another visit and do the reading she'd promised.

There was a small amount of flour remaining from her pa's last trip to the mercantile, so she decided to bake bread and hoped that when he came home he'd give her some of the money he'd won to purchase more provisions. She was tired of being hungry.

She had just pulled the loaf of bread from the oven when the door opened and her pa stepped through.

"Pa? I didn't think you'd be home so soon," she said, setting the bread pan on the table. He was carrying a large brown-paper-wrapped package and she was instantly curious.

He looked over his shoulder, then quickly closed the door. Forcing a smile, he moved toward her and kissed her on the cheek.

She drew back. "Pa? What was that for?"

He unbuttoned the top button on his shirt, then ran his hand over the top of his head. "I love ya, Cora. You know that, right?" He extended the package to her. "I got this for ya. Can you forgive me for actin' so poorly last night?"

"Course I can, Pa." All he had to do was ask. She always forgave him.

Without a moment's hesitation, she untied the string and opened the paper. "Oh, Pa ..." she gasped, staring at the silk fabric.

Her rough skin made a light scratching sound as she ran her hand over the material. The dress was red, trimmed in delicate white lace. The skirt was full and layered, unlike anything she'd ever seen. Noticing the wide, scooped neckline, she was certain it would be the type of dress that sat off her shoulders and exposed her neck. Her everyday dresses were much more modest.

Her heart raced. "Pa! It's beautiful! You *did* win big, didn't ya?"

He scratched his head, then crossed to the table. A pitcher of water sat next to the freshly-baked bread. He poured a glass and drank it down. "I want you to come with me to the boat. You need to fix yourself up. I want you to look nice."

She was speechless. All of her dreams were finally coming true.

"I'll step outside so you can change," he said and walked away.

She couldn't wait to tell Mrs. Moss, knowing full well that she'd been wrong about the steamboat. There were so many wonderful things she was about to see.

Quickly, she removed her worn out garment. As she lifted the shiny red dress over her head, her heart continued to thump. Her pa had done a fine job selecting it. It fit her perfectly. But where did he get it? There was nothing like it at their mercantile.

Sitting on the edge of her bed, she took a brush and groomed her long hair. Good thing she'd just washed it. She fumbled through an old box of trinkets and found a single satin ribbon that she tied around her hair. Pouring water into a wash basin, she scrubbed her face, then cleaned her teeth. And finally, she chewed on a mint leaf to freshen her breath. This was something Mrs. Moss had taught her and she encouraged her pa to do on a regular basis.

Twirling in a circle, she watched as the layers of fabric floated on air. She giggled with joyful anticipation. Looking down at herself, she finally felt like a woman.

Her pa rapped at the door, then opened it a crack. "Are you ready, Cora?"

Was his voice quivering? Maybe he was as excited as she was about the prospect of showing her off to his newly-found friends.

"Yes, Pa," she chimed. She glanced at the loaf of bread on the table. "Oh, Pa? Do you want some a the bread I baked 'fore we go?"

"No, Cora. I ain't hungry. I'll have some later." A pained look covered his face.

"What's wrong, Pa?" She crossed to him and placed her hand on his arm. "Don't you like the dress on me?"

"You look beautiful. You remind me of your ma."

She moved her arms around his body and held him close. "Thank you, Pa. Thank you for the dress."

"You're welcome, Cora." She could barely hear the words.

Taking his arm, she began to chatter, giddy about what was to come.

He pulled the door shut behind them and cautioned her to lift her skirt so she didn't get it dirty.

She grimaced as she looked at her worn shoes beneath the splendid dress. "Guess I need new shoes, too, Pa. Do you have enough money for 'em?"

He patted her hand and swallowed hard. "Yes, Cora. But don't worry 'bout your feet. No one will be lookin' at 'em." He turned his head and looked over his shoulder.

She followed his gaze. Trailing a short distance behind them were two gruff-looking men.

"Who are those men, Pa?" Her heart beat faster and she clutched his arm tighter.

"Men from the boat. They ..." He licked his lips and tried to smile. "They wanna make sure no one bothers ya. I told 'em how purdy you are."

Letting out a puff of air from her nose, she giggled. "Oh, Pa ... I ain't purdy."

He stopped and looked squarely into her eyes. "You're beautiful, Cora. Just like your ma. Don't you ever forget it."

"Thanks, Pa," she whispered, lowering her eyes. She looked back at the men and her stomach twisted into a knot. "I don't like the way they're lookin' at me."

He didn't respond, but encouraged her to press on down the shore.

The sun shone brightly above them and the water sparkled under its light. The Mississippi was wide at Plum Point and a bit higher than normal from all the heavy rain.

As they rounded a bend, the *Bonny Lass* appeared before her, in all its glory. Her heart leapt and she forgot about the men following behind.

"Pa! It's even better than I thought! When I saw it from afar, it was grand, but *dang*!"

Her pa stopped and scolded her with his eyes. "Cora! You're dressed like a lady. I won't have you swearin'!"

"Sorry, Pa. But—I ain't never seen nothin' like it. I can't find the right words to say how I'm feelin'."

She looked about. The boat was anchored and a long, wooden platform extended from the bow and rested on the shore. Men bustled around loading large stacks of wood.

Her pa nodded toward the sweaty men. "Them colored's is makin' sure there's enough fuel to get her to Memphis. That's where the boat's fixin' to go."

Memphis. If only she could go there, too.

The closer she got to the boat, the bigger it was. Three levels tall and longer than any steamboat she'd seen on the river. *Bonny Lass* was painted in red and black at the pinnacle of the front. The rest of the boat was sparkling white, clean, and spotless, with the exception of the paddlewheel which was brilliant red. Carved wooden rails encircled every level, and at the very top were two tall, black smokestacks.

"Why ain't there no smoke comin' out, Pa?" she asked, gazing upward.

"Soon, Cora. Once they're loaded, they'll start 'er up." He motioned again to the hard-working men. "The colored's will keep her goin'. It ain't easy, but as you can see, they're able."

She stared at their shirtless bodies. Their dark skin was covered with beads of sweat and their muscles rippled as they lifted the wood and carried it on board. One of them caught her eye and offered her a smile.

As she began to return it, her pa jerked her around to face him.

"Ignore the colored's, Cora." He held her arm firmly and led her toward the loading platform.

"Yes, Pa." She looked down at her arm. "Pa, you're hurtin' me."

Immediately, he released his grip. "I ... I'm sorry."

Why was he acting so odd? She was used to him being out of character when he drank, but he was stone sober.

"Pull your shoulders back," he said as they set foot on the platform.

She obeyed and stood upright, then raised her chin and placed her shoulders as far back as she could, just as Mrs. Moss had taught her.

"Good girl," he praised and led her onboard.

Once again, she was aware of the two men behind them. The closer they got to the boat, the closer the men got to them.

The taller of the two walked up beside her pa. "O'Brien's waitin'." He nodded up the stairs. Then his eyes shifted to her, examining her form from the top of her head down to her toes.

She looked away, uncomfortable with his gaze.

"Fine," her pa said, and gently took her arm and escorted her up the flight of stairs.

As they ascended, she took it all in. The boat lilted back and forth and the movement would take some getting used to. There was a lot of activity as men pushed by them going up and down the stairs.

He pointed to one of the men in uniform. "That man there's what's called a cabin attendant. He ain't too happy cuz some a the passengers are complainin' 'bout bein' in Plum Point so long. They want to get to Memphis. I heard 'em talkin' 'bout it." He puffed up like he was proud to know about the goings on here. And truthfully, she was proud of him for knowing it. This was the most exciting thing they'd ever done together.

"Why do some a the slaves wear uniforms, Pa?" Several had passed by her dressed as fine as the cabin attendants.

He stood even taller. "Most a the slaves are kept in the belly of the ship to keep her runnin', but some a them help in the dinin' hall servin' food. They also use 'em to clean cabins and tend passengers. Course it's only the ones they can trust."

She was about to ask him how they decided which ones were trustworthy, when he stopped her cold.

They'd arrived at the top level and stood in front of an open doorway. "Captain's cabin," he mumbled and froze. No longer full of confidence, her pa appeared edgy. His shoulders drooped and he didn't utter another sound.

The cabin had two chambers. The first held a roll-top desk with papers scattered about, several wooden chairs, and a long oak table. A map of the river lay open atop it. Large windows lined the wall on the far side, giving him a fantastic view.

As she craned her neck, she stared into the next chamber, in awe of the furnishings. A large bed, topped with a fancy quilt and decorated with embroidered pillows, centered the room. Pretty little rugs covered the floor, perfectly matching the swirled design of the quilt. Shades of blue were everywhere. Obviously his favorite color.

Captain O'Brien himself wasn't so fancy. He was shorter than her pa, twice as big around, and almost completely bald. To make up for the lack of hair on his head, he had bushy reddish-gray sideburns that came down nearly to his chin. Though he obviously shaved his face, his whiskers were scruffy. Perhaps his large jowls kept him from getting a good shave.

He looked at her, then moved his attention to her pa. "The dress fit, I see," he said with a heavy Irish brogue.

She turned, questioning her pa with her eyes. *Didn't you choose the dress?*

"Y—Yes," he stammered.

She froze where she stood. Something was terribly wrong.

The captain rubbed his chin, then circled her.

As his gaze moved over every inch of her, her stomach twisted, and she lowered her head.

"Where are her breasts?" he asked coldly.

Her face flushed and her heart raced. Instinctively, she crossed her arms over her chest. As her mouth became dry, she thought she was going to be sick.

"She has breasts!" Her pa's tone rose defensively. "She's only seventeen. They're still growin'."

The captain's assessment moved further down her body. He tilted his head, then reached out his hand and touched her face.

She jerked back, away from his touch. "Pa? I don't understand. What's happenin'?" Her voice trembled, as she swallowed the bile that rose in her throat.

The captain chuckled. "He didn't tell you?"

"Tell me what?" she asked, looking into the man's eyes.

He didn't answer her. Instead, he turned his attention once more to her pa. "Are you certain she's unspoiled?"

Her pa nodded rapidly. "She's not learnt the ways a the world. Never been with a man."

"And what of her hips? Are they wide?" Captain O'Brien moved behind her. "I can't tell through all this fabric."

Her breaths became rapid, the more they spoke.

"They're wide," her pa said and ran his hand over his head. "Wider than her ma's was."

The captain grinned, then motioned for the other men to come into the room. Trailing behind them was a man clutching a Bible.

She wanted to flee. Every part of her screamed that something was wrong. "Pa?" she panted, but her feet remained frozen to the floor.

He looked at her and she saw the same pain in his eyes that she'd seen earlier.

"It's gonna be all right, Cora," he whispered. "You're gonna have all you ever need."

The captain sneered. "Tell the lass the truth. Don't be making her believe you did this for her. It's your own neck you're savin'."

Though frightened, she was becoming impatient. "Pa! Tell me what's happenin'."

Everyone looked at her pa. "Give me a minute alone with 'er," he said.

Captain O'Brien lifted his chin in the air, then motioned for the other men to follow him out of the room. "We'll be right outside the door. You'll see this through." With his final words, he pressed his forefinger into her pa's chest, and received a simple nod of agreement.

They left, shutting the door.

With the men out of the room, she finally took a deep breath, but still didn't move. "Pa?"

He pulled out a chair and motioned for her to sit.

With trembling knees, she almost fell into the chair. Her ruffled skirt fanned across the floor.

Her pa knelt down in front of her, taking her hands in his own. "I'm in trouble, Cora. You was right, I shoulda left well enough alone. But-"

"What did you do, Pa?"

"They caught me cheatin'." He looked away from her, but continued holding her hands.

Her heart thumped hard. "They get the law?"

He shook his head. "No. They wanted the money. But, I'd been drinkin' and ..." He stopped and tried to look her in the eye. "I don't remember what I done with it."

Her eyes grew wide. "You lost the money? Pa! How could you?"

"It was the whiskey." He lowered his head. "You know what it does to me. Cora, they was gonna hang me! They was fixin' to get a rope, an I begged 'em. I told 'em I'd pay it all back, but they knew I was poor. So I told 'em I had sumthin' valuable. Sumthin' I knew O'Brien wanted."

The truth of his words slowly sank in. "Oh, Pa ..." She clutched her stomach, knowing she was going to vomit.

He looked around the room, then brought her a spittoon he found in the corner. He held it for her while she heaved.

Tears trickled down her cheeks. "You sold me, Pa?"

"No, it ain't like that. I done sumthin' I thought was good for ya. O'Brien's got money." With his thumb, he tried to smooth away her tears. "You won't never be hungry again, Cora."

She wiped her mouth with the hem of her skirt. Swallowing hard, she choked back tears. "No, Pa. Please— don't make me do this. We'll find the money. Tell 'em to give you time to find it. Please, Pa?"

"My time done run out. I don't know where it is. I reckon someone coulda taken it. If you don't do this, you won't have a pa no more."

"But—I can't ..." Her tears came readily.

"He aims to marry ya." He said the words with firmness as if it made a difference. "He wants a son."

She stared at him, feeling completely betrayed. "How? I don't know how to make a baby. I asked Mrs. Moss, but she hemmed an hawed and didn't tell me. How can I give him a baby?"

Her pa closed his eyes and lowered his head. "He'll learn ya."

"But—but he's Irish. You said you hate the Irish. How can you make me do this, Pa?"

He stood and his expression suddenly hardened. "It's the only way, Cora. Now, stop your cryin' and act your age. You're a grown woman and it's time you marry. Be thankful I'm givin' you to a man that can provide for ya."

She placed her head in her hands and rubbed her temples with the tips of her fingers. This had to be a dream. Squeezing her eyes tight, she took in even, deep breaths. All would be well once she reopened them. Slowly, she lifted her lids, only to see her pa standing there in front of her with his arms crossed over his chest. This was no dream. She knew that stance.

"Why me, Pa? Can't he marry someone else?" She sniffled and wiped her nose with her hand.

"Women don't take to life on the river. His wife died of the fever, with his child in 'er belly." He pulled up a chair and sat beside her.

She couldn't control the quiver in her voice. "H-How do you know 'bout that?"

"Men talk when they play cards and drink whiskey."

Her shoulders jerked forward as she sobbed, again. She covered her face with her hands, wishing Mrs. Moss was there to help her. "I j-just wanna go home ..."

"This is your home, now." He was blunt and harsh. Could she ever forgive him?

The captain pushed the door wide open. "I see you told her." He then nodded at the man with the Bible.

The man, whom she now recognized as a local preacher, strode swiftly into the room and cleared his throat. "Are you ready?"

"Aye," the captain said, pulling on his lapel with both hands.

Lord, no. I don't wanna marry this man ...

Her pa lifted her to her feet and held her up next to her husband-to-be. She couldn't breathe and wavered against him. After that moment, everything became a blur.

Chapter 3

The cool water soothed Cora's dry throat. As she set the glass down beside her bed, she caught a glimmer from the gold band on her finger.

"Ms. O'Brien," a tiny voice called out from the other side of the door.

"Huh?" she asked, dreamily.

Knuckles rapped hard against the wood. "Ms. O'Brien? I's told to empty your chamber pot."

Cora cast her eyes around the room, then jumped to her feet.

Opening the door, she found herself looking into the darkest eyes she'd ever seen.

A small-framed colored girl stared back at her. She was wearing a dark blue cotton dress and a gray bibbed apron. Her hair was wrapped in a gray scarf that tied in back at the base of her head, which she tilted, studying her. "Why ... you ain't no older than I is." She scratched her head, then pointed into the room. "Your chamber pot full?"

"What's a chamber pot?" Cora's eyebrows knitted together, totally bewildered by this young girl.

The girl let out a laugh. "For you to ... relieve yourself. Thought for shore you'da already used it." She crossed the room and lifted the ceramic pot, showing it to her. "Don't you gotta go?"

Cora felt heat rise into her cheeks. "I've been holdin' it. I figgered I'd wait 'til we get to land and find an outhouse."

The girl laughed again. "You'd hafta hold it for near two days. Cain't no one do that."

"Course not." Cora lifted her chin into the air, not wanting to be thought foolish. "So, what do you do with it? I mean ... where do you empty it?"

"Over the side a the boat." The girl shrugged, then leaned in toward her. "I make shore no one's below, if'n I heave it from the top."

A grin emerged on Cora's face. It felt good to smile. She'd feared she may never smile again. "What's your name?"

The girl bit her lip in a nervous gesture. "Bessie."

"Bessie, it's might nice to meet you. You can call me Cora."

"I cain't do that!" Bessie rapidly shook her head. "Mista O'Brien would tan my hide if'n I did. I's told you's the missus, and I hasta call you, *Ms.*"

Cora understood and certainly didn't want to get Bessie into trouble. "All right, then." She paused and looked toward the open door. "Do you know what Mr. O'Brien is doin' right now?"

"Yes'm. He's havin' the cook fix you a meal. An' he told me to get you a bath. I'll be bringin' up water soon."

Cora thanked her, then Bessie briskly left the room. The click of a key followed the shutting of the door. She must have locked it to keep Cora's privacy.

Had circumstances been different, she would have thought she'd died and gone to heaven. The room she was in was incredible. Bright-colored paintings of brilliant flowers hung on the walls, with brass oil lanterns to each side. There was one large window overlooking the river, covered with navy blue curtains that billowed from the gentle breeze blowing through.

Her bed was as glorious as that of Mr. O'Brien's. A soft, down-filled mattress perched high upon a wooden platform, covered with the finest bedding she'd ever felt. Satin and lace were everywhere. Obviously, she wasn't the first woman to bed down here.

She was still confused as to why she was given this room. The ring on her finger was proof that she'd married the man. The only words she remembered from the brief ceremony were those of her pa as he was escorted off the boat, "Be good to 'er."

She wished he'd followed his own request. Though her new room was more than fine, she'd have given anything to be with Mrs. Moss having tea, instead.

Thankful that Bessie told her what the chamber pot was for, she readily relieved herself. A soft sigh left her body with gratitude for the modern invention.

It wasn't long after that Bessie returned with a bucket of water and crossed to a long bathing tub, sitting behind a changing screen in the corner of the room.

As Bessie passed by the chamber pot, she grinned. "I's shore you feel better now, Ms. O'Brien."

Her frankness was something Cora would have to get used to. "I do. Thank you, Bessie."

Bessie paused and took a deep breath. "Ms. O'Brien. I's glad you stopped cryin'. 'Twas hurtin' my heart hearin' you go on the way you was."

It hadn't even occurred to her that someone might have been listening. "That's right kind a you to say. I ain't never been away from home before. Or married, neither."

Setting down the pail of water, Bessie placed a hand on her arm. "Don't you worry none. I'll look after ya." She smiled warmly, then lifted the pail and poured it into the tub.

After several more pails of water, Bessie left her alone to bathe.

Relieved to be by herself once again, Cora removed her rumpled dress and slipped into the warm water. Even the bathing tub was more comfortable than the small tub she'd used at home. It was large enough for her to recline and lay her head back.

Her head ached from all the tears she'd shed. Bessie was right; she'd gone on for hours before falling asleep. When she'd woke, the boat was moving, and the vibration of the vessel was something she didn't expect. It was noisier than she thought it would be, but after a while, she shut it out. Laying in the steaming bath, she tried to shut *everything* out ...

A much heavier fist rapped on her door.

She cast her eyes nervously around the room, then noticed a white, cotton robe draped over the changing screen.

Another thump on the door ...

"I ain't dressed!" she yelled, putting her arms through the sleeves of the robe. Her wet skin instantly dampened the material.

A click in the lock and the door opened. William O'Brien entered.

She ducked down behind the changing screen. "I said, I ain't dressed!"

"I'm your husband. I can enter your room when I please." He crossed to the bed, tucking a key into his pocket.

Her heart raced. "You said this is *my* room. You have your own room." She stood and peered around the edge of the screen, only to find him grinning at her.

"Aye, this is your room." He sat in a heavy oak chair, then took a pipe from his pocket and lit it.

"You're gettin' awful comfortable in my room. I'd like to finish gettin' dressed."

"I'm not stopping you." He blew a large puff of smoke into the air, then nodded toward a tall, oak wardrobe standing next to the bed. "You'll find a nightgown in the wardrobe. Belonged to me wife." He paused and grinned. "Seems it still does."

She swallowed hard. Staring at the man she must now call her *husband*, she pulled the robe tightly around her body and crossed to the wardrobe. Inside were an assortment of dresses, coats, and scarves. She pushed them aside, looking for the gown.

"It's folded on the bottom shelf," he said, and again exhaled smoke. "It's pink."

Locating the pink fabric, she lifted it from the shelf. It was long, but somewhat sheer, made from thinly-woven cotton. "Ain't much to it." She held it up in front of her.

He chuckled. "It gets very warm on the boat. You don't need much to sleep in. You may prefer nothing at all."

Jerking her head to look at him, she scowled. "I'll wear the gown. 'Fida known what was happenin', I'd a brung my own."

"Your father should have told you. But, then again, I doubt you would have come willingly."

She took a step closer to him. "If you know that to be so, then why don't you let me go?"

He grinned and raised his eyebrows. "You're me wife. You belong to me now. And ..." He stood from the chair and moved to her, staring deeply into her eyes. "I expect you to behave. I can still have your father hung. Don't ever forget that."

She met his gaze, but then lowered her eyes. "I won't," she said, and returned to the changing screen.

Once again, there was a knock at her door.

She peered over the screen just as Captain O'Brien opened it. He took a silver tray from the hands of a steward, then motioned for him to leave. The steward pulled the door shut, and the captain placed the tray on a small round table on the other side of the room.

"I hope you're hungry, Cora. My cook knows how to make a fish taste like something other than fish." He laughed heartily.

She peered at him from around the corner of the screen. Though she found him completely unattractive, he had a nice laugh. "So, what's it taste like?"

"Food." He motioned her to come closer. "Come see for yourself."

She covered the gown with the robe, trying to remain as modest as possible. Her hair hung loosely on her shoulders.

As she approached the table, he pulled out a chair. Surprised, she looked up at him and he smiled, nodding for her to take the seat.

Leaning toward the plate, Cora inhaled deeply. "Dang!" She immediately caught herself and covered her mouth. "I'm sorry."

O'Brien sat in the chair across from her and cleared his throat, but didn't scold. Then he motioned toward the food. "Go on ... eat it."

Along with the fish, there were sliced potatoes, creamed corn, and green beans. A small glass bowl sat just above her plate containing something she didn't recognize.

"What's that?" she asked, pointing to the bowl.

"Ah ... Francine's favorite. Bread pudding with caramel sauce." He patted his belly. "One of my favorites as well."

She dipped her finger in the creamy caramel, then licked it clean. "*Da-*"she stopped short of cursing for the second time. Her face flushed. "Can't seem to stop myself. Sometimes I don't know what to say and it slips out. I'll work on stoppin'."

He leaned back in his chair. "You don't offend me."

She looked directly at him. His softened eyes and warm smile affirmed that he meant what he said. "Who's Francine?"

"Francine DuBois. She works for me. Entertains me guests."

"How?" She took a bite of fish and closed her eyes, savoring the incredible flavor.

"Let's just say that she has many talents. She's French. From New Orleans. I found her there and she's worked for me this past year. You'll meet her soon enough."

Cora shoveled food into her mouth. Bite after bite, grateful for every morsel.

When she stopped to take a deep breath, her husband was shaking his head. "Slow down. You'll give yourself indigestion." Lifting a cloth napkin from the silver tray, he dabbed at the corner of her mouth.

His tenderness caught her by surprise. She sat back in her chair with her fork held in mid-air. "Pa said you married me cuz you want a son. That so?"

He lowered his eyes. Were they glistening with tears? "Me wife," he said in a whisper, "died. Me child with her. I'm getting old, and yes, I want a son."

"Seems you could a married whoever you wanted." She didn't take her eyes from him and stopped eating.

"No," he said, raising his eyes to meet hers. "I gave up. Look at me ... I'm not the finest catch in the sea." He forced a smile, then patted his belly.

"You seem nice enough." She leaned forward. "Would you really a hung my pa?"

His demeanor instantly changed. He sat up rigidly and folded his arms firmly across his chest. "Aye. I would have. Your *pa* cheated me and me passengers. By law, he should have hung. Only in his, and *my*, drunken foolishness, did I tell him me heart's desire. When he was threatened with a noose, he used me words against me and told me about you. We came to a gentleman's agreement."

She poked the tip of her fork into the pudding. "I don't like bein' bartered with."

"Cora," he spoke gently, then touched his hand to her cheek, "I won the finest prize I could have asked for." He withdrew his hand and eased back in his chair. "And you *did* cost me dearly. To appease me passengers, I paid them their losses out of me own pocket."

Her eyes widened. "You did?"

"Aye. But you have to follow through on your father's promise. I want a son."

"And if I give you a son, what do I get?"

He laughed and waved his hands around the room. "Is this not enough? Fine food, a comfortable room, slaves to draw your bath. What more do you need, Cora?"

She sat there, thinking. The first thing that came to mind was *love* ...

Clearing her throat, she finally spoke. "Nothin' I reckon. But ... will you let me go see my pa ... and Mrs. Moss?"

He stood from the table. "I'm afraid not. I can't risk you running away. I'm sorry Cora, but you can't leave the boat."

"You mean, I gotta stay here all the time?" She raised her voice, causing him to take a step back.

"You'll do as you're told. Now, finish eating and I'll return shortly. 'Tis our wedding night and I intend to take what's mine."

"What you gonna take?" The way he spoke made her stomach jump.

He once again touched her cheek. "You *are* naïve, aren't you, lass?" He turned and walked out of the room, locking the door behind him.

She pushed back her plate. Her appetite had been squelched. Even so, she'd eaten plenty.

What did he intend to take from her? She had nothing to give ...

* * *

The sun had set and the room would have been completely dark had it not been for the oil lanterns.

Cora's stomach was still in knots as she waited for her husband. She wanted to be angry with her pa for putting her into such a horrible mess, but something kept her anger at bay. Perhaps she was simply used to forgiving him for everything he did when he drank. She blamed the alcohol and forgave him.

But this was much worse than having him vomit on her bed quilt or spend the money she was saving for winter provisions; this time, he'd spent *her.* How could a pa do that to his only child?

She had to admit that the meal had been wonderful. Seasoned to perfection—even better than what she could do herself. And the bedding cradled her body in comfort. Things could be much worse.

The gentle rocking of the boat made her sleepy, but she remained awake and sat upright in bed, waiting to see what her husband wanted from her.

Without knocking, he turned the key and opened the door. The simple sound made her heart flutter. With a sudden need for privacy, she pulled a light-weight blanket up over her body and held it snug.

He locked the door and crossed to her. "Do you know why I'm here?" He loosened the top buttons of his shirt.

She shook her head. "I ain't got nothin' to give ya."

His eyebrows drew in. "You truly don't know what a man and woman do when they're married and alone?"

The heat in her cheeks made her glad that the room was dimly lit. "My ma died birthin' me. Pa never remarried. So, I don't know what married folk do ... alone or not."

Letting out a long breath, he sighed. "Is it your time, Cora?"

"Huh?"

"Your *time*? Your *woman's* time?"

"I don't know what you mean."

"Are you bleeding?"

She pulled the blankets around her even more tightly, drawing them high up on her neck. "How'd you know 'bout that? Did Pa tell you 'bout my ailment?"

"Ailment? Cora, I know about this because I was married. I know all about a woman's cycles."

"Cycles? Did your wife have the same ailment? Mine comes every month and sometimes hurts worse than other times." She loosened her grip on the blanket and leaned toward him.

"Me wife was the same and I'm quite certain it's that way for all women."

She wrinkled her nose and stared at him. "Mrs. Moss didn't have it."

"Who is Mrs. Moss?"

"The woman who raised me up for the most part. She's old ... but she was like a ma to me."

He grinned. "She didn't have it because she's old. When *you're* old, you'll stop having it, too."

"But ... I thought there was sumthin' wrong with me." She licked her lips, waiting for his response. Could he possibly have the cure she'd been wishing for, for so many years?

"No. Everything is *right* with you." He moved closer and stared at her. The flickering candlelight lit his face. "You're quite lovely, Cora. We'll make a handsome son."

She didn't respond, but gulped, as her throat became dry. Her heart thumped ... harder and harder, making breathing difficult.

"So," he said, taking another step closer, "are you bleeding?"

She shook her head. "No, sir."

"Call me William." He reached out and placed his hand on her leg.

Though the blankets were covering her, the touch of his hand made her jerk away.

"I'll try not to hurt you," he said in a whisper, "but the first time can be uncomfortable."

"What are you gonna do?" Her voice shook and her heart wouldn't rest.

"Give you my seed." He moved beside her and rested his hand on her shoulder. "Lie back."

His words were a gentle command which she dutifully obeyed. However, lying on her back and staring up at him, she was helpless. Her legs quivered, almost to the point of being out of control.

"You're much too small for me to lie on, so I'll stand." He flipped the blanket from her body, then grasped her trembling legs and pulled her to the edge of the bed.

Though frightened, she didn't resist him. Unsure *why*, something in his manner calmed her. Besides, her pa told her that O'Brien would teach her. So why was this lesson making her entire body shake?

"Close your eyes, Cora," he said soothingly, and she did as she was told.

The rustling of fabric seemed unusually loud. Even with her eyes closed, she could tell that he was removing his trousers. The only other sound at that moment was her heartbeat reverberating in her ears.

He pushed her gown up to her waist, then with his large, rough hands, removed her undergarment with surprising tenderness.

She grabbed hold of the gown, in order to keep him from pushing it any higher. Though the light was dim, there was one thing she didn't want him or anyone else to ever see.

He placed his hand over hers, stroking it with calm reassurance. Then, taking her by the hips, he pulled her even closer to him and hoisted her long legs onto his shoulders. His hands glided up and down along her legs, and by the time his body was pressed to hers, her quivering limbs had stilled.

Her eyes remained shut tight as she felt him move into her. Jerking slightly, she muffled a whimper, not wanting him to think her childish. Always curious as to how Mrs. Moss's cat continued to grow kittens inside of her, now she knew. This was how the male planted his seed. This was how she would give William a son.

Trying to ignore the discomfort as his movement became more rapid, she thought about skipping stones, and drinking tea, and even the first glimpse she'd had of the *Bonny Lass*. Her hands remained securely clasping her nightgown.

How long's this gonna take?

His grip on her hips became tighter. Trusting the fact that she believed he was doing his best not to hurt her, she breathed deeply, hoping it would ease the pain. He moaned, and she was quite certain by the tone, that *he* found pleasure in what he was doing. Suddenly, with an even louder moan, he seemed to swell inside her. He came to a slow halt, as he held her fast against him. His breathing slowed, his grip loosened, then he withdrew.

Gently laying her legs down on the bed, he muttered, "'Twas good," then proceeded to put on his trousers.

Thankful it was over, she scooted back and rested her head on the pillows. A trickle of warm liquid flowed from between her legs.

"I'll let you sleep now," he said, and began to walk away. "The next time should cause no pain. We'll carry on each night until we succeed."

Each night? She swallowed hard, but couldn't speak, having no idea what to say ...

"Goodnight, Cora," he said, and walked out, locking the door behind him.

Chapter 4

Somehow, Cora was able to sleep. Perhaps it was the soft down that cradled her body, or maybe it was the silky sheets caressing her skin. It could even have been the gentle motion of the boat as it glided along the waters of the Mississippi. Since the storms had let up, the river gave the boat little resistance.

Thinking about the activity of the previous night, Cora sat upright and blinked slowly, gazing at her room. No, it hadn't been a dream. The pain hadn't lasted long, but the memory of the strange way in which their bodies joined, lingered.

She knew that men and women were made differently, but didn't fully understand why. Until now …

It made sense, and she wasn't ashamed.

The last time Muffin had a litter of kittens, she'd watched. Would it be the same for her when it came time to have William's baby? How would it ever come out of her? She reached her hand down and touched herself, then quickly withdrew it. She had plenty to fret about and wasn't going to start worrying herself over something as distant as childbirth.

Yet, it *was* how her ma had died ...

Her heart fluttered. Confusion caused her head to reel. She couldn't understand why she wasn't angry with William, or why she'd resigned herself to accept the situation she'd been thrown into. Had her luxurious surroundings and full belly already taken hold of her? She needed to remind herself that she hadn't willingly gone into the marriage. Her pa had sold her.

A knock on the door brought her fully awake.

"Ms. O'Brien," Bessie's tiny voice called out. The key turning in the lock made a pronounced *click*.

Cora swung her legs over the side of the bed and stood. Once upright, she realized just how much the boat was moving and swayed for a moment, until she steadied herself by resting her hand on the bed.

She crossed the room and opened the door to find Bessie there with a tray of food in her hands. Gratefully, she took it from her.

"Bessie, this smells ..." She leaned toward the tray and inhaled deeply, "wonderful."

Bessie giggled. "You act like you never ate before. Biscuits, eggs, an grits is all it be." She stared at the tray, then pointed to a mug set above the plate. "Oh, an coffee. Not shore if'n you likes coffee, but I brung cream."

Cora set the tray of food on her table and instantly thought of the previous night—eating, with William watching her. "Thank you, Bessie. Has Mr. O'Brien had breakfast?"

"Yes'm. Long time go. He said for me to wait to bring you your food. Said you was tired." She grinned broadly.

Heat rushed to Cora's face. Was it possible that he told Bessie what they'd done? Why did the thought of someone knowing bother her? Obviously, it was what all married folks did. Otherwise, there would be no children to speak of.

"I *was* tired," she said, and quickly took a bite of grits. "Thank you for lettin' me sleep."

"Shore, Ms. O'Brien." Bessie nodded toward the door. "I gots to go, now. More chores to do."

Bessie smiled one more time, then walked quickly from her room, shutting the door behind her and locking it once again.

Cora didn't like the idea of being locked inside and decided she would speak to William and request to roam freely. Whether or not he would grant her request was another issue.

* * *

Pacing in her room became monotonous. It had taken many years for her to memorize the grain patterns of Mrs. Moss's floor, but only two days on board the *Bonny Lass* and she was already familiar with the throw rugs that covered the floor of her room. The green and blue swirling patterns made her nauseous. This was not what she'd had in mind when she'd dreamed of traveling by steamboat.

Bessie had come back more than once to check on her, empty her chamber pot, and bring her more food. Even though the girl was kind, Cora felt more like a caged pet than a wife. She couldn't believe that all wives were treated this way.

As Bessie began walking out for the third time, she grabbed her by the wrist. "Bessie, I don't like bein' locked in. Can't you please leave it unlocked?"

"Mista O'Brien would tan my hide! He say to me, *Bessie, now you be shore an lock the door.*" Her eyes were wide with fear. "I gots to do what he say."

Cora loosened her grip. "It's all right, Bessie. Just tell Mr. O'Brien I need to see 'im."

"Yes'm. I will." Letting out a long breath, she moved out the door and dutifully locked it behind her.

Cora flopped down on the bed, fully dressed, and lay back against the pillows. Even staring out the window became dull. Everything about the boat and the river had lost its charm. She closed her eyes, hoping that perhaps she could sleep and help the time pass quicker.

It was late afternoon and she'd just drifted off into a light sleep when the key clicked in the lock. She was instantly alert.

"You asked for me, Cora?" William crossed the room, neatly tucking the key into his pocket.

She sat upright on the bed and smoothed her dress with her hands. "Y-Yes ... William." Hearing the sound of her own voice trembling, she took a deep breath and continued. "I don't like bein' locked in my room."

He pulled a chair up beside the bed and sat, then tilted his head, studying her. "Is there something you need?"

"Course there is!" She found her courage and her voice grew even louder. "I ain't your pet! Mrs. Moss's cat has more freedom than I do. Dang!"

A light chuckle rose out of him. "Oh, my dear, dear, Cora." He touched her cheek. "You have to understand. I don't know that I can trust you."

"I'm your wife." She crossed her arms over her chest. "May not a been my choice, but by law I'm yours." Lowering her arms, she stared at her lap. "This is my home, now. If you won't let me leave the boat, least let me walk round it. I like my room an all, but dang!"

He scratched his chin and shook his head. "Cora." His eyebrows drew in. "I believe you need someone to teach you how to be a lady."

"My swearin'?"

He nodded.

"I'll try harder." She sighed, then realized he'd changed the subject, and sat even more upright. "So, are you gonna let me outta this room?"

"Can you swim?"

She knew immediately why he asked and chose to lie. "No, sir. Never learned. I'm good at skippin' stones, but put *me* in the water and I'd sink to the bottom."

He stood from the chair and walked to the window. The curtains had been drawn back so that she could look out, but he pulled them closed.

"I'm playing cards tonight," he said, moving toward her.

"Gamblin'?"

"Aye. After supper, we clear the dining room and lay out the cards for the men. We'll be in Memphis tomorrow, but tonight I intend to empty the pockets of me guests." He smiled a wry smile. "Your father is not the only man capable of good fortune."

Does he cheat, too?

"Are they important men?" She wasn't about to ask him about his gambling habits.

"Some. Mostly businessmen. More importantly, *wealthy* men."

He unbuttoned the top buttons of his shirt.

She swallowed hard. "Are you warm?"

"Since I'll be busy this evening, I thought I would take you now." He nodded at her. "Go on and remove your dress. You don't want to soil it."

"You wanna do that *now*? It ain't dark."

"It can be done in the light. Sometimes I prefer it that way."

She didn't move. "If I do this, will you let me leave the room?"

"On one condition," he said, unfastening his trousers.

"What?"

"You'll have to remain with Francine. I'll entrust her to look after you. And I'll have her groom you before you make an appearance. I can't have me wife looking like a river rat."

She pushed her hair behind her ears. "I thought you said I was *lovely*?"

He dropped his trousers and moved to the edge of the bed. Reaching out his hand to touch her face, he said, "You are. But I know you can look even better."

Tentatively, she removed her dress. As she lifted it over her head, his hands moved to help her.

When he tried to remove her chemise, she grabbed his hand. "No!"

"Why? Are you ashamed of your breasts?"

"*You* said I don't have none." She pierced him with her eyes.

Her look only made him grin. "Aye, I did. So, prove me wrong."

"No. I don't want it off."

He pushed the chemise up higher on her waist, but stopped when his eyes rested on it. "What is that?"

Quickly, she pushed the garment down, covering her mark. "It—it's a birthmark. Been there all my life. I didn't want you to see it."

William raised his chin in the air, studying her face.

She hated the mark. It covered a span across her abdomen the size of her hand; a purplish-red mark that was slightly raised from the rest of her satiny-smooth skin. As a young child, she thought nothing of it until her pa said hateful things about it in one of his drunken rants. After that, she made certain to always keep it covered.

She grabbed her dress and attempted to put it back on. "I know. You don't want me now."

William took the dress from her hand, and set it aside. "You're being foolish. Of course I want you." Without hesitation, he removed her undergarment, and as before, positioned her at the edge of the bed.

Chapter 5

"I ain't never smelled nothin' like this before," Cora said, wiggling her nose like a rabbit.

"I'll leave the two of you alone for now," William said, grinning as he watched her breathing in the scent of Francine's perfume. The smell hovered in the air surrounding them. He nodded to Francine, then looked directly at Cora, "Remember our agreement."

"Yes, sir ... William," she replied shyly. She raised her eyes to meet his gaze. "I promise."

He touched her cheek with his hand, then walked out of the room.

Cora had noticed from the corner of her eye that Francine watched William leave before turning her attention back. Francine's eyes had seemed almost *sad*, but then brightened once she gave Cora her full attention.

"You are very small," Francine said with a heavy French accent, "but I can see that William likes you."

Cora smiled at her remark, then lowered her head. Something about Francine intimidated her and she drew her shoulders in, attempting to hide herself.

Francine laughed softly. "You are shy, no?"

"I ain't never been called *shy* before. I just feel kind a funny bein' in your room. It's a might fancy." She smoothed her plain, cotton dress, and gazed around the room.

Cora thought her own room quite feminine, but Francine's went beyond the word. Mostly in shades of pink and everything accented with dainty lace. Francine's bed was lower to the ground than hers and covered in soft satin. It beckoned to anyone who gazed at it.

Francine herself also beckoned with her appearance. Her rose-colored dress was form-fitting to the waist and scooped low in front, accentuating her large bosom. Around her neck was a blue satin ribbon, centered with a cameo. The ribbon cascaded down her back, beneath her long, brown ringlets. Full dark lashes framed her deep blue eyes and fluttered every time she spoke. She was beautiful.

"Cora," Francine said, gently taking her hand. "Come sit."

Cora willingly followed her, determined to obey her husband. She would be allowed to leave her room, only if she stayed with Francine and did as she was told.

Francine motioned to the bed, where Cora gingerly sat down. She looked behind her at the overly large bed, then ran her hand across the smooth satin. "It's nice."

"Only the best on the *Bonny Lass*," Francine replied, and sighed with contentment.

Sitting in front of Francine, she got a wide-eyed view of her bosom. "You got big breasts."

"*Oui*, I do." Francine covered her mouth with her hand, stifling a laugh.

"I'm sorry, Miss Francine, but sometimes I talk before I think." She stared down at her own breasts, wishing for even *some* of what Francine had.

Francine lifted Cora's chin with her hand. "All women are different." She brushed a strand of hair off of her forehead. "Breasts do not make a woman, a woman. I can teach you how to be a lady."

"That's what William wants. But I gotta tell ya. Mrs. Moss has been tryin' for years. It ain't done no good." She looked away from Francine.

A bookcase caught her eye and she sprang from the bed. "Dang! Look at all the books!" She ran her fingers over the spine of every book on the shelf.

"*Oui*. I have many books."

Cora turned her head, taken by the change of tone in Francine's voice. It was soft and not nearly as confident. "You like to read?"

Francine pulled her shoulders back and lifted her chin. "No."

Eyeing the books once again, Cora let out a large breath. "Do you know how?" With a slight turn of her head, she looked back toward Francine. "Well, do ya?"

Francine's cheeks turned as red as her dress. "No. I keep the books to make men think I am smart. I do not want them to think I am only beautiful."

Cora faced away from her, tilting her head sideways to read the titles on each spine. "I know how."

"You do?"

"Course I do." She giggled at the surprise in Francine's voice. "Mrs. Moss learned me how to read from the Bible. I was just tellin' her a few days back how much I wanted to read some other stories ..." Her voice faded away. The realization of how much her life had changed in only a few days' time struck her.

Francine moved across the room and placed her hand on her shoulder. "You miss her, no?"

Her eyebrows knit together at the strange way in which Francine asked a question. "I miss her ... *yes*."

Francine nodded toward the books. "Choose one. I will not miss it. And if you find it good, perhaps you can share it with me."

Cora's heart pounded. She reached out, gently touching the books. Her eyes scanned the titles. "Wuthering Heights?" Wrinkling her nose, she looked at Francine. "What's a wuthering?" Francine shrugged, so she moved on to another. "Hmmm ... Three Musketeers." Opening the book, she realized that this was not for her. "Uh-uh ... no swords." Then her eyes popped at a very appealing title. "A Christmas Carol." She smiled at Francine. "I like the sound a that."

"*Oui*." Francine laughed. "Christmas is one of my favorite times of year. I like presents."

"Presents? Mrs. Moss always gave me a new pair a socks. Guess that's a nice present."

"Some presents are much finer," Francine said, fingering the cameo at her neck.

"I'll be real careful with it," Cora promised, holding the book against her chest.

"For now, set it on the bed stand. We have work to do."

Cora did as she was told, not wanting to damage her new-found privileges. Suddenly, the thought of having to spend hours on end in her room wasn't so unappealing. But for now, the book would have to wait.

Once again, Francine motioned for her to sit on the bed. Then she moved to her bureau, where she lifted a porcelain brush.

"Your hair," Francine said as she began brushing, "needs some tending." She jerked the brush through several tangles, causing Cora to grunt and wince.

"What you gonna do to it?" Cora pulled her head away against each stroke.

"First, make it smooth, then ..." Francine stopped, then stood back and evaluated her face. "I will part it and twist it so that it rounds over your ears. It will give your face more shape. You will not appear so thin." She began brushing once again.

"As for the rest of you," Francine continued, "you are fortunate that a flat bosom is in style. Many women wear garments to flatten them."

"Huh?" This made no sense to her. "Why don't *you* wear one?"

"It may be in style for women, but I find that *men* prefer to see how much a woman has to offer."

"Men like William?"

Francine hesitated before answering. "*Oui*. Though, now that he has you, he has no further interest in me."

There was a hint of disappointment in Francine's words. "You like William?" Since the tangles had been removed from her hair, the sensation of the gentle brushing was now calming her. She waited patiently for an answer, but heard nothing more than breathing.

Cora cleared her throat. "Did you hear me? I wanna know if you like my husband?"

"Husband ..." Francine whispered. "William has been good to me."

"Why didn't he marry *you*?"

Again, Francine didn't reply. She tucked pins into Cora's twist, holding it in place, then stood back admiring her work. She made her way to a tall wardrobe and thumbed through a selection of dresses. After choosing a blue satin gown, she returned.

"This should do," Francine said. "It may not fit you as it does me, but we will make it work."

"Francine?" She wasn't about to let the subject go away. "You didn't answer my question. I reckon if William expects me to learn from you, then you should be honest with me."

Francine took a seat beside her on the bed, holding the blue dress folded over her arms. "I am not the kind of woman any man marries."

"Why?"

Francine's head rose proudly. "I choose not to marry."

Sensing that Francine would give no further details, Cora let it go. "Oh," she said simply, then reached out to touch the blue dress. "I like blue."

"It will look lovely with your coloring."

"My colorin'?"

"*Oui*. You are fair. Blue looks nice with fair skin."

"Oh. I got freckles. Is that all right?"

Francine giggled. "*Oui.* Men find freckles ... charming." She stood and held up the dress. "Here. Let me help you."

Cora backed away. "I'd ruther do it myself." She took the dress from Francine and crossed to the changing screen. Even Francine's changing screen was trimmed in lace.

Men may find freckles charmin', but no one likes to look at my mark.

"Take care not to mess your hair," Francine cautioned.

Heeding the warning, she carefully pulled the dress up onto her body from the floor, rather than over her head. The satin was cool against her skin and the dress fashioned very much like the dress her pa brought her the day she'd married William. Though layered, the fabric was light and the short sleeves kept her arms cool. She didn't fill out the front the way Francine did, but it was reassuring knowing that flat chests were in fashion. And she didn't need a garment to help achieve it.

She stepped out from the screen and faced Francine. Cora's lip curled as she placed her hands on her hips. "Well?"

Francine crossed her arms over her bosom. "Cora. Put your arms down."

She obeyed.

"Now ... I want to see you smile."

She rolled her eyes, then flashed a toothy grin. "I feel silly."

"No. Do not. I'm making you into a lady, and ladies are *not* silly."

Francine moved around behind her and pulled her shoulders back. Then she took the back of her hand and tapped it under Cora's chin. She returned to face her.

"Now," Francine said, looking into her eyes. "A *real* smile."

Cora licked her lips and forced herself to smile. When Francine smiled back at her, her forced smile became real.

Clasping her hands together and holding them to her chest, Francine laughed. "*Oui*! That is what I want to see!" She leaned in toward her. "You have beautiful teeth. No need to hide them."

Lessons continued as Francine taught her how to walk like a lady. The new shoes William gave her were uncomfortable, but Francine assured her they would become more pliant the more she wore them, and therefore more comfortable.

"And," Francine continued, "when you speak, speak softly."

"Whisper?"

"No. Simply lower your tone. Use more breath when you speak. A woman should not sound like a man. Most importantly, *do not curse.*"

Cora lowered her head. "Guess William told ya." She sighed.

"*Oui.* The best advice I can give is ... speak as little as possible. If a man compliments you, then say, *thank you* and nothing more. Though, I find I can say a lot with my eyes." To demonstrate, she fluttered her lashes.

Cora leaned in and watched their movement. "Dang," she whispered, "you're good at that."

Francine waved a finger at her. "No. No *dang.*"

Changing years of speech behavior was not an easy thing to do. So, she made up her mind to take Francine's advice and only speak if she was spoken to, and even then, keep her words very limited.

Several hours passed. Cora was surprised when William returned to check on their progress. She gave him a genuine smile after seeing his eyes light up upon sight of her.

He nodded his approval. "Francine has worked her magic." He looked at Francine. "Haven't you, lass?"

"Your wife has everything a woman needs to work her *own* magic," Francine replied.

Cora released a chuckle, but promptly stopped herself from snorting.

"You are still missing one thing," William said to her. He reached into his pocket and removed a necklace made of tiny white seed pearls.

Cora's eyes opened wide, staring at the magnificent piece of jewelry.

"Turn around," he said, as he held it up to her.

She turned and he fastened the necklace. The simple, but elegant design made her feel like a princess in a fairy tale.

She smiled at Francine, who immediately shifted her gaze, all the while touching the cameo at her neck. Cora may have been simple-minded in the ways of the world, but she knew hurt when she saw it.

"Are you ready for supper?" William asked them.

"I ain't ready to go back to my room just yet," Cora said, as disappointment set in. "I was hopin' to see the rest a the boat."

William laughed heartily and extended his arm. "I'm not returning you to your room. Tonight, you'll eat with me in the dining hall."

Her stomach flipped at the thought of an evening spent outside of her room.

He extended his other arm to Francine, who smiled and willingly took it.

Cora stood tall as the three of them walked down the stairs and into the dining hall. She'd never felt more beautiful. Her life suddenly did seem like a dream. Maybe her pa knew what he was doing after all.

The room was bustling with colored waiters dressed in crisp, white uniforms, filling water glasses and laying down plates of food.

She gazed upward at the high ceiling, sparkling bright from the glow of the candelabras.

Dang ...

She giggled. Cursing to herself couldn't hurt. William couldn't read her thoughts.

All eyes turned to them when they entered the room. She bit her lip nervously, realizing they were the center of attention. William patted her arm and she oddly felt reassured.

They crossed the room to the head table. William pulled out a chair for her, then in turn, one for Francine. She noticed the men in the room raise their eyes, then giggled quietly and wondered if she would grow accustomed to the attention.

The meal was laid before them on ornate china plates embossed with gold piping. She'd never seen such a thing. Completely entranced with the dinnerware, she barely noticed the food, until the aroma drifted into her nose.

The dining hall held at least seventy passengers and the abundance of food overwhelmed her. The meal tonight was chicken—one of her favorites—but made in a way she'd never had before. It was coated in corn meal and fried, but what confused her was the smell. She leaned close to her plate and inhaled.

Leaning toward William, she whispered, "What spice did they use on the chicken?"

He dabbed the corner of his mouth with a napkin. "Curry. It's in the gravy on your potatoes as well."

"Curry? Never heard of it."

"It's yellow in color." He pointed at the gravy.

"Oh ... I thought maybe they over-cooked it. Burnt it a might."

"Taste it, Cora," he said quietly.

She dipped her fork into the potatoes covered in yellow gravy and lifted a small portion to her mouth. Instantly, she decided she liked curry. She began to form her favorite word, but caught herself just in time and said, "I like it," instead.

William chuckled.

She looked beyond William and watched Francine. Amazed at how she carried herself, even while eating.

Cora did her best to imitate her. She kept her shoulders back and her napkin draped across her lap. She sipped the water in her glass, rather than gulping it down in one swig. Most importantly, she kept her voice low and spoke only to William and only when necessary.

As the meal progressed, she became even braver and looked at others in the room. On one side of the dining hall was a bar, which she was told offered some of the best alcohol available, as well as simple beer and wine. Something her pa must have enjoyed.

She squinted, studying the barkeep. Then it dawned on her that he was the tall man who had followed her and her pa from their house to the boat. Unfortunately, he caught her looking at him. His eyebrows rose, then danced up and down a few times. He puckered his lips and winked at her.

She quickly turned her head and returned her attention to her husband. "William, who's that man?" She nodded in the direction of the bar.

"The barkeep? Name's Giles. Marcus Giles. He's tended bar on the *Lass* for six months now."

"Oh." She nibbled at her food and tried not to look at Marcus.

"Why do you ask?"

"He was lookin' at me," she said from the side of her mouth.

William took her hand in his. "Of course he was. Francine did a fine job of grooming you. Don't be surprised when the men notice."

"But ... he looked at me when I got on the first day. 'Fore Francine did anything to me. He makes me nervous."

William glanced over at Marcus, who nodded in return and smiled.

"Don't worry about Marcus. He knows you're me *wife* and won't bother you. Rest assured."

As soon as the meal ended, the tables were quickly cleared. The ladies present went to their rooms, while the men lit cigars and waited for the cards to be set. Close to Francine's side, Cora watched as the transition took place. It was well orchestrated and took very little time. It seemed that the men in the room were anxious to lose their money.

"Ain't you goin' to your room?" she asked Francine.

"No. Now is when I work." Francine took her hand and led her to a chaise. "Sit here. You can watch for a short while, but then I know William will want you to go to your room. This is not a place for proper women."

"Ain't you proper?"

"No. Not like the other women who dined here tonight. My virtues lie elsewhere."

Cora tipped her head. She didn't understand. But she sat as she was told and watched.

It didn't take long for the men to choose their tables. Many of them first made their way to the bar and began a night of drinking. Sounds of laughter, and soon after, anger, erupted from the room. Gambling could be a very dangerous sport.

But she was most intrigued by Francine, who floated across the room from table to table. Sometimes she would bend and whisper in the ear of a particular gentleman. Other times, she noticed that she would run her hands over a man's shoulders, causing him to look up into her eyes.

What kind a work is that?

William cleared his throat. "Francine should have taken you to your room."

Cora twisted her mouth. "She said I could watch for a spell. I find this all excitin'."

Holding his hand out, he lifted her to her feet. "'Tis not the place for me wife."

"Yes, sir." She couldn't have been more disappointed, but wasn't about to cross him and damage her newfound freedom.

He held her hand and led her across the floor to the stairwell. "Can I trust you to go to your room?" He dipped his head just slightly and raised his eyebrows.

She looked over his shoulder into the dining room, which was now an active gambling hall. Smoke billowed over the heads of the men seated at the tables, and every now and then Francine's laughter added a melodic accent to the grumbling gamblers.

"I'll go," she said, frowning.

"That's my lass," William said, then brushed his hand across her cheek.

As she turned to ascend the stairs, he patted her bottom. Turning her head sharply, she caught him winking. The wink was followed by a gracious smile and she was compelled to return it.

"G'night," she said, and continued up the stairs.

Before going to her room, she went to Francine's room and retrieved her book. Though it was dark outside, she intended to keep her lantern lit and start reading. The boat had pulled into shore for the night, but she had no idea where they were. It didn't matter. The book would take her somewhere else entirely.

She propped up a few pillows against the wall at the head of her bed. The lantern gave off a pleasant glow.

Quickly, she changed into her nightgown, wanting to throw herself into the story. Her hand caressed the cover, then slowly opened the book. She found herself smiling uncontrollably, then stopped before she read the first word.

Thoughts of her pa emerged. Guilt crept into her like a thief trying to take away something precious. How could she be so happy? She'd been sold, and a man she'd never met before took her body to himself. But William was gentle, and kind, and though not an attractive man, he was by law her husband. Was it wrong to make the best of a bad situation?

Her belly was full of the finest food she'd ever eaten. She was sitting on the softest bed that ever held her frame. She wasn't being abused by the bitter words of a drunken pa. And in her hands was a book. A *real* book. Yes, she was very happy. And she would not let herself feel guilty.

Chapter 6

Finally docking in Memphis, the *Bonny Lass* bustled with activity. Cora closed her book, carefully marking her place with a satin ribbon. She hated putting it down. It seemed that Mr. Scrooge was doomed. However, the sounds coming from outside her door screamed of excitement. Mr. Scrooge would have to wait.

Entering the common hallway, she rushed to the exterior door. She blinked in the bright sunlight, then moved to the rail and stared down at the many people exiting the boat. The ladies were all dressed in their finest dresses, and the men wore suits and top hats. The porters hoisted their bags onto their shoulders and escorted them to the waiting buggies.

She flew down the stairs to the second floor, then rounded the corner to descend to the exit platform.

William stopped her abruptly. "Whoa now, lass," he said, grabbing her by the arm.

She pointed to the platform. "But ..."

He placed his hand on her lips. "I never said you could leave the boat."

"I thought ..."

He shook his head. "No, Cora. Return to your room. I'll come to see you later."

Her heart sank. The joy that surged through her was doused by a few simple words from her husband. Out of the corner of her eye, she spotted Bessie walking down the platform with a basket on her arm. *Even the slaves have more freedom than I do!* None of it was fair.

When William came to her room that night, she planned to refuse him. But after he presented a bag of chocolate candies to her, she changed her mind. He knew how to win her over.

She'd become used to coupling with him, and as the weeks passed it became routine. To her it was no different than ritualistically cleaning her teeth or brushing her hair. It was part of the daily schedule, and one meant to have a rewarding outcome; a child they would both love.

She couldn't hide her disappointment when her cycle came. When William came to her that night, she had just cause to refuse him. He, too, looked deflated. So deflated that she offered him a kiss on the cheek to ease his sorrow. He accepted it gratefully, then turned and silently left her room.

In desperate need of someone to talk to, she made her way down the hall to Francine's room and knocked. Francine opened the door with an enthusiastic smile that suddenly dimmed, but she waved her into the room.

"Cora? Why are you here so late?" Francine grabbed a robe and put it on to cover her sheer nightgown. Her eyes moved over Cora's shoulder as if she was looking for someone else.

"I need to talk. Am I botherin' you?"

"No. But I am expecting someone. What is wrong?"

"I got my cycle," she muttered. "I ain't gonna have a baby."

"Oh ..." Francine swallowed hard. "You always say what is on your mind. Sometimes you surprise me."

She took Francine's hand. "William wants a son. How long's it s'pose to take to make one?"

"Well, as long as you do what is necessary," Francine cleared her throat, "then—one day—it will happen."

Francine hadn't closed the door, and within minutes a handsome young man appeared in the hallway and looked into the room. He was well-groomed, wearing a three-piece, brown suit.

"Looks like you got a caller," Cora said, nodding toward the man.

"*Oui*." Francine primped her hair. She passed by her and went to the man at the door, took him by the hand, and pulled him into the room. With wide eyes, she motioned Cora to leave.

Cora grinned and bit her lip. "I best be gettin' back to my room."

The man said nothing to her, but nodded as she left. As soon as she was out the door, it was pushed shut. The lock clicked. She leaned against the wall next to Francine's room, saddened that she couldn't talk more with her friend and teacher. *So many unanswered questions.* She was certain Francine had all the answers ...

Laughter erupted through the closed door, followed by the sound of shuffling feet. Soon after, there was a noise she recognized without any doubt. It was the steady, rhythmic reverberation of the bed moving, accompanied by a low, guttural moan from the man.

"Oh my ..." she muttered.

Francine should a told me she'd got married.

Smiling and happy for her friend, she returned to her room.

* * *

Having finished *A Christmas Carol*, Cora was anxious to choose another book from Francine's collection. She'd stayed up late and was relieved that the book ended as it did. All was well and Tiny Tim would live. Assuming Francine and her new husband might sleep late, she waited until well past daybreak to go to her room. She knocked softly on her door.

"Who is there?" Francine called out.

"Cora." She clutched the book against her chest, the excitement of getting a new one to read outweighing the sadness of giving this one back.

"Come in."

She slowly pushed the door open and peered toward the bed. Expecting to see the man there with her, she was surprised when Francine was sitting up in bed alone. Cora glanced around the room, then moved toward Francine when she realized they were alone.

Francine began to laugh. "What is wrong with you? What are you looking for?"

"Your husband. Thought he'd be here with you. I didn't wanna bother you, but I finished the book and hoped for another." She held up *A Christmas Carol* and smiled at Francine.

Francine cocked her head. "My husband?"

Cora lowered her eyes as she crossed to the bookcase. "I reckon it wasn't right, but I heard you last night. You must a changed your mind 'bout havin' a baby. Sounded like you was tryin' real hard."

"You listened?" Francine's eyes opened wide, then she covered her mouth, muffling a laugh.

Cora slid the book into its place. "I'm sorry. Your husband was kind a loud."

"Come sit," Francine said, patting the spot next to her. Despite her reluctance to leave the books, Cora obeyed. Francine took her hands. "Cora. That man is not my husband."

"Huh?" Cora tipped her head and wrinkled her nose. "But ... he was-"

"Enjoying himself," Francine said, finishing her sentence.

"I know that. I heard 'im." Heat rose in Cora's cheeks. "But, why were you tryin' to make a baby?"

"We were not." Francine looked at her with soft eyes. "Men like to do that for pleasure. Not just to make a baby."

"And you let 'em?" None of this made sense.

"*Oui*. I do." Francine waved her hands around the room. "It is how I can afford all this."

"They pay you?"

Francine nodded. "*Oui.* I find it hard to believe you know not of such things."

Cora stared at her hands. "Mrs. Moss never told me anything like that. And Pa didn't neither. You're the only one ever learned me 'bout men."

"Be thankful you have William. He will always treat you well. Some men are not so gracious." Francine rubbed her cheek. "Some have bad tempers."

Twisting her fingers together, Cora decided to be brave. "Francine? Do you *like* doin' what you do?"

"Most of the time. I like to make men happy." Francine pushed the blankets to the side and rose from the bed.

"That man last night sounded happy. Guess you done good." Cora stood and returned to the bookcase. "Can I take another one?"

"*Oui.* You may. But later, you must tell me about the one you finished. That was our bargain."

"I will. It was real good." She selected *Jane Eyre*. What sort of adventure would she be in this time? She turned to go to her room, then stopped and faced Francine once again.

"Francine?" Her heart pounded, afraid to ask what she wanted to know.

"*Oui?*"

She cleared her throat. "Did you ever make William *happy?*"

Francine took a deep breath before answering. "*Oui.* But that was before he had you."

Cora's body folded into itself, and Francine took hold of her shoulders, pushing them back.

"Cora." Her voice broke as she spoke. "He takes his marriage vow to heart. He will not have me again."

Cora lifted her gaze to meet her friend's. "I don't know why I feel like this, but I'm glad to know that."

"You care for him, no?"

She nodded. "I reckon I do ..." With that realization in her heart, she returned to her room.

She set the new book on the stand beside her bed and turned her thoughts inward. *Why* did she care for William? He was only a few years younger than her pa. Perhaps he was the pa she'd always wanted. She knew she wasn't in love with him, but she certainly didn't want to share him.

Thinking of how Francine made her money bewildered her. Wondering just how many men Francine had made *happy* over the years, she decided to begin reading and take her mind off things. It was much easier reading about someone else's life than living her own.

Chapter 7

Cora pursued William once her cycle ended, anxious to get back to their routine. Astonished that she missed having him close, she questioned what she was truly feeling and realized ...

Something deep inside her feared that if she denied him too long, he might be tempted to return to Francine.

William wasted no time resuming their activity. He chuckled when he came to her room and found her at the edge of the bed waiting for him.

"Why are you laughin', William?" she asked as he prepared himself for her.

"My dear lass, I believe you've grown fond of this."

She lay calmly, waiting with her hands folded over her belly. She had never allowed him to see her upper body, and he never objected.

"I want a baby," she whispered.

"Good. So do I."

Nothing more was said ...

* * *

"He's lookin' at me again, William," Cora said from the side of her mouth. They were in the dining hall enjoying a delicious roast pork supper, when she realized that Marcus had his eyes on her.

"You're imagining things, Cora," he said and nodded toward Marcus. "You see, he's cleaning the bar glasses."

She followed William's gaze and sure enough, Marcus was busily using a bar towel, wiping away as if it was what he'd been doing all along. William continued to eat, but she couldn't. Butterflies fluttered in her belly. She knew that she was *not* imagining things. She'd lost her appetite and lay down her fork.

"Can I-"

"*May* I," he corrected.

"*May* I go to my room, now?" She looked at him with soft eyes, hoping to be excused.

He nodded. "Cards tonight. I may come to you after."

"All right," she said, and stood to leave.

She cast a weak smile in the direction of Francine who was occupied in a conversation with an elderly gentleman. She hoped Francine wouldn't try to make *him* happy. It could kill him.

Unfortunately, she had to pass the bar on her way to the stairwell. Moving as fast as she possibly could, she passed Marcus, and as she did so she could have sworn he smacked his lips. Not wanting to encourage him, she didn't look his way and continued on to the stairs.

Her room was her refuge. Knowing that she intended to read well past sundown, she lit a lantern, put on her most comfortable nightgown, and propped herself up on the bed.

She didn't always understand everything she read. Some words she'd never heard before, so she did her best to assume their meaning by the other words surrounding them and the emotions of the paragraph. What gripped her about *Jane Eyre* was not only the mystery of the story and underlying secrets, but more than anything ... love.

She wanted to be in love.

She was pulled from her thoughts by the sound of footsteps approaching her room. Her door slowly opened.

"You win big tonight?" she asked with a soft laugh in her voice, not looking up from her book.

The door shut and was locked. "Not yet."

She swallowed hard, her heart raced, and she found breathing difficult. Without even marking her place, she laid the book aside and pulled the blankets around her body. When he stepped into the light, her fears were affirmed.

"Mr. Giles?" Her voice shook. "What are you doin' here?"

A sinister smile covered his scruffy face. "I'm gettin' my money back."

"Not in my room. I ain't got none. You need to leave." She tried to be firm, but couldn't hide the quivering in her words. She swallowed again and made every effort to control the rapid rate of her heart.

He moved a step closer. "You got sumthin' else I want. O'Brien's been tappin' it for two months now. Figger it's my turn."

She licked her dry lips only to regret it.

"I see you want it, too." He grunted and smirked. "It must be good. O'Brien's been smilin' more since he had you."

She shook her head. "No. You can't have me. I'm *his* wife. Only *he* has me."

Marcus laughed. "Wife? Winnin's is more like it. Your pa traded you cuz he didn't have nothin' better to barter."

He inched even closer, as she scooted her body to the head of the bed. "I'll scream. Go now or I swear I'll scream."

He pounced on her. His full weight covered her body as his hand clasped across her mouth. He bent his head and put his lips to her ear. "You scream and it'll be the last sound you make." His eyes pierced her. She knew he meant what he said.

Jerking the blankets back, his hand moved down her body. He was breathing hard and the unmistakable stench of alcohol filled her nose. As his hand neared her breast, he chuckled and grinned.

Her stomach churned. She didn't want him on her. Touching her. Taking her. He had no right. Forcefully, she drew up her knee, aiming it directly between his legs. His body doubled as he groaned in pain.

She tried to move away from him, but her gown was pinned beneath his body. As she yanked on it, he regained his composure and slapped her hard across the face. Even her pa, in all his drunken fits, had never struck her. Covering her face to prevent another strike, the door knob jiggling caught her ear.

"William!" she cried out, no longer afraid.

"Cora?"

There was fear in his voice, then the click of the key in the lock.

"William!" she screamed again as he entered the room. Pushing against Marcus's shoulders, she looked at her husband for help.

William's eyes filled with fury. Grabbing Marcus by the back of the shirt, he wrenched him from the bed in one effortless motion. Though William was a large man, until that moment, she hadn't realized just how strong he was.

Marcus stumbled backward and fell to the floor.

She jumped from the bed and wrapped her arms around William's bulging waist. Her pounding heart began to slow. He would protect her.

He tenderly stroked her hair, air hissing from his nostrils. "What are you doing in me wife's room?"

"Wife?" Marcus pulled his shoulders back and straightened his clothes. "She's no more your wife than this boat! She's a piece a property. A payment for a debt." He became bolder. "I want my pay, too. I was here to take it."

William gently pushed her to the side and crossed to Marcus. Wrapping his large hands around the man's neck, he shoved him against the wall, then pressed his huge body against him, pinning him where he stood. "I should kill you now!" He began to squeeze, and in no time, Marcus's face started to change color.

Marcus gripped William's hands, trying to pry them from his neck; struggling to free himself.

Though she despised Marcus for what he'd planned to do, she didn't want him murdered here in front of her.

"William," she whispered. "He ain't worth it."

William looked at her, his eyes on fire. "No man will have you, but me." He returned his attention once again to Marcus and his knuckles whitened as his grip tightened further.

She laid her hand on William's arm. "William ... don't."

William closed his eyes, then his hands eased, but he didn't let go. "I paid you what Craighead took. You're out nothing."

Marcus snarled. "I'm gettin' bored with Francine. I want sumthin' new. You don't love 'er. Why can't I have 'er?"

"I thought you had more sense!" William took him by the shoulders and dragged him across the room and out the door.

With a racing heart, she followed them, watching as William pulled him with ease down the hallway to the exterior door.

"I was only tryin' to take what I deserve!" Marcus yelled. He tried to struggle, but William's strength overpowered him.

"I'll give you what you deserve," William snapped.

They reached the outer rail. The sun was setting and a small amount of light glistened on the dark water.

As William lifted Marcus off his feet, he struggled even harder. "Don't do this, O'Brien! You do, and you'll regret it! I know what you do, and I'll see you hung!"

"All you'll see is the bottom of the Mississippi!" William lifted him up and over the rail and hurled him into the water below.

A loud scream was followed by a large splash, then nothing more than the ongoing thrum of the paddle wheel.

She raced to William's side. Looking over the rail, all she could see was dark water. "Where'd he go?"

"To Hell," William muttered, then turned and walked back toward her room.

She scurried after him. "But ... can he swim?"

"Doubtful." William continued. Doors opened, then quickly shut as they made their way past guest rooms. She looked down at herself and realized she'd gone out in her nightgown. In all the chaos, she hadn't even considered what she was wearing.

Closing her door, she crossed to William, who had seated himself in a chair at her table.

"Why'd you do it?" She could barely get the words out.

He looked up into her eyes. "No man will take what's mine. You're me wife, Cora." He took her hand and kissed it.

"It was a miracle you came to my room. When you play cards, you never leave so early." Tears pooled in her eyes, and when she blinked, a stream trickled down her cheeks.

"I went to the bar and Giles wasn't there. I followed me gut and came to your room. Had I listened to your worries, he would have been released before this happened."

She placed her hand on his shoulder. "I ain't angry, William. You came in time. He didn't hurt me ... much." Remembering the sting of his hand, she touched her wet cheek, which was bound to show a bruise.

"I'm sorry, Cora," he whispered.

She took his hand and lifted him to his feet. Then she led him to the bed.

"Give me a baby, William." She took her position at the edge of the bed, knowing it would give him pleasure. She looked deeply into his eyes. "Please, William?"

"Aye," he said, and dimmed the lantern. "Aye ..."

Chapter 8

"Mista O'Brien told me to bring you water for a bath," Bessie said, holding a pail in each hand.

Cora gratefully let her in the room. It was mid-July and blistering hot. The water Bessie poured into the tub was cool and she couldn't wait to dip her body into it.

"I'm covered in sweat." She wiped her brow. "I reckon I could fill the tub myself given time."

The girl giggled. "I'll bring more water."

"Thank you, Bessie." Cora held the door as she left with the empty pails.

Three full months on the *Bonny Lass,* and as much as she had longed to travel by steamboat, she wanted off. She'd forgotten what it felt like to have her legs on steady ground. Her body had grown accustomed to the movement of the boat.

Bessie returned with two more pails and added them to the bath. "Few more should be 'nuff." She smiled at her. "I's shore glad you're happy now, Ms. O'Brien. Mista O'Brien be happy, too."

Cora gave her a slight smile in return. "Bessie? Do you know where we're goin'?"

"Shore do. We's headin' for N'Orleans. Din't Miss Francine tell you?"

"No."

Bessie placed her hands on her hips. "I don't like that Mista O'Brien don't let you leave the boat. It ain't right."

She didn't respond, rather turned her back not wanting to show her disappointment.

"I's sorry, Ms. O'Brien. Sometimes I speak my mind."

Cora lowered her head. "It's all right."

Bessie left to get the last two pails of water. When she returned, Cora was staring out the window. "Is New Orleans as fine as folks say?" Cora asked without shifting her gaze.

Bessie emptied the pails into the tub. "Some folks likes it."

From the sound of her voice, she assumed Bessie was not one of those folks.

Since the night of Marcus Giles *disappearance*, there had been rumors circulating the boat. Of course, Cora knew the truth, but in order to preserve the good name of her husband, she kept that knowledge to herself. The only person she'd told about that night was Francine.

"I'll ask Francine 'bout it," she said, turning to Bessie.

"Mmm, hmm," Bessie muttered. "You an Miss Francine has become friends."

Again, the girl's tone indicated disapproval.

"Yes, we have," she said defensively. "Don't you like her?"

Bessie lifted her chin and rolled her eyes upward. "Not my place to say."

"Why?"

Bessie set the empty pails on the floor and crossed her arms over her chest. "I's been taught what she do ain't right. I likes you, Ms. O'Brien, an I don't want her teachin' you bad things."

She stared blankly at Bessie.

"Ms. O'Brien, you gots a husband. Miss Francine don't. But she act like she do with any man she please." Lifting the pails from the floor, she stared downward. "I say too much. Mista O'Brien find out I been talkin' bad 'bout Miss Francine, he'd tan my hide."

"I won't say nothin', Bessie." Cora gently touched her arm.

Bessie nodded her head and scurried out the door.

Cora was glad to be alone, again. She liked Bessie, but she also liked Francine. Confused by Bessie's admonishment, she wondered what Mrs. Moss would have to say about the situation. At times like this, she missed her more than ever.

It felt good to shed her garments and slip into the cool water. She glided a bar of lye soap across her skin. Looking down at her body, she was well aware that her form had changed in the time she'd been on board. The abundant food had plumped her in all the appropriate places, giving her more of a womanly shape. She smiled as she ran the soap across her breasts. They, too, had *plumped.*

Thankful that she was handy with a needle and thread, she altered most of her own garments. Francine had graciously given her some of her dresses, telling her that they were easily replaced. Francine liked to shop and knew of all the finest boutiques at every port. The only part of her body that hadn't changed was her mark. It was there for good and nothing she could do would ever change it.

Dressing in a light-weight, cotton dress, she made her way down the hallway to Francine's room, making sure to knock before entering. Upon seeing her at the door, Francine pulled her eagerly inside the room. "Cora," her voice was full of excitement, "William said we will stay in New Orleans for three days! I plan to go home. I want you to come with me."

"But ..." Her heart raced. *Will he let me go?*

"But nothing," Francine said. "I want you to meet Madame Beaumont. She knows many things."

Cora plopped herself down on Francine's bed. "You know William won't let me leave the boat."

Francine sat beside her. "I will ask him. As long as you are with me, then he should trust you. Besides, I believe he knows you will not leave him."

Cora stared at her hands and nervously twisted the wedding band around her finger. "He's my husband. I *can't* leave him."

"Then it is settled." Francine took her hands, forcing her to stop fidgeting. "When you told me about your mark, I knew then that you must meet Madame Beaumont."

Cora jerked her hands away. "I told you, cuz I trust you. I don't want some stranger knowin' 'bout my mark."

"You may find that your mark means something more than you realize." Francine's eyes were wide with intensity, and a small amount of fear.

"How can sumthin' on my skin mean more than just an ugly thing my pa used to fret over?"

Francine bit her lower lip, and blinked several times. "Madame Beaumont will tell you."

Slowly, Cora let out her breath. "Will you come with me to ask William?"

"*Oui*. Let us go now. He is at the wheel." Francine's eyes regained their sparkle.

The two went hand-in-hand to the bow of the ship and the small room which housed the wheel. William stood, gazing across the glittering water, with his hands firmly clutching the wooden wheel. He turned his head as they approached and let out a chuckle. "And what are the two of you up to?"

Francine gave her a gentle nudge.

"William," Cora said with as much bravery as she could muster. "I hear we'll be in New Orleans by nightfall."

"Aye," he said, raising his eyebrows. "And what of it?"

"Well ..." She cleared her throat. "I was just wonderin'. Ah, heck. William, I'd like to go ashore."

Again, William raised his brows, then looked out across the water. "You know the rules."

She defiantly crossed her arms over her chest. "Course I do! And I don't like 'em none! I've been on this boat for more than three months. Dang! Even the slaves get to leave every now an then. I'm your wife, and you treat me like ... like ... well ... a caged animal!"

Francine stood frozen, and when Cora looked to her for help, she cast her eyes downward.

Cora shook her head, disappointed in her friend.

William cleared his throat. "The last time you told me that you felt like a *pet* I allowed you to roam the boat. So now, you say 'tis not enough?" He wouldn't look at her.

She stepped forward and placed her hand on his shoulder. "My legs have forgotten what land feels like. I won't leave you, William. I belong here, but dang ..." Her voice was a whisper. "I need to use my land legs."

His shoulders shook as a deep laugh emerged and bubbled out of him. "Your land legs?"

Francine giggled. "*Oui.* Her land legs."

William narrowed his gaze and looked directly at Francine. "Can I trust you to look after her?"

"*Oui.* Of course! No harm will come to her."

Turning his face toward the river, William sighed. "Very well. But only in the light of day. At night, she must return to the boat."

Cora couldn't believe what she was hearing. Her heart pounded at the thought of walking on land. Jubilantly, she wrapped her arms around his massive body. "Thank you, William!" She kissed his cheek, then grabbed Francine's hand and fled with her down the hallway before he changed his mind.

* * *

"*Vieux Carre,*" Francine said in an angelic whisper. "The French Quarter."

Cora's *land legs* were still wobbly, but her eyes were sharp as she looked in every direction.

"Dang," she whispered, holding firmly to Francine's arm. Her eyes popped at the ornate buildings with intricate wrought iron railings and window baskets full of brightly-colored flowers.

"My home," Francine said, taking her by the hand and leading her down the cobblestone street.

"Where?" she asked, wide-eyed.

"Everywhere," Francine laughed.

Wanting to make a good impression for her homecoming, Francine wore a brilliant red dress made of shimmering satin. Cora chose a more modest blue cotton dress, with a dainty floral print. The heat of the summer couldn't be squelched and she wanted to be as comfortable as possible. They were an attractive pair and caused the men passing to take a second look.

It was obvious to her that Francine enjoyed the attention by responding to every glance with fluttering lashes and a coy tilt of the head. Cora, on the other hand, looked away from the eyes that followed her, reminding herself that she was a married woman.

"This way," Francine said, pulling on her hand. She led her to a two-story brick house sitting on a corner lot.

Cora stood in awe of the beautiful house. "This ain't nothin' like what I grew up in."

"*Chez moi*," Francine said, dreamily. "My home."

"Is your ma expectin' you?" Cora asked as they walked up the groomed sidewalk.

Francine giggled. "No."

As soon as the door opened, Francine was pulled into a warm hug and quickly surrounded by young women fawning over her.

"We have missed you," one young blonde said as she kissed Francine on the cheek.

It went on this way for several minutes until everyone had welcomed her home. Cora counted at least fifteen women. When she wasn't looking at the pretty smiling faces, she took in the fabulous décor of the living room. Everything was clean and tidy and looked new. Upholstery had no tears and every brass lantern shined as if recently polished. The window dressings were light and airy and fluttered gently against partially-opened windows. The floor was covered in woven carpet that matched the shades of green in the furniture. She looked down at her feet, thankful that there had been no rain. Never would she dare soiling such fine carpeting.

Francine proudly presented Cora to her family. "This is my dearest friend, William's wife," she said with a broad smile.

There was a series of surprised gasps and a stifled giggle. But soon after, she, too, was welcomed with kisses and warm embraces.

"You got a big family," Cora said after the last squeezing hug.

"*Oui,* I do."

"Are your folks home?" She looked around at all the faces, none of which was old enough to be her parent. Again, tiny giggles erupted from the girls. Francine led her away to a small sitting room and motioned her to a chaise. Cora sat and folded her hands in her lap. "Did I say sumthin' wrong?"

"No," Francine replied and sat beside her. "Cora, these are not my *real* sisters. I worked here with them before William asked me to work on the boat."

Cora gulped, suddenly realizing what work she was referring to. "They do that here?"

"*Oui.* This is where William found me. And I am happy he did."

"He must a really liked you. He had a lotta girls to choose from." Cora sat quietly, staring at her wedding band. She assumed he could have had any of these pretty girls as a wife, but he'd chosen *her*. Though the result of a bet, he still could have refused her.

Francine stood and reached out her hand. "I will take you to Madame Beaumont."

"She don't live here?"

"No. But she is not far." Francine pulled her to her feet. "Come."

Even though all the young women had been kind, Cora was glad to be leaving their house. It may have been Francine's *Chez moi*, but it felt nothing like home to her.

Several blocks down the road, they stopped at a much smaller house. It was older than the pleasure house, and covered with climbing vines. The side yard held a small vegetable garden with tomato plants and herbs. It was in need of weeding, but otherwise the plants looked healthy.

"She loves tomatoes," Francine said, pointing to the numerous plants.

Cora nodded. Her stomach churned as they approached the woman's door. Before Francine could knock, the door opened.

Cora stared at the odd looking little woman. Deep wrinkles covered her face, and her eyes were crystal blue. Her head was wrapped with a turban-like cloth, in brilliant colors of red, orange, and green. The woman raised her bony hand toward her, pointing a long, ring-laden finger.

"I see you," she rasped, through dry cracked lips. Her accent was unlike any she'd heard before. A trace of French, similar to Francine's, but much more gruff. Cora's breath hitched in her throat. Her first instinct was to turn and run.

"Madame Beaumont." Francine held her hand firmly. "Don't frighten her."

Madame Beaumont turned and grinned. She was missing a front tooth.

"Come in," the woman said and motioned them inside. Her wrist jingled with the sound of multiple gold and silver bracelets. As she stepped back, allowing them to enter, Cora marveled at the caftan she wore. The long, flowing robe-like dress was not something a proper woman would wear. Like her headwear, it, too, was multicolored and vibrant.

Cora wrinkled her nose at the unusual odor in the old woman's home. A strange, spicy scent filled the air. They were led to a round table and told to sit. Madame Beaumont excused herself to make tea.

She thought about Mrs. Moss, but tea was the only thing she and Madame Beaumont had in common. The tiny house Mrs. Moss inhabited was simple, with very little furniture. This house was just as small, but crammed full of everything imaginable. The living area had two small sofas, an over-stuffed chair, two round end tables, and a large book case. All of the furnishings were topped with jewel-toned coverlets. The room flowed into the dining room where they were seated. The tiny table was surrounded by four captain-style chairs made of carved wood. A two-eyed black stove sat perched in the corner of the room, and Madame Beaumont was poking sticks of wood into the chamber, stoking the fire. It crackled and popped and the old woman muttered as she went about preparing their tea.

A collection of assorted figurines were scattered here and there. The largest, resembling an ape, sat beside a window next to one of the sofas. Multi-colored candles flickered around the room, sitting on any surface flat enough to hold them.

The walls were decorated with swirling turquoise and blue wallpaper, and framed artwork all around. Most were florals, but one was a nude dancer discreetly turning her back to the artist. Cora cocked her head sideways, staring at the woman's bottom, and wondered if her own looked similar.

When Madame Beaumont returned, she handed each of them a cup. Cora thanked her and took a sip.

It was all she could do to swallow and not spit out the nasty liquid. She doubted she wanted to know exactly what she was drinking.

"Madame Beaumont," Francine began, "I brought Cora to you for-"

Madame Beaumont put her hand up. "I know why you are here." She shifted her eyes to Cora. "I knew you were coming."

Cora felt her eyes widening. "How'd you know?"

The old woman reached out her hand and placed it over Cora's, then closed her eyes and tipped her head back. "I feel you ..." She began to hum.

Cora tried to withdraw her hand, but the woman tightened her grip. Francine leaned toward her. "She will not hurt you. She is a seer."

"Huh?" she asked, swallowing another large lump in her throat.

The woman brought her head forward, then lowered it and continued humming. Without warning, she stopped. Her eyes flew open and she stared directly at Cora. "You have a mark."

Cora's head turned sharply toward Francine. "You told her?" She took in a deep breath, willing back the tears that stung her eyes.

Francine rapidly shook her head. "No. It is as I told you. She is a seer."

Cora looked at Madame Beaumont through blurred vision. "How do you know 'bout that?" she said a little too harshly, but she couldn't stop herself.

"I feel it. I must see it with my eyes." Madame Beaumont rose to her feet and stood beside her. "Show me your mark."

"Uh-uh." Cora glued her eyes to the table, hoping the woman would go away. Her heart beat so rapidly that she thought any minute now it might burst from her chest.

"Cora," Francine said with compassion, "I told you she can tell you things. You do not have to be afraid. She will not hurt you, I promise."

For some reason, she believed Francine and suddenly wanted to know what the seer would say. Cora stood, towering over the little woman.

"Come." Madame Beaumont grasped her hand, leading her into her tiny bedroom. Like the rest of the house, it was filled full and there was scarcely room to walk. She unfolded a changing screen that had been leaning against the wall, and stood it erect. Then she nodded at Cora and motioned behind the screen.

This woman scared the fire out of her, but she followed her direction and removed her dress, then draped it over the screen. She stepped out in her undergarments.

Every window in the old woman's house was covered with heavy drapery. The only thing illuminating the room were the candles, eerily flickering.

"Show me," Madame Beaumont commanded, lifting a candle toward her.

Cora tentatively raised her chemise, exposing the mark.

"Ah ..." the woman gasped. With one hand holding the candle, she took her other hand and ran her fingers lightly over the mark. "Oh ..." she moaned.

Cora wanted to jerk away, but stood firmly, trusting Francine, who stood beside them and leaned in looking at the mark.

"Well?" Francine asked Madame Beaumont.

The old woman didn't answer. Her hand moved further down Cora's body and came to rest on her lower belly. "A boy," she whispered.

Francine's mouth dropped. "A child?"

The woman nodded.

"What's she mean?" Cora asked.

"You are going to have a baby," Francine said. "She can feel it."

Cora looked down at her abdomen. "How? I don't feel nothin'."

The woman's hand moved upward again. She laid it flat against the mark. Instantly, her expression changed to one of pain. "Oh ..." she moaned, just as she had before.

"Why's she doin' that?" Cora asked. "It sounds like it hurts her."

"Madame?" Francine asked. "Are you in pain?"

The woman continued to moan and tears trickled down her cheek. Her body shook until finally, she pulled away. "I must sit," she said and moved toward one of the sofas.

Francine followed her and Cora returned to the changing screen to dress.

When she came out, Francine and Madame Beaumont were talking in whispers. She became aware of something else that reminded her of Mrs. Moss. Madame Beaumont had cats. Not just one, but she counted at least four. They prowled around the house as mysteriously as Madame Beaumont herself.

Francine patted the sofa, beckoning her. "Come sit."

Cora nearly sat on one of the cats, but it sprinted away before her bottom touched the fabric. She looked at Madame Beaumont, bit her lip, and waited to hear what she had to say.

"You will have a son," Madame Beaumont said matter-of-factly. "A good son."

Cora smiled. "That's what William wants."

Closing her eyes, the old woman moaned. "Beware the mark."

"Why?" Cora was tired of the wailing.

"It means death," Madame Beaumont said, opening her eyes.

"*My* death?" She squeaked out the question.

"You died already."

Cora stood. This woman obviously wasn't in her right mind, and all she was doing was scaring her.

Madame Beaumont grabbed her arm, pulling her down. "Let me explain."

"*Oui*, Cora. Let her explain," Francine urged.

Madame Beaumont lifted her hands, spread her fingers, and wiggled them through the air. "In your previous life, you were pierced by an arrow. A savage took your life, and the mark remains as a warning. It is where the arrow entered your body, and its essence carried over when you were reborn."

Cora was speechless. This was the most ridiculous thing she'd ever heard. "So ... what's it warnin' 'bout?"

The old woman closed her eyes and began rotating her head in slow circles. "You must protect the child. At all cost ... protect the child."

Cora covered her belly with both hands. If there was a child growing in her, she'd protect it. No crazed woman had to tell her to do it.

"Francine?" she whispered. "Let's go back to the boat. I wanna see William."

Madame Beaumont grabbed her hand and squeezed. "At *all* cost!"

Cora jumped to her feet. "I wanna go *now*, Francine."

Francine led her to the door. "Wait here."

Anywhere but near that woman ...

Within moments, Francine returned and they left the old woman's house.

"What did you tell her?" Cora asked, as they walked briskly down the street toward the shore.

"I thanked her," Francine said.

"Thanked her? She's not in her right mind."

"Oh, but she is. You will find out soon enough." Francine offered a smile, but Cora couldn't return it. She'd never been so frightened, and was anxious to feel the comfort and security of her home ... the *Bonny Lass*.

Chapter 9

Cora stood in her room, looking out the window. Though they were docked in New Orleans for three full days, she wouldn't venture out again. Memories of Madame Beaumont haunted her.

"I allow you to leave, yet you come back to me even before I require it," William said as he walked up behind her and turned her to him. He tenderly touched her face. "Why, Cora?"

"I didn't like it there." She closed her eyes, soothed by his gentle touch. "I ... I feel safe here. 'Sides, I didn't want you to think I might run off."

"I'm glad you returned early. Though I trust Francine, I don't trust others in the city."

She lowered her hands and rested them on her belly. "William?" She moved them in a circular motion. "An old woman said I have a baby growin' in me. She said she could feel it."

"What woman?"

"Francine said her name's Madame Beaumont. She scared me."

William placed his hand over hers. "I know of her."

"But—how would she know? She said other things, too, but I don't believe her."

He took her by the hand and led her to a chair. "Don't think about it. I will speak to Francine about her actions. She should have asked me before taking you to her."

"Don't be mad at Francine. She thought she was helpin' me."

"Helping?" William's eyebrows knit together as he sat down beside her.

"The woman wanted to see my mark." She went on to tell him all that Madame Beaumont had said. He listened closely, and it seemed that her words made him sad, as the sparkle in his eyes she'd grown to love disappeared.

"A son?" he asked. "Let me see."

She stood and he helped her remove her dress, then she pulled up her chemise and he placed his hand over her belly.

"Your hand's warm," she said, smiling at him.

He closed his eyes and warmth covered his face. "You're not as thin as you once were. However, unlike Madame Beaumont, I cannot tell that our son is inside you. But I have hope."

"If you ain't sure, then I reckon we need to keep tryin' ... just to be sure. I don't mind." She looked into his face until he opened his eyes and met her gaze.

"To be certain," he whispered, and they moved to the bed.

* * *

Months passed and there was no denying the certainty of her condition. Cora was without a doubt carrying William's child. He doted on her, bringing her everything she craved. If they didn't have it on board, he would go into port and find it for her. Luckily for William, her cravings were simple. The most common craving was fried chicken. With curry.

Bessie also doted on her and expressed her excitement over the coming baby. She took time to teach Bessie how to knit, and they would spend hours in her room making tiny items for the baby. She also read to Bessie and tried to encourage her to learn how to read. Bessie preferred knitting.

As her belly grew, William no longer took her to himself. She feared he might return to Francine in order to be kept *happy*, but he assured her that he had no interest in Francine.

If anything, Francine became more distant the further her pregnancy progressed. Maybe Francine was jealous. Though she claimed not to be interested in being a wife or mother, Cora believed it was what every woman truly wanted. At least, that's what Mrs. Moss had always told her.

The first time she felt the baby move, she went as quickly as possible to find William. He was at his post manning the wheel, and when he saw the look on her face, he immediately called for his cub pilot to relieve him. There was concern in his eyes as he led her down the hallway to her room.

"William, nothin's wrong. I was just excited, that's all. I felt it move." She took his hand and placed it on her abdomen.

It shook. "Cora ... I don't feel it." His eyebrows knit with worry. "Are you certain you felt it?"

"Yes, sir. Here, try a little lower." She moved his hand to a new spot. "Push a little. You won't hurt me."

With hesitation, he pushed against her, then rapidly withdrew his hand. "I felt something."

She giggled. "I've been feelin' it from the inside flutterin' 'round for quite a spell, but this is the first time I could feel it on top a my skin. I wanted to wait to tell you 'til I knew you could feel it, too." She grinned at him, and brightened even more when a tear trickle down his cheek. "William, the baby's fine."

Later that night, as they went to dinner, William walked taller than ever. He proudly paraded her on his arm and showed her more attention than the other husbands on board showed their wives.

"Tonight," he announced, winking at her, "I will play cards for me son."

"Huh?" she asked, confused. She protectively covered her belly.

"What I meant to say was ... my winnings will go to our son. It's high time you buy some furnishings for the lad. He'll need a proper cradle." He took her hand and kissed it sweetly.

She released a relieved sigh.

* * *

Another month passed and William had not yet provided a cradle. She thought about her pa and knew that if she could see him, he could carve a beautiful cradle for the baby. However, when she suggested they stop at Plum Point, William's demeanor instantly changed and he told her firmly, "no."

When she was nearly in her ninth month, and still had no bed for the baby, she decided it was time to push the issue with William. He'd stopped going into port for some unexplained reason and he'd become more distant from her. She knew that she'd grown as big as a cow, but never imagined that William would turn away from her for that reason. After all, she was carrying *his* son in her humongous belly.

They would be docking in Memphis tomorrow, and from all that she'd been told, it had a very busy port. Merchants set up their wares close to the docks, hoping to attract travelers leaving the boats.

Being that it was February, trade was not centered on cotton and most merchants were more inclined to bargain. She believed she could get what she was looking for at a reasonable price.

"I can't leave me boat, Cora," William said to her when she asked to go ashore.

"But we need a cradle." She rubbed her huge belly with both hands. "Can't you go just for a spell?"

"No. I have to take a look at the boiler. Been told it's out of sorts."

"What if Francine goes with me?" She pleaded with him. She hadn't left the boat since New Orleans, almost six months ago.

William placed his hand on the large bulge. Almost instantly, the baby kicked. "The lad wants out," he chuckled.

"So does his ma." It was the first time she'd heard him laugh in weeks. She tilted her head and looked at him with soft doe-eyes. "Just to buy a cradle. I can take Bessie, too. Would that make you feel better?"

William rubbed his hand over the top of his head, but then nodded. "Just promise me you'll take care. You're carrying the most precious cargo on this boat."

His words touched her heart. "I will, William."

With permission granted, she left him to find Francine and Bessie so they could make plans for their outing.

* * *

"Now, Ms. O'Brien, you take care and let me help you," Bessie fussed, as they walked down the platform. She held onto Cora's arm, steadying her.

Cora grinned, held her belly, and waddled one step at a time.

Francine followed after them, pulling her coat tightly around her body. "Cora, it is not the best time for shopping. It is far too cold for my liking."

"I'm glad it's cool," she said, taking in a deep breath. "Carryin' this extra weight makes me hot." She wore a heavy wool coat over her long, full dress. Her baby bulge was obvious and kept her from fastening the buttons around her middle.

They walked the short distance onto shore and cast their eyes around the long line of vendors. Even without the cotton trade, there was bustling activity. As with any city along the Mississippi, every port had its share of saloons and gambling halls. William had cautioned her that many of the men on board spent the winter months looking for easy money, and once off the boat were lured to the darker sides of town where shady activities bade them in.

The women had no interest in those things, but wanted to spend their money on goods. Things they could hold onto and not fritter away.

"The mercantile is this way," Francine said, nodding to the left.

Cora had seen mercantiles before, and hoped for something a bit more exciting. "Ain't there any street vendors that might sell things for babies?"

"The mercantile would be the best place for you to go," Francine insisted.

Cora looked down the street to the right and noticed a small shop with brightly-colored cloth flags billowing in front of it. The color caught her eye, but then it was a wood carving that kept her attention. Someone had taken great care in carving out a tall figurine of an angel. "I wanna go this way."

"But you need to go with me," Francine said. "I told William I would look after you."

Cora glanced again at the flags. "Tell you what ... Bessie can stay with me. You go to the mercantile and see if they have a cradle, all right?"

Francine crossed her arms. "William will not like it."

"I'll be fine. 'Sides, I don't think I'll be able to be out long. I'm already gettin' tired and we just left the boat."

Bessie jumped in, "I'll look after her, Miss Francine. I won't let nothin' happen to her."

Francine shook her finger at Bessie. "You had better not. William will take a switch to you if she is harmed."

"Yes'm," Bessie said, lowering her head.

Francine cinched her coat tightly once again and shivered. "I will find you a cradle. I do not know why you must go the other way."

Cora stepped up to Francine and kissed her on the cheek. "I can't explain it, but sumthin' 'bout that angel is callin' to me."

Bessie linked her arm in Cora's. "We be fine, Miss Francine."

Francine offered a weak smile, then headed off in the opposite direction.

Cora's mind drifted to thoughts of her pa. When she was a very young girl, he'd carved a small angel for her. She wondered if it was still tucked away in the box beside her bed. Maybe that was why she was drawn to this little shop.

As they got closer, there were pieces of furniture strewn about. The workmanship was fine, but the woodcarver needed someone to tidy up. There were small tables, chairs, and ornate boxes, as well as an assortment of figurines. Mostly animals, but also a collection of angels. Then, as she opened the door and entered the shop, there was the most beautiful thing of all; a wooden chain spanning the perimeter of the small room.

Her pa had carved a wooden chain out of an old oak block, and it had always been her favorite piece. She was fascinated with the way it could go on forever and never be broken. It had to be completely thought through before the knife touched the wood. Each link had to magically entwine with the others but also become separate in its own right. The end joined with the beginning, and he was forever carving out the middle. Maybe with her gone, he'd finally finished it.

Sitting on a stool in the corner of the tiny shop was a man with a whittling knife. He hadn't bothered to look up when they entered. All she could see of him was the top of his white-haired head.

Cora cleared her throat, drawing his attention.

"Let me know if you wanna buy sumthin'," he said, without raising his head, and continued whittling. He appeared to be sculpting a cat.

"You wouldn't happen to have a baby cradle, would you?" Cora asked.

"Nope. But I can make one if you want." He continued to stare at the cat, moving the knife with skill and patience.

She wandered to the corner of the shop and gazed at the wooden chain, then reached her hand up to touch it. The door opened, but she was so enthralled with the chain that she didn't bother looking to see who had entered.

She glanced at the woodworker. "My pa's been makin' a wooden chain for years now. Someday, I reckon it'll look like this one."

"Elise?" A crisp, deep voice filled the little room.

Cora turned her head and looked toward the sound.

"Elise?" he repeated.

When she realized he was speaking to her, she bit her lower lip and grinned. He couldn't be real. No man could look this fine. He wore a well-fitting black suit and hat, but it was his facial features that captivated her. He was clean-shaven with a firm jawline and a cleft in the middle of his chin that intrigued her. She had no idea that any man could be carved so perfectly.

His eyes met hers. "Elise, what are you doing here? I thought you were going out of town this week with your mother."

She turned around completely and faced him. "I reckon you must a mistook me for someone else. I ain't Elise." She placed her hands on her belly and smiled. "I came in here lookin' for a cradle."

His big brown eyes opened wide as he stared at the bulge. "Oh ... I'm so sorry ... But ... you look ..." His face twisted as he tried to understand his error.

She dipped her head. "I'm Cora, an this here's Bessie." She nodded toward Bessie who was instantly by her side.

The man removed his hat, exposing hair similar in color to hers. He nodded courteously to both of them. "Douglas. Douglas Denton. And this is my uncle, Harper."

The old man on the stool bobbed his head, but continued carving.

Douglas smiled. "He doesn't talk very much, but as you can see he's quite talented."

A spark of unexplained energy pulsed through Cora's body. A simple smile from this stranger made her heart flutter. She liked the way he talked. It reminded her of

Mrs. Moss—proper and well-spoken—though he didn't have the same accent.

"Yes, he is talented," she agreed. "My pa is a wood-carver. Been workin' on a chain like that one for years."

Douglas stared at her, and shook his head. "I'm sorry ... Mrs. ..."

"O'Brien," Bessie interjected. "Her name's O'Brien."

"Mrs. O'Brien," Douglas said, nodding at Bessie. "Forgive me for staring, but you look very much like a friend of mine. Her name is Elise. Elise Peck. Do you know of her?"

Cora shook her head. "Nope. I ain't never heard a no one named Peck." She looked at the floor, then slowly raised her head, meeting his gaze. "Can't imagine anyone lookin' like me."

"She's lovely," he said and again smiled his more-than-gracious smile.

She gulped, knowing that his compliment of Elise was actually a compliment for her. *He has the nicest eyes ...* She stood entranced for what seemed like an eternity. It wasn't until Bessie cleared her throat that she snapped to attention.

"Ms. O'Brien, we needs to go. Miss Francine will be worried." Bessie tugged on her arm.

Without warning, a sharp pain shot through Cora's lower abdomen. "Oh!" she cried out, and nearly fell to her knees.

Douglas grabbed her arm, holding her steady. Bessie already had a firm grip on the other.

"What is it?" he asked, wide-eyed.

"I don't know ..." Cora tried to explain but then another pain struck. "Oh ... my ..." She doubled over, holding her belly. "Dang!"

"We gots to get her on the boat!" Bessie yelled. "Mista O'Brien will have a fit!"

"The boat?" Douglas asked.

"Yessa," Bessie whimpered. "Her husband owns the *Bonny Lass*. We gots to get her to him!"

"Woman needs a doctor," Harper muttered. "Douglas, get the woman a doctor."

"He may not talk much, but he has sense," Douglas said, holding onto Cora. "Miss Bessie, I'll help you get her to the boat, then I'll get a doctor. I know of a good one."

"Thank you." Bessie held back tears. "I don't wanna make Mista O'Brien angry."

With Cora between them, Bessie and Douglas headed out the door and into the street. It didn't take long before another pain came and she crumpled.

Douglas wasted no time lifting her into his arms, then carried her the rest of the way. Once on the boat, William was alerted to her condition and was instantly at her side. He thanked Douglas for bringing her to him, then Douglas left to fetch the doctor. Bessie went with him to find Francine.

"William?" Cora said, as she opened her eyes and realized she was in *his* arms. William's arms were different than the arms that had carried her to the boat. Arms which for some unexplained reason she wished still cradled her.

William took her to her room and gently laid her on the bed. "He's bringing a doctor."

"It hurts, William," she muttered.

He stroked her head and soothed her with his words. "You'll be fine. I believe our son wants to be born."

"You think it's time?" she rasped.

"Aye ... the babe knows."

Chapter 10

Douglas had a horse and buggy at the livery stable not far from his uncle's shop. More than anything, he wished that Elise and her mother weren't out of town. Mrs. Peck was a midwife and exactly what he needed. Doctor Mitchell would have to do, but he needed to get to his office quickly.

Though Harvey Mitchell was young—only a few years older than himself—he knew him to be capable. He had tended his mother through a serious bout of pneumonia recently. After losing his father when he was a very young boy, Douglas was exceedingly grateful that Dr. Mitchell was able to save her.

"Is it your mother?" Dr. Mitchell asked when he opened the door and saw him standing there.

"No, sir," he replied, shaking his head. "There is a woman on one of the steamboats—a woman with child. She's having pains."

"What of Mrs. Peck?"

"She's away." Dr. Mitchell's hesitation was apparent, so he pressed on. "Please, Doctor. She's young. I'm quite certain it's her first."

Dr. Mitchell scratched the back of his head, then adjusted his wire-rimmed glasses. "I've not delivered many babies."

"Harvey, please?" He stared into his eyes, pleading with the doctor.

Dr. Mitchell cleared his throat. "I'll get my bag."

Douglas didn't move from the doorway. Wringing his hands, he had no idea why he was so anxious over the woman. She meant nothing to him. Yet, he found himself smiling, remembering the way she'd looked at him.

So uncanny ... the resemblance between her and Elise. Perhaps that was what drew him to her. He'd always been fond of Elise. However, just like his step-father, she'd always paid more attention to his step-brother, Cameron.

Dr. Mitchell grabbed his coat and hat as they rushed into his buggy and headed toward the boat.

"I'll pay you," Douglas said. He stared straight ahead and drove the horses as hard as he could.

"I know you will. I have you to thank for my new dining room table."

Douglas chuckled. He knew Harvey Mitchell well enough to know that it wasn't the money that led him to practice medicine. He genuinely wanted to help people. "Perhaps you'll be able to add a few more chairs. My uncle will gladly make them."

"Keeping things in the family?"

"Of course." He laughed aloud and found it eased his nerves.

* * *

Bessie was waiting for them at the loading platform. She shook her hands, then waved them frantically. "Hurry! Her water done broke!"

Dr. Mitchell clutched his bag and briskly walked up the platform with Douglas right on his heels. Douglas's eyes were drawn to another woman standing just over Bessie's shoulder. As he reached the top of the platform, he nodded at her and smiled. She smiled back, completely focused on him, and ignored the doctor.

"I am Francine DuBois," she said, extending her hand.

"Douglas Denton." He took her hand and raised it to his lips.

She giggled. "A true gentleman, I see."

"Acknowledging a true lady." Again, he dipped his head.

Bessie stomped her foot. "We ain't got time for this! Ms. O'Brien needs the doc!"

"Take me to her," Dr. Mitchell said.

Bessie jerked her head toward the stairwell and they all followed. As soon as they neared Cora's room, her cries filled the air.

"Dang!" she yelled, followed by loud, heavy breathing.

Bessie rapped on the door, then opened it a crack. "Mista O'Brien! I gots the doc."

William was sitting on the bed, perched beside Cora. He jumped to his feet and took Dr. Mitchell by the arm. Then he closed the door, leaving the rest of them standing in the hallway.

Moments later, the door opened again. "Bessie! Have the cook boil water. The doctor needs it!" The door slammed shut.

Bessie stammered, "I gots to go!" She raced away, leaving Douglas alone with Francine.

"So," Francine said, moving toward him, "how did *you* become drawn into this affair?" Her voice had a seductive lilt.

He took a step back, second-guessing his first impression of her. "I was at my uncle's woodshop when she began having pains."

"I see." She stepped even closer. "So, you have a big ... *heart*?" She ran her tongue around her lips as her eyes moved over his form.

He swallowed hard. "She needed help. I had to do something."

They were interrupted by another loud, "Dang!" from Cora.

Francine laughed softly. "She tends to curse. Her upbringing was not refined. But I am quite certain you already realized that, no?"

"No," he said, casting his eyes toward the door. "She's in pain. I hope she'll be all right."

"*Oui.* She is young. She has wide hips." Francine took another step forward and placed her hand on his chest. "You are a good man. I see that. Do you have a wife?"

His heart raced. "No. I've not yet fallen in love."

"*Oui. Amour* ..." Holding her hand to her breast, she batted her eyes, looking into his.

"Are *you* ... married?" he asked, and tried to steady his breathing.

"No. I do not marry. But ..." She ran her hand down his arm. "I know how to love."

When Cora yelled again, he was thankful for the interruption. He was even more grateful when Bessie arrived with the water.

"Mista O'Brien!" Bessie yelled, pounding on the door. "I gots the water!"

William opened the door, took the water from Bessie, then shut it again.

Bessie lowered her head. "I's never gonna have no babies."

He moved away from Francine and rested his hand on Bessie's arm. "Dr. Mitchell is a good doctor. She's going to be fine." Hearing himself say the words, he actually felt better.

"Hmmph," Francine whimpered. "That is what *I* told *you*."

He cocked his head and looked at her. "Yes, you did. And, I believe it to be so." He leaned in toward the door and grinned. "She stopped cursing."

The sound of a shrill baby's cry made him jump, then he laughed. "Now that's a welcome sound!"

The door opened enough for them to see William's shining face. "'Tis a lad!" He looked upward and shook his fists in the air. "I have a son!"

"Congratulations, sir," Douglas said. "And ... how is your wife?"

William closed his eyes and sighed. "I have a remarkable wife. She is quite well." He opened his eyes and smiled. "Thank you for all you did."

Douglas nodded and William closed the door.

"William has his son," Francine said, crossing her arms over her chest.

"Yes. It's what every man wishes for," Douglas whispered. Then, he remembered Cora's reason for going to his uncle's shop. "She needs a cradle."

"*Oui*. I did not acquire one. When Bessie came for me, I was trying to work out an arrangement with the shopkeeper." She grinned devilishly. "But, we did not come to an agreement."

He knew very well what she was implying. His brother had similar skills. "My uncle can make one. I'll go to him now." He turned his attention to Bessie. "Do you know how long you'll be in port?"

"Uh-uh," Bessie replied, shaking her head. "But, I reckon Mista O'Brien will stay 'til Ms. O'Brien's well. He won't go far from the doc." She looked longingly at the closed door. "I wants to see the baby."

"I'm certain you will, once they're ready. You care about her, don't you, Bessie?"

"Yessa! I love her! She been good to me."

He smiled and patted her shoulder. "I'll be back with a cradle."

"Want me to come with you?" Francine asked, reaching out her hand.

"No. Thank you, but no." This time he had to force himself to smile, then he walked away.

As he was leaving, he heard her muttering something in French.

* * *

"How did you craft this so quickly, Uncle Harper?" Douglas asked as he ran his hand over the tiny cradle.

Harper rubbed his bristly chin. "Knew she needed it. Knew you'd be back."

"How?"

"You like her. I could tell."

"Uncle Harper, have you forgotten that she's married, and just gave birth to her husband's son?"

"Didn't forget. Don't matter none. Man can't help how he feels. Best take care." He perched himself on his corner stool and picked up a knife.

"Thank you, Uncle Harper." Douglas lifted the cradle into his arms.

"Welcome." Harper lowered his head and went about his work.

It was a ridiculous thought. He didn't *like* her. How could his uncle say such a thing? But the excitement he felt just thinking about giving her the cradle, confused him. It had to be her similarity to Elise. Nothing else made sense.

And yet, she was so unlike Elise in every way *but* her features. Though there was a similar tone to their voices, their use of words was nothing alike. Never had he heard Elise curse. She spoke with refinement and proper upbringing. Cora, on the other hand, was obviously raised in the back woods. But something about her had charmed him from the moment she'd addressed him. He shook his head and chuckled.

Dang!

Chapter 11

"It's beautiful, William," Cora said, turning her head to look at the cradle. Her voice was weak and raspy, but she'd never been so happy. "Where'd you get it?"

He wasn't looking at her or the cradle. His eyes were affixed on his son. "That man. The one who brought you home. He brought the cradle."

She tried to rise up in the bed, but immediately lay back down. Little William squirmed in the crook of her arm. She closed her eyes, remembering the man her husband referred to. "Denton? Name's Denton, right?"

"Aye. Douglas Denton. You were sleeping when he brought it by. He didn't want me to wake you. He said to tell you that his uncle sent it with his compliments."

When she opened her eyes, William was stroking their son's cheek with his finger and he began to whimper.

"I can't imagine that man sayin' nothin'. He didn't talk much when we was in his shop." With great effort, she scooted up onto the pillows and opened the front of her gown. Her breasts bulged, already filling with milk.

William grinned. "Not so shy now, Cora?"

"Billy needs it. Mrs. Moss told me that's what God made 'em for." She moved Billy onto her breast where he eagerly began to suckle.

"Aye." William nodded. "Your Mrs. Moss is a very smart woman."

"Yep. Even though she never told me how to *make* a baby, she told me how to care for them. She had a baby that died ..." Tears pooled in her eyes. "William? I don't never want Billy to die."

"Billy won't die. Now, don't worry yourself."

She sniffled and gazed down at her tiny son. "Ain't he the most beautiful thing you ever did see?" She ran her hand over the light tuft of reddish-blond hair.

"Aye," William whispered.

"It didn't hurt much. Worse than goin' in, but not much."

William's shoulders shook as laughter bubbled out of him. "My dear, dear Cora. I never know what you might say."

She wrinkled her nose and grinned, though she didn't know why he was so amused. Then she turned her attention to the cradle. She believed in her heart that it was a gift from Douglas, even though he said that his uncle sent it with *his* compliments.

* * *

The *Bonny Lass* remained docked in Memphis for a full week. Dr. Mitchell came by daily to check on Cora and the baby. He reiterated to her just how much she looked like Elise, Douglas's friend. She couldn't comprehend such a thing.

Feeling at ease with him, she thought that perhaps he could tell her more about Douglas. She tried to convince herself it was simple curiosity, but it was more than that. Something about Douglas tugged at her from the inside out.

"Have you known Douglas long?" she asked, while trying to sound only mildly interested in his answer. She eased up in her bed and rested her back against the wall. Doctor Mitchell sat comfortably in a chair beside the bed.

"Yes, for some time now," he replied. "I tended his mother when she was quite ill."

She nodded, hoping he would continue. "Does he have a large family?"

"No. A step-brother, but no other siblings."

She sensed a tone of dislike at the mention of the step-brother. "You don't like his brother, do you?"

Harvey chuckled. "You're quite perceptive." He took a deep breath, then sighed. "Douglas's father died when he was a toddler. His mother married Arthur Wellesley, who was himself a widower. His first wife died in a carriage accident. A horrible thing."

She listened more intently as he opened up to her. "Terrible," she muttered, not wanting to say too much and cause him to stop speaking.

He nodded. "Yes. But the saddest thing of all is that Mr. Wellesley never took to Douglas. He needed a father, but Arthur already had a son and never gave Douglas a chance. He doted on Cameron and sadly spoiled the boy rotten."

"How could he not care for Douglas? He seems like a nice man." She leaned in toward the doctor. "He helped me."

Doctor Mitchell patted her hand. "Yes, he did. And you're right again. Douglas Denton is one of the finest men I've known." He rose from the chair. "I've probably said too much."

"No." She rapidly shook her head. "I'm glad you told me." She glanced in Billy's direction and smiled. "I ain't never gonna spoil *him* rotten. I might spoil 'im ... but never rotten."

Harvey rested his hand on Billy's head. "Just love him. Your love is the greatest gift you can give."

"That's the easy part," she said with a smile.

He grinned at her and told them both to get some sleep. Then he bent his head and walked out her door. She'd never known a man quite so tall and thin, or as smart as the doctor. But as she laid her head back onto her pillow, all of her thoughts were about Douglas.

* * *

On their final night in Memphis, William asked the doctor to return after his regular visit and join them for supper. Doctor Mitchell gladly accepted.

"Oh, and please bring Mr. Denton with you," William said as the doctor prepared to leave. "It's the least I can do to show my appreciation."

"Of course," Dr. Mitchell replied, and tipped his hat to Cora. "We'll see you this evening."

"Five o'clock," William added.

Cora fidgeted with her blanket as she watched Doctor Mitchell leave. Why was it so hard to ask this question? She took a deep breath of courage. "You reckon Mr. Denton will come?"

"Aye, he'll come," William said. "Francine tells me that she's taken a fancy to him. Most men can't resist her."

William kissed his son on the cheek, then smiled at her as he made his way out of her room. "Are you certain you'll be up to eating in the dining room tonight?"

She nodded.

"Then get some rest and I will see you later." He looked in Billy's direction one more time before pulling the door shut behind him.

She couldn't utter a sound. It felt as if a dagger had pierced her heart.

Francine? Francine's taken a fancy to 'im?

The last thing she wanted to think about was how easily Francine could make Douglas Denton *happy.* Though she knew it shouldn't matter; it did. She held Billy on her shoulder and stared out the window, gently patting his back. Unable to erase the thought of Francine entertaining Douglas, she decided to take William's suggestion and laid down for a nap. Billy cuddled his little body up next to hers, and in no time both of them drifted off.

"Ms. O'Brien," Bessie whispered in her ear, "you gots to wake up."

Cora's eyes popped open. "Did I miss supper?"

"No'm. But you will if'n you don't get dressed." Bessie lifted Billy from the bed. "You should put him in his cradle. Tired as you is, you might roll on him."

Cora gasped. "I never thought a that." She placed her hand on Billy's head. "I won't do it again."

"Tell you what," Bessie said, swaying with Billy in her arms. "After you feed him, I'll care for him. That way you can enjoy your supper."

She liked the idea. Her heart fluttered, thinking about Douglas.

After feeding Billy, she went to her wardrobe and selected a royal blue dress. She slipped into it, and had Bessie tie the bow in the back. Then, she sat down and brushed out her long hair. Since the weather was cool, she chose to leave it down, even though Francine insisted it was more stylish *up*.

Bessie giggled. "I ain't never seen you so excited 'bout supper. Guess you been cooped up in your room too long. What with the baby an all."

"That's right, Bessie. I wanna look real nice for ... William." Her face flushed. Could Bessie see through her words?

"Course you do! I ain't never seen Mista O'Brien more proud. He love this baby!" Bessie bounced him in her arms, patting his back and encouraging a burp.

"Yes, he does," she whispered. He loved the baby, but did he love her? She respected William, and was grateful for the life he'd given her, but her heart had never fluttered until the day she looked into Douglas's eyes. Shaking her head as if coming out of a deep sleep, she scolded herself.

I ain't got no right thinkin' 'bout another man.

So, she pinched her cheeks to give them color, licked her lips, kissed her son, and made her way to the dining room.

* * *

"Douglas," Francine chirped, "you truly are the kindest man I've ever known."

He thanked her, then pulled out her chair, allowing her to sit. He scanned the dining room, hoping to see Cora.

"Please ... sit by me," Francine said, patting the chair next to her.

Standing over her, he got a remarkable view of her cleavage. He couldn't deny that she was attractive, and as she looked up at him through her long lashes, he decided to comply and sat down beside her.

Immediately, she turned to face him, pursing her lips, and batting those incredible lashes. "You won't be disappointed," she said, leaning into him. Her words were followed by a light squeeze of his leg.

Not wanting to encourage her, he chose to ignore the gesture and again looked around the room. Dr. Mitchell stood by the stairwell talking to Mr. O'Brien. O'Brien acknowledged Douglas with a nod, indicating that they would be taking their seats soon. He was relieved. He didn't know how long he could entertain Francine.

And then Cora descended the stairs, slowly and gracefully, one step at a time. She showed no indication of discomfort and he assumed she was fully recovered from the delivery.

"You would never know she just had a baby," he muttered under his breath.

Francine leaned against him. "I heard you." She rested her hand on his leg. "She may look fine, but I assure you ... once a woman has had a baby, her body is never the same."

He glanced sideways at Francine. "A small sacrifice for bringing a new life into the world. Wouldn't you agree?"

Rather than responding, she took a sip of wine from her crystal goblet.

He rose to his feet and walked toward Cora. William and Dr. Mitchell were already by her side.

"You're well, I see," he said, nodding politely to her.

"Yep," she replied, and smiled timidly.

William put his arm around her and gave her a gentle squeeze. "Me wife is a strong woman. I'll forever be indebted to her for me son."

"What did you name him?" Douglas asked.

O'Brien puffed out his chest. "William Casey O'Brien the second."

"We call him *Billy*," Cora added. She looked directly into his eyes, then quickly shifted her gaze and stared at the floor.

Dr. Mitchell stepped up beside Douglas. "You were right about the similarity. If Elise could see her ..." He rubbed his chin and shook his head.

"Elise is still out of town. By the time she returns, the *Bonny Lass* will be long gone," Douglas said. "It's a shame ..."

William tucked Cora's hand into the crook of his arm, and led her across the room toward the table. Douglas and Dr. Mitchell followed. Cora looked over her shoulder and gave Douglas another timid smile. Something about her made his heart skip a beat, then race as if it had to catch up. She captivated him.

Francine looked up and smiled, once again patting the seat beside her.

"Douglas and I are old friends now," she said, looking at Cora. "It was good you chose not to go with me to the mercantile. I would have never met him."

He couldn't help but notice the expression on Cora's face. Francine's words clearly disturbed her. "I believe everything happens for a reason," he said. And when Cora lifted her head and smiled at him, his heart melted.

Throughout the meal, he couldn't stop himself from glancing in Cora's direction. Everything she did charmed him; the way she closed her eyes and savored every bite of food that entered her mouth, the way she giggled at simple things that no one else found amusing, but most of all the way her eyes sparkled when they met his.

He scarcely noticed anyone else or the remarks they made, and before he knew it everyone had finished their meal.

"I reckon I best go an tend to Billy," Cora said, scooting her chair back.

Every man at the table stood.

Cora giggled. "I ain't never seen nothin' like that. Takes a might gettin' used to."

William helped her to her feet. "I'll be up later. Cards tonight."

Cora nodded. "Night y'all."

Everyone politely told her goodnight.

"Mrs. O'Brien," Douglas said, moving toward her. "I hope the cradle is working out well for Billy."

"Yessir," Cora said. "I reckon what your uncle did was one a the nicest things ever done for me."

"He was happy to do it." He noticed that her brown eyes had tiny flecks of gold, then blinked rapidly, realizing he'd been staring far too long.

"Thank him for me, all right?"

"I will. Goodnight, Cora." He watched her as she ascended the stairs. She stopped halfway up and looked directly at him. Quickly, he took his seat and hoped that no one saw into his heart.

"Are you playing cards?" Francine asked him, as he pulled his chair closer to the table.

"No. I don't play. My brother, however, never passes up the opportunity."

Francine placed her elbows on the table, then rested her chin in her hands. "And where is your brother now? Why did you not bring him?"

"He wasn't invited. I assume he's home."

"Such a shame. Is he as handsome as you?" She seductively bit her bottom lip.

"We look nothing alike," he said, brushing aside her compliment. "He has blond hair and blue eyes. He's my step-brother." It was time to leave, though he didn't want to rush the doctor.

He caught Harvey's eye and realized that he too was ready to go. Harvey Mitchell was not a card player, either.

"'Tis a shame I can't convince you to try your hand at poker," William said boldly.

Dr. Mitchell wiggled his fingers in the air. "I have to keep my hands clean. One never knows when they might be needed for something more delicate."

William patted Dr. Mitchell soundly on the back. "Aye!" He chuckled heartily, then turned to bid Douglas goodbye. "Francine hoped to get to know you better," he said, leaning closely to him. "You might want to reconsider leaving." William winked and slapped his back.

"I appreciate your hospitality," Douglas said, "but, we must go. Perhaps another evening?"

The two men moved across the floor and in no time were on their way home.

Douglas sat quietly with reins in hand, as he guided the horse down the street. It would be dark soon, and he needed to get Dr. Mitchell home.

"What's bothering you, Douglas?" Harvey asked.

He shook his head. "It doesn't fit ..."

"What?"

"The two of them. He's old enough to be her father." He didn't shift his gaze, blankly staring forward.

"I agree. But it's not our place to judge love. It's obvious he cares for her."

"Cares. Yes, he gives her what she needs. But I can't imagine that *she* loves *him*. Truly *loves* him."

"Douglas." Harvey's voice was firm, so he turned to face him.

"Yes?"

"She gave him a child. There's no greater love."

He faced forward again and didn't respond. Instead, he clicked to the horse and snapped the reins. He needed to get home ...

Chapter 12

"Shhh," Cora soothed Billy. "Your ma's right here."

Billy fussed only briefly and was soon comforted against her breast.

She gazed down at his little face, marveling that she'd been a part of creating something so perfect. It made her sad to know that her ma never had the chance to experience such a blessing. It led her to wonder who had suckled her. Her pa never spoke of it.

Sounds of muffled voices seeped in through her closed door. She was propped up on her bed, leaning against the soft pillows. In the morning, the thrum of the engine would begin and the boat would leave Memphis. She would probably never see Douglas Denton again.

The voices became louder. She recognized one as William, but was unsure about the other. The angry tone in William's voice disturbed Billy. His tiny face wrinkled and his little legs kicked.

"It's all right, Billy," she whispered. "Your pa ain't mad at *you*."

Not wanting him to cry, she decided to get out of bed and ask William to keep his voice down. Covering herself, she cradled Billy and walked toward the door. Her intent was to open the door just enough to speak to William, but when she began to open it, she stopped, and decided to listen to the conversation.

"Don't waste any more time," William said.

She widened the opening enough to see that William had his finger pointed in the man's chest. The man was Leonard Gaines. She'd come to know him during her stay on the *Bonny Lass*, but would always remember him as the *other* man who followed her to the boat along with Marcus Giles.

"I'm sorry, sir," Gaines said. "We thought he'd been taken care of."

"Next time, *I'll* do the thinking." William's breath came out in heavy bursts through his flared nostrils. Her heart pounded. *Why is he so mad?*

"But ..." Gaines continued, "... he didn't make it to Memphis. Not this time."

"And the next time?" William asked. His voice was much softer.

"He'll be waiting."

There was a brief silence and she feared she might be discovered. She was about to close the door, when William spoke again. "I know what I have to do." William's voice broke as he spoke.

She held Billy firmly against her. She'd never heard William sound so defeated. Closing the door, she returned to bed. Now that there were no longer voices being raised, she comforted Billy against her breast. Tending to him gave her peace and purpose, but it didn't soothe the ache in her heart.

* * *

His home was unusually cold. Douglas made his way into the living room to warm himself by the fire, only to find Cameron lounging back on the sofa with a cigar in one hand and a glass of wine in the other. The fire crackled and pulsed warmth through the room. Had it not been for Cameron, the ambience would have soothed him.

"You're home early," Cameron said, then blew a ring of smoke into the air.

Douglas moved closer to the fire, and lifted his hands to warm them. He rubbed them together, then turned them with open palms to the heat of the flames. "It was supper ... nothing more."

Cameron sat upright. "How was it?"

"Very good. They have an accomplished cook." He sighed, certain that Cameron had no interest in the menu. Why had he even bothered speaking to him?

"A Negro?" Cameron asked, and took a sip of wine.

Douglas turned his head sharply. "How would I know the color of his skin? Or *her* skin for that matter. I didn't meet the cook."

Cameron chuckled. "What's got you so ill? I merely asked a question."

"Forgive me. I'm very tired." Douglas lowered his head. He wanted nothing more than to be left alone with his thoughts.

"Then go to bed." Cameron rose and stood beside him. He was tall, though several inches shorter than Douglas. "I wish *I* was tired. I'm afraid I can't sleep."

"Why?"

"Father has been pestering me about marriage again. Damn him." He tipped up his glass, emptying it.

This time *Douglas* chuckled. "Can you blame him? You're nearly twenty-four."

"But I'm not ready to marry." Cameron crossed the room to a small table which held a half-full decanter. Resting his cigar in an ash tray, he opened the vessel and filled his glass full.

"What about Elise?" Douglas asked. He looked away from Cameron and stared into the fire, waiting for his response.

"Elise?" Cameron crossed once more to him and took a long drag from the cigar, then blew it out above his head. "I have no interest in Elise *Peck*." He spit out her last name as if trying to discard her.

Douglas was plenty warm, now and moved away from his brother, taking a seat on the sofa. "She cares for you."

"Most women do. That doesn't mean I want to marry them. I enjoy women, but care nothing for commitment. If you think so highly of her, why don't *you* marry her? You're almost as old as I am." Cameron sat on the sofa on the opposite end from him.

"Me? It's not me she wants."

Cameron snickered. "Of course not. You're not in line to inherit Father's money. I believe that's what all women truly want. They claim love, but their love is not for any man."

He had no desire to talk about Cameron's wealth, so he rose and turned to leave. "I'm tired, Cameron. Good-night."

"Wait! I'm not finished talking."

Not wanting to be rude, Douglas sat down. "Forgive me. What do you wish to speak of?"

"You didn't tell me about the boat—aside from the good food. Tell me about the women." Cameron jiggled his eyebrows, then sipped his wine.

Immediately, Cora came to mind. "None of interest to you. As I told you, the woman who gave birth looks very much like Elise, and you've established how you feel about *her*. Besides, you just said that you believe women only want you for your money. So why the sudden interest?"

Cameron grinned and took another drink. "Women always interest me. They have *attributes* I appreciate."

"There was a French girl you may have found attractive," he whispered, but then wished he hadn't said it.

"French?" Cameron asked, sitting taller. "Tell me ..."

Douglas wanted to brush aside his words, but could tell that Cameron wasn't about to let him. "She's lovely. I believe I disappointed her when I didn't agree to stay and play cards."

"Cards?" Cameron's face lit up even more than at the mention of a French woman.

"Yes ... poker. Mr. O'Brien runs a gambling boat."

Cameron jumped to his feet. He snuffed out his cigar in the ash tray, then downed the remaining wine in his glass. "You should have told me immediately. Why do I always have to pry things out of you?"

"You're going to the boat?"

"Of course, I'm going. Today has been boring. You've given me a craving for French poker." Cameron snickered as he crossed the room and retrieved his hat and coat from a wooden stand in the corner.

Douglas heard nothing more out of him than the slamming of the front door. In many ways he was relieved that Cameron left, but felt guilty for steering him in the direction of the *Bonny Lass*.

I hope Francine slept well last night. She certainly won't sleep tonight.

* * *

Cora doubted she'd slept at all. Tending a baby was more difficult than Mrs. Moss ever let on. *What did she know anyways? She ain't never raised a baby.* The sun had just begun to peek over the horizon and she wished she could crawl back into bed. Billy had other things on his mind.

"All I seem to do is feed you, an change you," she muttered, holding him close. Then, seeing his tiny little form completely dependent on her, she softened and kissed him on the top of his head. "I love you, Billy. Forgive me for bein' so cross."

It was very early in the morning, so the laughter coming from the hallway surprised her. Instantly, she recognized the high-pitched giggle of Francine.

She stood, holding Billy, and crossed to the door. She pressed her ear to it and waited.

"I can't stay," a tenor voice said in a loud whisper.

"Why not?" Francine asked, with a pronounced pout in her voice.

"Because ..." he stopped, and she believed them to be kissing, "the boat will be leaving port. I never intended to stay all night."

Cora sighed and rolled her eyes. It seemed Francine had found another man to please.

"But you did," Francine said, followed by another giggle.

There was silence for a few moments. *They must a left ...*

But then, the silence was broken by a low moan, and a few defined *smacks*. They were caught up in some strange physical behavior.

"Now, I must go," he said. "When will you return to Memphis?"

"Four weeks. Will you come to me again?"

"Again," he kissed her, "and again."

Did he growl? Dang ... he's a strange one.

"*Adieu,* Cameron," Francine said. Another kiss.

He chuckled. "A-doo."

He ain't French.

She listened as he walked away, followed by Francine's footsteps, returning to her room. She moved away from the door and stood in front of the window. The rising sun was beautiful and took her breath away. She couldn't help but think about Douglas. Where was he at this very moment? Was he watching the same sunrise?

She raised her hand to her lips. No man had ever kissed her the way that man was kissing Francine. She bent down and kissed Billy one more time. Kissing him came naturally. So why hadn't William ever tried to kiss her on the lips? As far as she could recollect, there hadn't even been a wedding kiss.

Francine confused her. How could any woman give herself so easily to so many men and enjoy it as much as she seemed to? Sighing, she moved from the window and perched on her bed. When the familiar hum of the boat filled her ears, she knew they were once again on their way.

A single tear trickled down her cheek. Quickly, she brushed it away. She had everything she could possibly need, and more than she ever imagined she'd have. And yet, she felt sorry for herself. Her heart was heavy and she couldn't stop the low, dull ache of loneliness.

Chapter 13

Douglas opened the front door and gasped, thinking Cora had somehow found him. He stepped back and took a deep breath, calming his heart.

Elise laughed. "You look like you've seen a ghost!" She tossed a bright red wool scarf over her shoulder.

He shook his head and closed his eyes. "Uncanny," he muttered, then opened his eyes again.

"It's cold out here, Douglas. Aren't you going to let me in?" She stared at him and placed her hands on her hips.

"Forgive me." He stepped aside, allowing her to enter. "I didn't expect you back so soon."

She had no difficulty making herself at home, immediately removing her white cotton gloves, and heavy gray wool coat. The scarf was the last to go, and she made a point of flinging it onto the chaise in the entryway, while she draped her coat over her arm. She peered around the room, craning her neck as she glanced up the stairway to the second floor.

"Where's Cameron?" she asked.

"Not home yet," he replied, and took her coat.

"What do you mean? It's nine o'clock in the morning. I've never known him to go out so early."

He felt a bit sorry for her. She was smitten with Cameron, and he wasn't about to let her know that he'd been out all night and most likely with a woman. He looked away from her, afraid she might guess that what he was about to tell her was a lie. He crossed to the cloak-room and hung up her coat. "He went for a walk," he said, over his shoulder. "Thought the cold air might be good for him."

"Oh." She sat on the chaise, folding her hands in her lap.

Looking at her once again, he got that same strange feeling that he had the first time he saw Cora. His stomach fluttered. Elise had never affected him this way before.

"Douglas Denton," she scolded. "Why do you keep staring at me?"

"You won't believe me ..."

She tilted her head and grinned. "Tell me. I can see that you're up to something."

"I ... met someone," he said, then realized how foolish he must sound. "What I mean to say is ..." He stopped, feeling his cheeks becoming warm.

Elise sat perfectly upright. "Douglas. Did you meet a woman while I was away?"

"Yes. The strangest thing ... She looks very much like *you*."

"Like me?" She coyly turned her head and giggled. "Douglas, dear ... I know that you've always cared for me, but to fabricate a woman in my place is a little odd."

"No, you don't understand." *She thinks I'm daft.* "She's no fabrication. She was in my uncle's woodshop, and began having pains. You see ... she was heavy with child. I helped her return to the boat she arrived on."

"A boat?" She toyed with her scarf. "The woman came off a boat?"

"Yes. The *Bonny Lass.* Her husband is the pilot ... and owner."

"So, she has a husband?" She stood and crossed to him. "Unfortunate for you. From the way you're behaving, I believe you have feelings for the girl."

How could he be so obvious? "No. I'm only telling you about her because ... well ... she could very well be your twin."

"Twin?" She burst out laughing. "Oh, my, Douglas. Mother will enjoy hearing that you've fabricated a woman *and* another child for her as well."

"Why do you insist this is a fabrication? I'm telling you the truth." He stepped toward her and compared the height of the top of her head to where it met his. "You and she are even the same height. She came up to here." He placed the back of his hand under his chin. "So do you."

"And did she have my eyes?" Batting her lashes, she gazed deeply into his eyes.

Leaning in, he peered into them. "Yes. Brown with gold flecks." *Though hers sparkled more ...*

"And what about her lips?" She grinned, pursing her lips. "Or, did you get close enough to examine them?"

"She's a married woman, Elise." He cleared his throat. "But, I'm telling you—the two of you are identical. I didn't realize just how much, until you walked through my door."

"That's simply foolish!" she raved, waving her hand in the air. "No two people can look *exactly* alike."

He chuckled, then stopped when he realized she was becoming irritated. "Oh, Elise, don't be angry. I was laughing because I thought of the one thing that makes the two of you very different."

She touched her finger to the tip of her nose. "My adorable nose?"

"No, not your nose." He looked closely. "That's the same as well."

"Then what?" she asked, placing her hands on her hips.

"You speak differently." Thinking about it made him chuckle again. "She's much more ... *colorful.*"

"Colorful?"

"Yes. Colorful. And, sometimes ... she curses."

"Curses?" Her eyes widened and she clutched her hands to her chest. "Oh, my, Douglas. Mother would never allow such a thing."

The door opened and Cameron appeared in the same clothing he was wearing when he'd left last night. His eyes were puffy and he was obviously in need of sleep. He stopped abruptly when he saw Elise.

Her eyes popped open even further. "My, Cameron. That must have been a very brisk walk."

"Walk?" Cameron asked, and shifted his eyes to Douglas.

"Yes, walk," Douglas said, raising his eyes at his brother. "Did the cool air help your headache?"

"My head ..." Cameron touched his fingers to his temples. "Oh ... yes ... my headache. Much better. Thank you for asking."

Elise crossed to Cameron and rested her hand on his arm. "It *must* have cured it. You'd nearly forgotten you even had a headache."

Douglas watched the two of them, feeling very guilty. He shouldn't have covered for Cameron's activities. But then again, Elise was also quite good at playing games, so perhaps he wasn't completely out of line.

"I need to wash," Cameron said, dryly. "Excuse me." He walked away, without acknowledging Elise any further.

She sighed and returned to the chaise, plopping down soundly upon it.

Douglas offered her a smile. "You know very well that Cameron is not sociable."

Her eyes remained affixed to the floor. "He used to be."

Feeling sorry for her, he sat and took her hand. "Elise, you'd do much better to put your heart elsewhere."

"Where? I love *him* ..."

He wanted to tell her that he was not worth loving, but instead, patted her hand in a gesture of reassurance.

"I suppose I'll go now," she said as she stood and moved toward the door. "He has no interest in seeing me."

"Perhaps he's simply tired. Didn't get much sleep ... because of his headache."

She stared at the floor.

"Elise," he said, and approached her, waiting for her to look at him. "I'll speak to him."

Her face brightened. "Thank you, Douglas."

He opened the door and she was gone as quickly as she'd arrived.

He had always found her attractive, and yet she showed no interest in him. Her words confirmed what he'd always thought. *She's in love with Cameron.* However, Cameron insisted that what Elise Peck loved was money. Her parents were wealthy. Her father had inherited his fortune, and her mother earned hers by making an honest living as a mid-wife. The idea that Elise was a fortune seeker didn't fit. She had all that she could ever need, so why search for more elsewhere?

"Was that Elise I heard?"

"Yes, Mother," he said, and kissed her cheek.

Mary Wellesley rarely came out of her room. The house was large enough that everyone in it had plenty of their own space, but Mary kept to herself more than the others.

"She didn't stay long," Mary said, and nervously twisted a strand of hair around her finger.

"She was here to see Cameron. He gave her no reason to stay." He took her by the arm and guided her down the long hallway to the kitchen. "You've not eaten, have you, Mother?"

She shook her head. "I wish your father hadn't sold Rosie. I liked the way she cooked."

He helped her to a chair at the round table, situated in a brightly-lit corner of the kitchen. Knowing she preferred it to the formal dining room, they often sat here while enjoying a cup of tea.

"I'll make tea," he said, grinning at her.

She nodded her gratitude, then stared out the window while twisting her fingers together.

He couldn't remember a time when his mother wasn't edgy. From listening to some of the slaves talk, he assumed that she had been witness to a disturbing crime when he was a very young boy. She never spoke of it and he didn't press the question. She was a kind and loving mother and he would never force her to reveal something she didn't want to openly share.

"Your father works too much," she said with a sigh.

Though Arthur Wellesley was his step-father, she'd never referred to him that way. And he aptly called him *Father*. It was Arthur that caused the barrier between them.

"Yes, he does," he agreed. "But owning a textile mill can be very demanding. Even when he's not trading cotton, there's a lot of business to take care of." He added wood to the stove, then sat beside his mother while the water heated.

"You'd think that in the off-season, he would stay at home more often." She stared at her hands. "You don't suppose he's seeing someone else?"

"Mother!" He wrinkled his brow and took her hands in his. "Don't say such a thing. He loves you."

"I'm not the woman I once was."

He moved closer and kissed her forehead. "You're more."

She raised her eyes and smiled at him.

Cameron entered the kitchen, and the mood instantly changed. "Making tea?" he asked.

"Yes. Would you like some?" Douglas offered as politely as he could.

Cameron looked nervously around the room. "Is she gone?"

"Elise?" Douglas asked, knowing very well who he meant.

"Of course, Elise!" Cameron folded his arms, and flared his nostrils.

Douglas considered toying with him, but didn't want to waste his energy. "Yes, she's gone."

"She's a fine girl, Cameron," Mary said quietly.

"Girl, yes. Fine, *no*." Cameron strutted across the room and peered out the window. "I suppose I should go into town and speak with Father. I need to borrow some money."

Douglas watched his mother stiffen. "What do you need money for?" He took his mother's hand and gave it a gentle squeeze.

"I borrowed some from Lloyd Phillips on my way to the boat. I thought I would win enough to pay him back, but unfortunately, luck was not on my side." Cameron flicked his fingernails against each other as he spoke.

That habit of his always annoyed Douglas. "So, you want to *borrow* money from Father to pay back money you *borrowed* from Lloyd Phillips?"

Cameron whipped his head around. His lip curled into a scowl. "It will all be *mine* eventually. In actuality, it's more of an *advance* than a loan."

Douglas chose not to respond. The water was boiling on the stove, so he rose in order to prepare his mother's tea.

Cameron walked to him and leaned in, whispering. "I always get what I want." He cocked his head to the side. "The French girl was good, but you don't understand those things, do you?" He grunted and walked away.

Douglas wasn't about to let Cameron upset him, but his mother's dour look indicated that she could not so easily dismiss him.

"Don't let him upset you, Mother," he said as he set a porcelain cup of tea in front of her.

She patted his hand, then took a sip. "He won't get all of it. I'll see to it."

He sighed. The money didn't matter. All he wanted was a simple life with a loving wife and a family of his own. He'd never belonged on the Wellesley estate.

"Douglas, have some tea," Mary whispered.

He poured himself a cup and sat beside her. In no time at all, he was telling her about Cora. His mood changed and he smiled. And when his mother also smiled, Cameron was forgotten.

Chapter 14

Billy was sound asleep in his cradle, so Cora took a very welcome break and walked out of her room and into the open air. She wanted to stay close enough so that if Billy woke she would hear him. But she needed the air.

She leaned against the railing, breathed deeply, and gazed out over the water. After months on the Mississippi, she knew it well. Every turn, every sandbar, and every shallow. William ably piloted the boat through all of them.

The only time she became angry with him was when they passed Plum Point and he refused to let her disembark. He claimed it was for *her* own good, but she knew it was for *his* peace of mind. After almost a year together, he still didn't trust her.

They were nearing Plum Point, so she stayed at the rail, hoping to get a glimpse of her old home or maybe even Mrs. Moss. But because of her interest in it, William steered the boat as far from shore as he possibly could. Maybe he thought she might try to jump.

Plum silly. I'd never leave Billy.

Ever since she'd overheard William and Leonard Gaines, William's demeanor had changed. Though he was overly attentive to her and the baby, she always sensed a deep sadness behind his eyes. That night, when he came to visit her, she decided to confront him.

No longer did he come to her room to couple, but instead came to play with Billy. She sat comfortably on her soft bed, but her heart was heavy. Since he wasn't enjoying her that way, maybe he was visiting Francine for pleasure. She certainly wasn't going to ask either of them about it.

I ain't even gonna think 'bout it.

"William?" Her voice shook, but he was paying little attention to her. He moved around her room, bouncing Billy in his arms. "William?"

"Aye?" He didn't look at her, but kept his eyes on their son, smiling all the while.

"I ..." She fidgeted with the blankets. How would she approach this? "I ... uh ..."

He looked up and gazed at her with concern.

"Few weeks back—right after Billy was born—I heard you talkin' to Leonard Gaines."

William stopped the movement of his arms and held Billy still. "What did you hear?"

She cleared her dry throat. "Well ... I ..." Nervously, she smoothed her nightgown. "Are you in some kind a trouble, William?"

He stared at the floor, then gently laid Billy down in his cradle. He pulled up a chair next to her.

"I never wanted to do this," he said in a whisper. "But, 'tis time I tell you."

Feeling his pain, she scooted close to him and placed her hand on his shoulder.

He turned his head and smiled at her. "You've been good to me, Cora. I know 'twas wrong for me to take you against your wishes." He gazed at Billy. "But I'm glad that I did. I hope I've treated you well."

She nodded rapidly. "I ain't hungry. That's for sure."

He chuckled, but then grew quiet. "Marcus Giles lived."

Every bit of air was sucked from her body. She tensed up, knowing what it meant. "How do you know?"

"Gaines heard talk while we were in Memphis. We left just in time. Giles was bringing a lynching party."

"Lynchin' party?" Her heart thumped. "Why?"

William stood and began to pace. "I'm not a good man, Cora."

"Course you are." Her throat was dry, and she swallowed hard. "You take good care a me an Billy."

Freezing in the middle of the floor, he placed his hands over his face, and his shoulders shook.

Her heart ached for him. His large frame suddenly seemed small and helpless. She hopped off the bed and crossed to him, placing her hand flat against his back.

His breath was staggered as he stood upright, attempting to regain his composure. "The cards I use are marked."

"You cheat?"

"Aye. I cheat." He turned to face her. "I'm no better than your father. A cheat recognizes another cheat. I played him, Cora."

All the sympathy she held for him left her in an instant. Her head reeled and she gritted her teeth. Then, without a second thought, she slapped him hard across the face.

He didn't budge.

Her head dropped and she began to cry.

"Forgive me, Cora," he said pulling her into his arms, then gently stroked her hair.

"You was gonna hang ... my pa," she sniffled, and tried to back out of his embrace. "And all the while, you was cheatin' too. It ain't right."

"No. It's not right. And now, I'll pay for it." He kissed her forehead and released her.

She wanted to remain angry with him, but having him harmed didn't set right with her. "What'll they do?"

"What they set out to do in Memphis. Giles won't stop until he sees me hung."

She stumbled back toward the bed. William was there quickly to catch her before she fell and helped her to sit.

She touched his cheek, still red from the strike of her hand. "Then, don't go back to Memphis." Tears fell of their own will down her face.

"It won't matter where I go." He took her hand and held it against his chest. "He knows our course. Eventually, he'll find me."

"That why we're goin' so slow? It ain't never taken us so long to get back to New Orleans."

"Aye. But the passengers are becoming angry."

Her mind raced. There had to be some way to stop Marcus Giles. "Can't you get someone to *make* him stop?"

"I'm surprised at you, Cora. What you're implying ..."

"But—I don't want him to hurt you. Billy needs his pa."

"You have to protect him, Cora. At all cost. Make certain no harm comes to me son." He crossed to the cradle and lifted him into his arms, then closed his eyes and gently swayed.

His words flashed a memory. *Madame Beaumont* ...

"Cora," William's voice was firm, "I want you to leave the boat when we get to New Orleans. Take Billy and never return."

Her eyes popped open wide. "What? No. I don't like New Orleans! It scares me! I won't do it, William!"

He stared at her without saying a word. She could tell that his mind was racing. His brow furrowed, and he breathed rapidly. Finally, he spoke. "If they don't come for me in New Orleans, then ... you'll leave when we return to Plum Point. You're going to need help. I hope that your father will provide it."

"I getta go home?"

"Aye. Against me better judgment. Giles knows where you came from. He'll be looking there. When you go, you can't stay. Get your father's help and leave as soon as possible. I don't want to know where you plan to go. It's best that way."

"But—why would Giles want me? I never cheated him." This was too much for her to handle.

"He wants you in other ways. If he knows we have a son, then he'll want him, too. He thinks I owe him everything I have because he hid what I was doing for a very long time. By now he's told every gambler I ever cheated. Men don't like to have their money taken. And don't forget, I tried to kill him. Most men wouldn't fault him his revenge."

Seeing William broken tore at her heart. "I can't leave you, William. I can't ..."

"You have to. It's the only way to protect our son."

"Madame Beaumont," she whispered.

He nodded. "She may seem odd, but somehow she knows things."

"You knew her before. What did she tell you that made you believe in her?"

"She met me wife. Though she didn't tell *her*, she told *me* that me wife and child would die. As I said, she knows things ..." His voice drifted away.

She took Billy from his arms and returned him to his cradle. She then took William by the hand.

"William," she whispered, "I'm all better. You can have me if it'd make you feel better." She moved toward the bed.

He stopped. "No, Cora. It wouldn't be right."

"But ... I don't mind."

"No," he said, firmly. "I won't risk giving you my seed. It will be hard enough for you to tend to *Billy* without me."

As she released his hand, tears pooled in her eyes. "I can't think 'bout you that way. I don't want you to die ..."

"Sometimes, things are out of our hands. Often times, we create our own end. Me hand has been dealt." He turned to walk away.

"William?" She reached out to him.

He returned to her and held her close. "You're a fine lass, Cora. Someday, you'll find another husband."

Another husband?

Letting her tears freely fall, she tried to sort through everything he'd told her. And as her mind drifted from one thought to another, her sorrow turned to guilt. She thought about Douglas ...

* * *

"And you should have seen her face when I told her about my *twin*." Elise placed her hands on her cheeks and laughed. "I expected her to laugh, but she looked horrified!"

Douglas watched as Elise recanted the story. He'd done as he'd promised and spoken to Cameron about her, but Cameron showed no interest or concern. He indicated that he had other plans for his future, but wouldn't elaborate.

Elise had stayed away for some time and he knew her feelings were hurt. So when she'd arrived this morning, he was surprised to see her.

"Why would she be horrified?" he asked.

They made themselves comfortable in the living room, while she continued her tale.

"I don't know." She shrugged. "She acted very strange and later insisted that I didn't disturb her with my news.

She said she was thinking about something else at the time."

"You don't believe her?"

"No, I don't. I know Mother well enough to know when she's lying. The problem is that I don't understand *why* she would lie."

His mother entered the room. "Did I hear you mention your mother?" She was wearing a long nightgown, covered with a heavy blue robe. Her light brown hair was twisted into a knot at the top of her head.

Elise smiled. "Yes. She asked about you." She stood and crossed to her. "She told me to tell you that she would very much like to see you sometime."

Mary looked away from her. "Perhaps ..."

Douglas rose and took his mother by the hand. "Would you like to join us? Elise was telling me about her mother's reaction to the news of the woman I met on the boat."

Mary shook her head. "No. I need to dress. I'm meeting your father for dinner." She turned and smiled at Elise. "Tell your mother ..." she hesitated. "Tell your mother that I'm thinking of her." Without waiting for a response, she left the room.

He and Elise returned to the sofa. He watched with sadness, as his mother exited.

"Didn't they used to be good friends?" Elise asked.

"I believe so. A very long time ago."

"Something must have happened between them." She lifted her chin into the air. "It could have something to do with Cameron. Mother thinks he's being cruel to me."

He doubted that would be the reason his mother would discount their friendship. "Then why do you continue to pursue him?"

"I told you," she said firmly. "I love him. Eventually, he'll feel the same."

"You can't force love, Elise. If he doesn't feel it now, he may never."

She stood. "Well, then. I was hoping to see Cameron, but it seems he has other things to occupy his time. So ... I'll be leaving."

"I didn't mean to upset you," he said, rising to his feet.

"Douglas Denton. I'll have you know that I'm not a quitter. Mother taught me to pursue whatever I want. I want Cameron. Tell him I came by."

She marched to the front door and he traipsed behind her.

"Oh—one other thing," she said, holding the door knob. "If you see that *woman* again, Mother would very much like to see her. I don't think she believed my story."

"I doubt I'll see her. She lives on the boat. I don't know when she'll return to Memphis." The truth of his words sunk deeply into his heart.

"Oh, well. There's not much we can do about it then, is there? So, I guess I'll just say *goodbye*."

She left without looking at him.

Why would her mother want to meet Cora? Was it simple curiosity, or was it something more? He believed it was something much more.

Chapter 15

The *Bonny Lass* left New Orleans without any trouble, staying only long enough to allow passengers to exit, restock their supply of wood and provisions, then board new passengers.

Cora stayed in her room with Billy the entire time. William had instructed her not to let anyone know of their plans, including Bessie and Francine. "If no one knows, it's best for all of us," he had said. She took his words to heart.

As the days passed and they neared Plum Point, her heart ached even more. Leaving the *Bonny Lass* both saddened and terrified her. Hopefully her pa would welcome her home, but she'd more than likely find him drunk and disoriented. She much preferred her life on the boat.

Then, she thought about Mrs. Moss. She hadn't even been able to tell her goodbye and knew she must have been horribly worried about her. Surely her pa had told her what happened. At least, she hoped he had.

William timed their arrival in Plum Point at dusk. Though they normally docked for the night, he intended to keep on going after he left her there. The moon was full, lighting the water. Besides, he knew the route. He could have piloted it in his sleep.

Her hands shook as she packed her bag with as many items of clothing as she could. Looking around the room at all the lovely things, tears started to form. She placed the copy of *Grimm's Children's Tales* on the bed and was certain William would return it to Francine. She had borrowed it to read to Billy, but found the stories disturbing, so she hadn't read them aloud.

She ran her fingers lovingly over the cradle, closed her eyes, and thought about the man who'd given it to her. *So kind.* There was no way for her to take it with her. She'd have to find some other place for Billy to sleep. Maybe her pa could make another. Besides, Billy would soon outgrow the cradle and would need a larger crib.

William stood in her doorway. His eyes were red and she knew he'd been crying.

She wrapped her arms around him. None of this felt right. There had to be another way. "I can't do it, William." She couldn't stop herself from sobbing.

He took her arms firmly in his hands, holding her away from him. "You have to." His eyes penetrated her.

She shook her head. "Don't go back to Memphis. He won't find you if you stay away."

"I can't run forever. I have to face him." William loosened his grip and lowered his head. "Besides, he's ruined me already. Haven't you noticed that we don't have many passengers? No one wants to gamble. Me reputation—well—no one trusts me."

Billy began to cry, so William lifted him into his arms. "Hush now, lad," he soothed him, "and grow into a fine man."

She sobbed even harder. "I'm scared, William."

"You're strong, Cora. One of the strongest lasses I've known." He pulled a cloth bag from his pocket. "Take this. It will get you by for some time."

As he placed the bag in her palm, she felt the coins through the fabric.

"What if you change Giles' mind? If you can talk him outta hangin' you? Give him money ..." She sniffled and had a hard time saying what she wanted to say. "Can't you come an find us?"

"I don't want to know where to look. Remember ... tell no one. And Cora," he gently touched her cheek, "don't use me name. Not even for Billy. Use a different name. Do you understand me?"

"Yessir," she said, wiping the tears from her face.

The hum of the boat slowed.

"'Tis time," he said, and led her from the room.

* * *

The warmth from Billy's tiny body was welcome, and comforting. Cora stood on the shore and waited until the *Bonny Lass* was out of view. The sky was painted beautifully tonight in colors of orange and bits of lavender. But it was hard to appreciate with tear-filled eyes. Though she didn't love William, she cared for him deeply, and feared for him.

Why ain't he afraid to die?

She kissed Billy's cheek. "Your pa loves you. Someday, I'll tell you all about him."

Francine had been in her room and Bessie was already below deck when Cora left the boat. She had wanted to tell them *goodbye,* but William insisted she not say a word. Even though she and Francine didn't always see eye-to-eye, she considered her a friend, and she would miss her. More than anyone, she would miss Bessie. She hoped William would be good to her.

She gasped. *What will happen to them when William's gone?*

She couldn't think about it. There was too much else to deal with. Standing upright, she put her shoulders back and trudged down the shore to her old house.

It was mid-March and quite cold. She kept a blanket tucked firmly around Billy. At only one month old, he was still very fragile. "Soon we'll have a nice fire to warm by," she said to him, and hoped her pa had learned how to keep it going.

As she approached the house, she slowed. It didn't look right. She tipped her head and stared at the old bathing tub, which was upside down and lying in front of the doorway. Blocks of wood were scattered about. Even though her pa wasn't much of a house-keeper, he always kept his wood in order. He liked to select just the right piece for each of his projects.

She set down her bag. Her heart pounded as she pushed aside the tub in order to enter the house.

"Pa?" she called out, but no one answered.

The door creaked as she pushed it open. A large rat scurried across the floor in front of her and she jumped back, startled.

Billy jerked in her arms, wakened by her movement.

"It's all right, Billy." She was trying to convince herself even more than him, but her rapid breathing and pounding heart didn't help.

She found a lantern and lit it, then held it up to peer around the house.

The beds had been turned upside down; the mattresses cut open. All of the dishes were off the shelves and broken into pieces on the floor. She moved around the room carefully, fearing what she might discover next.

Her thumping heart shattered. In the corner of the room, the wooden chain was in pieces, as if someone purposefully cut every link. She lifted a piece of it from the floor and held it in her hand. Once again, she couldn't hold back her tears.

Using a corner of Billy's blanket, she wiped her eyes, then in panic crossed to the remains of her bed. Dropping to her knees, she placed Billy as gently as she could on the floor. Where could it be? Frantically, her hands moved through the rubble as she searched for her box. It kept all her special things; most importantly, her angel. Realizing that it was nowhere to be found, she sobbed, and in turn Billy let out a loud bawl.

"H-Hush ... Shh ..." she whispered, lifting him into her arms and placing tiny kisses on his precious face.

Rising to her feet, she bounced him in her arms and patted his little back. A racing heart brought her back to her senses. Someone had been here. Someone looking for something.

Giles ...

But, where was her pa?

She clutched her chest.

Mrs. Moss ...

Spinning around, she flew out the door, snatching up her bag as she exited. She raced down the shore to the home of her dear friend.

A sigh of relief left her body as she saw smoke billowing from the chimney. Her spirits lifted at the clean-swept porch; an indication that Mrs. Moss was inside.

Butterflies fluttered in her belly as she rapped on the door.

"Who is it?" Mrs. Moss asked, timidly.

She could hardly speak. "It's me ... Cora."

Silence.

Cautiously, the door opened.

Light from inside the house cast shadows behind Mrs. Moss. Though it was hard to see her face clearly, Cora believed she wasn't looking at her. "Mrs. Moss?" she asked, tipping her head. She wanted to reach out and hold her, but something held her back.

Mrs. Moss stared vacantly forward. "Cora, is that really you?" She lifted her hand and touched Cora's face. Gently, she moved it across her skin, feeling every curve. Her hand shook as she drew it back. "It *is* you!"

Cora waved her hand in front of Mrs. Moss's face, but she didn't flinch. "You can't see me, can you?"

Mrs. Moss shook her head. "Not with my eyes. But I've kept your image in my heart." Tears trickled down her cheeks, falling from her cloudy eyes. She took her arm. "Come in out of the cold." As she said this, her hand brushed across Billy and he whimpered.

Mrs. Moss drew back. "A baby?"

"His name's Billy. He's mine." Her face flushed and it was one time she was thankful that Mrs. Moss couldn't see her.

With a long stick in her hand, Mrs. Moss tapped her way across the floor to the kitchen table.

Cora watched her, dumbfounded, then scolded herself for not assisting her. "What's been goin' on here?" she asked as she sat down at the familiar table.

Mrs. Moss closed her eyes. "Much has happened. But as many questions as you have for me, I have many more for you." Her chin quivered and she started to cry. "I thought I'd never see you again."

Being that she *couldn't* see, her words were even more disturbing. Cora stood, moved to the old woman, and wrapped her arm around her. *Her* troubles now seemed very small. Mrs. Moss needed her. "I'm home. I ain't goin' nowhere again. Well ... I reckon that's not exactly true. But, when I leave I wanna take you with me." She kissed her lovingly on the cheek, then returned to her seat.

Before Mrs. Moss could respond, she jumped in. "Where's Pa? The house is a real mess."

Mrs. Moss lowered her head. "Cora ..." her voice crackled and broke. "Your ... *pa* ... is dead."

As if sensing her sorrow, Billy let out a wail. "Hush, now," she said, choking back tears. In an effort to keep from falling completely to pieces, she quickly unbuttoned her coat, then unfastened the front of her dress, allowing him to nurse.

Mrs. Moss turned her head to the sound and managed to smile. "A hungry boy. That's good."

"Yes'm," she said, looking down at her son. She sniffled and tried to steady her breathing. "How'd he die?"

"As I told you, much has happened ..." Her facial expression immediately changed, as sadness gripped her once again.

"I need to know."

"Yes, you do. Then, you will tell me about you. *I* need to know as well."

Cora stroked Billy's cheek while he eagerly suckled. He was the only thing at this moment that felt right.

Mrs. Moss folded her hands on the table. "Your father told me what he did. It took an entire bottle of whiskey for him to tell me, but as you know that was not uncommon for him."

Cora nodded, but then realizing that Mrs. Moss couldn't see the gesture, added an, "Uh-huh."

"As you can imagine, I was angry. I always thought of you as mine. My own daughter." Her body shook and her voice wavered. "Bartering you away like he would an old watch or a piece of silver. Damn, him!"

Cora's eyes widened and she gasped. She'd never heard Mrs. Moss curse.

"Yes, I said what I meant! No man has the right to give away another human. You were his daughter and he discarded you like an empty whiskey bottle!"

She reached across the table and took Mrs. Moss's hand. "But ... I'm all right. William was good to me. I was angry in the beginnin', but ... he gave me Billy. He treated me good, Mrs. Moss."

Mrs. Moss's shoulders dropped and her face softened. "I'm glad to hear this. Yet, it was still highly improper."

"Please, tell me what happened after ..."

Mrs. Moss nodded and continued. "He kept on drinking after he left here. Several days went by and I didn't see him, so I went looking for him." She raised her head, staring into nothingness. "I found him at home, slumped in the corner. He wasn't breathing."

Cora covered her mouth with her hand, as her heart tightened in her chest.

"I sent the Negro boy who helps me to find a doctor. But, of course, it was too late. He was already dead. The doctor said it appeared he had choked on his own vomit." Her face wrinkled at the memory. "I'm sorry, Cora, but whiskey killed your father."

Crying openly now, Cora continued wiping away the tears so as not to dampen Billy.

Mrs. Moss pulled a handkerchief from her pocket and waved it in the air. "It's clean."

Cora took it and blew her nose. "All this time, an Pa's been dead ..."

"There's more to tell, Cora." Mrs. Moss patted her hand.

"What more can there be? My Pa's dead ... the house is a mess ... and you're blind. Dang!"

"There is something good." She smiled in Cora's direction.

"Good? What can be good?"

Mrs. Moss nodded toward the kitchen shelf. "Behind the shelf is a box. Get it."

Cradling Billy, she stood and did as she was told. The wooden box was wedged between the shelf and the wall, obviously meant to be hidden. With a gentle thump, she rested the box on the table.

"Open it," Mrs. Moss said, nodding.

As the metal clasps were unhooked and the lid raised, Cora's eyes popped open wide. "Where'd you get all this money?" She ran her fingers through the silver and gold coins.

"Your father."

"The money he lost? But—why didn't you remind him you had it? He could a got me back!"

"When he came to me and told me what happened, the boat was long gone. Then, when I reminded him of the money, he finished off the bottle of whiskey and left." Her vacant eyes welled with tears. "He hated himself for what he'd done to you, child. As angry as I was with him, I was grateful for the money. I had no intention of spending any of it, hoping you would return. But when my sight began to fail, I used it little by little. The old man up the road would send his Negro to look after me. I gave him money for food. We helped each other."

Cora calmed down and realized it wasn't the fault of Mrs. Moss. Reaching her hand across the table, she took hold of the old woman's frail hand. "I'm sorry. We can't change what happened." She stared at the large sum of coins. "This'll help. We gotta leave here soon as we can."

"There you go again, talking about leaving. Why leave? You're welcome to stay with me. It would help me more than you realize. I believe that Negro boy tires of me."

Cora decided it was best to tell her everything. Since she was determined to take Mrs. Moss with her, she would have to know what could or couldn't be said.

"So, they intend to hang your husband?" Mrs. Moss asked, and placed her hand on the old Bible.

It was the first time that Cora noticed it sitting there, and it saddened her even more knowing that Mrs. Moss could no longer read it.

"Yes'm," she replied in a whisper. "William's bein' right brave about it. I told him he should stay away from Memphis, but he insisted on goin'. Little Billy will never know his pa."

"Cora," Mrs. Moss said, pushing the Bible toward her. "Read my favorite chapter."

Cora's eyes misted over as she opened the large book. The satin ribbon was still in the same place. As she began reading the twenty-third Psalm, it touched her heart more than ever. "I shall fear no evil, for thou art with me ..."

She stopped and Mrs. Moss tipped her head ... waiting.

"Mrs. Moss? You reckon God's with William?"

"Of course He is, child."

"I'm glad a that." Cora finished the chapter and closed the Bible. "Reckon Pa's in Heaven, Mrs. Moss?"

"He believed, didn't he?"

"I reckon so. He always said Ma was with the angels. Now he's with her. I just hope there ain't whiskey in Heaven."

Mrs. Moss blinked her empty eyes. "It's quite doubt-ful." She offered her a sweet smile. "I'm glad you're home, Cora."

Mrs. Moss went on to tell her that they buried her pa in the woods behind the house. A small wooden cross marked the grave. Before they left Plum Point, she'd stop there so she could pay her last respects. He may not have been the best pa, but she loved him.

That night, she stayed with Mrs. Moss, but couldn't sleep. After folding blankets to make a pallet on the floor, she curled up with Billy. But every sound she heard brought her instantly awake. She envisioned Marcus Giles hovering over her and the image was haunting. Even worse was the thought of her husband with a noose around his neck. Every time that thought drifted into her mind, her eyes filled with tears.

She twisted the gold band around her finger, knowing that in the morning she would have to remove it. She would place it in the wooden box with the money and forget that she was ever married.

Chapter 16

"What's all the commotion about?" Douglas asked his uncle. He crossed to the shop window and peered into the street.

"Don't know," Harper replied, and moved his knife around the wing of an angel.

Yelling and cursing filled the street. People came out of every shop, intrigued by the noise. Douglas decided to join them.

"What's going on?" he asked one of the men walking down the street in the direction of the docks.

"Gonna be a hangin'," he replied, and grinned.

The man quickly left and Douglas stood there, shaking his head. *He grinned about a hanging?* There was something terribly wrong about that.

Returning inside, he told his uncle what was said.

"Lynch mobs are dangerous," Harper muttered. "Best stay in."

With his curiosity piqued, he chose to ignore his uncle's suggestion and grabbed his coat. "I'll be back."

People were coming from everywhere, making their way to the docks. Most of them were men. He'd never seen so many people in this part of the city. Craning his neck, he looked up and around the multitude, trying to see where the event was taking place. The city marshal was nowhere to be seen. Obviously, the mob had formed quickly, and someone wanting swift justice was forgoing the use of the law. The noise rose even louder the closer he got to the dock. Then his heart thumped when he recognized the *Bonny Lass*.

Cora?

He quickened his pace.

"Cheat!" one man yelled and shook his fist.

"Bastard!" another man hollered, and was encouraged by others around him. "String him up!" he added, and the crowd cheered.

Thankful for his height, Douglas was able to see above most of the crowd. Jeers and curses flew every which way. He gasped.

O'Brien ...

With a man to each side of him, William O'Brien was being forcefully led off the *Bonny Lass*. Another man walked behind him, holding a rope in his hand and wearing a very broad grin. He held the rope into the air and the crowd yelled louder than ever.

Douglas swallowed the lump in his throat and looked further behind William, anxious to find Cora. She was nowhere to be seen.

The man with the rope shouted. "He's been cheatin' you for years! Every one of ya!" He swung the noose back, then whipped it forward, striking it across the back of William's head, causing him to cower. "I want justice!" the man roared and spat at William's feet.

"Hang 'im!" someone hollered.

People pushed and shoved, trying to get close to the action. Their eyes were wild, as they shook their fists and cursed. Harper was right, this was a dangerous mob, hungry for blood.

Douglas couldn't stand and do nothing, so he ran to the livery stable and retrieved his horse. Jumping on his back, he sped away to the marshal's office, all the while wishing it wasn't on the other side of the city.

Marshal Underwood was seated behind his desk when he arrived. Douglas quickly told him about the mob and the marshal wasted no time. He patted the gun at his side and grabbed his coat.

But they were too late. By the time they returned to the dock, the crowd had disbursed, the *Bonny Lass* was already on its way down the Mississippi, and the body of William O'Brien swung from a live oak.

Douglas dismounted and fell to his knees.

Marshal Underwood followed and stood over him. "You know him?"

He nodded.

"I'm sorry."

"It's not right," Douglas muttered. "What about the law?"

"Some folks reckon they have the right to carry out punishment." The marshal walked toward O'Brien. "You told me there was a mob, but if you look around, you'll see that most folks don't care. They want to see the hangin' but pay no mind to the man danglin' from the tree once he's dead."

The marshal was right. Everyone was gone. They returned to their business with no more thoughts of William O'Brien. How could they be so unfeeling?

"Do you know who did this?" the marshal asked, laying a hand on Douglas's shoulder.

Douglas pictured the man holding the rope. Composing himself, he rose to his feet. "I saw a man that appeared to be leading them to do this, but I don't know who he was."

"Reckon he's on one a the boats?"

"Yes," he whispered. He feared for Cora and the baby.

The marshal looked up at O'Brien. "He's a big man. I best be gettin' the coroner. I'm gonna need help gettin' him down."

"I'll stay here until you return."

Marshal Underwood nodded and mounted his horse.

Knowing the body of a dead man was so close made him shiver, but Douglas wasn't about to leave him. So he took a seat beneath the tree and waited. He looked upward at the massive body hovering over him. This was one of the most unpleasant things he'd ever had to do, but he believed every man deserved dignity in death and William was given none. Staying with him was the least he could do. He closed his eyes and tried to imagine what he'd been, not what he was now.

Remember his life and laughter ... not this.

* * *

Cora tried to describe everything to Mrs. Moss. She waved her hands in the air and pointed to the trees, and the sky, then realized that her gestures were pointless. So she used every word imaginable to describe color and form. She even ventured to describe the smells in the air, which only made Mrs. Moss laugh and remind her that there was nothing wrong with her nose.

She had purchased a horse and buggy in a town not far from Plum Point. Careful not to show that she had a large sum of money, she skillfully bartered with the blacksmith.

Since she'd never been far from home, no one knew her, and that was to her benefit.

Though she didn't tell William exactly where she planned to go, she knew where her heart was leading her; Memphis, Tennessee. Yes, it was not the brightest idea, but then again she was convinced that Marcus Giles would assume she'd stay away from Memphis and wouldn't look for her there.

Crossing the Mississippi by ferry was frightening—especially for the horse—but it was necessary and her determination kept them going.

"We're almost there, Mrs. Moss," she said.

"I certainly hope so," she replied and clung to Muffin, whose head was buried in the folds of her skirt.

When the ferry finally docked, Cora let out a heavy sigh. "Dry land, Mrs. Moss."

"Thank the Lord!" She raised her face to the sunshine.

Cora stepped off the ferry and took the reins in hand, urging the horse onto shore. The chestnut mare gingerly stepped and pulled the buggy behind her. Billy was wrapped in a blanket snugly held in a wicker basket on the floorboard.

"How's my baby?" Cora asked.

Mrs. Moss reached down and touched his tiny body. "Still asleep. He's a good boy."

Cora paid the ferryman and he thanked her. She made a point of not becoming too friendly with anyone. William's words of warning echoed in her mind.

"Where are we?" Mrs. Moss asked as Cora hopped up beside her and snapped the reins.

"Memphis," Cora said the word with a heartfelt sigh. "Memphis, Tennessee."

It had taken them three weeks to get here. They intentionally traveled at a slow pace. Some nights they were forced to sleep in the buggy, but when they came to a town that offered lodging, they took advantage of it.

"It's a miracle we didn't get robbed ... or worse," Cora said as she led the horse down a familiar-looking street.

Mrs. Moss smiled and patted the Bible. "I did a lot of praying."

"Least it's warm. I was tired a wearin' a coat."

"Where are we going now?" Mrs. Moss tipped her head, waiting for a response.

"I think we'll stay here. Feels like home." She suddenly realized she'd driven the horse down the street where she'd met Douglas. Her heart pounded as she passed Harper's woodworking shop. It was all she could do to keep going. It wouldn't be wise to make her presence known.

Continuing down the street, she stopped the buggy to ask about a boarding house and was directed to *Miss*

Daisy's. It was an old home, owned by a widow, and they supposedly had a vacancy.

The two-story house was pristine and she immediately liked it. Painted white with green shutters and surrounded by trees. A sign reading *Miss Daisy's* over the front door confirmed she was in the right place.

"Wait here," she said to Mrs. Moss, and jumped out of the buggy.

Mrs. Moss chuckled. "I will. And Billy, too."

Cora rapped on the door and was greeted by a smiling, dark face. The young boy looked over his shoulder. "Ms. Daisy ... you gots guests."

Cora smiled at him and waited with her hands folded casually in front of her.

A short woman with gray hair and a very large belly came to the door. "Yes?" She eyed her up and down.

"I need a room," Cora said, and looked back toward the buggy. "That is, I need a room for me, my baby, and Mrs. Moss. Oh—and her cat, Muffin, too."

The old woman peered toward the buggy. "A baby?"

"Yes'm. My son, Billy. He's just a few months old."

"And your husband?"

She stared at the ground, already having concocted her lie. "He died, Ma'am."

"Oh, my dear. I'm so sorry." Daisy clutched her breast. "I know what it's like to lose a husband. Please bring them in."

"What 'bout my horse?"

"There's a livery stable up the road. I'll have my boy take it for you." She motioned to the little boy, then eyed Cora once again. "You *do* have money, don't you?"

"Yes'm."

"Well then!" Daisy clasped her hands and laughed. "Toby, take this woman's horse to the livery stable."

Cora pulled a coin from her pocket and handed it to Toby. His eyes lit up.

"That's too much!" Daisy exclaimed.

"Oh," Cora said. "Tell 'im I aim to keep it there for a spell."

Daisy grinned and patted Toby on the back. "Go now."

He skipped out the door and to the buggy.

"My friend will need help gettin' down," Cora said, following the boy. "She's blind."

"A child widow and a blind woman with a cat," Daisy muttered.

Cora looked over her shoulder. "And a baby," she said with a grin.

"And a baby." Daisy fanned herself and sighed.

* * *

Daisy gave them two adjoining rooms. She went on about how fortunate they were that she had enough space. They were also lucky that the rooms were on the main floor. Climbing stairs would have been difficult for Mrs. Moss.

Cora rearranged the furnishings in order to make things as simple as possible for Mrs. Moss. The beds were shoved against the walls and the stuffed chairs were pushed to the far side of the room. Muffin promptly made one of them her bed, curled up into a ball, and fell asleep.

For the time being, the wicker basket would have to do for Billy. In the back of her mind, Cora knew where she could go to get a crib, but that would have to wait. Beneath the window in her room was a bookcase. Sadly, it held no books. That wouldn't do. A trip to the mercantile would fix that problem.

"I'm puttin' your teacups on this shelf," she said to Mrs. Moss. "I reckon Miss Daisy won't mind us havin' tea in our room."

Mrs. Moss sat on the edge of her bed. Her lip quivered, but she didn't speak.

"Are you cryin'?"

Mrs. Moss wiped her eyes. "I miss my house."

"I'm sorry." Cora moved next to her and wrapped a loving arm over her shoulder. "I didn't think you'd mind so much. Least we're together."

Mrs. Moss nodded. "Yes. That's what matters the most." She patted her leg. "Now, please lead me to the outhouse."

Mrs. Moss's face turned a bright shade of red. It occurred to Cora that that was what was truly bothering her. Never before had she had to ask the way to such a private place, knowing her way perfectly at home.

"C'mon. We'll find it together." She helped Mrs. Moss to her feet, checked to make sure Billy was still sleeping, and after Daisy pointed the way, they took turns using the facility.

When they walked arm-in-arm back inside, Toby grinned at them. Cora lifted her head and paraded on by. Once again, she was thankful that Mrs. Moss couldn't see.

* * *

"Are you still thinkin' 'bout that man?" Harper asked Douglas, who was staring out the shop window.

"It's difficult not to." It had been more than three weeks since the hanging, but Douglas couldn't shake the memory. Once the coroner had arrived, he'd helped them bring the body down, and lift it onto the back of a wagon. No one claimed his body or showed any interest in offering a burial, so he'd paid for the service and had William buried in a local cemetery. Not knowing his date of birth, he had a stone carved listing only his date of death, March 20, 1851, as well as his name; William Casey O'Brien.

"I know you, Douglas," Harper said, rising from his stool. "You're thinkin' 'bout *her,* too."

He turned and faced his uncle. "I'm worried for her. Her husband is dead. She has a baby to care for, and ..."

"And you like her."

He did a double-take. Since Harper seldom left his stool, seeing him standing beside him took him by surprise. But even more than that, Harper was grinning.

"Yes," he admitted, "I like her. I like many women. I find them pleasant."

Harper chuckled, turned, and returned to his stool. "You ain't Cameron."

"You know very well that's not what I meant. I simply find women enjoyable to be around. Elise, for example." He stopped, when the door opened, and Elise stood there in front of him.

Harper sat upright.

"Douglas Denton, were you talking about me?" she asked with a coy smile.

Still chuckling, Harper began to whittle.

"Elise?" Douglas stared at her. "I didn't think you ever came to this part of town."

"Your mother told me you were here. Truth be told, I'm looking for Cameron. Have you seen him?"

Harper started to cough, then excused himself. "Nature," he muttered, and walked out the back door of the shop.

Elise cocked her head, watching him leave. "Is he always so outspoken?"

Douglas covered his mouth, amused by her question. "No, Elise, I haven't seen Cameron. He doesn't advise me of his whereabouts."

She wandered through the shop, lifting figurines and examining them. When she looked overhead and admired the wooden chain, he was once again reminded of Cora.

"He's very good," she said. "But I don't understand why he lives here. This isn't the best part of Memphis."

"He likes it here ... near the water. Mother once asked him to live with us, but he refused. I don't think he appreciates the Wellesley estate." Douglas understood his uncle's reasons. Living by the water appealed to him as well.

"I'd give anything to live on the estate," she said, dreamily. "I truly *must* find Cameron."

He hated to tell her what he knew she needed to hear. "Elise ..." His voice cracked.

"What is it?"

He took a deep breath. "Cameron is engaged." She buckled at the knees, so he rushed to her and caught her before she fell to the floor.

She fanned herself. "Engaged?"

"Yes. Just this past week. I'm so sorry."

"Who?"

"Vivian Stamford."

"Vivian?" She breathed heavily. "She's wretched! How could he ever choose her over me?" Her head rested against his shoulder and she blubbered into tears.

"Please ... don't cry." He looked around the room, hoping to be rescued. "I don't know why my brother does the things he does, but I assure you, you're better off."

She stiffened and backed away from him. "How could you say such a thing? I love him!" Again, she swooned.

Though she tried to push him away, he steadied her. "Let me take you home. I'll get my buggy."

Tiny whimpers were her only response.

"Wait right here," he said, pointing a stern finger as he positioned her in a chair not far from Harper's stool.

Her lower lip quivered. "I don't have anywhere else to go."

He left her there and hoped that when Harper returned he wouldn't upset her further. Walking briskly to the livery stable, he kept telling himself how unfair it was that he had to be the one to tell Elise about Cameron and Vivian.

Cameron should have had the decency to do it himself.

"Hey, Mista Denton," Toby said, grinning. He was busily brushing a mare.

"Hello, Toby. Whose chestnut?"

"New boarders. Paid me to come hep with the horse. Real nice. Purdy, too."

Douglas grinned and patted Toby's head, then bent down, leaning in close. "Tell Rosie my mother misses her. The new cook isn't nearly as good."

"My mama's cookin' for Miss Daisy now that we gots more boarders." He grinned from ear-to-ear. "She be fine. I'll tell her what your mama said."

"Thank you, Toby." He led his horse from the stable. "I'll be back soon. I have to take a friend home."

"She purdy?" Toby asked, wrinkling his nose.

He shook his head. "How did you know she's a *she*?"

"Cuz men can walk." Toby placed his fisted hands on his hips and lifted his chin as if it was a fact everyone knew.

Douglas chuckled and hopped into the buggy.

"Bye!" Toby waved and yelled as he rode off.

When he returned to his uncle's shop, Elise was still sitting where he'd left her; shoulders drooping almost as low as her bottom lip. He crossed to her and extended his hand, helping her to her feet. Harper had returned and was perched on his stool, paying no attention to Elise.

"I'm taking her home," Douglas said over his shoulder.

"Good place for her," Harper said, without raising his head.

He hoped Elise didn't hear his uncle's remark.

* * *

The Peck home was located near the Wellesley estate, but was in a neighborhood not quite so grand. However, their home was fine and much more impressive than

MARKED · 179

most of the homes in Memphis. Elise chattered non-stop the entire way and he was anxious to leave her in the care of her mother so he could return home for some peace.

"Cameron is by far the most horrid man I've ever known," she proclaimed amidst her one-sided conversation. Through the course of her tirade, Cameron had consistently dropped rank. He'd gone from being the love of her life to someone completely unworthy of anything. She turned and looked at him, raising her eyes as if waiting for him to remark. He scratched his head and looked away.

"Douglas," her voice softened. "Is it true that all of your father's money will go to that *wretched* brother of yours?"

Her comment caught him off guard. "Who told you this?"

She folded her hands in her lap. "Mother."

He was silent for a moment, wondering how her mother knew. But then again, since their mothers had been friends at one time, they must have discussed it. He sighed. "I don't care about the money."

"So it *is* true?" She sat more upright and defiantly pulled her shoulders back. "It's terribly wrong!"

"It's the way it is. As long as Arthur Wellesley has a living, breathing son of his own, I don't exist in his eyes." He realized after he said it that his tone was a bit cad, but he couldn't take his words back.

"Do you mean that if something were to happen to Cameron, *you* would be his heir?" She placed her hand on his arm. Slowly, her eyes lifted to meet his; long lashes fluttering.

"Nothing will happen to Cameron. And as much as you've decided you dislike him, it's not a very kind thing to say or even think about, for that matter."

She lowered her head and feigned regret. Because he knew her well, he was certain there was more to her comment than she let on. Her mother appeared to be waiting for her and was standing on the front porch with her arms casually folded across her chest.

He smiled warmly and watched as she lowered her arms and walked toward them. Lena Peck was attractive for her age; however, she looked much older than his mother, even though only one year separated them. Her overly-wrinkled skin was evidence that she'd spent much too much time in the sun.

"Douglas," she chirped and extended her arms upward as if waiting for him to jump into them.

"Hello, Mrs. Peck." He casually stepped from the buggy, then helped Elise down to the ground.

Lena scooted in beside him, offering her hand.

He forced a smile and lifted her hand to his lips out of courtesy.

"That's better," she said, grinning.

"Mother," Elise said, pushing herself between the two of them. "Douglas was kind enough to bring me home. He had horrid news and I didn't take it well." She lowered her head and stared at the ground.

Lena stiffened. "Is it your mother?"

"Oh, no ..." he said, rapidly shaking his head. "It's my brother." He paused, wondering if Elise would jump in and spill the news, but she remained silent.

Lena questioned him with her eyes.

"Cameron is engaged," he said, and waited for the backlash. He expected an outburst of some sort, but instead, Mrs. Peck deflated.

She mumbled something he couldn't make out, then Elise jumped in and began ranting again about how horrible Cameron was.

Finally he couldn't take anymore. "I really must be going. Mrs. Peck, please look after Elise for me."

Lena reached out and rested her hand on his shoulder. "You've always been the good boy." She put her arm around Elise and the two of them walked slowly into their house.

* * *

"It's not my fault," Cameron mumbled as he reached across the table and nabbed another biscuit.

Ada, the new cook, was pouring water into his glass. Her entire arm shook and she looked as though she was having difficulty breathing. As Cameron pulled his arm back, he bumped into her and she spilled a small amount of water on the table.

"Be more careful!" Cameron yelled, dabbing up the water with a cloth napkin.

"I's sorry, Mista Wellesley."

Her voice trembled and Douglas feared she was going to cry. "It was an accident, Ada," he said, trying to ease her. "Cameron should be more careful."

Cameron scowled at him in response and Ada hurriedly returned to the kitchen.

"Good help is so difficult to come by," Arthur Wellesley muttered. "I paid a lot of money for her. After the disappointment I had with Rosie, I'm thankful I could barter her away for something better. That woman at the boarding house bought her back from me."

Douglas couldn't remain silent. "She wanted Rosie to be with her son. I saw Toby at the livery stable. He was beaming. Grateful to have his mother with him again."

Arthur curled his lip. "They're slaves, Douglas. They have no feelings."

"They're people, Father." His heart pounded so hard, it caused his neck to throb. "With deeper feelings than many other people I know." He looked directly at Arthur, then glanced at Cameron.

Mary twisted her fingers together. "Now ... please. Let's enjoy our supper." She swallowed hard, then turned her attention to Cameron. "What was it you were saying?"

Cameron broke off a piece of the biscuit and popped it into his mouth. "I was saying that it isn't my fault that Elise Peck is upset. I never gave her any indication that I would marry her. Besides, Vivian and I are better suited."

Arthur smiled at his son. "You made a wise choice."

"Of course, I did," Cameron said, smugly. "Douglas may disagree, but I know what I'm doing."

Douglas held back what he truly wanted to say to his brother. "Do you love her?"

Cameron snickered. "With every part of me."

Mary smiled timidly, then lowered her head and continued eating the roast pork and potatoes mounded on her plate. "Ada did a fine job with the meal."

Arthur spooned a large amount of potatoes into his mouth. "Yes. Perhaps I'll keep this one."

Douglas ate as quickly as he could, wanting very much to escape. He loved his mother, but had no respect for the man he had to call *Father.*

He was grateful that his bedroom was in the west wing of the house, far away from the rest of the family. It offered solace—something he desperately wanted tonight.

* * *

"Moping?" Cameron asked, peering into his room.

Douglas sat upright on his bed, surprised to see Cameron standing there. "No, just enjoying the quiet. What are *you* doing?"

Cameron sauntered into the room and sat down in a carved wooden chair. "What was it like, seeing that dead Irishman?" He crossed his legs and leaned in toward him.

"You disgust me."

Cameron laughed. "You've been moping about it for weeks now. So, I assume it must have bothered you. Did he smell?"

Douglas stood and pointed to the door. "Get out."

Cameron stood. "If you insist. But I was hoping you could tell me more about what you know. Why they killed him? Aside from the fact that he was a cheat. And ... where did they take the boat? I would very much like to know."

"Why do you care?" He couldn't help being cold to Cameron, who always brought out his worst side.

"Because ..." Cameron smiled wryly. "I'm fond of a certain French whore, who gave me one of the best nights of my young life. I hope to see her again."

"You're engaged. Or did you already forget?"

Cameron smirked. "Engaged, but not married. I still have time."

Without speaking, Douglas again pointed to the door.

"Fine. But please, if you hear of the *Bonny Lass* coming to shore, let me know." Throwing his shoulders back, he strutted out the door.

Douglas happily slammed it behind him.

Chapter 17

Cora's heart thumped. She breathed deeply, making every attempt to steady herself. Gaining courage by holding onto Billy, she opened the door to Harper's woodshop.

He was in his usual spot and didn't bother raising his head. For a brief moment, she considered turning around and running as fast as her legs could carry her back to the boarding house, but she took another step forward.

Timidly, she cleared her throat.

Harper raised his head to the sound, glanced at her, then lowered his head and began whittling. "Didn't think you'd be back so soon," he grumbled.

She was taken aback by his icy tone. "I ... I ... never got the chance to tell you how much I liked the cradle." She patted Billy's back in an attempt to remain calm.

Harper's head snapped upward, then he jumped off his stool, setting aside his knife.

Her eyes widened at his strange behavior. "I reckon I came at a bad time. I best be goin'." She turned to walk away.

"No!" Harper yelled, then his voice softened. "I want you to stay."

She faced him, but couldn't understand the awkward expression on his face. After their previous brief encounter, she knew him to be an unusual man, but he was behaving more oddly than ever.

"Why you lookin' at me like that?" she asked, then soothed Billy with a gentle kiss on his cheek.

"Thought you was that *other* woman." He scratched his head. "Didn't see the baby."

She looked down at the floor. "I shouldn't a come here."

"Don't say that. Glad you came. Glad you liked the cradle." He turned his attention to Billy and wiggled his finger under the baby's chin.

Billy squirmed in her arms. "He done outgrew it already. I came to ask you to make him a crib." She looked around the little shop nervously. "But ... you can't tell no one I was here."

"No one?"

She shook her head. "If my husband knew I was here, he'd be right angry with me." She leaned in close to his ear. "There's folks that might try to hurt me an Billy."

Harper stared blankly at her.

"I reckon I said too much already." Opening a small cloth purse hanging from her wrist, she pulled out several coins. "Here. When you got the crib done, can you bring it to me at Miss Daisy's boardin' house?"

He nodded without saying a word.

"Thank you." Again she leaned into him. "I go by *Smith* there. Can't let no one know my real name." She softened her voice even more. "William says it's too dangerous."

She smiled, nodded, and left as quickly as she could.

Her heart slowed the further she got from the woodshop—grateful that Billy would soon have a crib, but disappointed that Harper's nephew was absent today.

* * *

"I can't believe she was here," Douglas said, pacing Harper's floor.

Harper bobbed his head. "Day before yesterday. Said I shouldn't tell no one." He rubbed his chin. "Oops ..."

Douglas grinned at him, then became somber. "She had no idea that her husband is dead?"

"Nope."

It made no sense. Cora was in Memphis using an alias and she didn't know that her husband was hung and buried?

He crossed to the crib which was nearly complete. "How soon will it be ready?"

Harper looked upward, then scratched his head. "T'morrow."

"Good." He ran his hand over the smooth wood. "I'll take it to her." He looked at his uncle who was grinning from ear to ear. "*What?*"

"You like her. Knew you did."

"She needs to know about her husband." The thought of telling her upset him, but it was the right thing to do.

"She *deserves* to know and to see where he's buried." He paused, walked across the floor, and gazed out the window. "I want to know who she's afraid of.

Harper followed him. "Careful. Don't know what kind a trouble she's in."

"I will be. But I believe she needs help and she may not even know it."

He walked to the door and opened it, then turned and smiled once more at his uncle. "And yes, I do like her."

* * *

As soon as Douglas walked through the front door, female voices rose from the kitchen. He recognized his mother's voice and could tell she was upset, but couldn't make out her words. Walking briskly down the hall to the kitchen, he realized the other voice was that of Lena Peck.

Why is she here?

"You owe it to me!" Lena yelled as she hovered over Mary, but then drew back when she saw him standing in the doorway.

"Mother?" He went quickly to her side.

Mary sat at the kitchen table, twisting a cloth napkin around her hand. He stared at Lena, then looked again at his mother. Her eyes were wide with fear.

"What's going on here?" he asked, and sat beside her.

Lena feigned a chuckle. "Oh my dear, Douglas. Your mother and I were having a simple conversation." She looked at Mary. "Weren't we, Mary dear?"

Mary cleared her throat, then took his hand, setting aside the napkin. "Yes ... simple." She patted their joined hands and looked into his eyes. "You're home early."

Feeling his mother's hand tremble in his grasp, he looked sideways at Lena. "What did you mean? What does my mother owe you?"

Lena placed one hand at her breast and laughed. "Oh! It was a little wager your mother and I made. I told her that I knew that cook of yours wouldn't last, and when I came here today and found Ada preparing dinner, I told her that I was right all along. She owes me two bits." She leaned forward and smoothed his hair. "We never gamble large sums of money."

His brows furrowed. "Mother? Is this true?"

"Y-Yes." Mary swallowed the lump in her throat. "I was about to go to my room to get the money."

Lena continued laughing. "Don't bother, Mary. The wager was in good fun. I never intended to take your money." With her final words, her upper lip twitched. He knew her words were false, but he couldn't understand why his mother was defending her.

"Yes ... good fun," Mary muttered, then grabbed the napkin, twisting it again.

Lena placed her hand on his cheek. "Elise hasn't stopped talking about you since you brought her home. I believe she's finally realized that her eyes were on the wrong brother. You *must* call on her." She looked deeply into his eyes.

"I consider her a dear friend, Mrs. Peck. Nothing more." He would not be manipulated.

"Friends can easily become *more,*" she replied, then looked sharply at Mary.

He watched the two of them exchange glances, then how rapidly his mother shifted her gaze downward.

"Mary," Lena said, "I'll see you again soon. Perhaps another wager?"

Silently, Mary shook her head.

"I'll see myself out," Lena said, while walking away. She paused at the door and turned to face him. "Douglas," her upper lip twitched, "I've been meaning to ask ... Have you seen that woman again? The one whom you said looks like my daughter?" Her tongue flicked anxiously out of her mouth.

"No, I haven't." Lena's interest in Cora bothered him, causing his heart to increase its pace.

"Well ... if you do, remember that I would very much like to meet her." Her mouth twisted into a smile. She turned, waved, and walked out the door.

He returned to the kitchen. "Mother, what was that all about?" He looked over his shoulder making certain Mrs. Peck was gone.

When his mother didn't respond, he turned to look at her, only to find her with her head in her hands on the table.

"Mother?"

She lifted her head, just enough to look at him. "I need to lie down. My head aches."

He helped her to her feet, then walked her to her room.

"Pull the drapery, Douglas," she said as she stepped out of his grasp and onto the bed.

He did as she asked. "Get some rest. I'll check on you later."

She nodded, then rolled over on her side facing away from him.

As he left the room, he pulled the door shut. Why had Lena emerged after so many years of absence? Now his mother was more withdrawn than ever. *What kind of friend would cause such behavior?* The answer was obvious ... no *true* friend.

Chapter 18

Cora sat in the common living room mending a dress. Daisy had been kind enough to bring her a number of garments from the charity box at church. Since she was in hiding, she didn't want to draw any attention to herself, so she only brought one of the fancy dresses from the boat and kept it stored away.

Toby popped into the room with his ever-present wide grin. "Ms. Smith, Mista Denton is here with a bed for Billy."

She froze. "Mr. *Denton*?"

"Yes'm. Said his uncle sent him." His toothy smile lit up his face. "Said he wants to give it to you his self."

Mrs. Moss sat next to Cora, with Muffin curled up on her lap. "Who is Mr. Denton?"

"No one special." Cora jerked the needle through the fabric and with her mind elsewhere jabbed it into her finger. "Dang!"

"Cora!" Mrs. Moss scolded. "Control your temper!"

"Shh!" Cora fussed. "You'll wake Billy!"

Mrs. Moss sat perfectly upright, while stroking the cat. "It is you who will wake your son if you don't mind your temper. Now ... see to this *Mr. Denton*, and try to act like a lady."

Cora set aside the dress, then while nursing her finger, stood. Pulling it from her mouth, she examined it. The bleeding had already stopped. "I'm sorry, Mrs. Moss. Excuse me." She scurried out of the room, but in the opposite direction of the front door.

Toby followed her. "Ms. Smith. Mista Denton is out *there*." He pointed the other way, then wrinkled his face and stared at her.

She stopped, smoothed her dress, then ran her fingers through her hair. "There?" she asked, nodding toward the front room.

"Yes'm."

She passed by Toby and walked one step at a time toward the front of the house. All she had to do was round one corner and she would be face-to-face with Douglas Denton. Her mouth was dry, her palms sweaty.

You're a silly girl, Cora.

Before rounding that corner, she closed her eyes and took a deep breath. Then, she took the last step.

"Mr. Denton?" She crossed to him and tried to plaster a casual smile on her face. Could he see that her entire body was trembling?

"Hello, Cora." He smiled at her and she nearly fell to the floor. He was dressed more casually than the last time she'd seen him. Unable to help herself, she scanned him from head to toe. He looked more comfortable in these

194 · Jeanne Hardt

clothes; simple chocolate-brown cotton shirt and tan
pants.

Sure fits his colorin'. His eyes is the same color as his shirt.
Her heart fluttered. *So fine to look at …*

Douglas took her hand and gave it a gentleman's kiss.
When Toby snickered, she jerked her head to look at
him, then motioned with her eyes for him to leave. He
complied, sniggering all the while.

She pulled her hand back, hoping he didn't notice just
how damp it was. "I see you brought the crib." She nodded toward the piece which he'd placed next to the wall
in the entryway. "It's real nice. Please thank your uncle
for me."

"I will." He folded his hands comfortably in front of
himself, then silently stared at her.

"Is sumthin' wrong?" She gulped and looked down at
herself.

"No … well …" He sighed. "Cora? Can we sit? I need
to speak with you." He nodded toward a sofa in the sitting room.

Her heart thumped even harder. "I reckon so."

She passed by him and as she did so, breathed in
deeply. He smelled clean and fresh, unlike any man she'd
been close enough to smell. Leading him to the sofa, she
gestured for him to sit.

"Thank you," he said, and patted the spot next to him.
"Please … sit. It'll make this much easier."

Completely confused, she did as he asked.

Before he could speak, she jumped right in. "Mr. Denton, you probably shouldn't be here. You see …" She

leaned in closely to him. "I'm not s'pose to let anyone know I'm here. They think my name's *Smith.*"

"I know. Uncle Harper told me."

Of course Harper told him she was there. Even though she'd told him not to tell anyone, she'd secretly hoped he would. Timidly, she looked around the room and softened her voice. "Still ... might not be a good thing havin' Toby know that you an I are ... *familiar.*"

"Cora ..." He spoke her name so gently that she felt her heart might burst.

Something was troubling him, so she decided she should let him speak his mind. There had to be a reason why he chose to bring the crib in his uncle's place. "Yes, Mr. Denton?"

"Douglas," he said, and reached for her hand.

She stared at his hand, holding hers. Tiny tingles trickled across her skin. "Douglas," she whispered.

"I have so many questions." He stopped, struggling to speak.

"It's all right. I reckon we're safe enough. You see ... William's worried 'bout this man named Giles. He's tryin' to hurt us. Well, hurt *me,* that is. My pa cheated him and he decided he could get back his money by havin' me." She stopped, feeling the heat in her cheeks, and looked into his eyes.

"And your husband stopped him from doing that," he said, urging her on.

"Uh-huh." His thumb moved back and forth, caressing her skin. She closed her eyes, savoring the sensation. *How can a simple touch feel so good?* She shook her head, forcing herself to focus on her words. "William threw him overboard."

The caress abruptly stopped, but he didn't release her hand. "Overboard?"

"Yep. William said he deserved it. He wasn't gonna let him hurt me."

"So, why did you leave the boat?"

The memory of that night flooded her mind and she couldn't stop tears from filling her eyes. "William said I had to. He's runnin' from Giles. He got word that Giles was puttin' together a lynchin'. He feared that they'd do sumthin' to him, then come after me an little Billy."

He squeezed her hand. "Cora ..."

With her free hand, she wiped the tears from her eyes, then sniffled. "Yes?"

"I'm so sorry—but—your husband was hung. More than a month ago. I helped bury him."

Her chest tightened and all the breath in her lungs seemed to escape all at once. Though William had warned her it could happen, she still held on to hope that maybe he could stop Giles. She trembled, as tears readily fell from her eyes. "Where?" She couldn't manage another syllable.

He pulled her into his arms and let her cry. As she dampened his shirt, he soothed her with soft words, telling her she would be all right.

William had never held her this way. Even when he offered her comfort, it felt nothing like this. Douglas was strong and firm-bodied, but gentle and kind.

Her heart thumped harder and faster; a mixture of emotions pushing the blood rapidly through her veins.

She slowed her breathing, lifted her head from his shoulder, and tilted it upward to look into his face. Blinking away the tears, her eyes locked with his. Swallowing hard, she fought an unusual urge to kiss him.

"Cora?" The tapping of Mrs. Moss's walking stick caused her to pull away from him. "Cora," Mrs. Moss persisted, "are you crying?"

She sniffled, then wiped her face with the sleeve of her dress. "I'm fine, Mrs. Moss."

Slowly, the old woman crossed the floor, all the while tapping the stick in front of her. "No, you are not fine." She tipped her head and sniffed the air. "Who is that with you?"

Douglas rose from the sofa, then helped Cora to her feet. "My name is Douglas Denton."

"Denton?" Mrs. Moss asked. "Your family must be from England."

"Yes, Ma'am," he replied, "but my grandparents settled in Tennessee many years ago. I've always lived here."

Mrs. Moss smiled, staring vacantly beyond his face. "That explains why you have no accent. But I will assume you behave as an English gentleman."

"Yes, Ma'am." He folded his hands in front of his body.

Mrs. Moss turned her attention to Cora. "Now, why were you crying?"

Cora's chin began to quiver, so Douglas stepped in. "I'm afraid I brought bad news."

"Oh?" Mrs. Moss inched closer to her.

"Yes. Her husband was killed. I tried to stop it." He looked at Cora and his eyebrows knit together as he spoke. "I saw the mob forming and went for the marshal, but when we returned, it was too late."

"You did?" Cora asked him, placing her hand on his arm. "You tried to help William?"

"Yes." His hand covered hers once again.

She looked up into his eyes and for a few moments they said nothing. Clearing her throat, she pressed on. "Why'd you do it?"

"No man should be punished without a fair trial. I saw him being led from the boat." He paused, looking upward as though he were deep in thought. "Strangely, he didn't appear to show any resistance."

She let out a long breath. "William knew they'd kill him. He told me that all he cared 'bout was keepin' me an Billy safe. He wanted me to forget we was ever married."

"But how can you? He was your husband. You can't forget someone you love."

She stared at the floor. How could she tell him that she didn't love him that way? He would think poorly of her if he knew she gave him a child, but didn't love him. *Wouldn't he?*

"I reckon you're right," she muttered under her breath.

Mrs. Moss reached out to her and she moved into her arms.

"My poor, poor dear," Mrs. Moss said, stroking her hair, then tilted her head, looking toward Douglas. "Thank you for bringing the news. I know it's not easy telling someone such a horrible thing."

He nodded toward the crib. "I brought a crib for Billy. My uncle made it."

Cora raised her head and looked at him. "I'll show it to her later. Let her feel it. She's blind."

Mrs. Moss managed to chuckle. "I'm quite certain he's already realized that, Cora."

A different kind of cry filled the air, causing her to stand erect. "I gotta get Billy."

"May I see him?" Douglas asked.

"You wanna see my baby?" she asked, wrinkling her nose.

He nodded. "Yes, I do. Very much."

Mrs. Moss patted her arm. "Bring him, Cora. Show Mr. Denton what a fine son you have."

Cora rushed from the room. Her head was spinning with thoughts she couldn't control. Sorrow mixed with desire; a very unusual combination.

Lifting Billy from the wicker basket gave her a sense of normalcy. She changed his wet diaper, then carried him to the front room, so that Douglas could see him.

"He's hungry, but since you wanna see him, I reckon he can wait." She cradled him in her arm.

Douglas smiled as she pulled back the blanket from his tiny face. "He looks like you," he said, and touched his finger to Billy's cheek.

"Oh," Mrs. Moss said, "I'm happy to hear you say this. Cora neglected to tell me what her husband looked like. But I'm glad to know the baby favors her. She was a beautiful child."

Cora didn't say a word. She was caught up watching Douglas enjoy her son.

"She still is," he said, smiling at her.

Mrs. Moss blinked her empty eyes. "Yes ... she is."

200 · Jeanne Hardt

Cora knew what Mrs. Moss was thinking. Douglas was being a bit *too* familiar.

"I ... I better take Billy an feed him." She placed him over her shoulder and patted his back. "Thank you again for bringin' the crib. And ... I appreciate the news of my husband. If you have time one day, I'd very much like to see where he's buried. Pay my respects. Mourn ..." Her voice drifted off as she struggled with what to say. Though she shed tears upon hearing the news, why wasn't she more grief-stricken?

"I can come back tomorrow," he offered. "Just tell me a convenient time."

"How 'bout nine in the mornin'?"

"I'll be here." He turned toward Mrs. Moss. "It was nice to meet you, ma'am."

Mrs. Moss nodded her head and smiled.

"And you, too, Billy," he said, and patted his back.

Cora's eyes met his one final time, then he turned and walked out the door.

* * *

Douglas let out his breath with a long sigh. As he climbed into his buggy, he looked over his shoulder at the boarding house. Toby's large, dark eyes peered at him through the sitting room window, accompanied by an even larger grin glowing with sparkling white teeth. He acknowledged Toby with a nod, then headed toward home.

Why did he feel so strange? Though he'd never before had to tell a woman that she was a widow, he knew it was something much more than that. When Cora looked at him through her misty eyes, he'd felt more than pity. He'd fought the urge to pull her even closer and press his lips against hers. And what was even odder to him, was that he believed she *wanted* him to.

She's a widow, Douglas. You've no right to think such thoughts. Scolding himself seemed to help, so why did he wish he could turn the buggy around and go back to her?

He pressed on, and in no time at all was on the long, winding path which led to the estate stables.

The heavy scent of hay and horses filled his nose. Stepping down, he handed the reins to the stable slave, Jeriah, then walked toward the house.

"There you are!" Elise lifted her skirt and shuffled toward him.

"Elise?"

"Yes, it's me, silly." She giggled, then stumbled and fell into his arms.

He knew exactly what she was up to, but caught her regardless. "You need to be more careful, Elise."

She tilted her head coyly and looked up at him. "As long as I have you to catch me, then why should I be?"

Looking down at her—for a brief moment—he saw Cora. But she was nothing like Cora and he pushed her away. "I may not always be here to catch you."

"What if I wanted you to be?" Her eyelashes fluttered as she moved a step closer to him.

"What about Cameron? Or did you forget that it is *he* whom you love?"

"Cameron, who?" She took a step even closer and their midsections were almost touching. Tilting her head upward, she closed her eyes and pursed her lips.

He stared at her. *So much like Cora ...* Slowly, he lowered his head, inching closer and closer. He closed his eyes...

"No," he said, and stood upright.

"No?" Her eyes popped open wide, and her fists rested on her hips. "And why not? Haven't you ever thought of kissing me?"

"Yes, I have. But that was a long time ago. When you gave your heart to Cameron, I knew I had to dismiss any thoughts I might have of you." He resumed walking toward the house.

She followed him and grabbed his arm. "I don't want Cameron any longer." She jerked, forcing him to face her. "I want *you*, Douglas."

Pulling away from her, he crossed his arms over his chest. "And why is that? Does your heart so easily change its course?"

"I was confused," she pouted. "Mother believes I've always loved you, but didn't realize it because I was blinded by Cameron."

"I see. And now that Cameron has decided to marry Vivian, you're no longer blind?"

"Mmm ... hmmm." She batted her eyes.

"You *do* remember that I have no inheritance?" He cocked his head, waiting for her response.

Her jaw dropped as she stood there, aghast. "Douglas Denton! How could you ever think that money has anything to do with my heart?"

He forced away the smirk which *so* wanted to appear on his face. "Forgive me, Elise."

She held her hand to her breast. "Very well. I imagine I'll have to show you just how much I care." She sprang on him, wrapped her arms around his neck and pressed her mouth to his. "I love you, Douglas!"

He peeled her hands away, and as gently as he could, pushed her aside. "No, you don't. Now please ... go home."

"But ..." She looked as if she was going to cry.

His heart softened and his voice calmed. "Elise, please go on home. You're confused. I know how much you care for Cameron and he hurt you. But I'm not him, and I never will be."

"I'll prove to you that he means nothing to me." She sniffled. "I was foolish. I'll show you that you and I are meant to be together. You may not want me now, but one day ..." Her face brightened with a generous smile. "You will."

She flitted away, down the path to the stables.

He shook his head as he opened the door and went in-side. It took him a few moments to digest what had just happened, and he knew that Elise wasn't in her right mind. *Her mother believes that she's always loved me?* That fact in itself was disturbing. Then he thought of the con-versation that Lena Peck had with his mother. This was a puzzle he wanted to solve. More than that, he *needed* to solve, and somehow Cora seemed to be one of the pieces.

Chapter 19

April rains returned to the South.

When Cora woke, rain pattered against the window. She let out a sigh, but nothing would stop her from going to William's grave. In many ways the rain fit her mood.

"I'm comin', Billy," she said, swinging her legs over the side of the bed.

He had just begun to whimper and she wanted to reach him before his whimpering became an out-and-out bawl. Though no one in the house had complained about Billy waking them, she tried to be courteous.

The new crib was beautiful; sanded to a smooth finish and painted white. Harper had even carved the letter 'B' on one end and outlined it in blue.

"Your Grampa woulda liked this," she said, lifting him into her arms.

He responded by moving his lips, and thrusting his tongue.

"I know ... you're hungry." She walked with him to one of the stuffed chairs and sat, first making sure that Muffin wasn't there. "You're always hungry."

She smiled as she watched him suckle. "I know what it's like bein' hungry, and I swear to you ... I aim to make sure you never are."

The sound of shuffling feet caused her to lift her head. "Mornin' Mrs. Moss," she said, then turned her attention back to Billy.

"Good morning, Cora." Mrs. Moss clicked her way across the floor, then felt her way down the arms and seat cushion of the other chair. Finding it empty, she sat. "I see that Billy is having his breakfast."

Cora laughed. "You see with your ears, don't you, Mrs. Moss."

"Yes, I do." She chuckled. "God blessed me with fine hearing."

"Ain't you mad He took away your sight?"

"I don't blame God for my loss of sight, Cora. Our bodies are imperfect. One day I'll see again." Mrs. Moss startled for a moment when Muffin jumped into her lap. "Oh, my! I didn't see her coming!"

"We need to give her a bell 'round her neck."

"That's a fine idea, Cora. Perhaps the next time you're at the mercantile, you can purchase one."

They sat silently for a while, enjoying the quiet of the morning. The rain came down harder.

Mrs. Moss cleared her throat. "It's pouring. Are you certain you want to go out in the rain?"

"Yes'm." She gently released Billy from her nipple and put him over her shoulder. After several pats on the back, he expelled a sound burp, then she moved him to her other breast. "I wanna see William's grave. He'll always be Billy's pa, even though Billy won't remember him."

"Are you ready for this, Cora?"

"What do you mean?"

"Did you love him?"

She rubbed her hand over Billy's head. His fine hair was soft as silk.

She couldn't lie. "He took care a me an Billy. I cared 'bout him, but I don't think I loved him."

Looking over at Mrs. Moss, she could tell that she was thinking about what she said. When she didn't respond, she decided to go further. "Ain't you supposed to wanna be with the man you're in love with? Be with him all the time?"

Mrs. Moss nodded.

"Well, it didn't bother me none when he didn't come 'round. 'Cept for when I thought he might be seein' Francine. Then, I wanted him to see me."

"Francine?"

She folded her hands in her lap. How would she tell Mrs. Moss about Francine? Some things were too delicate for Mrs. Moss's ears.

"Francine's a woman that works on the boat. I reckon she cared for William. But ... she didn't wanna marry him." She scratched her head. "Ah heck, Mrs. Moss. It's hard to talk 'bout!"

"If it's hard, then perhaps you loved him? At least, *somewhat* ..."

"But he didn't make my heart thump." She stared at her, waiting to be scolded.

"Has your heart *thumped* for someone else?" Mrs. Moss leaned toward her. "Hmmm?"

"Dang, Mrs. Moss. How'd you know?"

Mrs. Moss lifted her finger and shook it at her.

She immediately apologized.

"I was in love once," Mrs. Moss said. Her hand moved mindlessly over Muffin's fur.

"So, you know what it feels like?"

"I know that it's raining, and yet you're willing to go into the downpour in order to see your husband's grave. You tell me that you didn't love him, which makes me wonder what is truly pushing you out the door. Or shall I say *who* is pushing you out the door?"

Cora straightened her body. Billy wiggled briefly, then nestled down again and resumed eating his breakfast. "I don't wanna be rude to Douglas. I mean ... *Mr. Denton.*"

"Douglas?" Mrs. Moss smiled. "Is he handsome, Cora?"

Unable to hold back, she blurted out. "Most handsome man I ever seen. Has the brownest eyes, an dusty-blond hair. Keeps his face shaved clean ... an ... he's real tall ... an ..." She stopped and placed her hand over her mouth, sucking her breath in with a loud gasp.

Mrs. Moss chuckled. "And does he make your heart *thump?*"

"Yep. First time I seen him I thought my breath had been sucked outta me. An then ... well ... Billy started comin' an Douglas carried me to William."

"Oh, my," Mrs. Moss gasped, and held her hand to her chest. "He carried you?"

"Uh-huh." She stared dreamily. "He has the strongest arms ..."

"Cora Craighead!" Mrs. Moss raised her voice a little too loudly, startling Billy, who immediately cried.

"Shh," Cora soothed him. "Mrs. Moss, you know you ain't s'pose to use that name."

"What name?" Toby entered the room without knocking.

"Toby," Cora said sternly, "You're s'pose to knock."

"I heard Billy cry," he said. "What's a Craighead?"

"None of your concern," Mrs. Moss said.

He shrugged. "Mama gots breakfast ready. I told her Mista Denton was comin', an she made extra for him." He grinned. "She likes Mista Denton." He turned around and left the room.

"She's not the only one," Mrs. Moss mumbled, then stood. "I'll see you at the breakfast table."

"Wait," Cora said, reaching out to her.

Mrs. Moss stopped. "What is it, dear?"

"Do you think I'm awful? William ain't been dead long. But ... I can't help how I feel. I can't explain it. Sumthin' happened to my insides soon as I saw him the first time."

Mrs. Moss extended her hand and Cora pulled it lovingly to her face, cradling it against her cheek. "You're not awful, Cora. But ... be careful. The heart can be easily broken. I don't want you hurt. You've been through too much already."

Mrs. Moss left her alone to finish with Billy. She was relieved that she didn't think poorly of her for caring for Douglas, but chided herself nonetheless. She laid Billy long-ways across her lap, admiring him. He blinked his green eyes at her and she could have sworn that he smiled.

"Your ma's gonna go see your pa's grave. I'm sorry you won't never know him."

Billy kicked his feet and bobbled his head as though listening to every word. She placed her fingers into his grasping fists and stared at his tiny features. Bending down, she kissed his chubby cheek, then whispered in his ear, "You were worth it, Billy."

* * *

Toby opened the door and grinned at Douglas. "Mama saved some food for ya. She made them butte'milk biscuits you like."

"She did?" He looked Toby in the eye. "And what about her strawberry preserves?"

Toby nodded. "Them, too."

"Well then ... Show me the way."

Toby took his hand and led him through the short hallway to the kitchen. Rosie had a cloth in her hand, wiping down the kitchen table.

"I should have come sooner," Douglas said, crossing to Rosie and extending his hands. She took them in her own and gave them a tender squeeze.

Daisy entered the room and smiled up at him. "You know you're welcome anytime," she said, then turned her attention to Rosie. "Pork roast for supper, Rosie." She hurried out of the room.

"Off to church," Rosie said, watching Daisy leave. "They's makin' baskets for the poor."

He nodded. Daisy Phelps had always been a gracious woman.

After drying the table with a towel, Rosie dipped her hand into a sack of flour, then sprinkled it on the wood. She then took a large mound of bread dough from a bowl and set it on the dusting of flour.

"I love your bread, Rosie," he said, taking a bite of a biscuit that Toby had given him.

"I know you do. Too bad your daddy didn't feel the same."

Toby watched as his mother kneaded the dough.

"I'm glad he didn't." Douglas couldn't have been more serious. "Toby needed you. Everything worked out for the best."

She stopped what she was doing, smiled, and nodded. "And what 'bout you? That brother a yours makin' your life miserable?"

"I try to ignore him." Douglas froze and stared when Cora entered the room. She was dressed in a forest green cotton dress with tiny white roses dotted around the fabric. It was modest but fit her form. Her body was quite different than Elise's. Motherhood had caused her figure to fill out in all the appropriate places.

"Am I interruptin'?" Cora asked, slowly stepping forward.

He shook his head. "No. You see ... Rosie and I are old friends. Aren't we?"

Rosie smiled at Cora. "Yessa, we is."

"Mama's makin' bread!" Toby chimed. "Can Mista Denton eat supper with us t'night, Mama?"

Douglas looked at Cora, then at Rosie. "I wouldn't want to impose."

"Miss Daisy'll just charge you for it," Rosie said, with a chuckle. "She let anyone eat, if'n they pay."

"Ain't no better food to be had," Cora added.

He found the idea appealing. Not only would he be able to eat Rosie's cooking, but he would have more time with Cora. He turned to respond to her and discovered that she had her eyes on him. Was it possible that she felt something for him, too?

Digging into his pocket, he produced a nickel. "Will this do?"

"Shore nuff," Rosie said. "Corn puddin'?"

He nearly melted into the floor. She remembered that it was his favorite. "Rosie, you know how to make a man weak in the knees."

Cora cleared her throat. "Are you 'bout ready to go?"

"Forgive me. Yes." Without a second thought, he took her hand. "Rosie, I'll see you later. You too, Toby."

They exited the kitchen and proceeded to the front door. Then it dawned on him, "Where's Billy?"

"Sleepin'. I fed him, then put him in his crib. Mrs. Moss is gonna watch him for me." She stared down at their hands.

He followed her gaze and quickly released her. "I'm so sorry. I don't know what I was thinking." It seemed a natural thing to do ...

"Pay it no mind." She pointed to the door. "You know, it's still rainin'."

"Yes, I know. My buggy is covered. It's plenty warm, so I don't believe we'll be too uncomfortable." He gave her a reassuring smile. "I brought an umbrella for the cemetery. As long as there's no lightning, we should be fine."

"Don't like lightnin' none." She looked over her shoulder.

He sensed her trepidation. "Are you all right? I know this must be difficult for you."

"I ain't never left Billy before."

"Would you rather take him with us?"

"No. He's too little to understand. 'Sides, I don't want him out in the rain."

He nodded, then extended his arm. "It's not far. We should be back before he wakes."

As she took his arm, some of the tension in her body vanished.

"Douglas?" A trace of shyness was evident in her voice. "What's an umbrella?"

She was completely adorable. "I'll show you. It's a device that covers you and prevents the rain from dampening your skin."

"I need one a them," she giggled. "Mrs. Moss always fusses at me for gettin' wet an muddy."

Helping her into the buggy was effortless. "She cares a great deal for you." He made sure she was comfortably seated before stepping up into the buggy beside her.

"Yep. She's kind a like my ma. She raised me for the most part."

"Has she always been blind?"

Cora shook her head. "No. Lost her sight just this past year. Not sure how it happened. Don't seem quite right."

"But now, *you* can care for *her*. It's good that she has you."

She dropped her eyes, and stared at her hands. "We have each other." Raising her head, she smiled at him. "Oh ... don't worry 'bout her tendin' Billy. Long as he's sleepin' she does fine with him. She ain't too good at diaperin'."

He grinned at her and was repaid with a generous smile. As he snapped the reins, she looked up into his eyes in a way that made his heart race. Her body was warm beside him and there was a hint of sweet flowers on her skin. The rain didn't trouble him. Cora herself was all the sunshine he needed.

* * *

Cora wished the journey to the cemetery had been longer. Sitting next to Douglas gave her more joy than she knew existed. Yet she was a grieving widow and needed to act appropriately.

Her thoughts kept returning to the feel of his hand in hers. He had taken her hand without reservation and she held his without giving it a second thought. *Does he hold hands with all women?* She wished he hadn't pulled it away.

"I hate that you hafta go outta your way to take me to the grave," she managed to say through her overly-dry mouth.

He looked at her and smiled, causing her heart to double its pace. "I don't mind. Honestly, it makes me feel better knowing that you'll see where he's buried." He faced forward, becoming somber. "I never understood why no one claimed his body."

The sorrow in his voice compelled her to touch him. She tenderly rested her hand on his knee. "It was good a you to help bury him."

"It was the right thing to do. He didn't deserve what happened to him."

"You might a felt different if you'd a been one a the folks he cheated."

"Are you certain he cheated?"

She nodded. "He told me so. Said the cards was marked." She turned her head. "Just like me," she added, under her breath.

"What did you say?"

"Oh ... nothin'. Pay it no mind." She folded her hands in her lap.

He stopped the buggy beside a large, white brick church. A wooden sign displaying the name, *St. Peter's*, was in the forefront of the building.

"The cemetery is behind," he said, lifting his chin.

He stepped out of the buggy, then extended his hand to her once again. She gladly took it. "Catholic?" she asked.

"Yes. He was Irish, I assumed he was Catholic." Unfolding the umbrella, he held it over her head. Her eyes widened as she scanned the device. It was probably one of the greatest inventions she'd ever seen. He beamed as if he could read her thoughts. "This will keep us dry."

"I feel silly," she muttered.

"Why?" He tipped his head, then raised her chin, looking into her face. "Is it the umbrella?"

"Uh-uh. I like the umbrella. I'll hafta get me one at the mercantile."

"Then what's wrong?"

She gazed around the yard and stared at the building. "Cuz—I ain't sure what he believed. We never talked 'bout it. Never talked 'bout much at all."

He guided her down a side-path to the grave. The rain danced off the top of the umbrella. "But you married him. Obviously you must have had something in common to speak of."

She took a deep breath. Was this the right time to tell him about how she became William's wife?

"Over there," he said, pointing to a tombstone on the far side of the graveyard.

"Thank you." The distraction was welcome.

The wet ground had become muddy, making the plot even more dismal. She read the inscription on the stone and a lump rose in her throat. Tears formed. Tears she didn't fully understand.

Her breathing grew rapid and her body shook.

He placed his arm around her. "What can I do to help?" His voice flowed with compassion.

She tried to steady her breathing. "Hold me," she whispered. "Please?"

He didn't hesitate. Just as he had so easily taken her hand, he pulled her against his chest. "It's all right, Cora. Go on and cry." Holding the umbrella with one hand, he cradled her body with the other.

"Why does it hurt, Douglas?" she asked, sniffling.

"Because you loved him." His hand moved across her back, stroking her with reassuring tenderness.

"No," she whispered. "That's just it. I *didn't* love him."

The movement of his hand stopped. "I don't under-stand."

"My pa made me marry him." She turned her head and looked up at him, waiting for a reaction. His face held no expression, so she continued. "See ... Pa gambled. He won big on the *Bonny Lass* and when they found out he was cheatin', they wanted the money back. But Pa liked to drink more than he liked to gamble, and he drank so much he forgot where the money was. They was gonna hang him, but he made a deal with William."

When she stopped to take a breath, he spoke. "You were his prize." His tone was matter-of-fact, with a hint of anger.

"My pa sold me. Tried to make me believe it was best for me. I blamed the whiskey. I don't reckon he would a done it if he'd a been sober."

"Cora, I've never heard anything so horrible. How could he do that to you?"

"He didn't. The whiskey did."

He took her chin in his hand and made her look at him. His eyes were filled with pain. "He chose to drink."

"You're right, but he drank cuz my ma died birthin' me. He was lonely." She paused, and nervously bit her lip. "I reckon everything happens for a reason. Least that's what Mrs. Moss says. I see it this way. If Pa hadn't a given me to William, then I never would a left Plum Point. I wouldn't have Billy, and ..." She stopped and swallowed hard. "I never would a met you."

Their eyes locked.

"Cora," he said, breathlessly.

"Uh-huh?" She licked her lips, and waited.

The umbrella slanted sideways as he bent down and kissed her. Cool droplets of rain fell on their faces.

She closed her eyes and savored every precious second. His lips were warm and full, drawing her into a place she never wanted to leave.

When he pulled back, she stared at him, breathing heavily. "Where'd that come from?"

"I'm sorry." He lifted the umbrella into place over their heads.

"No, don't be sorry. It's just that ... I ain't never been kissed before."

His brow wrinkled. "Never? But ... how?"

"William never kissed me. Least ... not like that. He'd kiss my forehead or my cheek, but never my lips. I may a been his wife, but he didn't marry me cuz he loved me. He just wanted a son."

He lifted his free hand and pushed aside a strand of wet hair from her face. "You deserve so much more."

"I don't reckon I deserve much a anything. But I gotta tell you ..." A heavy sigh left her body. "Sumthin' happened to me the first time I saw you. I don't understand it. And the way you just kissed me ... I reckon the same thing happened to you." She stared into his eyes. "That is, unless you always kiss women when you take 'em to a cemetery."

He chuckled. "No, Cora. Only you."

"Then ... do you mind so much doin' it again?"

He didn't waste any time. This time, he kept the umbrella firmly overhead, covering them as they locked together in a deeper, more passionate kiss.

She'd have given anything at that moment to be in a closed room. She moved her hands around his body and pulled him even closer to her. His body was firm, and his chest rose and fell rapidly as the rate of his heartbeat increased. Her own heart thumped just as hard. Could he feel it? Overwhelmed with new feelings, a strange sensation swept over her; a desire to couple.

"Dang ..." she panted.

"I agree." He took a step back, but kept the umbrella over her. Then he nodded toward the grave. "This is inappropriate. Being that you came here to pay your last respects, my actions were out of line. Mrs. Moss believes me to be an English gentleman. She would be disappointed in me."

"Douglas?" She took a step closer to him. "I asked you to do it." Turning her head, she looked at the gravestone. "William ain't comin' back."

"No, he's not. But-"

"All you gotta tell me is that you wanna keep seein' me. I just gotta know that you're not simply tryin' to take advantage of a grievin' widow."

He took her hand in his, then raised it to his face. Closing his eyes, he said, "I haven't stopped thinking about you since the first day I met you. I don't understand all this—but—God forgive me, I'm grateful he's not coming back."

Her heart jumped. "Why me? I ain't nothin' special."

"You're wrong, Cora," he said, touching her cheek.

"I reckon Mrs. Moss ain't the only blind person I know."

He shook his head, then pulled her close once again. "I'm not blind." He bent down for another kiss.

She liked kissing him. Truth be told, she *loved* kissing him. But then, as the rain pelted harder and harder, and the thunder grew louder, she knew that it wasn't wise to stay.

Her hand shook as she placed it flat against his chest. "I'd best say *goodbye* to William and get back home to Billy."

He nodded and held the umbrella for her as she bent over the grave.

"I did like you told me, William. I'm takin' care a Billy and Mrs. Moss is helpin' me." She turned her head and looked up at Douglas, then looked back at the grave. "Mr. Denton is helpin', too. He brought me to you."

The realization that her dead husband was buried deep beneath her feet sank in. She slowly stood and wavered enough that Douglas placed his arm around her waist.

She stared at the muddy ground. "I'm sorry, William," she whispered. "I know I didn't love you like I should a, but dang ... we didn't have a real marriage. Maybe now you're with your wife and your other baby. I hope so."

She took a step forward and placed her hand on the wet stone. Then she traced her fingers around his name. "Goodbye, William."

Douglas stood behind her, remaining silent.

"I don't got nothin' else to tell him," she said with a sigh. "One day, when Billy's old enough to understand, I'll bring him here."

"I'll take you home." He extended his arm. "The storm is getting worse."

Taking his arm, she lowered her head. "Was I wrong to kiss you? Right in front a William's grave?"

"If you were wrong, then so was I."

She could feel his eyes on her and lifted her head. "I know I'll never forget this."

"Neither will I." He walked with her to the buggy.

Sitting beside him once again, she wanted to nestle her body into his. She didn't understand what was happening to her, but the one thing she was certain of was that she wanted to be near him. In every way possible.

He cleared his throat and glanced in her direction. "I'm curious ..."

"'Bout what?"

"What became of your father? You haven't mentioned him, other than telling me how he gambled you away. I can't imagine that you have a good relationship with him. Believe me, I understand what it's like to have no respect for your father." He stopped. "Or, *Pa*, as you call him." He smiled at her.

It was easy to talk to him, even about difficult things. "Pa died," she said, sitting fully upright. "It happened while I was on the boat. I didn't know 'til I went home. Mrs. Moss told me."

His face fell. "I'm so sorry, Cora. I shouldn't have been so unfeeling."

"You sure do a lot a apologizin'!" Trying to ease his discomfort, she lowered her voice. "Pay it no mind. Pa drank himself to death." Gently, she rested her hand on his leg. "You're a good man, Douglas."

He covered her hand with his and gave it a gentle squeeze. His simple gesture made her heart flutter.

She didn't wait for him to help her from the buggy when they reached the boarding house. Her breasts were telling her that it was time for Billy to nurse. Of course, even though she was outspoken, she knew it would be impolite to relate that detail.

The rain pelted on her head, causing her to laugh. "Should a waited for the umbrella!" She held her hand palm up, catching the drops. "Mrs. Moss is gonna fuss!"

He was by her side within moments, covering her with the umbrella. "Why didn't you wait?"

"I need to see Billy. Can you come in for a spell?"

He stared at her damp face, then lifted a handkerchief from his pocket and blotted the water from her face. "I promise you, it's clean."

"Mrs. Moss always tells me the same thing," she said with a laugh.

"Cora," he whispered her name. "I have some things I need to do, but I'll be back for supper. I'm looking forward to Rosie's pork roast."

"All right, Douglas." She turned from him, but hesitated, not wanting to tell him goodbye. "Douglas?" Her breath caught as she turned to face him once again.

"Yes, Cora?"

Her heart pounded in her chest. He looked directly into her eyes as he stepped closer to her. What was it about him that was so different from every other man she knew?

"I'll see you t'night," she said, unable to move her eyes from his.

He leaned closer to her, but then stopped and stood upright. His lips curved into a bright smile, then he nodded, bowed slightly, and returned to the buggy. As he hopped up into the seat, he looked at her one more time before snapping the reins.

She let out a long breath and walked through the door.

Chapter 20

"Yes, I kissed her," Douglas said, pacing Harper's floor. "More than once."

Harper sat perched in his usual spot. Without looking up, he chuckled. "Knew you liked her."

Stopping in the middle of the floor, Douglas placed his hands over his face. "I shouldn't have kissed her." He shook his head and again paced.

"She slap ya?"

"Of course not." He stood firm and pulled his shoulders back. "Truthfully, she *asked* me to kiss her the second time."

"Then what's the trouble?"

"I ... well ... she's a widow."

"Yep." Harper once again began to chuckle. "Her husband won't mind."

"Why do you find this so amusing? I'm trying to do what's right by her. She just found out that her husband is dead and I kissed her in front of his grave! And ... I wanted to kiss her again when I took her home. What's wrong with me?"

"Nothin'. You're a man. You like the woman. Nothin' wrong in that."

His uncle made everything seem so simple. Was it so unusual to want a woman who had already shared her life with another man? But, as Cora reminded him, William would not be coming back.

Uncle Harper cleared his throat. "You all right?"

He wasn't sure how long he'd been staring blankly at his uncle. "Yes ... I'm fine."

"Don't look fine."

"I believe ..." *Oh, God ... it's all making sense ...* "I believe ..." His voice fell to a whisper. "I'm falling in love with her."

Harper smacked him hard on the back. "Knew it all along."

Having an uncle who rarely spoke made anything he said worth listening to. However, he found it hard to believe that his feelings for Cora had been so transparent. "How could you know it, when I just came to realize it myself?"

"I'm an old man. Seen a lot in my life. Know love when I see it."

He tipped his head and looked directly into his uncle's eyes. "Have *you* ever been in love?"

Harper froze. "Got work to do," he said and walked briskly to his stool.

Douglas followed directly behind him. "I'm not letting you get away from me that easily. Tell me."

Reaching out to a small angel figurine, Harper took his knife and began carving. His breathing became labored.

"Uncle Harper?" He placed a gentle hand on the man's shoulder.

Slowly, Harper raised his eyes to meet his. "If you love her, do sumthin' about it."

The pain in Harper's eyes told him that he need not ask anything further. He patted his shoulder and nodded, sharing an unspoken understanding. "I will. Thank you, Uncle Harper."

Harper forced a smile and continued his work.

Douglas stood watching him, unable to walk away.

After several minutes of silence between them, Harper stopped working. "What you waitin' for?"

"I ..."

"I'm fine. Go." Harper nodded toward the entrance. His demeanor proved he *wasn't* fine, but his respect for his uncle led him out the door.

* * *

"How's supper comin'?" Cora asked Rosie, who was bent over checking the pork roast in the oven.

"Still cookin'," Rosie replied, then stood upright and called out for Toby.

He was there almost instantly. His face was smudged with dirt. "Yes, Mama?"

Rosie cocked her head. "You been messin' with them horses again, ain't ya?"

Toby kicked at the floor. "I like 'em."

"Don't like 'em when it's rainin'! Go wash!" Rosie shooed him out the door. "Cora, girl ... you just wait 'til Billy gets old nuff to get dirty."

She laughed. "He'll be just like his ma!"

Mrs. Moss entered the room. "Rosie, no one knows mud like Cora. I assure you."

After tending Billy this morning, Mrs. Moss had laid down for a nap and slept most of the afternoon, so Cora was glad to see her up and about. Anxious to talk to her, she took her by the arm. "Don't tell all my secrets, Mrs. Moss. Let's leave Rosie to cook. I need to talk to you."

"Yes, please take her outta my kitchen, Mrs. Moss," Rosie said with a chuckle. "She been poppin' in an out all afternoon. Like I don't know how to cook!"

Rosie's laughter followed them down the hallway, as they moved to the sitting room and sat on the sofa. A light rain pattered against the roof. Any other rainy day might have made her glum. However, her heart had never been lighter. All she could think about was the memory of Douglas's eyes and the feel of his kiss.

It didn't take long for Muffin to leap into Mrs. Moss's lap.

"That cat loves you," Cora said, reaching out and stroking her fur. A loud, grateful purr filled her ears.

"Cats are loyal. They also appreciate a warm lap." Mrs. Moss raised her eyebrows. "Cora, I doubt very much it was Muffin you wished to speak to me about."

Cora stopped petting the cat and immediately began twisting her fingers together. "Dang ..." The word left her mouth in a puff of air and she wished she hadn't said it.

Before she could be reprimanded, she apologized. "I know ... you don't hafta tell me."

"I know what's bothering you, my dear." Mrs. Moss reached out and found her hand, forcing her to stop fidgeting.

"You do?" Her heart thumped.

"Yes, I do. You said very little when you returned from the cemetery. And ... what I sensed in your voice was not grief, but joy."

Cora's shame at that moment was overwhelming. Mrs. Moss saw her better with her heart than with her sightless eyes.

Mrs. Moss pressed on. "Is it Mr. Denton you wish to speak to me about?"

How'd she know?

"Your silence tells me everything, Cora."

"Mrs. Moss ..." *Please don't scold me ...* "Douglas kissed me." She said the words quickly, hoping the scolding she was about to receive wouldn't be too harsh.

"I see ..."

"Three times."

Mrs. Moss was silent.

Not knowing what else to do, she began to fidget once again, and when Mrs. Moss still said nothing, she blurted out. "Don't think bad a Douglas. I asked him to do it the second time."

Mrs. Moss drew back. "Cora! Do you want him to believe you're a harlot?"

"A what?"

"A woman who throws herself at men. One who willingly kisses a man who is not her husband."

Like Francine? No, she was nothing like Francine. "I ain't no harlot, Mrs. Moss. Fact is ... I reckon I love him." For a moment she paused, wondering if she would be scolded again. "Please don't be mad at me, Mrs. Moss."

"I'm not *mad*, Cora. But, I don't want to see you hurt."

"I reckon he feels the same way 'bout me. I feel it in here." Taking Mrs. Moss's hand, she placed it against her breast. "My heart tells me he does."

Mrs. Moss sighed. "I hope you're right, my dear. But promise me that you'll slow down. Give things time. If necessary, *I'll* talk to Mr. Denton."

"No ... no ... Please don't." The thought of her discussing something so private with him made her terribly nervous. "It'll be fine. I won't kiss him again, less he marries me. All right?"

"Don't make a promise you can't keep." Mrs. Moss smiled at her, then turned her attention to Muffin, scratching her under her chin.

"All right. How 'bout ... I'll do my best."

Mrs. Moss nodded. "That's all I ask."

Cora started to stand, but then plopped back down again with a thump.

"More on your mind, dear?" Mrs. Moss asked quietly.

"Yep." There was so much on her mind that she thought it might burst. "I'm worried 'bout Douglas."

"Worried? Why?"

She lowered her head, wishing that her life wasn't so complicated. "Well ... now that he knows I'm here, then it's likely other folks will figger out who I am ... and who I was married to. What if Giles finds out and comes lookin' for me?"

Mrs. Moss wrapped an arm around her shoulder and gave her a gentle squeeze. "Mr. Giles would be foolish to come looking for you. You've done nothing wrong and the law will protect you. I believe Mr. Denton will also look after you. That is ... if he feels about you as you believe he does."

"I don't want him hurt, Mrs. Moss." A pool of tears filled her eyes. "He's been awful nice to me ... an Billy, too."

Leaning toward her, Mrs. Moss placed her hand against her cheek. A single tear trickled down and dampened the old woman's hand. "I believe you truly do love him, Cora."

She nodded into her palm. "I do."

"Then follow your heart and pray that God will see to Mr. Giles."

"Giles scares me, Mrs. Moss."

"No man is bigger than God. Now ... go wash your face and get ready for supper. You don't want Mr. Denton seeing your tears."

She slowly stood. "He already has."

* * *

"Rosie," Douglas said, leaning back in his chair, "that was the best meal I've had in a very long time."

Rosie chuckled and shook her head. "You're good at payin' a compliment. But I knows Ada is a fine cook. You ain't goin' hungry."

"No, I'm not going hungry, but no one cooks like you do. You have a gift." He looked across the table to Cora, meeting her gaze. This had been going on throughout the meal. He was unable to take his eyes from her and wanted to hold her again.

They sat in the common dining room around a long wooden table, which could accommodate up to ten people. It was simpler than what he was used to, but he preferred it. He was relaxed and knew that if he happened to belch, he wouldn't be admonished.

Toby reached to the center of the table and grabbed the corn pudding. The bowl was nearly empty.

"Now, Toby," Rosie said, "Mista Denton might want that. You knows better than to hep yourself."

Toby sheepishly lowered his head, and withdrew his hand. "Sorry, Mama."

"I'm as full as can be," Douglas said, lifting the bowl toward Toby. "He's welcome to it."

"Thank ya, Mista Denton!" Toby chimed, and spooned the small amount onto his plate.

Daisy clasped her hands together, tilting her head. "This is what I've always wanted. A table full of boarders with full bellies."

"Mista Denton ain't a boarder," Toby said through a mouthful of corn pudding.

Douglas grinned when Rosie shook her finger at Toby, scolding him for speaking with a full mouth. This meal had been more than just good food. The people he shared it with were more enjoyable than his family had ever been.

"I know that Mister Denton is not a boarder," Daisy continued, "but I believe we'll be seeing more of him." She winked at him, then smiled at Cora.

Cora shyly lowered her eyes. She'd been very quiet throughout the meal and he hoped he would have time to speak with her alone.

"Cuz a Mama's cookin'?" Toby asked.

Rosie released a hearty laugh. "That's right, Toby. Cuz a your mama's cookin'."

A loud cry erupted from the other room and Cora jumped to her feet. "'Scuse me. I gotta get Billy."

Douglas stood and watched her walk away.

"She won't be long, Mr. Denton," Mrs. Moss said. "Why don't we go to the sitting room and wait for her?"

"I'd like that," he replied, then helped her to her feet.

"Thank you again, Rosie ... Miss Daisy ..." he said as he walked away. "It was wonderful."

As he helped Mrs. Moss take a seat, she thanked him, then motioned for him to sit. Trying to get comfortable, he readjusted himself more than once in a large chair and attempted to understand what was making him ill at ease.

Mrs. Moss chuckled. "You fidget as much as Cora."

"Forgive me ..."

"Why are you uncomfortable, Mr. Denton? You certainly don't feel threatened by an old blind woman."

He was beginning to understand why Cora was so fond of Mrs. Moss. Her gentle manner was endearing, but he believed that she was about to interview him.

"Again, I apologize," he said. "I don't find you threatening, however ... I ..." What would he say to her? Not wanting to lie, he was at a loss for words.

"Yes, Mr. Denton?"

He let out a long breath. "I admit ... I'm nervous."

"Oh, my." She laughed and raised her hands to her face. "Now I will ask for *your* forgiveness. I didn't intend to make you nervous. However, I care for Cora and I would like to know your intentions."

"I ..." His stomach knotted.

"Mrs. Moss!" Cora scolded, entering the room with Billy in her arms. "What are you doin'?"

He released a relieved sigh and stood acknowledging Cora.

"I'm speaking with Mr. Denton," Mrs. Moss replied, sitting fully upright.

"I can see that," Cora said. She leaned in toward Mrs. Moss and lowered her voice. "I thought I asked you not to talk to him."

"Ever?" Mrs. Moss pursed her lips.

"You know what I mean."

Mrs. Moss smoothed her dress, then pulled her shoulders back. "Yes, dear."

Enjoying the interchange, the knot in his core began to untie itself. "It's all right, Cora. She was being hospitable. I don't mind."

"Well," Cora replied, "*I* do. I ain't ready for her to pick you apart. She may seem harmless, but I know she has a way of gettin' things outta you."

"I have nothing to hide." He crossed to her and took her hand. When she lifted her eyes to meet his, they sparkled.

"Well ..." Cora swallowed hard, leaving her eyes locked on his. "Even so ... there may be some things you don't wanna tell her just yet."

"Excuse me," Mrs. Moss said. "Would you like me to tend Billy so that you and Mr. Denton can have some time together? Perhaps a short walk?"

"Huh?" Cora asked dreamily, blinking slowly at him. "Oh ... yes, Mrs. Moss ... I'd like that. Is that all right with you, Douglas?"

He nodded without speaking. But then, so as not to be rude, he said, "I'd like that very much. Thank you, Mrs. Moss."

After placing Billy into the arms of Mrs. Moss, Cora led Douglas toward the front door. Toby came around the corner and grinned at them, but then was called back into the kitchen by his mother.

It was a pleasant evening. The rain had stopped and there was a clean fresh scent in the air. The sun was about to set and filled the sky with wisps of red, purple, and orange. But the most beautiful sight of all was the woman next to him in the simple green cotton dress.

As they walked down the street, he wanted to take her hand, but decided to wait to make certain it was something she wanted him to do. Her hands were folded in front of her rather than at her side, which he took as an indication that she was keeping her distance.

After walking silently for a while, she let out a sigh.

"Are you all right?" he asked.

"Yep."

Placing a hand on her shoulder, he stopped her. "Cora, you've been so quiet all evening." He couldn't help himself and released a small chuckle. "It's very unlike you."

She giggled. "I reckon you know me perty well. I *do* like to talk."

"Then why have you been so quiet?"

She turned away and wouldn't look at him. "I'm kind a scared."

Gently, he took her chin in his hand, turning her head. "Of me?"

"No. You don't scare me at all."

"Then I have to assume it's that man ... *Giles*, isn't that right?"

Her face fell. "Yes."

Without even considering the fact that they were in public, he pulled her into his arms and held her close. "I won't let him hurt you, Cora."

The tension melted away from her body as she conformed to his. She rested her head against his chest and just stood there, saying nothing.

A man and woman approached, and as they passed by, gave them a scornful look. He was grateful that Cora hadn't noticed.

"Let's return to the boarding house," he said.

She lifted her head, then pulled away from him. As if she knew what he'd been previously thinking, she left her arm at her side and her hand close to his. He took it and squeezed it tenderly. His gesture said more to her than any words he could have spoken.

By the time they reached the house, it was time for him to leave. "I'd like to see you again soon," he said, thinking about the advice Uncle Harper gave him.

"I'd like that. Forgive me for being so ... *unlike* myself. I'll do better next time."

"You've had a difficult day. Considering all you've had to deal with, I think you've done remarkably." Lifting her hand to his lips, he kissed it, then held it for a moment longer. "Would it be all right with you if I come by on Saturday?"

"I'll be waitin'." She gave him her biggest smile of the day.

He opened the door for her, then followed her inside. Mrs. Moss was sitting where they'd left her, gently rocking Billy in her arms. Drawn to the little boy, he walked across the sitting room and offered to take him from her.

"If it's all right with you, Cora," he added, and she nodded her approval.

Such a small bundle to hold in his arms. Billy cuddled into his body, just as his mother had only minutes before. It was natural holding him and he was drawn to kiss his tiny face. "You're a very lucky little boy," he said, looking into those baby green eyes. "You have a wonderful mother."

Billy's tongue thrust out of his mouth and he craned his neck toward Douglas's chest. He held in a laugh and looked at Cora. "I think he wants something I can't give him."

Cora's face flushed. "Reckon you're right. I'll take him."

"I should be going," he said, placing Billy into her arms. "But I'll see you on Saturday."

Mrs. Moss cleared her throat.

"I'll see you as well, Mrs. Moss," he said. "And, thank you again for tending Billy."

"Of course," she replied. "Billy is *no trouble* at all. A *very good* baby."

"Yes, he is," Cora agreed, and with Billy in her arms, she led Douglas to the front door.

Placing a warm hand on Billy's head, he leaned forward and kissed Cora on the cheek. "Saturday," he whispered, then bowed slightly and turned to leave.

"Saturday," she rasped, and her eyes sparkled.

He continued on to the livery wearing a grin that wouldn't go away.

Chapter 21

"Douglas," Mary said, with a bright face. "I believe you're smitten."

He couldn't hide the truth from his mother. Even though he had spent very little time with Cora, there was no doubt how he felt about her. "Yes, I believe I am."

Pouring their afternoon tea, he set a cup in front of her. She took a sip, then sat back in her chair and smiled. "I'm happy for you. When do I get to meet her?"

"Oh ..." he hesitated. Not wanting to rush Cora, he wasn't certain if bringing her to meet his mother was a good thing to do.

Mary patted his hand. "It's fine, dear. Bring her when you're ready. Perhaps to Cameron's engagement party?"

"Perhaps. Though I'm not sure I want her to meet him."

"Douglas, I believe that even Cameron can be well behaved at his own engagement party. Give it some thought."

"She and I aren't officially courting ... yet." He stared at his teacup. "I don't know how long I should wait, since she's recently widowed."

"You'll know when it's time." His mother gave him a warm smile.

She appeared to be more relaxed than he'd seen her in quite a while. He loved to see her smile. Since she seemed open to conversation, he decided this might be a good time. "Mother, I told Uncle Harper about my feelings for Cora."

"You did?"

"Yes. Truthfully, he guessed at my feelings. It seems I'm quite transparent."

Softly, she chuckled.

Hearing her laugh warmed him even more. "He made me believe that he'd been in love. Do you know anything about that, or why he never married?"

The warmth on her face melted into sorrow as the corners of her mouth softened. "Yes, I know."

"I'm sorry. I've obviously brought up a bad memory. All these years and I simply accepted the fact that Harper never married. But now ... I'd like to know *why?*"

"It's all right, Douglas. I don't mind telling you. You're old enough now to understand." She paused for a moment, took another sip of tea, then a very large breath. "It was more than thirty years ago ... before I met your father." She stopped and smiled.

He relaxed, knowing that not all of her memories were painful.

"Her name was Iris and she was quite lovely. Harper fell for her almost instantly, but because we came from a poor family, he thought she would never consider him as a suitor."

"Money shouldn't matter." He shook his head and cradled his cup.

"But it did. And you'll find it still does to many people."

He knew exactly whom she was speaking of.

"So Harper kept his distance," she went on, "and even though Iris showed every indication that she was open to his affections, he wouldn't ask to court her. Iris had her heart set on marriage and when Harper pulled away from her, her eyes turned to another man."

"You believe she loved Uncle Harper?"

"Oh, yes." Again, she breathed deeply. "He told me that she kissed him one day, while they were talking together at the river front. But he didn't return her kiss ... Something he's always regretted."

"What happened to her?" He leaned in, intrigued by the story.

"She gave her heart to a traveler. A man who came to Memphis peddling his wares. When he left, she went with him." She blinked slowly, fighting back tears.

"And Harper never loved again ..." he sighed, and sat back in his chair.

"No. He's never stopped loving Iris. Why do you think he stays in his home by the water?"

"Hoping she might return?"

She nodded. "That, and it reminds him of her kiss. He began carving the wooden chain a short time after she left. You see ... her *peddler* was a wood carver. Harper was determined to become whatever it was she saw in him. To be even better than he was."

Now he understood the advice his uncle had given him in regard to Cora. Never again would he see him with the same eyes or his carvings as simple sculpture. It was much more than that. Every piece held his heart.

"Thank you for telling me, Mother," he said, kissing her on the cheek. "I won't let on to Harper that I know. I don't want to cause him any more pain than he already suffers."

"He loves you, Douglas. You're the son he never had."

"He's been good to me. I intend to take his advice. And, if Cora is agreeable and things progress as I hope, it would mean bringing a child into our family as well. Could you love him?"

She cradled his cheek with her hand. "If you love him, then I'll love him."

He hoped it would be that easy. One thing was certain, if he was to raise a child not of his own blood, he would vow to be much better at it than his own step-father.

* * *

"Over here," Douglas said, guiding Cora along the rocky shoreline. He pointed across the water to the far bank.

"You're right." Cora cupped her hand over her brow. "It's beautiful."

He'd taken her to his favorite spot on the river. From their viewpoint, they were able to see a wide expanse of the water and a cluster of trees on the opposite side.

"One day, I'd like to build a house over there," he said.

"Right in the middle of the trees."

"But then you'd hafta take a ferry to get over here to the city."

He chuckled. "That's part of my dream. To be far away from everyone else. I wouldn't be troubled with dinner parties or business affairs. I could live simply, right on the water."

Bending down, she picked up a flat stone, drew her arm back, then pitched it across the water. It skipped three times before falling below the surface.

"I'm impressed," he said, picking up a stone. He made an attempt to duplicate her skill, but after one skip the stone fell.

She pulled her shoulders back and grinned. "I've had lots a practice. I grew up in a place that sounds like the kind a home you've dreamed of. Guess it was kind a nice livin' a simple life. But bein' fond of a good meal, I prefer to have the means to eat. It can't be all bad livin' where you live."

"No, it isn't *all* bad. I believe what makes it slightly miserable is the people I share it with. I love my mother, but-"

"That step-brother you mentioned, right?" She picked up another stone and had even more success; this time skipping it four times.

"Cameron. Yes."

She wrinkled her nose and stared upward. "Cameron? I remember someone named Cameron. I heard Francine talkin' to a Cameron on the boat. They was bein' ... well ... *very* familiar with each other."

"Sounds like my brother. And he *was* on the boat. The

night your husband invited me and Doctor Mitchell to dinner. After I returned home and told him about the *Bonny Lass*, he couldn't stay away. From what he told me, he found Francine very much to his liking."

They crossed to a large flat rock, which they sat upon simultaneously.

"Most men like Francine." She stared downward and twisted her fingers together. "I know *she* liked *you*."

He took her hand, then pulled it to his lips and kissed it. "I had no interest in Francine."

"I'm glad." Her words came out in a breathless rasp and her hand trembled in his. Oh, how he wanted to kiss her ...

A rumble of thunder filled the air. Dark rain clouds gathered in the distance.

"It seems we attract rain," he said, lifting her to her feet. "I had better get you home before it falls."

"I wish we didn't hafta go back. I like bein' here with you."

"Cora." He took a deep breath. "I truly am sorry if I took advantage of you at the cemetery. I was out of line and I'll make an effort to restrain myself."

She licked her lips and swallowed hard. "What if I don't want you to?"

"I doubt Mrs. Moss would approve." He grinned, but was quite serious.

"I'm a grown woman, Douglas. I love Mrs. Moss, but it's time I make up my own mind 'bout things. I was forced to marry William. Didn't have a choice. But now, *I'm* makin' the choices. I want you in my life."

Rain pelted down from the sky. Cora let out a burst of

laughter and raised her hands upward. He grabbed her hand and they ran down the shore to his waiting buggy. Even though it was covered, the rain had already dampened their clothing and hair. They laughed as the horse pulled them along the road to the boarding house.

"I forgot the umbrella," he said as he helped her step down.

"Too late to do any good," she laughed. "Mrs. Moss is gonna fuss!"

* * *

Cora was so happy that she giggled all the way to the front door. Douglas followed directly behind her and moved to open it. A loud gasp coming from behind them drew their attention.

"Douglas?"

Cora froze. Douglas reached down and took her hand in his.

"Elise," he said, then cleared his throat. "What are you doing here?"

The woman's mouth hung wide open and Cora realized that her own was as well. She quickly closed it, but couldn't move another muscle. Douglas squeezed her hand, bringing her out of the trance. She'd seen her reflection in a mirror, but this was no mirror, and yet she was looking at her own image. She finally managed to turn her head enough to look at Douglas. "Douglas ... I ..." She couldn't finish her sentence.

He put his arm around her, steadying her.

"Douglas Denton," the woman said. "Who is *she*?"

"Elise," he said, moving Cora a step closer to the other

woman. "This is the woman I told you about. Her name is Cora."

She couldn't take her eyes off of Elise. The closer she got to her, the more nervous she became. "She the *Peck* woman you told me 'bout?"

"*Peck* woman?" Elise mumbled. "Is that how you referred to me, Douglas?"

"No," he replied. "Not exactly."

Elise crossed her arms over her chest. Her wet hair was matted against her head and her clothes were soaked through. "This isn't right. How could she look like me?"

Cora pitied her. "Let's go inside. I can get you sumthin' dry to wear. You don't wanna get sick."

Elise wrinkled her nose and looked at her from head to foot, dissecting every part of her.

"It doesn't seem we have the same taste in clothing," Elise huffed. "But something dry is much better than something wet."

Cora managed to smile. "C'mon then. 'Sides, I gotta feed Billy." Without thinking, she cupped her breast with her hand, and winced.

Elise's eyes widened. "Have you no modesty?"

"Huh?" Cora looked at Douglas, who seemed to be uncomfortable by the entire situation.

"Let's go in," he said, and motioned to the door.

Cora held tightly to his arm as they proceeded to the house. She turned her head and looked behind them. Elise trailed, looking a bit put out. Cora's stomach twisted. Though completely drenched, she could still tell that this woman was her twin.

But that was impossible.

Chapter 22

"Mama!" Toby yelled. "Mista Denton an Ms. Smith is home!"

As Elise stepped through the door behind Cora and Douglas, Toby's mouth dropped. "Mama!"

Rosie entered the room and shook her head. "Now that I sees 'em together, they's no doubt. First time I saw Ms. Smith I thought she look like her." She nodded toward Elise. "Course, Miss Peck never gived me the time a day, so I didn't get a chance to look at her close."

Elise lifted her nose into the air. "You're a slave. I'm not supposed to give you the time of day."

Rosie's eyebrows furrowed and she frowned at Elise. Then she turned her attention to Douglas. "She comin' to supper, too?"

He shook his head. "No—but—Rosie, could you please get her a towel?"

"Course I could." She looked over her shoulder. "Toby, get Miss Peck a towel."

Toby hadn't stopped staring at the two women. "Yes'm," he said, and left the room.

"Why did you call her '*Smith*?'" Elise asked, and glared at Cora.

Cora looked wide-eyed at Douglas.

He cleared his throat. "Elise, let's get you dry, then we'll talk."

"But ... her name is *O'Brien*. You told me that her husband was the pilot of the *Bonny Lass* ..." Her voice trailed off, then her eyes opened wide. "The pilot that was hung!"

Rosie stared at Cora. "Your husband was that man?"

Cora stammered. "Well ... I ... I need to check on Billy." She rushed out of the room.

Douglas stood there shaking his head. He'd never imagined that he could be in such a predicament. Elise needed to know the truth in order to protect Cora. But would Elise be cooperative?

First, he wanted to ease Rosie's concerns. He placed his hand on her arm. "I'll explain more later. I promise."

"You better! Ms. Daisy ain't gonna like this none." Rosie frowned and returned to the kitchen.

Toby came back with a towel in his hand and gave it to Douglas. "She shore do look like Ms. Smith."

Elise yanked the towel out of his hand and wiped her face. "Smith!" Moving the towel over her arms, she snapped at Douglas. "You had better explain this to me. First of all, I'd like to know why you were holding her hand."

He needed to remain calm. "Elise, I—I care for her."

Toby grinned, watching the two of them, but stopped when Elise glared at him. "Mama needs my hep." He skedaddled out of the room and left them alone.

Tapping her foot soundly on the floor, Elise crossed her arms over her chest. "But what about me?"

"You're my friend, Elise. And I hope you always will be. But I've made it clear to you that my feelings for you go no deeper."

Elise turned her back on him. "How can you care for her? She's ... simple ... and uneducated." She whipped around to face him. "I know! It's because she looks like me. You said so the first time you told me about her. I thought you were making her up, but now I know you were telling me the truth." She beamed. "I understand now. You care for her because she was my replacement when you thought I loved Cameron."

"No, Elise. She's not a replacement. I care for her because ..." He paused, pondering how much he should tell her.

"See!" she chirped. "You don't know why."

They turned to the sound of Mrs. Moss's walking stick.

"Mr. Denton?" Mrs. Moss asked, tilting her head sideways.

"Yes, ma'am?" He took her arm and led her to a chair.

"Who is that with you?"

Elise remained silent.

"Her name is Elise Peck," he said.

"She's very loud," Mrs. Moss said, taking a seat. "She disturbed Billy."

Elise placed her hands on her hips. "Who is Billy?"

"He's my baby," Cora said, entering the room with Billy cradled in her arms.

Mrs. Moss smiled. "And he's a dear."

"Oh, yes," Elise said with a sigh. "I forgot you gave birth. My dear Douglas brought the doctor." She crossed to him and placed her hand on his arm, all the while looking at Cora.

He promptly removed her hand and went to Cora. "May I hold him?"

Cora looked up into his eyes. "Course you can." She passed Billy into his arms. "I'll get Elise a dry dress." She started walking out, but turned to look at him and Billy one last time before leaving the room.

He held Billy close. He was wide awake and looking directly at him. His head bobbled, so he firmly cupped it in his large hands. "Don't worry, Billy, your mother will be back soon."

Billy wrinkled his nose and wiggled his body as if he understood.

"You're full of surprises, Douglas," Elise said. "Now tell me, why isn't she using her *husband's* name?"

"Because," Cora said, walking into the room with a red and white dress draped over her arm, "there's folks that wanna hurt me an Billy. I don't want them to know I'm here." She extended the dress toward Elise.

Elise reluctantly took the garment. "Who would want to hurt you? Or your baby?" She cast her eyes toward Douglas, then rolled them upward. "Douglas, what's gotten into you?"

"Nothing. I'm enjoying Billy. He's a good boy." He was talking baby talk to Billy and bounced him in his arms.

She rolled her eyes again. "Where can I change?" she asked Cora.

"My room. C'mon." She waved her arm and motioned for Elise to follow her.

As the two women exited, Douglas marveled at the fact that they were exactly the same height. There was even a similarity in the way they walked.

Uncanny ...

"What can you tell me about that woman?" Mrs. Moss asked.

"I wish you could see her." He took a seat beside Mrs. Moss, but continued swaying with Billy. "She looks exactly like Cora. And I mean *exactly*. They look like twins."

"How much do you know about her?"

"I've known her as long as I can remember. Our mothers have been friends since before Elise was born."

"Tell me what you know about her mother." Mrs. Moss spoke with an urgency he'd not heard from her before.

"Well ... she's middle-aged. My mother's age. She's a midwife. I think she's brought more babies into this world than any doctor."

"What's her name?"

"It's Lena. Lena Peck. I don't know her maiden name, but if it's important, I can ask my mother."

Mrs. Moss's face went ashen.

"Are you all right?" he asked, reaching out to her.

"Please, bring me a glass of water." Her hand trembled as she patted his arm.

He stood and placed Billy over his shoulder. Quickly, he returned with the water and placed it in her hand, before sitting down beside her.

She sipped slowly. "I always believed something wasn't quite right."

"What do you mean?"

"I knew Cora's mother. She was small-framed like Cora and when she was heavy with child, she was larger than any expectant mother I'd ever seen."

He listened intently, while Billy was lulled to sleep.

Mrs. Moss sighed. "I told her that I thought she was having twins, considering her size, but she laughed at me. Then she begged me not to tell Clyde. He'd been worrying over the idea of one more mouth to feed. She feared that adding even another would push him to the bottle."

"What does Lena Peck have to do with this?"

"Lena is not a common name. It was the name of her midwife. I never saw the woman, but she told me about her. Angela was afraid of giving birth and she told me that when Lena offered to deliver the baby, her heart eased."

"Cora's mother's name was Angela?"

"Yes. And Clyde began carving angels after she died." She sighed. "He was an accomplished wood carver, but a horrible father."

He looked at the sleeping baby in his arms. "How could any man treat a child poorly?"

"Oh, he wasn't so bad when he was sober. Had Angela lived, Cora would have had a much better upbringing."

His head reeled. "Mrs. Moss, do you believe that Lena Peck *took* Elise from Mr. Craighead?"

She craned her head, then lowered her voice. "It's the only logical conclusion. If Elise looks like Cora and Mrs. Peck is the same woman who tended Angela, then yes, I believe she kept her."

"Kept her?"

"When Angela died, Lena offered to nurse the baby until she was weaned. Of course, we had no knowledge that there were actually *two* babies."

He scratched his head, trying to make sense of everything she was saying. "But how could she nurse them? She'd have to have had a baby herself."

"Yes. Clyde told me that it was a miracle when she came to them. He told me that her child had died and when she met Angela at the market, she told her that she wanted to help her so that Angela wouldn't have to experience the same grief."

Mrs. Moss reached out and placed her hand on Billy's sleeping form. "Losing a child is the most horrible thing any woman can endure." Her face was so filled with sorrow that he was certain she would cry.

He was about to say something, when she continued. "I think Lena sought out a woman whose child she could take. She then raised her as her own. And since there were twins, Clyde was none the wiser. She was very clever."

"But how did he not know there were two?"

"Whiskey," she replied, spitting out the word.

"So he was drunk when she gave birth?"

Mrs. Moss nodded and closed her eyes. "And when he realized that she'd died, he stayed on the bottle for

months. I didn't see Cora until she was weaned. Then ..."
Her face lit up with a smile. "She became *my* girl."

"She was the lucky one. To have you for a mother." He
meant every word. No one could have loved a child
more.

"I *do* love her." She felt her way up his arm, until she
reached his face. "Douglas, please don't hurt her. I believe
you've seen that she has a gentle heart. I couldn't bear to
see it broken."

He cradled her hand against his face. "I won't hurt her.
I ..."

"Love her, too?" Her vacant eyes looked through him.

He nodded and the movement of his head made her
smile.

"I may be blind, Douglas, but I'm not *blind*." Her
hand moved down from his face, to his arm, then she
rested it on Billy's head. "Can you love her child?"

He took a deep breath. "I already do."

* * *

"You don't intend to watch me dress, do you?" Elise
asked, with her hands on her hips.

Cora bit her lip, then turned around. "Sorry. I just
can't stop lookin' at you. Don't you find it odd that we
look so much alike?" The lush fabric of Elise's dress
swished as she removed it.

Reminds me of them fancy dresses Francine gave me. The
thought tugged on her heart. She didn't miss the dresses
so much, but ached for her friends—fearing what had become of them.

"I don't think we look *that* much alike," Elise replied. "My hair is much nicer."

Cora didn't know what to think of Elise. But since she was Douglas's friend, she would do her best to be kind. "Hard to tell with it soakin' wet."

"It wouldn't have been wet if Douglas hadn't run off and left me."

"What do you mean?"

"Didn't he tell you that we're courting?"

Cora gasped, but then covered her mouth and shook her head.

Elise giggled. "Dear, dear Douglas. He's rather shy about letting people know. You see ... for the longest time, everyone thought I would marry his brother, Cameron, but just recently we came to realize that Douglas and I are far better suited for one another." She sighed. "You can turn around now. I'm dressed."

She didn't want to turn around. She didn't want Elise to see the tears in her eyes. Forcing her tears to stop, she wiped them away, then put a smile on her face.

"How do I look?" Elise asked, primping her still-damp hair.

"Just like me." Pushing aside her emotions, she had many questions to ask. "How old are you?"

"I just turned eighteen." Elise stood perfectly upright.

She's proud a hurtin' me. Being nice to this woman wasn't going to be so easy.

"Me, too," Cora said. "March the sixth."

Elise's body folded and she sat down hard on the edge of the bed. "That's my birthday."

254 · Jeanne Hardt

Cora sat beside her. "Don't you see? Somehow, you an me are twins." Her heart raced. Could her ma still be alive?

Elise laughed. "Twins? You are *not* my sister." She turned her head and looked deeply into Cora's eyes. "You have flecks of gold in your eyes. And freckles."

"Yep."

"So do I," Elise muttered. "But—Mother would have told me if I had a sister. When I told her about you, she laughed. But she also said that she wanted to meet you if you ever returned to Memphis."

"She wants to meet me?" The thought of meeting her ma overwhelmed her. "I reckon I ain't ready to meet my ma."

Elise stood and defiantly crossed her arms over her chest. "She's not *your ... ma*! She's *my mother.* And I have a father, too. You *can't* be my sister!" Flinging open the door, she exited the room and left Cora standing there wondering ...

* * *

"Douglas," Elise said. "I'm ready to go home, now."

He covered his mouth, hiding a grin. The simple cotton dress she was wearing would have looked perfect on Cora, but it was definitely *not* Elise.

Mrs. Moss shook her head. "No, you can't go just yet. I need to speak with you."

He was grateful that Mrs. Moss couldn't see the daggers that Elise released with her eyes. "Elise," he said, as calmly as he could, "you need to hear what Mrs. Moss has to say."

Cora crept into the room. When he turned to look at her, he could tell she'd been crying. He placed Billy in the arms of Mrs. Moss, then crossed quickly to Cora. "What did she say to you?"

Cora lowered her head. "She told me 'bout you." Her eyes lifted. "Why did you lie to me?"

"Lie to you?"

"She said you was courtin'."

Her voice was so low that he could scarcely hear her, but he understood. Sharply, he turned his head to face Elise. "Why did you tell her that we're courting?"

Elise flitted across the room and took his arm. "Douglas, dear. I told her how *shy* you are, but you shouldn't mislead the poor girl."

With blood boiling in his veins, he jerked his arm away from her. "We are *not* courting. Truthfully, I'll have you know that if there is anyone I wish to court, it's Cora, not you."

"Huh?" Cora asked, stumbling backward.

He caught her by the arm. "Yes, Cora. I would very much like to court you."

"No!" Elise yelled, stomping her foot. Her scream prompted Billy to cry.

"I told you she's too loud," Mrs. Moss said, juggling Billy and trying to calm him.

He took him from her, placed him over his shoulder, and patted his back. "It's all right Billy," he whispered, then kissed his cheek. "So, are you agreeable to my proposal?" he asked Cora.

She nodded and gulped. Then her face lit up with a bright smile.

Mrs. Moss cleared her throat. "Excuse me, but there are important things to discuss."

"Dang, Mrs. Moss, what's more important than havin' a man court me?" Cora sat down beside her.

Elise clasped her hand over her mouth. "She truly does curse."

"We're working on that, aren't we, Cora?" Mrs. Moss said.

"Yes'm," Cora said, with a calm nod.

Mrs. Moss moved her hands over the seat of the sofa until she found Cora's hand. "I need to tell you about your mother."

"She didn't die, did she?" she asked, looking toward Elise.

Mrs. Moss patted her hand. "Yes, she did."

"But ... I thought ..."

Douglas took a seat beside her, with Billy comfortably quiet on his shoulder. "Listen to what she has to say, Cora." He nodded to Elise. "You may want to sit. This involves you, too."

Elise scowled, crossed her arms with a huff, and sat down hard in a chair.

As Mrs. Moss retold the story of their mother and the midwife who delivered her, he turned his attention from Cora to Elise, waiting for their reactions. As expected, Elise appeared horrified, while Cora was simply astounded.

Elise tried to maintain her composure, but was fighting back tears.

"So," Cora whispered, "you figger Elise and I are sisters."

"Oh, yes," Mrs. Moss said. "I wish I could see you with my own eyes, but my heart is telling me it's so."

"They's sistas, all right," Rosie said.

Douglas looked up. She'd been standing in the hallway, listening.

"Just look at 'em, Mista Denton," she continued. "They's just like two peas in a pod."

Tears finally flowed from Elise's eyes. "But ... if she and I are sisters, and her mother died giving birth ... I mean ... *our* mother died ..." She stopped and covered her face with her hands.

Douglas was compelled to comfort her, but before he could do anything, Cora was on her feet moving toward her.

"Elise," she whispered. She extended her hand and rested it on Elise's leg.

Elise lowered her hands from her face, then blinked several times, causing tears to trickle down her cheek. "My life's been a lie," she said and sniffled.

Cora wrinkled her nose. "It might a been a lie, but least you haven't wanted for nothin'. I reckon the Pecks took good care a you. You're far more a lady than I am."

Elise's chin quivered. "The *Pecks*. That's all they are. They aren't my parents." Once again, she covered her face and cried. Her shoulders shook as she sobbed.

"But you got a sister you didn't know 'bout. Don't that help none?" Cora spoke with compassion.

Elise looked beyond Cora and directly at Douglas. "I need to go home, Douglas. Please?"

"Are you certain you're ready to do that?" he asked, calmly. "What will you say to your mother?"

Elise stood, giving no regard to Cora. "She's not my mother. My parents are dead."

"*Our* parents are dead," Cora said in a whisper.

"Douglas, *please*?" Elise walked toward the front door.

He stood from the sofa and placed Billy tenderly in Cora's arms. "I'm going to take her home, but I'll be back for supper."

"I wanna go with you," Cora said boldly. "I need to meet Mrs. Peck. She was the last person to see my ma alive. I gotta know things."

"Yes, Douglas," Mrs. Moss piped up. "Cora deserves to know everything. I'd like to go as well. I owe it to Angela."

Elise threw her hands in the air. "Do *you* want to come along as well?" she asked Rosie.

"Uh-uh," Rosie said. "That's the last place I'd wanna be."

"Can I go?" Toby asked, popping his head into the room from around the corner.

"How long you been there?" Rosie asked.

"Awhile," he said with a toothy grin. "Can I go, Mama?"

"No. You get your tail back in my kitchen. We gots work to do."

Toby hung his head and left the room with his mother behind him.

When Douglas opened the door, he was grateful that the rain had finally stopped. But he knew that a much worse storm was coming.

Chapter 23

"Where did you get that ghastly dress?" Lena asked, looking up at her daughter as she entered the room.

Cora stood timidly behind Douglas, holding Billy tightly against her, but suddenly became bold and stepped out to confront Mrs. Peck. "I let her wear it," she said, swallowing hard.

Lena's mouth gaped open. Her upper lip twitched as she rose to her feet.

Cora stared at the woman. She was pretty, but there was something ugly lying beneath her beauty. Her hair was neatly twisted atop her head and the dress she wore looked expensive.

Lena nervously fingered the pearl necklace that circled her slender neck. Cora watched her as she moved her gaze to Douglas, then lastly to Mrs. Moss.

"What's going on here?" Lena asked. Her chest rose and fell rapidly as she passed breath through her nose.

"We've come for answers, Mrs. Peck," Douglas said. "May we sit?"

"Of course," Lena said, with a hint of nervous laughter. She motioned them into the living room.

Cora was in the presence of a very wealthy woman. The furnishings were even finer than those on the *Bonny Lass*. The sofa was upholstered in a deep, lavish red fabric with gold brocade trim. The wood accent tables were dark stained oak. She tipped her head upward and admired the candelabra that flickered with a dozen lit candles.

Douglas took her arm. "Let's sit, Cora." He led her into the room.

Elise hadn't acknowledged her ma. It was understandable. Everything she believed about her family had been false. However, in addition to not acknowledging her ma, Elise hadn't said a word to *her* the entire way here, even after Douglas told her in detail why she was using a fake name. She'd hope it would draw even a morsel of sympathy out of Elise, but she was sadly disappointed. And even though Elise hadn't been kind, Cora was grateful to know that she had a sister.

Lena was the last one to sit down. She took a chair on the far side of the room, closest to the door, looking as though she wanted to bolt at any moment.

"So, Douglas," Lena said, through pinched lips, "I see that you found my daughter's look-alike."

"Mrs. Peck?" Mrs. Moss tilted her head to the side and gazed in the direction of Lena's voice.

"Yes? And who might you be?" Lena spoke with forced kindness.

"A friend of Angela Craighead," Mrs. Moss said. She sat upright and raised her chin into the air.

Cora had never been more proud of Mrs. Moss and promised herself that when they returned home, she would give her an overdue hug.

"Craighead?" Lena asked. "I don't believe I know that name."

"Stop it, Mother!" Elise yelled. "Mrs. Moss told me the truth! How could you?"

Lena once again rubbed her pearls. "How could I *what*, my dear?"

"You took me from my family! My *real* family!" Elise stood and crossed the room to her mother. "You never told me I had a sister!"

Lena gripped Elise's arm. "Lower your voice," she snapped. "I'm your mother and you'll show me respect."

"No, you ain't." Cora couldn't sit there and say nothing. "She an I had the same ma and she died birthin' us. But you already know that, don't you?"

"How dare you say such a thing?" Lena glared at her. "Who do you think you are?" She rose to her feet and strode toward her. "How dare you come into my home and spew horrid lies to my daughter!"

As Lena raised her arm Cora drew back, expecting to be slapped. She protectively covered Billy.

"That's enough, Lena!"

All heads turned to the deep, gruff voice.

"Edward?" Lena took a step back. "This is no concern of yours. Go back to your bookkeeping."

Standing before her was a short bald man, wearing an expensive-looking black suit. For a brief moment, Cora thought he was going to turn and leave, but after puffing out his chest, he stepped further into the room.

"I said you can go back to your bookkeeping," Lena said, fluttering her hand as if trying to shoo him away.

"No!" He pulled on his lapel and crossed the room until he was facing her. She towered over him, but he held his ground. "Tell her the truth!"

Lena's upper lip twitched. "Damn, you," she muttered, then seated herself once again.

Elise's eyes popped. "Mother?"

"What?" Lena threw up her hands. "Can you honestly tell me that you would have rather grown up in *Plum Point, Arkansas*?" She spoke the name with a crude accent, mimicking Cora. "And would you rather have had a father like Clyde Craighead, who would drink himself into oblivion and vomit at your feet?"

"Thought you said you didn't know no Craighead," Cora stated boldly.

"Oh, shut up!" Lena barked.

Douglas stood. "I won't have you speak to her that way."

"Why are you so concerned with this little ... ragamuffin?" Lena asked, cocking her head.

Cora looked up at him and wondered what he would say.

He sat closer to her than before, then smiled a broad smile. "We're courting."

Looking as though she'd swallowed a chicken whole, Lena choked. "Courting?" She clutched her chest. "Oh, dear Lord."

Edward rushed to her side. "Are you all right, dear?"

"Oh … go count something!" she yelled, pushing him aside.

Mrs. Moss beat her walking stick on the floor. "What is this? Was I taken to a circus, rather than a civilized home?"

Lena leaned forward in her chair, looking closely at Mrs. Moss. "Are you blind?"

"Course, she's blind," Cora said. "But she's also right. We came to find out 'bout our ma. I think you need to calm down and tell us what happened to her."

Lena smirked. "She died."

Douglas squeezed Cora's hand. "Mrs. Peck, Cora deserves a better explanation."

Cora could tell he was becoming impatient and returned the squeeze with one of her own. "It's all right, Douglas," she whispered in his ear. "She's a bitter woman."

"I heard you," Lena said smugly.

"Lena, tell the child what you know," Edward said. He looked at Cora with pity in his eyes.

"I ain't no child," Cora said. "Billy here's a child."

Edward smiled, but said nothing more.

"Your mother," Lena said, "had narrow hips. It was all I could do to expel the two of you. She bled out soon after you came." She folded her hands in her lap. "There. Now you know."

"But—when did you take Elise?" Cora asked. She was determined not to let this horrid woman upset her.

"I kept both of you in my care until you were weaned. Yes, I suckled both of you." She smirked. "You'd have died without my breast."

"Reckon I would a," she responded, undaunted by her coldness. "So, you took me back to my pa and kept Elise. How'd you choose which a us to keep?" Mindlessly, she placed her hand on her abdomen, protecting her secret mark.

Lena's tongue flicked out of her mouth, licking her lips. "She was a better baby. You cried all the time. I didn't want to raise a cry-baby."

Cora looked at Mr. Peck, who immediately cast his eyes downward. She doubted that Mrs. Peck was telling the truth.

"You know that kidnapping is a crime, don't you?" Douglas asked.

"Will you bring the marshal, Douglas?" Lena waved her hand in the air and laughed. "What would your mother say? Your mother is my friend. I doubt she would want you to have me put away."

"Elise?" Douglas looked at Elise with concern. "What would you like to do? You're the one who has suffered from the crime."

"Crime?" Lena shrieked. "Saving her from a life of back-woods drudgery is a crime? I made her life far better than it ever would have been. All you have to do is look at her sister and you can see which child had a better life. At least my daughter didn't breed with a man old enough to be her father!"

Cora wanted to run and the gentle way Douglas stroked her hand was the only thing that kept her seated.

"We've heard enough," Mrs. Moss said as she stood. "Douglas, please return us to our home. I'm feeling ill."

Cora nodded. "Billy's gonna need to be fed soon."

Elise hadn't budged.

"Elise," Douglas persisted. "Do you want to press charges?"

Elise faced her mother.

Lena offered Elise a tender smile, then tipped her head, and with slow batting eyes extended her arms.

Elise stood and went to her. "No, Douglas," she said with a sigh. "I don't want to do anything like that." She looked around her expensive home. "She's given me a good life. Better than what it could have been. I can't fault her for that."

"Oh, my sweet girl," Lena chirped.

"Let's go, Douglas," Cora said, feeling that she was going to be sick. Mrs. Moss was right, they'd all heard enough.

* * *

After Douglas returned Cora, Billy, and Mrs. Moss to the boarding house, he went home to look in on his mother, with a promise to Cora that he would be back for supper.

Glad to have some time to gather his thoughts, he drove the horse at a slow pace on his way back. His grumbling stomach reminded him that it was nearly supper time and the thought of eating Rosie's cooking caused him to push the horse a bit faster.

He'd told his mother about Lena and the fact that she'd stolen Elise as a replacement for a child she'd lost. He assumed his tale would trouble her, but she sat and listened quietly, showing no surprise. It was as if there was nothing that Lena could do that would astonish her.

All she had said to him was that it was *a shame* for Elise, then quickly changed the subject and told him the details of Cameron's upcoming engagement party. She urged him to invite Cora, since they were officially courting. His mother's dismissal of Lena's criminal activity bothered him, but as he neared the boarding house he returned his thoughts to Cora.

Aware that she had *known* another man troubled him, but his heart spoke louder than his mind in this matter. *She'd never been kissed before. How could he have coupled with her without kissing her?* He squeezed his eyes tightly shut, trying to erase the vision of William and Cora together. Unlike his brother, he was saving intimacy for marriage. He believed it to be the appropriate thing to do. Besides, he would never risk creating a child with a woman who was not his wife.

"Stop thinking about it, Douglas!" he scolded himself, shaking his head as rapidly as he could.

Unfortunately, ever since he'd kissed Cora in the cemetery, he couldn't *stop* thinking about it. His body cried out to him, begging to be close to her.

He wiped his brow with the back of his hand, only to dampen it more. His hands were sweating as much as his heart was pounding.

"I will remain a gentleman," he said aloud, sitting up tall.

If not, Mrs. Moss will likely beat me with her walking stick ...

* * *

"Rosie," Douglas said, patting his belly. "Once again, you've outdone yourself."

Rosie waved her hands in the air. "Weren't nuthin'." She chuckled as she returned to the kitchen to bring dessert.

"It seems you've had quite the day, Mr. Denton," Daisy said, folding her hands on the table. "Cora told me what happened with Mrs. Peck." She cast her eyes around the table. "I've never cared for that woman."

He shook his head. "I've lost what little respect I ever had for her. Honestly, I wish I never had to see her again."

"Why would you?" Daisy asked, tilting her head.

"She's my mother's friend and Mother invited her family to the engagement party."

"Dang," Cora mumbled, then clasped her hand over her mouth.

He chuckled. "I feel the same way, Cora."

They were sitting side-by-side, so he reached under the table and rested his hand on her knee, after patting it gently. Her body jerked and she released a small whimper. Then she placed her hand in his. He turned his head and smiled at her, wondering if she'd been having the same thoughts.

"Chess pie?" Rosie asked. She carried the dessert into the room and set it down on the table.

He thought he'd died and gone to heaven. "Corn pudding and now chess pie?" He couldn't hide the excitement in his voice.

Rosie released a hearty laugh. "Easiest man to please I ever know'd!"

He turned to look at Cora, wondering if she was as fond of chess pie as he was, only to find that her cheeks were bright red. She bit her bottom lip, then looked shyly downward. He'd never known her to be shy. Perhaps she *was* having similar thoughts.

"I'll have some," Mrs. Moss said. "Always did have a fondness for sweets."

Rosie cut the pie and placed it on individual dessert plates, then set one down in front of each person at the table. The slice she cut for Douglas was twice the size of the others.

Cora wrinkled her brow, staring at his pie. "Don't seem quite fair."

He rubbed his hands together and smacked his lips. "Rosie knows *my* fondness for sweets."

Looking into Cora's eyes, he was reminded that *she* was the sweetest thing he'd ever tasted and he wanted more of her. As her tongue came out of her mouth, wetting her lips, his heart thumped.

"You all right, Douglas?" Cora asked. "You're starin' at me."

"You're beautiful, Cora," he whispered. "It's difficult *not* to stare."

As if in perfect unison, Mrs. Moss, Daisy, and Rosie cleared their throats.

Mrs. Moss cocked her head. "Was that Billy I heard?"

He scooted his chair back and rose to his feet. "I'll check on him."

* * *

Cora watched him leave. "He's sure taken to Billy," she said, taking a bite of pie.

"Yes, he has," Mrs. Moss said. "And Billy has taken to him."

"I wish you'd told me the truth about your husband," Daisy said, leaning back in her chair.

"I'm sorry 'bout that, but William told me to be careful and not use my real name. Mr. Giles might still be lookin' for me an Billy."

"I don't want any trouble here, Cora," Daisy said sternly. But then her voice softened. "If you stay close to Mr. Denton, you'll be safe."

Staying close to Douglas was exactly what she wanted to do.

"Look who's awake," Douglas said, cradling Billy in his arms.

Cora stood. "I reckon he needs changin'." She reached out, only to have Douglas grin at her and hold him even tighter.

"I changed him," he said.

"You did?"

"Yes, I did." He proudly raised his chin in the air, then sat with Billy at the table. "Billy, would you like a bite of chess pie?"

She took her seat. "He's too little for chess pie. All he eats right now is ... *me*."

Douglas grinned at her with dancing eyebrows. There was a series of *throat-clearing* around the table.

Having finished her dessert, Cora stood and reached for Billy. "Time he has *his* dinner."

"If you insist." Before passing him to her, Douglas kissed Billy's cheek. "One day, you'll have chess pie and many other sweets."

"I don't want a fat baby," she scolded, but then softened when Billy cooed at Douglas. "It don't take him long to eat."

The way Douglas smiled at her made her knees weak. She left the room with Billy as fast as she could.

* * *

The evening progressed with no further excitement, which suited all of them. Rosie and Toby had already gone to bed, as well as Daisy. Billy fell asleep on Douglas's shoulder, so Cora lifted him gently and quietly carried him to his crib. When she returned to the living room, Mrs. Moss was chatting with Douglas. Mrs. Moss turned her head upon hearing her enter the room and announced she was going to bed. Before exiting, she glanced in Douglas's direction. "Remember, Douglas. You are courting, but you must remain a gentleman."

Mrs. Moss crossed the room to her. "Cora?"

"Yes'm?"

"He's not yet your husband."

She understood and kissed Mrs. Moss on the cheek. "Don't you worry none."

Mrs. Moss tapped her way out of the room. And then ... they were alone.

Douglas patted the spot beside him on the sofa. Cora gulped, but quickly sat down and was immediately aware of the warmth of his body and his incredibly clean scent.

"Today's been kind a troublin'," she said, and gulped again. His hand rested on her leg.

"I'm sorry, Cora." Her body tingled as his hand moved up and down along her thigh in a gentle caress.

She stared forward, afraid to look at him. "There you go again, apologizin'. Why do you do that, Douglas?"

"Because I *am* sorry." His voice was soft and low. "Sorry for the way you lived growing up. Sorry for all the heartaches you've endured. Sorry that you never knew your mother and ... I'm sorry that you lost your husband."

She had to look at him. "But none a that was your fault. That was my life before I met you. *You* ain't got nothin' to be sorry for."

He placed one hand on the side of her face and looked into her eyes. Her heart beat even faster and she got that feeling again deep within her belly. She wanted him ...

"Why me, Douglas?" she asked, blinking slowly. "Is it cuz I look like Elise?"

"What do I have to say to convince you that it's *you* I want to be with?"

"But—I know she likes you. And ... *wants* you. And she talks much finer than I ever will. She wouldn't embarrass you at the engagement party."

"You think that you'll embarrass me?" He took her hands in his. "I'll be proud to have you beside me wherever we may go together."

"But-"

"Cora," he interrupted her. "Yes, the two of you look alike, but there is one thing that is very different."

"My cursin'?"

He laughed and shook his head. "No. It's what's in here." He touched the tips of his fingers to the space between her breasts, making her breath hitch.

She shyly lowered her head, but he raised it and forced her to look at him. "Cora, you have the gentlest heart of anyone I've ever known. And—you make me smile."

"So, I don't embarrass you?"

He shook his head back and forth, penetrating her with his eyes. The air became thick around them as their breathing intensified. His hand moved along her arm and before she could say another word, his arms were around her and his mouth covered hers. She melted into his embrace and allowed her hands to grasp his back.

"Mmm," she moaned. "Douglas ..." His name rasped through her lips.

The kiss became different than anything she'd imagined when he opened her lips with his tongue and kissed her deeply. She grasped him even tighter and her tongue twirled with his. He tasted sweet, *like chess pie.* Devouring *him* would be much finer.

How she wished he was her husband. It would be easy now to take him by the hand and lead him to her bed. All the times she coupled with William, she never wanted him like this.

* * *

"Cora," Douglas panted. He couldn't stop touching her. His hands roamed across her back and as their kiss deepened, he moved one hand to her belly. His palm moved in slow circles inching upward toward her breasts. Dare he touch her there?

MARKED · 273

His mouth moved from her lips to her cheek, then to her ear. "Cora ... I ... love you."

"Douglas," she said, breathlessly. "I love you, too."

Unfastening the buttons at the front of her dress, he slipped his hand beneath the fabric and continued his circular caress across the curve of her ribcage. His fingers brushed along the base of her full breast, causing a low, guttural moan to rise from deep within her.

What are you doing? He stopped the motion of his hand and rose up to look at her face. Her eyes were closed and her head rested back against the sofa. She had succumbed to him completely.

Her hands moved into his hair, as she pulled him to her once again.

She wants this ...

He kissed her with a hungering kiss and pushed her dress open. He restrained from grasping her breast and moved his hand lower toward her abdomen.

She became rigid and sat upright. "No, Douglas." Her tone was firm—almost frightened.

What have I done? He should have known better than to compromise her. "I'm sorry, Cora." After running one hand back through his hair, he took several deep breaths and tried to calm his heart. He shifted his body, attempting to ease the tension in his lower extremities.

She refastened the buttons on her dress. "Don't apologize, Douglas. It ain't you ... it's me. There's sumthin' you gotta know 'bout me."

"What is it?" His heart ached for her. "You're shaking."

274 · Jeanne Hardt

"Another one a Mrs. Peck's lies." She looked away from him and fidgeted with the cushion on the sofa. At least she'd stopped trembling.

"I don't understand ..."

"She lied 'bout why she kept Elise 'stead a me."

Placing a loving hand on her arm, he questioned her with his eyes.

"Elise an me ain't the same all over. Least I reckon we ain't."

Even though it was taking Cora a long time to explain, what she had to say was important, so he remained quiet and waited for her.

"I got a mark," she said, and her face flushed.

"A mark?"

"Uh-huh. A birthmark. Here." She placed her hand on her abdomen. "I don't like no one to see it. Fact is William only got a quick glimpse of it." She paused, and gingerly touched his chest. "And—he never done what you just did to me, which—I gotta say—took my breath." She tentatively looked at him and his heart melted.

"So, that's why you stopped me? You don't want me to see your mark?"

"It's ugly. I'm ashamed of it."

He pulled her into his arms and she nestled into him, resting her head on his chest. Gently, he stroked her back. *Thank God my touch didn't offend her.* "Nothing about you is ugly, but if you don't want me to see it, then I won't. I respect you, Cora."

She giggled. "If Mrs. Moss walked in few minutes ago, she may a thought otherwise."

"But Mrs. Moss can't see."

She raised her head and grinned. "No, but she can hear. I reckon she would a figgered out what we was doin' by the sounds we was makin'."

Her arms encircled him and her strong heart beat against his chest. He kissed the top of her head. "I need to marry you soon, Cora."

Her head popped up. "You do?"

He nodded. "I'm being selfish. I want you terribly."

She rose up so that their faces were inches apart. "I want you, too."

"I want to make love to you," he whispered, and pressed his forehead to hers.

"Make love?"

"Yes, make love. I want to be as close to you as humanly possible."

Confusion filled her eyes. "You mean—you wanna try an make a baby?"

"Eventually, *yes*. But it's more than that."

"Oh. I know what you mean. You wanna do that cuz it'll make you happy, right?"

He touched his hand to her face, then slid it back through her hair. "I hope that when we do, it will make both of us happy."

She nestled down again into his arms and sighed. "Me, too..."

He leaned back and closed his eyes, pulling her with him.

* * *

Douglas woke with a start to the sound of Billy crying.

Cora lifted herself from his chest and stood. The room was completely dark.

"I can't believe we fell asleep," he said, then stood and straightened his clothing.

"I can. I was spent. I gotta get Billy. He's hungry."

He took her into his arms and kissed her sweetly. "Go to him. I need to get home."

"Douglas?" She tipped her head up, searching for him in the darkness.

"Yes. I'm here."

"Dream a me," she whispered.

"I have been." He kissed her one last time, then carefully walked out of the room, whispering *goodnight* as he left. It was good that his horse knew the way home.

Chapter 24

"Don't be so nervous, Cora," Douglas said as the buggy wound its way toward the stables. "Mother is going to love you." He turned and offered her one of his most infectious smiles, but Cora couldn't still her heart.

"You sure I look all right?" She asked him, while smoothing her skirt for the umpteenth time. Not sure if she was truly ready to meet his family, she couldn't overcome the butterflies.

He placed his hand on her leg. "You look beautiful. Now stop worrying."

Maybe leaving Billy at home with Mrs. Moss and Rosie wasn't the best thing to do, but she didn't want to bring him to an engagement party attended by adults only. Douglas promised her that he would take her home in plenty of time to nurse. Still, she'd never been away from him for such a long time.

Her gaze circled the large stable, then she smiled when Douglas handed the reins to a slave he called *Jeriah.*

The man nodded politely to her, as Douglas helped her from the buggy.

"Nice livery stable," she said to Douglas. "It's big." She counted at least ten horses, three buggies, two wagons, and one enclosed carriage.

"It's not a livery. This belongs to my father." Douglas took her hand and placed it into the crook of his arm.

She looked over her shoulder and watched Jeriah release their horse from the buggy. He grinned at her, having obviously heard their conversation.

"All this for your family alone?"

Douglas nodded. "I know what you're thinking."

She coyly tilted her head as he chuckled. "Not *that*."

She bit her lip and looked at the ground. It seemed that Douglas *could* read her mind.

"You're wondering how one family would need so many animals and means of transportation. Am I right?"

She nodded.

"We don't use most of them. Father likes to have them simply for show. He believes it impresses people."

"*I'm* impressed." She squeezed his arm, as he led her down the path to the house.

Then she stopped. She couldn't go another step further. "Dang, Douglas." She gulped. "I knew you had money ... but ... *dang*."

She took in the site of the estate. The house alone filled a full two acres of property. It was three stories high and had a large set of fanned steps leading up to the front door. Made from stone and white brick, the house appeared sturdier than any she'd ever seen.

Nothin' like my house at Plum Point.

"How many folks live here?" She asked, still frozen to the ground.

"Four. The slaves live in smaller houses behind."

She looked sideways at him. "I don't feel well."

He turned her to face him squarely. "Cora, it's a building. Nothing more. Believe me, I much prefer the boarding house. The rooms here can be very cold in the winter."

"Glad it's May." She lowered her head, shaking it slowly. "I don't belong here."

"Yes, you do. You're with me. And—if it makes you feel any better—when Father dies, all of this will go to Cameron. So you won't have to worry about it."

"All of it?"

"Yes, all of it. Are you disappointed?"

"Uh-uh. But, it just ain't right. What makes your brother more deservin' than you?"

"Blood," Douglas replied with a sigh. "Now then, let's go on and get this over with, shall we?"

"I reckon so." She took his arm and allowed him to lead her to the house. When the sound of music filtered out from the inside of the home, she smiled. "I like the sound a that."

"Father employed musicians for the affair. Do you dance?"

Horrified, her eyes opened wide and she pulled Douglas to a halt. "Nope. Never have. And please don't ask me to."

He patted her hand, then lifted it to his lips and kissed it. "If I dance with you, it will be in private. If you step on my toes, only I will know."

Pushing the front door open, he motioned her inside. There were people everywhere and she wanted to turn and run. But before she could leave, there was a tug on her arm and she turned to face her sister.

"Cora," Elise said in a sugary-sweet tone. "I'm so happy to see you again." She pulled her into a firm embrace, which caused her to lose her breath.

"Elise?" She stepped back, gaping at her.

"Aren't you happy to see me? It's been weeks."

Something was terribly wrong. Cora managed to smile, then looked over her shoulder for Douglas. He was caught up in conversation with someone she didn't recognize.

"Cora," Elise said again, and turned her to face her.

"Huh?"

"Aren't you happy to see me?"

Her persistence was something Cora was forced to address. "Uh-huh. Your ma here, too?"

"Of course, she is. This is the event of the year. Everyone of importance is here." Elise leaned in and whispered. "Have you seen Vivian?"

Cora shook her head. "We just walked through the door."

Elise took her by the arm and led her across the room to a large common area. Cora couldn't help but look up at the high ceiling. Someone had actually climbed high enough to paint it with an ornate swirling pattern. She was mesmerized, until Elise once again tugged at her arm.

"Cora! I'm trying to speak to you." Elise placed her hands on her hips and pursed her lips.

"Sorry, Elise. I just ain't never seen nothin' like this place."

"I know what you mean. This is the finest home in all of Memphis."

People passed by them and Cora imagined they were gossiping about them. Her stomach continued to churn and she wished that Douglas would finish his conversation and take her somewhere quieter.

"As I was saying," Elise said with her mouth close to her ear. "Vivian is wretched. I don't know what Cameron sees in her. But you'll see for yourself soon enough."

Cora rubbed her ear, then stepped away from Elise. "That ain't very kind."

"Cora, is everything all right?" Douglas asked, resting his hand on her arm.

She let out a relieved sigh and basked in the comfort of his presence. "I'm holdin' up." She leaned her head on his shoulder.

Elise forced a smile. "I see the two of you are even more familiar than the last time I saw you together. Obviously, you still think you care for one another."

"We do," Douglas said, and Cora added an enthusiastic nod of agreement.

"Sweet," Elise said. "If you'll excuse me, I need to check on Mother. I want to be certain she's enjoying herself." Flitting away as if she had no care in the world, Elise vanished out of sight.

Cora shook her head. "What's gotten into her?"

"I'm not certain," Douglas replied. "But I have a feeling it's not good." He took her by the hand. "Come with me. I want you to meet my mother."

They pushed past groups of people and made their way down a long hallway. She stared at everything they passed; gold-framed paintings on the walls, ornate statues and floral arrangements, and plush furnishings unlike anything she'd seen before.

"Father purchased the furniture overseas," Douglas said. "That's called a divan." He pointed at a piece in the sitting room.

Fancy word for a sofa.

Aromas of baking bread and cinnamon pastries filled the air. The scent was growing stronger, so she assumed they were nearing the kitchen.

"Mother is most comfortable here," Douglas said, pointing toward an arched doorway. "We enjoy having tea together in the afternoon."

"Just like Mrs. Moss," she said, wishing she was there.

There were a few guests standing on the far side of the kitchen, but mostly there were slaves bustling around with trays of food and dishes.

An attractive woman sat at the table cradling a teacup. She knew instantly that she was Douglas's ma. He looked very much like her.

"Mother?" he said, guiding her forward. "I'd like you to meet Cora."

Mary Wellesley stood and smiled at her.

"Mrs. Wellesley," Cora said, nodding her head and bending slightly at the waist.

"Please. Call me *Mary.*"

"All right. Long as you call me *Cora.*"

Mary motioned for her to take a seat at the table and Cora was grateful to be away from the busyness of the main house. But Mary's eyes were on her, so she looked away, uncomfortable about being measured up.

"I still can't believe the likeness," Mary said, in one of the softest voices she'd ever heard.

Douglas sat between them and nodded his agreement. "I told you. I couldn't believe it myself when I first saw her."

Mary leaned in. "Look at me, dear."

Cora raised her eyes to meet Mary's, then blinked slowly.

Mary's face warmed into a gracious smile. "Alike, but very different, Douglas." She stretched her hand across the table, palm up, and nodded to her.

Cora placed her hand in Mary's. With her other hand, Mary covered their joined hands. She closed her eyes and continued smiling. Tilting her head, Cora looked at Douglas, questioning him with her eyes.

"Mother?" he asked, "What is it?"

Mary let out her breath in a slow, steady pace. "I like her, Douglas. She has a loving spirit."

Cora gulped, but didn't pull her hand away. "How can you tell?"

"I saw it in your eyes." Mary patted her hand, then pulled back her own. "You can tell a lot by looking into someone's eyes. Did you know that?"

"Mrs. Moss told me that the soul shines through folk's eyes. That what you mean?"

"Yes. Douglas has told me about your *Mrs. Moss.* The next time you come for a visit, I would very much like to meet her."

"She's blind. I reckon Douglas told you that, too."

"Yes. But a person can see with their heart. I imagine she has very good sight."

All of the nervousness she'd had before they came, melted away. Somehow, Mary made her feel that she belonged. Cora took hold of Douglas's arm and gave him a squeeze. His smile affirmed that once again, he knew what she was thinking.

"Mary!" Lena's loud voice brought an abrupt end to her ease. Mary stiffened, then grabbed a cloth napkin and began twisting it.

"Why are you sitting in here?" Lena asked, crossing the room and towering over them. "The party is out there." She pointed a firmly-extended finger toward the hallway.

Mary looked down, staring at the twisted cloth. "I'm getting to know Cora."

Cora was amazed at how quickly Mary changed. She was not the same woman from only moments ago. Her face had gone pale and her shoulders slumped forward. She'd folded into herself. Lena Peck affected her in a way that no true friend ever should.

Douglas stood. "Mrs. Peck, I hope you won't mind, but could you please give us a bit of privacy? Cora and Mother were just now becoming acquainted."

Lena waved her hand in the air. "Nonsense! This is a party and Mary is supposed to be the hostess." She glared at Mary. "Have you forgotten how to entertain, Mary?"

Mary wouldn't look at her.

"You're being rude to your guests." Lena lifted her nose into the air. "Then again, you aren't Cameron's mother, so perhaps no one will care." Her upper lip twitched, she grabbed her skirt, then whipped around and left the room.

Tears filled Mary's eyes.

Cora scooted her chair out, moved behind Mary, then knelt down and placed her arm around her shoulder. "Pay her no mind, Mary. She's a cold, bitter woman."

Mary dabbed her eyes with the cloth napkin. "You've not known her long, how can you tell?"

"I've looked in her eyes."

Douglas knelt down on the other side of his ma. "I'd like to go after her and ask her to leave. Would you like me to do that, Mother?"

Mary shook her head. "No, Douglas. I invited her."

"I'll never understand," he said, rising.

Mary stared at her hands, but didn't respond. Loud laughter erupted from the hallway, followed by shouts of congratulations and cheers. Cora's eyes were drawn to a tall, handsome man who suddenly appeared in the archway.

"Mary," he said, extending his hand. "Cameron is about to speak."

When Mary didn't rise, he snapped his fingers, causing her to jump.

Douglas helped lift her to her feet. "You'll be fine, Mother," he said, and kissed her cheek. He then nodded toward the man in the doorway. "My father," he said stone-faced.

Mary hurried across the floor to her husband's side. She turned her head and glanced at the two of them standing there, before disappearing with him down the hallway.

"He snapped his fingers at her," Cora said, shaking her head in disbelief.

Douglas pulled her into his arms. "I promise you, I'll *never* snap my fingers at you."

"Better not."

He squeezed her waist, then bent down and kissed her gently on the lips. "Are you ready to meet my brother?"

"Do I hafta?"

He nodded. "It is his engagement party, after all. Just be warned, he may not be kind."

"Hmmm ... You sure Mrs. Peck ain't his ma?"

Douglas chuckled. "Let's go."

Though she'd worn her finest dress for the evening, Cora felt under-dressed. She gazed down at her dark green cotton print and doubted she should be here.

"Stop doing that, Cora," Douglas whispered in her ear.

"What?" She hadn't done anything.

"You look fine. I can read your thoughts." He jiggled his eyebrows at her.

How did he do that? Playing along, she jiggled her brows at him. "I reckon I can read yours, too."

He nonchalantly licked his lips.

"Told ya," she grinned.

It had only been a few weeks since their intimate encounter on the sofa at the boarding house, and in that time she knew he was trying to keep their physical activity to simple kisses and nothing more. She was definitely thinking about that *something more* every time they were together. And she assumed he was, as well. As his ma had said, "You can tell a lot by looking in someone's eyes."

She clung tighter to him as they moved into the large group of people. They gathered in the *concert hall*, as Douglas called it, which was also used for dancing.

Her jaw dropped, taking in the enormous room. Eight candelabras hung from the ceiling, each one lit with numerous flickering candles. Large tables mounded with food lined the walls and the slaves hovered, just waiting for a plate to be emptied so they could fill it. She'd never seen so many pastries.

At the opposite end of the room was a raised platform on which were four musicians. A pianist at a grand piano, two violinists, and a cellist ready to play once Cameron finished his speech.

"My brother," Douglas said to her, nodding toward the platform.

As they moved closer and closer, Cameron became clearer. "He's not bad lookin'," she said through the side of her mouth, "but you're much more handsome."

Mr. Wellesley led Mary up onto the platform beside Cameron and Vivian.

Vivian … hmmm … She was quite lovely, so why did Elise say she was wretched? She would make a point to look into her eyes and see for herself.

"His fiancée is purdy," Cora said. The satin gown she wore was soft pink, trimmed with fine lace. It was fully ruffled with layers of material. "Reckon she's warm in that dress?"

"I *reckon* so." Douglas grinned at her and she playfully smacked his arm.

"Learnin' to talk like me?" She lowered her voice. "You'll be sayin' ain't and dang 'fore you know it."

"Perhaps I will." His eyebrows drew close in. "Promise me that you'll never change. Please?" His tone became serious—no longer playful.

"You mean that? I figgered you'd *want* me to change ... be more like Elise. You know—my speakin' an all."

He shook his head. "Never. I love the way you are."

Their eyes locked together.

"Thank you all for coming!" Cameron yelled across the room.

She turned her body toward the stage, but still held tightly to Douglas.

"My bride-to-be and I are grateful to each and every one of you," Cameron continued. He took Vivian by the hand and pulled her to him. They were an attractive couple; both blond and blue-eyed, and seemed to be close in age.

She pulled on Douglas's arm. "They'll have purdy babies," she whispered, and smiled.

Douglas didn't respond, but patted her arm. She glanced around the room to see if she recognized anyone else. Strangely, she couldn't find Elise or Mrs. Peck anywhere.

Maybe they left ...

The other person missing was Harper.

"Douglas, where's your uncle?"

"Uncle Harper doesn't enjoy these sorts of affairs. He's probably on his stool, whittling."

"So, what you're tellin' me is that he's the smart one in this family. Ain't that right?"

Douglas covered his mouth to hold in a laugh. He shook his head, dropped his hand, and flashed a very broad grin.

"Douglas!" Cameron yelled, bringing them both to full attention.

"Yes?" Douglas replied.

"Come up here," Cameron demanded, pointing to the stage.

She looked at Douglas, shaking her head. "I ain't goin'."

She was relieved when Douglas waved his hand at Cameron indicating their decline, but Cameron yelled again. "Bring Cora with you!"

Shouts of encouragement rang out across the room. She held her hands to her face, feeling the heat rising in her cheeks. When she met Mary's gaze, she realized that they would have to comply out of respect to his family.

"Let's get this over with," Douglas said, and led her by the hand toward the platform.

She wanted to bury her head somewhere. Could she turn and run and have no one notice? It was doubtful. So, she took a deep breath and followed Douglas.

When they stepped up onto the platform, Mary gave her a reassuring smile, but that didn't stop the pounding of her heart. Then, when Cameron looked at her, she had to look away. His eyes moved over her in the same manner that Marcus Giles had looked at her.

Cameron was unsteady on his feet and when she got close enough to him, she recognized a familiar smell.

Whiskey ...

Cameron pointed at Douglas. "My baby brother," he said. His words were slightly slurred. "And his ... *woman* ... Cora."

Cameron covered his mouth and snickered. The air around Douglas became tense, as his body stiffened. He took a step closer to Cameron, but Cameron moved away.

Cameron leaned toward the on-looking crowd. "Yes, she looks like Elise Peck, but she's not. She's her sister!" He stood upright and looked at the many faces. "Where is Mrs. Peck? I have some questions for her."

Douglas grabbed Cameron's arm. "Don't do this, Cameron. This isn't the time or place ..."

Cameron jerked his arm away. "It's *my* party!" He looked at Vivian. "*Our* party. Isn't that right, sweetheart?" He pulled her to him and kissed her hard.

A mixture of snickers and laughs, as well as a few gasps, filled the air. Vivian stepped back once he released her and politely wiped her mouth. She smiled timidly at their audience, but didn't say a word. Finally, Arthur Wellesley stepped in to control his son. He pulled him to the side, but Cora couldn't hear what was being said.

After the encounter, Cameron stepped forward, unaffected by the obvious scolding. "Vivian and I will be leaving shortly." He put his arm around her waist. "Please stay as long as you like, and eat as much as you can." He pointed to a large woman who stood at the front of the crowd. "Except for you, Mrs. Donner. You've had enough already!" He burst out laughing, then Arthur took him by the arm and led him from the platform.

Arthur escorted Cameron from the room with Vivian and Mary following after. Douglas took Cora's hand and helped her down.

"I'm sorry, Cora. You shouldn't have had to endure that." Douglas placed his hand on her cheek and looked at her with the saddest eyes ...

"It wasn't your fault." She stood on her tip-toes and kissed his cheek. "I gotta tell you, I feel kind a sorry for Vivian."

He nodded his agreement. As the crowd disbursed to the food tables and the musicians began playing, Douglas took her by the hand and led her down the hallway.

"I want to show you something," he said, with a grin.

The excitement behind his eyes had her curiosity piqued. Thankful to be away from all the people, she would have followed him anywhere.

He stopped just short of opening a tall, wide door. "Close your eyes, Cora," he said, and she obeyed.

After pushing the door open, he guided her into the room. She breathed in deeply and recognized the smell of leather and something else familiar.

Books!

Her body trembled with excitement.

"Open your eyes," he whispered in her ear.

As she slowly lifted her lids, her heart raced, and her mouthed dropped open. There were rows and rows of books. Shelves lined the walls, two stories high, and every shelf was full. "Dang!" She raced toward the closest shelf, turning her head sideways as she scanned the titles.

"When you told me how much you enjoy reading, I couldn't wait to bring you here," he said with a laugh in his voice. "You can read any you'd like. Father won't miss them. I doubt most of them have ever been touched."

She moved across the room, running her hand across the bindings. "There are more than I could ever read in a lifetime."

"Then you should never find yourself bored."

She returned to him and held him close. "With you, I'll never be bored." Raising her head she looked into his eyes. "Even without *any* books."

He bent down and kissed her, and she grinned having proven her point. With a promise that he would return her to the library before taking her home, he led her out of the house into one of the many gardens circling it. The heavy April rains had done their job and the flower gardens burst with color and sweet smells. It was late afternoon and the temperature was perfect. Warm, but not hot.

She breathed in the aroma of a large, red rose.

"It's beautiful out here, Douglas," she said, taking his hand. "Can we stay here for a spell? I'd much ruther."

"Aren't you hungry?"

"Uh-uh. I ain't used to eatin' at such a strange time. I had dinner 'fore you picked me up and Rosie'll have supper ready when I get home." She stared at the ground. "I hope Billy's all right."

Douglas gave her a gentle squeeze. "I'm certain he's fine. I'll take you home soon."

They walked hand-in-hand around the perimeter of the house. For a short time, they said nothing. The sound of laughter turned their heads. Cameron was leading Vivian down a long pathway toward the stables.

"They really leavin'?" she asked, amazed that they would leave their own engagement party.

"Yes. I believe Father asked him to leave. Father has a lot of important people here today and didn't want to be embarrassed by Cameron."

Minutes later, the carriage emerged from the stable. The driver sat tall at the front, popping the reins to encourage the two horses pulling it.

"Your brother likes the carriage?" she asked, impressed by its magnificence.

He hesitated before speaking. "He enjoys the ... *privacy.*" He raised his eyebrows and she understood.

"They do *that* in there?"

He nodded, then shook his head. "A fact I wish he'd never shared with me."

She watched until the carriage was out of sight. Hard to imagine it would be comfortable for such a thing.

Douglas took her hands in his, then raised them to his lips and kissed them. "Cora, I don't want to speak about Cameron any longer. I want to talk about us."

The look in his eyes made her knees quiver. "Us?"

"Yes. I don't know if this is the proper time to do this ... but ..." He went down on one knee.

Her mouth was so dry that it felt as if it was filled with balls of cotton. "What, Douglas?"

Still holding one of her hands, he tenderly caressed her skin. "Cora, I'll love you forever ... if you'll let me." He paused and took in a large amount of air. "Please, tell me you'll be my wife." His unblinking eyes were locked with hers.

"I ... I ..." She held her hand to her breast. "I love you, too."

"So ... that means?"

"Course it means, *yes*."

He stared at her, but didn't move.

"I said, *yes*, Douglas." She swallowed hard and breathed slowly, steadying the beat of her heart.

He was still on one knee. His eyes closed and he shook his head.

She stroked the side of his face. "I don't deserve you, Douglas."

Standing erect, he pulled her into an embrace. "No, Cora. You and I are perfect for one another. And I know we're going to have many happy years together."

"Startin' now," she said, smiling.

With that, he kissed her, long and fervently, surrounded by beautiful blossoms and covered in warmth from the sun. Leaning back, she let out a stream of laughter and was instantly joined by Douglas.

"I love you!" he yelled, and held her close.

She giggled. "Someone might a heard that."

"I hope they did. I want them all to know."

As her heart steadied itself, she thought about Billy. "Douglas, you know if you marry me, you'll be a pa, too."

"I know. And I promise to be the best *pa* I can be to Billy. He'll always know that he has a father who loves him. And when the time comes for us to have children of our own, I'll love them just the same."

"You sure 'bout that?"

"Yes. I'll love each and every one of them. All *ten*."

"Ten?" *Is he serious?* "You want ten kids?"

"One at a time, of course," he replied, wiggling his brows.

"Dang," she said in a whisper, shaking her head. They'd need an awfully big house.

He took her hand and walked toward the front entrance of the estate. "Let's go see Mother. I know she'll be happy. Besides, you didn't get much of a chance to speak with her. Now that Cameron and Vivian are gone, we should be able to squeeze in that time."

She touched her hand to her breast. "I'll need to get home soon. I can tell that it's time for Billy to eat."

Douglas stared at her bosom.

Realizing that she'd drawn attention to her breasts, she lowered her hand. "I reckon I'm gettin' more at ease with you. I forgot 'bout bein' *modest*, as Elise called it."

"I'll be your husband soon. You won't have to be modest."

She grinned, but realized he was still looking at her bosom. Taking his chin in her hand, she raised his head until he met her gaze.

"Forgive me, Cora," he whispered. "I must admit I'm rather envious of Billy."

She promptly smacked his arm. "Shame on you, Douglas." Though she was scolding him, she couldn't help, but grin.

He looked at her sheepishly, but she knew that in many ways, he meant what he said.

"Ain't that Elise and her ma?" she asked, pointing to the front steps.

He turned his head and looked. "Yes, it is. They seem to be in a hurry."

Mrs. Peck had Elise by the arm, pulling her rapidly up the steps. Before entering the house, they both primped themselves and smoothed their clothing. Mrs. Peck grinned at her daughter before they slipped through the door.

Cora wrinkled her brow. "Sumthin' ain't right 'bout all that."

"Perhaps they were using the facilities."

"Together?"

He shrugged. "I'm done worrying about Elise and her mother. Though I know she's your sister, I hope you don't mind if we keep our distance from them for a while. Mrs. Peck has a way of upsetting my mother that I don't fully understand."

"I don't mind. Elise may be my blood, but I don't trust her. She's too much like her ma."

"Yes, upbringing has a lot to do with a person's behavior. Thank God for Mrs. Moss." He grinned at her, then took her hand and guided her up the steps.

Music filled the hallways, but they didn't stop at the concert hall. Instead, he took her back to the kitchen where they found Mary comfortably sitting at the table drinking a cup of tea.

Cora could tell that it was what soothed her, and in no time at all she and Douglas were sitting beside her sharing their happy news.

Chapter 25

A smile covered Douglas's face as he closed his eyes. He would dream about Cora.

His mother seemed to be the only one in the household who understood his feelings for her. She knew that love was much more important than social rank. He didn't care that Cora came from a small shack on the banks of the Mississippi river, or that her father was a poor woodcarver. What he cared about was that she had a pure heart. He trusted her and she would be a faithful and loving wife. And—she made him laugh.

He chuckled as he thought about some of the things she had said. *She was right about Uncle Harper.* He would have to pay him a visit and share the news of their engagement. Of course, Harper had expected it all along.

"No!"

Douglas jerked upright in his bed. His heart pounded, hearing his father scream.

Again, Arthur yelled, "No! You're lying to me!"

Douglas jumped from his bed and put on a light-weight robe over his pajama bottoms. After lighting a lantern, he rushed into the hallway and down the long corridor to where the shouting was coming from.

Marshal Underwood stood just inside the entryway, with his hat in hand. "I'm very sorry, Mr. Wellesley," he said, placing his hand on Arthur's shoulder. "There ain't no mistake. But I'll need you to claim his body. Since it's so late, you can come by t'morrow. Mortician has the bodies."

Douglas's chest tightened. *Bodies?*

His mother had her arm around his father, trying to offer comfort. Arthur's anger was rapidly changing to grief. His body shook and he let out a loud wail, shaking the air around them.

The marshal met Douglas's gaze and nodded at him. Douglas crossed to him. "What happened?"

Before the marshal could answer, Arthur broke in. "My son is dead! Do you hear me? My *son* is dead!"

His mother's eyes were wide and tear-filled. She whispered something into Arthur's ear, then took him out of the room. Arthur sobbed, harder and harder, the further they went.

Marshal Underwood shook his head. "Sometimes I hate my job."

Douglas was determined to remain calm and patted the marshal's shoulder. "I understand."

"Strangest thing I ever seen," the marshal said, looking up at him.

"What? Please ... I have to know what happened." He could tell that the marshal was tired, so he led him to the sitting room and motioned to a chair. "Can I get you something to drink?"

"No. Thank you, but no." Marshal Underwood set his hat on a small table beside him and ran his hands over the top of his head. "Somehow, your driver was able to get to my office. He's at the hospital now. Reckon he'll make it."

"Our driver? You mean, Mr. Sherman, the carriage driver?"

"Yep. That's him."

Douglas leaned in, folding his hands together. The glow from the lantern gave the room an eerie feeling. "And he told you what happened?"

"Yep. Told me where to find 'em."

"I know you've already told this to my father, but please tell me."

Marshal Underwood took a deep breath. "They wasn't far from the hospital. The carriage was upside down in a ditch on the side a the road. 'Fraid I had to put down one a the horses."

"But ... how?"

"The woman had been snake bit. Copperhead. I reckon she was dead 'fore the carriage flipped."

Douglas shook his head, not understanding how this all fit together. It wasn't easy staying calm. The more he heard, the more horrifying the story became. *Copperhead?*

Obviously seeing his confusion, the marshal went on. "Sherman said that they was drivin' to Miss Vivian's house, when Mr. Wellesley stuck his head out the winda and told him all in a panic that Miss Vivian had been snake bit. Said there was a package in the carriage they thought was an engagement present. Snake was inside."

"Good Lord!" Douglas was unable to hide his shock.

"So, Sherman drove the horses hard, tryin' to get to the hospital in time. He said Mr. Wellesley was screamin' and yellin'. Stomped the snake hard and killed it. But not long after, sumthin' went wrong with the carriage. They was drivin' so fast that there was nothin' he could do to control it. One a the wheels came plum off, flipped the carriage. Broke Sherman's leg when he was tossed off it. Then, when he stumbled back to check on Mr. Wellesley and Miss Vivian, they was both dead. Mr. Wellesley's neck was broke."

Douglas couldn't believe what he was hearing. His mind raced. "Who would put a snake in a box and disguise it as a gift?"

"Someone who wanted 'em dead." Marshal Underwood shook his head. "This was no accident."

Douglas placed his hands over his face and closed his eyes. "You know that Cameron's mother died in a carriage accident. That was many years ago ..."

The marshal stood and placed his hat on his head. "Reckon that wasn't an accident neither?"

Douglas's heart stopped. *No ... it couldn't be.* He lowered his hands and looked up at the marshal.

Marshal Underwood stared at him. "Sumthin' you need to tell me?"

"I don't know ..."

"Well, you think on it. If you think a anything that will help figure out who done this, you let me know."

"Yes, sir. I will." Douglas walked with him to the door. "It's very dark. Are you sure you'll be all right going home?"

"Reckon so. I got here just fine. Got me a good horse." He nodded his head and slowly made his way down the front steps to his buggy.

Knowing that this was not the time to speak with his mother or his father, he walked down the hallway to his room. His body was numb. Picturing what Marshal Underwood had told him about the accident, he envisioned the horror that Cameron and Vivian must have endured. As much as he disliked his brother, he didn't deserve to be ... *murdered.*

"Cameron and Vivian were murdered," he muttered.

Unable to sleep, he propped pillows up at the head of his bed, then dimmed the lantern.

His mind reeled.

Surely Arthur's first wife died accidentally.

He had so many questions to ask his mother. What did she know about that accident? Then, there was Lena Peck. Somehow she fit into all of it.

Elise and Mrs. Peck weren't in the concert hall when Cameron was making his speech, then we saw them rushing into the house shortly after Cameron and Vivian left in the carriage ...

His heart thumped—*pounded*—as reality set in. He didn't want to believe it, but somehow it all made sense.

* * *

Cora listened as Douglas retold the horrible story. Tears pooled in her eyes. *Vivian must a been so scared ...*

And poor Cameron. She scarcely knew him, but her heart ached for him.

She'd fallen asleep last night dreaming of the man she loved, who would soon be her husband. Never had she been so happy. Then, when Daisy had knocked on her door and told her that Douglas was here and the sun had barely risen, she knew something was terribly wrong.

Daisy held her hand to her breast. "Those poor children."

"Such a tragedy," Mrs. Moss said, shaking her head. "I've never cared for snakes. When I was a child, a snake was coiled in the outhouse. My father killed it, but from that day on I was terrified of them."

Cora shuddered. "Her folks must be heart-broke. Yours, too, Douglas. I know how much your pa loved Cameron."

"I don't believe he slept at all last night. I got very little myself." He paced the floor.

She watched him; wanting so much to take him in her arms and offer comfort. But what he needed now was to be able to talk about what had happened.

"When I tried to speak to him this morning," Douglas continued. "He dismissed me with a toss of his head. Mother told me that I need to give him time, but he and I have never been close. I doubt that this tragedy will bring us closer."

"We'll hold off on gettin' married," Cora said. "Don't seem right celebratin' when folks is grievin'."

He stopped pacing and pulled her into his arms, then kissed the top of her head. "Yes, we should wait. But I don't want to wait long."

She looked up into his eyes and offered a sad smile.

"So, the marshal believes someone planned this. That it was no accident?" Mrs. Moss asked.

"Yes. That's what he said," Douglas replied.

Cora took his hand and led him to the sofa. She was glad to have him sit beside her, no longer pacing the floor. "Douglas? I have this awful feelin' inside. I keep thinkin' 'bout seein' Elise an Mrs. Peck right after Cameron an Vivian left."

"I've been thinking the same thing," he said, squeezing her hand.

"Oh, my," Mrs. Moss said, bringing her hand to her mouth. "Do you believe that it was your sister and her mother who put the snake in the carriage?"

He cleared his throat. "The pieces fit. But I don't know why they wanted her dead."

"I do," Cora said. "Didn't you tell me that Elise wanted Cameron? She told me that she thought Vivian was *wretched*."

"Yes, but from what the driver said, someone tampered with the carriage wheel. Whoever did this wanted them both dead. Then there's the issue of Cameron's mother's death. She died in a carriage accident twenty years ago. I need to speak to mother about it. I want to know how it happened."

"I seem to remember that accident," Daisy said, sitting upright. "It happened near the river. Not long after—your mother married Mr. Wellesley."

Douglas nodded. "Yes, and he became my father."

"Did Mrs. Peck know his first wife?" Cora asked. Her stomach continued to churn.

"I don't know," he replied. "That's one thing I intend to ask Mother."

Cora snuggled down into his arms, resting her head on his chest. "It's all just awful. Is there anythin' I can do to help your folks?"

"I'll talk to Mother. She likes you. It might help her to have another woman at the house ... someone she can talk to."

She lifted her head and smiled at him. "Maybe I can take little Billy to see her. Sometimes babies can make folks smile, even when they're feelin' poorly."

A bell jingled and Mrs. Moss patted her lap. "Come up, Muffin." The cat leaped up and curled into a ball in the folds of Mrs. Moss's skirt.

Douglas lifted his brows. "The bell was a very good idea, Cora."

"Thank you. I know sometimes I don't talk right, but I got sense. And I've always been good at figgerin' things out." She let out a long breath. "I'm scared that what we're gonna find out 'bout Mrs. Peck and Elise won't be good. That's sumthin' I wish I *hadn't* figgered out."

Douglas tenderly stroked her back. "I agree. But no matter what we find, nothing will change the way I feel about you." He gave her a quick peck on the cheek.

Mrs. Moss chuckled. "I heard that," she said, and Muffin purred loudly.

* * *

"No, I don't want her here!" Arthur Wellesley yelled.

Douglas stared blankly at him. A week had passed since the *accident*. Though his father had been civil to

Cora at the funeral, when he'd suggested he bring her to their house to provide his mother with someone to talk to, Arthur snapped.

"Why, Arthur?" Mary asked, timidly.

Bursts of air puffed from his nostrils. "Because ..." Arthur pointed at him, shaking his finger, "How do we know it wasn't the two of them that orchestrated the entire event?"

"What?" Douglas yelled. "How can you even suggest such a thing?"

Arthur threw his hands into the air. "It finally makes sense! That night, the two of you left together after Cameron's speech." His eyes were wild-looking; wide and on fire. "You knew that you would inherit my estate if Cameron was dead. And that little ..." He shook his head and waved his hands as if he were crazed. His eyes rolled upward. "That little ... *woman* ... you brought into our home."

"Don't say anything against Cora. She makes me happier than I've ever been!" He'd put up with years of criticism and abuse from Arthur Wellesley, but he wasn't about to let him degrade Cora.

Mary placed her hand on Arthur's arm. "Arthur, dear. The doctor said you need to remain calm."

Arthur ignored her and continued glaring at him. "Happy? How can you say that word in this house? Happiness died with my SON!"

His mother cowered. Neither of them deserved this treatment, regardless of how grief-stricken Arthur was. Taking a deep breath, Douglas tried again and spoke as calmly as he could. "There are other people living in this house. You still have your wife and you're the only father I've ever known. Can't you for once recognize that I'm also your son?"

Arthur clinched his fists. "You've never been my son. I know it was you—you and that *woman* who did this." Arthur placed his finger in the middle of Douglas's chest. "Douglas ..." He sneered and pushed hard. "I'll see to it that you get nothing!"

"I don't want anything from you." He turned from Arthur and walked away.

"Don't come back!"

Douglas continued on down the hallway and out the front door, not caring whether or not he ever returned. His mother was crying, but she made no attempt to stop him.

He'd tried to talk to her about Lena Peck and the suspicions he had about her involvement with Cameron's death, but she wouldn't hear it. She said that she and Arthur had determined that it was a prank that got out of hand, most likely done by a drunken guest. They had told the marshal that they wanted the entire ordeal to be dismissed as a tragic accident, and asked to be given their privacy in order to grieve.

But *he* couldn't so easily dismiss the event.

Elise and her parents had attended the funeral. He believed her to be completely grief-stricken, and though her mother tried to give her comfort, he'd watched Elise push her away. It made him wonder if perhaps they *hadn't* been a part of it. Still, it was the only solution that made sense.

"Goin' for a ride, Mista Denton?" Jeriah asked, as he entered the stable.

He shrugged. "I'm not sure where I'm going. But for now, I can't stay here."

Jeriah hung his head. "Shame what happened to Mista Wellesley an Miss Vivian. I's told the wheel on the carriage done come off." He raised his head and looked at him. "I feels just awful. See ... I would a checked them wheels if'n Miss Elise hadn't come talked to me. She was goin' on 'bout how upset she was 'bout Cameron an Miss Vivian. I's tryin' to calm her down. For I know'd it, the carriage was goin' out the stable door. An when I turned 'round to talk to her again, she was gone."

Douglas's heart thumped. "Was her mother with her?"

"Ms. Peck?" Jeriah looked up into the air. "No, sir. I didn't see Ms. Peck. Why?"

"I'm simply trying to understand it all, Jeriah." He placed his hand on his shoulder. "Don't blame yourself for any of this. You're good at what you do. It wasn't your fault."

"But ... 'fida checked them wheels-"

"It wasn't your fault," he repeated, looking squarely into his eyes.

The man nodded, but hung his head.

Douglas looked around the stable, then pointed to one of the buggies. "I'll take that one. I think I'll go and spend some time with Uncle Harper. At least *he* appreciates me."

"What 'bout that fiancée a yours?"

"I can't stay with her. We aren't married yet."

He grinned. "What you waitin' for?"

"Honestly, I don't know."

Jeriah walked away to prepare the buggy.

While Douglas waited, he thought about what was said. He and Cora had agreed to postpone their wedding until things calmed down, but now that he was being sent away from his home, maybe it was time to make one of his own.

Chapter 26

"Wellesley finally give you the boot?" Harper asked, raising his eyebrows.

"I chose to leave," Douglas replied. "I won't stay with a man who blames me and my fiancée for a crime we didn't commit."

"You still work for the man. How you gonna manage that?"

"I can work at the mill and never see him. It's a big place."

Harper shook his head. "How's Miss Cora doin'?"

"She's troubled about all this, but she's still wonderful." He smiled for the first time all day.

Harper strolled across the shop to the window. "I seen her sister here few days back."

"Elise? She came here again?"

"Yep. She's a strange one. Looked upset 'bout sumthin. Reckon it was cuz a Cameron. Think she loved him. Didn't stay long. Don't know why she came." Harper craned his neck, looking through the glass and down the street. "You see the *Bonny Lass* when you came here?"

"What did you say?"

Harper left the window and perched himself atop his stool. "The *Bonny Lass*. She was docked last time I looked."

"Cora!" Douglas yelled and flew out of the woodshop.

Hopping into his buggy, he wasted no time snapping the reins. It lurched forward, jerking his body, but he didn't care.

First, he drove to the docks. The *Bonny Lass* was leaving ... *Yes, it had been here.* He knew that by the time he went to the marshal, the boat would be long gone. Turning around, he sped toward the boarding house, driving the horse as fast as it would go. He didn't bother knocking and burst through the front door. "Cora!"

She was standing before him in no time, holding Billy in her arms. Her eyebrows drew in. "What's wrong?"

He wrapped his arms around both of them, kissing them as he did so. "Thank God, you're all right."

"Your heart's beatin' plum outta your chest!" She placed her palm against him. "Why wouldn't we be all right?"

He cupped his hand over the top of Billy's head. "The *Bonny Lass*. She was docked. I don't know how long she was here, but Harper told me he saw her. I went to see for myself and she was heading downriver."

Cora's face went ashen. "Reckon Giles was lookin' for me?"

"I don't know. He doesn't know you're in Memphis." He pulled her even closer and kissed her forehead. "If he'd seen you ..."

She placed her fingers to his lips. "He didn't. Billy an me are fine."

They turned to the sound of Mrs. Moss tapping her way across the floor. "Come sit, Douglas. You don't sound well."

"I'm not," he said, and decided to take her up on her suggestion. He placed his head in his hands. "If anything had happened to-"

"Douglas," Cora whispered, sitting beside him. "Nothin's gonna happen to us." She rested her head on his shoulder. Billy wiggled in her grasp, kicking his feet.

"May I hold him?" he asked, holding out his hands.

"Course."

He took Billy into his arms and stood, then walked back and forth across the floor, speaking softly to him. "I'll protect you," he whispered and kissed Billy's cheek. He then turned and looked intently at Cora. "Let's get married."

"I already said, *yes,* Douglas."

"I know you did. But I want to get married *now.*"

"*Right* now?" Cora's eyes popped open wide.

He gazed down at Billy, whose tiny eyes looked up at him. "What do you think?"

Billy gurgled.

He cocked his head and grinned at Cora. "Billy thinks it's a good idea."

"But ... we'll hafta get a preacher. And ... where we gonna do it?"

She was right to ask questions. His sense of urgency clouded his mind. "Perhaps today won't be a possibility. We'll need to have some preparation." He sat beside her and began thinking aloud. "I know of a preacher at my mother's church who can perform the ceremony, but I don't think we should marry in the church. We shouldn't draw any attention to you. It's too dangerous."

"What 'bout in the garden where you asked me to marry you?"

He shook his head. "Father and I had words. I left home, and as I was leaving he told me that he didn't want me to come back."

"That ain't right."

"Why don't you marry in the yard behind the boarding house?" Daisy asked, entering the room.

Cora perked up. "The gardens here are lovely. If your pa don't want you there, then I don't wanna be there neither. And I reckon I don't need a church weddin'. I ain't never been in a real church. Mrs. Moss learned me everything I know 'bout the Bible."

"Yes, I did," Mrs. Moss chimed in. "And Cora was a fine pupil."

He took Cora's hand and rubbed it tenderly with his thumb. "I'd like my mother to be here. It's important, and I believe she'd want to be present."

"Then you need to ask her," Cora said.

He lifted her hand to his lips and kissed it, gazing deeply into her eyes. "I love you, Cora, and Billy, too. We'll be the family I always wanted." He paused, then turned his attention to Mrs. Moss. "Ma'am, I want you to live with us, too. You'll always be part of our family."

Mrs. Moss gasped. "Mr. Denton," she said formally, "I always knew you were a good man. But why would you want to be burdened with an old blind woman?"

"Because you're not just any *old blind* woman. You're Cora's mother and you belong with us."

Mrs. Moss wiped a tear from her eye. "So. Where will we be living?"

Cora giggled. "Didn't take her long to decide she's not a burden."

Mrs. Moss laughed with her.

"For now," Douglas said. "I don't know where we'll live. I may have to stay here with you until I get my finances in order. That is ... if Miss Daisy doesn't mind."

"Mind?" Daisy raised her hands and clasped them to her breast. "Of course, I won't mind!" She then lowered her voice and leaned in toward him. "It will cost more. But I'm sure you understand."

"Of course," Douglas said.

Daisy nodded toward him and the deal was made, even though he had no idea just how much more she would charge them.

Knowing he had a lot to attend to, he handed Billy to Cora and gave her a quick peck on the lips. "I'll return this evening. Hopefully Father will be out and I can speak to Mother. In the meantime, keep the doors locked. I had no difficulty coming in today, and if I could so easily barge in, anyone could."

Cora nodded, affirming that she understood just how serious he was.

After kissing Billy's cheek, he hurried out the door.

* * *

Cora rose from the sofa and walked toward her room. "I need to feed Billy," she said, then looked directly at Mrs. Moss. "Mrs. Moss, will you come to my room while I nurse him? I need to talk to you."

"Of course, dear."

Cora positioned herself in her favorite chair, opened the front of her dress, and nestled Billy into the crook of her arm. She enjoyed this time with him. Since Mrs. Moss couldn't see, she was not displaying herself, and having her in the room was no intrusion to her privacy or modesty.

Mrs. Moss smiled. "He's hungry." She felt her way across the room and sat in *her* favorite chair.

"Yep." She let out a long, loud sigh.

"What is it, dear? What's troubling you?"

Muffin's bell jingled and she jumped into Mrs. Moss's lap.

"Douglas," Cora said.

"Douglas? Why, dear? He loves you. He is out now making the arrangements to marry you. What can be wrong?" She stroked the cat while vacantly staring toward Cora.

Cora's chin quivered, then the tears came. "He's too good for me!"

Billy popped off her breast like a cork being released from a bottle. His tiny face wrinkled up and he let out a loud bawl.

"Now Cora, you've frightened Billy," Mrs. Moss said, scolding her with a loving voice.

She sniffled. "I didn't mean to. But I'm ruinin' his life. Since he met me, he's had to bury my husband *and* his brother. And now, his pa's done thrown him out!"

Billy cried even harder, so she lifted him onto her shoulder and patted his back, trying to soothe him.

"None of that was your fault, Cora. Now, stop crying, or Billy won't get a proper meal."

"An ... an what if Giles comes after me? What if he tries to hurt Douglas? Why can't nothin' ever go right for me?" She wiped her nose on Billy's bunting and sniffled again.

"Cora Craighead!" Mrs. Moss raised her voice in a way that startled her. "Shame on you! God has given you the opportunity to have a happy life with a man who loves you. Douglas is willing to do whatever he has to in order to take care of you and Billy. You should be grateful. I believe God brought you together. That child in your arms is a precious gift and you've met a man who realizes that. Don't throw it all away by feeling sorry for yourself!"

"Dang, Mrs. Moss," she said, through her tears. "I don't feel sorry for *myself*. I feel sorry for Douglas."

Mrs. Moss folded her hands on top of the cat. "He doesn't want your pity, child. He wants your love." Mrs. Moss was much calmer, and the gentle way in which she spoke her final words brought Cora's tears to an abrupt halt.

"I *do* love him." Her chest shook as she tried to regain her composure. As she calmed, so did Billy.

"Good girl," Mrs. Moss said. "No more tears, now. If you'll excuse me, I have to tend to private matters." She stood and tapped her way out of the room and out the back door.

Did Mrs. Moss truly have to use the facilities or did she leave the room to give her time to think? Whatever it was, she was glad to be alone. She mulled over everything Mrs. Moss had said and the words that stayed in her mind were the final words; *He doesn't want your pity, he wants your love.*

She thought about the first time she'd looked into his chocolate brown eyes and the feeling she had when his arms were around her, carrying her to the boat. It was as if she knew at that very moment that he would be something more to her than a casual stranger that passed through her life for a moment. He was so much more. He was the man she believed was created for her and her alone. Now, if she could simply allow herself to *deserve* him.

"Billy," she whispered, stroking his cheek with her finger, "you're gonna have a new pa. And I promise you ... I aim to make sure nothin' bad happens to this one."

* * *

"Yessa, Mista Denton," Jeriah said, while taking the reins from Douglas. "Your daddy been gone least an hour."

"Good," Douglas replied, jumping down from the buggy. "I won't be staying long. You might as well leave the horse with the buggy."

"Yessa." Jeriah scratched his head and pointed toward the front lawn. "Mista Denton? Miss Elise been lookin' for you."

"Elise? Why?"

Jeriah shrugged. "Just said she needs to see you."

He thanked him, then walked from the stable toward the front entrance of the house. He couldn't imagine what Elise Peck wanted from him. And he knew he had no interest in seeing her. Though he'd considered her a friend for a very long time, he knew that he couldn't trust her ... especially now.

He didn't bother knocking. It had been his home for much too long to start that ritual.

He stopped at the sound of women's voices. They spoke too low for him to make out any of the conversation. Chiding himself for being overly suspicious, he hurried on down the hallway to the kitchen.

"Douglas!" Elise cried out, then raced to his side and encircled him with her arms. "Your mother was just telling me that your father made you leave."

With a sideways glance, he indicated to Elise that he didn't appreciate her affections. She released him immediately.

"I chose to leave," he said, coldly.

She tilted her head and pouted. "Why are you angry with me? Did I do something to upset you?"

He thought of the many things that he could say, but didn't want to upset his mother. "Forgive me. I simply don't feel it's proper for you to hold me. Did you forget that I'm engaged to your sister?"

"I certainly did not forget. But, Douglas, as long as we've known each other, I didn't feel a compassionate hug would be out of line. You and I have gone through a horrid ordeal. I know that you and Cameron weren't close, but he was your brother. And you know how I felt about him."

"Douglas," Mary said. "Come have a seat so we can talk."

He gave his mother a kiss on the cheek before sitting.

She lovingly patted his hand. "That's better."

Elise wasted no time and sat beside her.

"Douglas," Mary said. "I'm happy that you came by. Your father has calmed down. You're welcome to come home."

Elise flashed a large grin. He wondered why *she* was so happy about the news.

"I don't believe I want to come home. He's made it clear how he feels about me. I'll continue working at the mill, but I don't want to live here."

His mother's face contorted and her chin quivered. "But the house is so large. It's much too empty with you and Cameron both gone."

"Mother, you couldn't expect me to stay here forever. I have my own life to live." Though he would have preferred not speaking about this in front of Elise, he pushed on. "Cora and I are proceeding with our wedding. We want to keep it as simple and quiet as possible. Daisy has offered the use of her garden, and Cora and I both feel it's a fine idea. I'll speak to Reverend Rogers about performing the rites. I'd like you to be there."

Mary smiled, but before she could speak, Elise jumped in. "When will you marry? I simply *must* be there. She's my sister, after all."

She was overly eager, which made him even more suspicious. "If I can finalize the arrangements, we're looking at Saturday."

"*This* Saturday?" Elise asked, leaning in. Her eyes were opened wide and she bit her lip nervously.

"Yes," he replied. "But please ... don't tell anyone. Not even your mother. I want to do this quietly."

Elise brushed her hair back from the side of her face, exposing what appeared to be a faint bruise. "Though I think you're being silly, I'll keep it to myself."

He took her chin in his hand, and turned her face into the light. "Elise? What happened to your face?"

She moved her hair to cover it. "I ... tripped. Fell and hit myself on the side of a chair. You know me—I can be clumsy."

Yes, he knew her well. And she was lying to him.

"You should be more careful," he said, releasing her.

"Douglas," Mary said, twisting a strand of hair around her finger. "Please reconsider coming home. There's plenty of room for you, and Cora, too."

"And Billy and Mrs. Moss?" he asked.

Mary hesitated. "Of ... of course. All of them."

"I'll think about it," he said, rising.

Elise stood as well. "You're not leaving already, are you?"

"Yes, Elise. I have many things to tend to." He looked at his mother, who continued twisting her hair so tightly that her finger was turning white. "Elise," he said with as much courtesy as he could muster. "Would you mind giving Mother and me a few minutes alone?"

Elise hesitated, but then nodded and walked out of the room.

He pulled a chair closely to his mother. Taking her hand, he made her unwind the strand of hair. "Mother, I know something is troubling you. Please talk to me."

She looked toward the doorway, craning her neck.

"It's all right, Mother. Elise has gone down the hallway."

"Oh, Douglas," she said, gripping his arm. "There's so much I need to tell you."

Her entire body trembled through her fingertips. "I'm listening."

Her head dropped and she shook it back and forth. "Lena." She stopped and her breathing became rapid. "Lena ..." She raised her head and stared into his eyes. "Don't trust her."

"Why? We all know about Elise and how she passed her off as her own. What more has she done?"

Mary began to cry. "I never knew about Elise. I was her best friend and she didn't tell me. When she left the city, she was heavy with child, and when she returned, she came to me with Elise in her arms. How would I have known it wasn't the child she bore?"

"Of course you wouldn't know. No one knew."

"But ... I was her friend." She stared at him, looking like a lost child with tears trickling down her cheek.

He wiped them with his fingertips. "Mother, what more do you want to tell me?"

"Don't blame Elise. She loved Cameron. I *know* she did. And ... Lena expected them to marry. Lena was angry. She said I owed it to her."

"So, that was what she said you owed her? To have Elise marry Cameron? What would cause her to believe you owed her a guarantee of her daughter's future?"

"Because ..." She began to sob and her words turned into unrecognizable mumbling.

"Mother?" He pulled her into his arms and gently stroked her hair. "It's all right. You don't have to tell me now."

Her sobs grew louder and louder.

Elise appeared in the doorway and stared at Mary.

He waved her away, hoping that she would understand that he needed more time with his mother. However, she continued on into the kitchen and showed very little regard for Mary's distress.

"So ... what time on Saturday?" Elise asked.

How could she be so unfeeling? Though he hadn't confirmed a time with Cora, he quickly calculated what he hoped would do. "We'll plan for one o'clock." He stared into her eyes. "Don't tell a soul." He enunciated every word.

She shook her head. "I won't. Thank you, Douglas. Everything is going to be fine. I'll see to it." Placing her other hand on Mary's head, she sighed. "Your mother needs rest. I can stay with her."

Perhaps he'd misread her. "Will that be all right with you, Mother?"

Mary didn't speak, but took hold of Elise's arm and nodded.

"You see," Elise said. "I'll take care of everything."

He nodded, then kissed his mother and walked away. *What did she mean by that?* His stomach knotted. Though his mother cast no blame on Elise, he still believed she was involved. He couldn't shake the memory of Elise and her mother rushing up the steps of the house, just after Cameron and Vivian rode away in the carriage. He had no doubt that they were to blame for their deaths.

Jeriah grinned at him as he handed him the reins. "You was right. You din't stay long."

"Long enough. Thank you, Jeriah." He pulled on the reins, turned the horse around, and headed out from the stable. It was time to have a talk with Marshal Underwood.

* * *

"How is it you're able to set yourself in the middle of these situations?" Marshal Underwood asked. He rubbed his chin and stared at Douglas.

"I'd like to know that myself," he replied. "I seem to attract trouble."

Marshal Underwood scratched his head. "Seems those twin girls are in the middle of all of it from what you've told me. And ... Mrs. Peck? You sure she took the girl without the consent of the daddy?"

"Yes. Elise had no idea that the Pecks weren't her true parents. But that happened so long ago, it's not the real issue now. What concerns me is that I believe they had something to do with the carriage *accident*."

"And your fiancée seen them acting suspiciously that day along with you. Ain't that what you're tellin' me?"

Douglas nodded. He'd tried to piece everything together for the marshal, hoping that telling him about it would somehow make it clear to both of them.

"And now, you're worried that this other man, *Giles*, wants to harm your fiancée? The widow of that boat captain, O'Brien." The marshal took a seat and crossed his arms over his chest.

"Yes. I'm certain he was the one who led the hanging."
He doesn't believe me.

Marshal Underwood shook his finger at him. "But you didn't *see* the hangin'. So, how can you be sure?"

Douglas sat down hard in a chair across from the marshal and placed his head in his hands. Slowly, he raised it and looked at him. "I feel it ... in here." He made a fist and tapped it against his chest. "I know I have no proof, but I'm afraid for Cora." A lump rose in his throat as the marshal studied him. "Marshal, isn't there anything we can do?"

The marshal leaned back in his chair and crossed one leg over the other. "After the hangin', I sent a man after the boat. All I can say is *that's one fast boat.*" He scratched his head. "Never did catch up with it. Fact is, he wasn't sure he was goin' the right direction. Mississippi is a big river. If a man wants to hide, he can do it ... even in a steamboat."

"So, why didn't her husband hide?"

"Maybe he was tired a runnin'. And ... maybe he did it for her."

"Gave his life to save her and the baby?"

"Wouldn't *you*?" Marshal Underwood uncrossed his legs and leaned forward, staring into his eyes.

"Yes, I would," he whispered. His heart fluttered. *I know I would ...*

The marshal leaned back again. "You tell that uncle of yours that if he sees the *Bonny Lass* again, to let me know right away. I'd like to talk to Marcus Giles. Feel him out."

Douglas wanted to do much more than that to Marcus Giles. Giles wanted Cora, and the thought of him trying to do anything to her set him reeling. "If the *Bonny Lass* returns, wouldn't it rightfully belong to Cora?" he asked, rising to his feet.

Marshal Underwood nodded. "Reckon it would. If they was legally married, then anything rightfully titled to O'Brien would belong to her."

"Then perhaps you'll need to do more than *talk* to Marcus Giles."

"Reckon so," Marshall Underwood said with a grin.

"As for Cameron and Vivian," Douglas said, feeling the issue wasn't resolved. "Is there anything else we can do?"

"Your folks insist it was an accident. All you have to indicate otherwise is a feeling and suspicion. There ain't much I can do when folks don't want to press charges. 'Sides, who would they press charges against?"

"Lena Peck," Douglas muttered. But that was never going to happen.

Chapter 27

"I'm nervous, Mrs. Moss," Cora said as she primped her hair and smoothed her dress.

"Don't be, Cora," Mrs. Moss said. "He loves you and will make a fine husband."

She couldn't believe that it was all coming together so easily. Douglas had arranged everything, and in less than thirty minutes they would exchange vows beneath a tall oak tree in the garden behind the boarding house. The weather was perfect; a bright shining sun and no rain.

A soft rap on the door turned her head.

"May I come in?" Elise asked with a timid smile.

Cora wasn't sure it was a good idea that Douglas told Elise about the wedding, but since she was her sister, she believed that he did it with her best interest in mind. "Course you can." She motioned Elise into the room.

"Mrs. Wellesley told me you were getting ready," Elise said, then crossed the room to her and kissed her on the cheek. "She's happy for you and Douglas. So am I."

"Thank you." Even though Cora said the words, she didn't feel them. There was something about Elise that made her uneasy, causing her stomach to flutter. She turned away and gazed into the standing mirror.

She wore white, as Douglas requested, though it seemed a bit inappropriate. Understanding that white was a symbol of purity, it didn't feel right. He told her they were starting over and in his eyes she was pure, but Billy was proof that it was not so.

Elise giggled nervously. "I believe I'd look about the same in that dress." She sniffled. "I suppose I'll never know."

Cora turned to her and took her hand. "You'll get married someday, Elise. It'll happen when you least expect it. Love just kind a sneaks up on you sometimes."

Elise looked down and away from her. A tug on Cora's heart proved she still had feelings for her sister, even without trust. She pitied her.

Another knock on the door, and this time it was Toby. "Miss Cora?" He wrinkled his nose. "A weddin' gift just came."

She grinned. Getting presents was one of her favorite things. "Can you bring it to me?"

"Well ... all right." Toby walked away, then returned, pulling a nervous-looking young colored girl behind him. "Says her name be Sophie."

"Someone gave us a slave?"

Elise clasped her hands together and laughed. "Surprise!"

"Why you givin' us a slave? We don't need no slaves."

"She's a wet nurse." Elise grinned from ear-to-ear.

"A what?" She couldn't be more dumbfounded.

Elise took her by the arm and sat her down on the edge of the bed. Cora looked at Mrs. Moss who was shaking her head from side-to-side.

"A *wet* nurse." Elise spoke down to her as though *she* were a child. "To feed Billy so that you won't have to."

Cora glanced at Sophie, who nodded and cupped her hand over her breast. She appeared to be barely old enough to have had a child. "You have a baby of your own?"

"No'm," Sophie said. "They took my baby. Say it died. Then Ms. Peck found babies for me to feed. Been heppin' feed babies for a long time, now."

Elise beamed. "Mother thought she'd be the perfect gift. Aren't you pleased?"

"But ..." Cora hesitated, not wanting to upset her sister. "I like feedin' Billy."

Sophie hung her head and stood in the doorway, rubbing her hand over her breast. "I needs to feed a baby soon. It hurts when I don't."

"Cora," Elise said firmly. "Wouldn't you rather spend time with your husband tonight, than have your entire wedding night used up by tending Billy?"

She had to admit that the idea of having all night with Douglas without the distraction of a baby was very appealing. However, she understood why Sophie was uncomfortable. If she didn't nurse Billy for a long period of time she, too, would be in pain.

Elise's bottom lip protruded. "You don't like our gift."

"No ... it was real nice of you. But ..."

"Tell you what," Elise said. "If you decide you don't want to keep her, give her back to Mother. But I know you'll find her very useful. Just look at her. Have you ever seen a sweeter face?"

The compliment made Sophie smile and Cora was instantly reminded of Bessie. Oh, how she missed her. She prayed she was well.

"All right," she said. "I'll keep her. Though I don't know where she'll sleep. Douglas an I plan to live here until we decide what we're gonna do. He's worried 'bout his ma and we may go live with her. Just for a while."

Elise jumped from the bed. "Good! As for where she'll sleep—for tonight—you don't have to worry about that. She can sleep in your bed close to Billy. You and Douglas will be staying at the Riverside Hotel, won't you?"

"How'd you know 'bout that?" No one was supposed to know.

Toby stood in the doorway. His eyes popped open wide, then he fled down the hall.

Elise laughed. "Little ears sometimes have very big mouths."

Cora wrinkled her brow. "That sounds kind a strange, but I know what you mean."

"Are you ready?" Mary Wellesley asked, peeking into the room.

Elise extended her hand to Cora and helped lift her from the bed. "Yes, she most certainly is."

"You're beautiful, Cora. Your hair looks lovely *up*," Mary said, dabbing at the corner of her eye with a handkerchief.

"I just hope Douglas likes it. Thank you for sayin' so." She gazed one last time in the mirror and touched her hand to the top of her head for one, final primp.

Mary gave her a quick embrace, then excused herself saying that she needed to go and take a seat.

Even though the wedding was simple and only a handful of witnesses would be present, Cora could not stop the pounding of her heart. When she'd married William it wasn't her choice and memories of that day weren't fully clear. But this time, she wanted to remember everything. Every sight, smell, and sound. And more than anything, she wanted to remember the look in Douglas's eyes when she walked toward him.

As she passed the kitchen, she inhaled deeply. Rosie had prepared a chicken dinner for all of their guests. The scent of curry filled her nostrils. It was something she'd passed on to Rosie, and she'd cooked with the spice ever since.

Loaves of cooling bread lined the countertop. Some were glazed with a mixture of sugar and milk, while others had been brushed with fresh butter. She smiled, knowing how much Douglas would enjoy the bread.

Douglas ... Just thinking of him made her heart beat faster. She would finally be able to give herself to him fully. Her mouth became dry and her palms began to sweat as she stepped out the back door and into the garden.

Mrs. Moss was already seated and Muffin was perched on her lap. Seeing the cat in attendance at her wedding made her giggle. She quickly covered her mouth, not wanting anyone to see her behave so.

"Take these, Cora," Daisy said, handing her a bouquet of red roses.

Tears welled in Cora's eyes as she took the flowers and breathed in their fresh scent. "Thank you, Daisy." She managed somehow to speak, though the words barely passed her lips.

With Toby's help, Daisy had set out chairs in a half-moon, facing the enormous live oak. Its branches stretched out high into the sky and shaded them from the heat of the sun.

Cora's gaze passed from one seat to the next, smiling at each of their guests as their eyes met. Her eyes lingered on Harper. He seemed out of place not being atop his whittling stool, but he was dressed in a fine, black suit and looked very handsome. His face lit up with a grin and she lifted her brows when he winked at her.

Mary sat in the center, nervously wringing her hands. She nodded at Cora, then tilted her head to the side. Cora's eyes moved to the man sitting beside her. "Mr. Wellesley?" she muttered under her breath, astonished that he was here.

Rosie took a well-deserved break from the kitchen, and she and Toby were there, *seated,* and a welcome part of the audience. Daisy bustled to the seat beside them after handing Cora the bouquet.

Though it was awkward for her, Cora allowed Sophie to tend Billy during the ceremony. It was strange thinking of him suckling another woman's breasts, but Sophie was gentle with him and would tend him well. Maybe Elise's gift wasn't so bad.

On the far end, Elise sat tall and proud, watching and waiting ...

But the most important person there—aside from the preacher—was Douglas himself. When Cora finally shifted her eyes from their guests to him, her breath hitched.

The suit he wore today was deep gray. Wanting to keep things simple, he wore no hat, just as she chose not to wear a veil. He told her once that it was how he always wanted to live his life, and that was what she would give him. Simplicity in the form of undying love and devotion.

She managed to keep her feet going forward and took one step at a time toward the man of her dreams. Had Jane Eyre felt this way? Suddenly, Cora was the heroine in her favorite book, living a happily-ever-after.

The minister nodded to her and she stood beside Douglas, who took her hand and smiled. His heavy breathing caused his chest to noticeably rise and fall.

He must be as nervous as I am.

Then, in a gesture of pure love, Douglas raised her hand to his lips and kissed it. "I love you," he whispered.

Once again, her tears began to pool. "I love you, too," she said, and squeezed his hand.

The minister opened the Bible and read. "Therefore, a man leaves his father and mother and cleaves to his wife, and they become one flesh." He paused, nodded at her, then at Douglas before proceeding.

She turned and looked up into Douglas's eyes. Then, everything the minister said went unheard. Her thoughts took over. She became lost in his eyes and wanted more than anything to be lost in his arms. She vowed her love to him and savored the sound of his deep voice pledging to honor and keep her. And as he slipped a gold band onto her finger, she thought she would burst. Happiness overwhelmed her.

"You may kiss your bride," the preacher said, and Douglas wasted no time.

He placed his hands on the side of her face, and covered her lips with his own. She wanted more. With Douglas, she would always want more ...

He must have felt the same, because even after he stopped kissing her, his hands remained on her face and his eyes locked with hers. His warm breath drifted across her skin.

"Douglas," she rasped.

"Yes, Cora?" He grinned broadly.

She swallowed the lump in her throat, then returned his grin. "We best see to our guests."

And as if they'd heard her, their friends and family surrounded them, offering congratulations and hugs. She took Billy from Sophie. He was too little to remember any of this, but it was important to have him be a part of this meaningful day.

"Wanna hold your son?" Cora asked Douglas, who took him into his arms and kissed his cheek.

"One day soon, you'll call me *Daddy*," he said to him, and Billy happily wiggled.

* * *

Douglas couldn't have been more shocked when Arthur Wellesley arrived with his mother. Why was the father who never gave him a second thought at his wedding?

Douglas hadn't spoken to him, but as the man approached, he couldn't be rude.

"Congratulations, Douglas," Arthur said, extending his hand.

Cora clutched his arm.

"Thank you, Father," he managed to say while shaking his hand, and Cora added a *thank you* of her own.

Arthur looked downward, then pulled an envelope from inside his jacket pocket. "This is for the two of you." He hesitated for a moment before handing him the envelope. "I hope you'll forgive me for my behavior. As you know, losing Cameron has not been easy for me."

Douglas nodded. "I *do* understand. It's not been easy for any of us, but I know how much he meant to you."

Arthur cleared his throat, then pulled a handkerchief from his lapel pocket and dabbed at his eyes. "Your mother and I would like you to come home. All of you." He directed his final comment toward Cora and Billy. "Whenever you're ready."

"Thank you, sir," Cora said. "Douglas an I are glad you came today."

His mother had been standing silently at Arthur's side, but leaned in and kissed Cora on the cheek. "I know you'll be very happy." She stroked Billy's face with her finger. "He's a sweet baby."

"A good baby, too," Cora said.

Arthur shook his head. "It's been a very long time since we had a baby in the house." After taking a large breath, he took Mary by the arm. "We should be going."

His mother stepped away from his father, wrapped her arms around him, and pulled him into a warm embrace. "I'm so happy for you, Douglas." With a final squeeze, she backed away, then they left.

Cora stood with him, watching them walk away. "I'm glad your pa came."

Douglas wasn't convinced that Arthur Wellesley had changed his opinion of them and wasn't ready to let his guard down and trust him again. After years of disapproval and no attention whatsoever, it was hard to believe Arthur's words. However, he wasn't about to let any suspicions or ill feelings interfere with his wedding day.

Picking Cora up off her feet, with Billy between them, Douglas kissed her sweetly. "I'm glad, too."

As he set her down again, she scanned the room. "You seen Elise?"

"No. Not since the ceremony."

Uncle Harper appeared over his shoulder. "Said she was sick. Left while back."

"Oh." Cora said. "That's odd. Before the weddin', she seemed fine."

Elise most likely left because she was still jealous of Cora, so Douglas dismissed her absence without much thought. Instead, he focused on the guests remaining and looked forward to the night to come.

"Uncle Harper," he said, patting him on the back, "I've never seen you look finer."

Harper grinned. "I clean up good."

"Yes, you do, *Uncle* Harper," Cora said with a smile. "Wish Mrs. Moss could see you. She might take a fancy to you."

Harper chuckled, then excused himself to go and get more food.

"Speaking of Mrs. Moss," Cora said, "I best check on her. I'll see if she'll take Billy for a spell, so we can eat."

"I like that idea." Douglas followed her to the sitting room where they found Mrs. Moss in her favorite chair. She gladly took Billy, and even though Sophie was close by and ready to *do her duty*, Billy was content for the time being.

They ate their fill of Rosie's fine food, then, after Cora nursed Billy one final time, they hopped into Douglas's buggy and were on their way to the Riverside Motel.

She scooted in close to his body, then nuzzled her head into his shoulder.

"Are you happy?" he asked softly.

"Happy ain't a good enough word." She raised her head and smiled.

"Do you have another word in mind?"

She giggled and bit her lip. "Dang ..." She burrowed into him once again.

He chuckled and his heart thumped with anticipation.

* * *

Their room faced the river. Douglas had chosen it for her, knowing how much she loved the Mississippi. They had talked many times about her life on the river and each time she spoke of it, her eyes lit up with wonderful memories. Even the sad memories of her father were outweighed by the happy memories of skipping stones and wading up to her knees in the cool water.

He turned his head to look at her.

God, she's beautiful ...

He'd never quite understood what first attracted him to her, but he'd accepted the fact a long time ago that she was something special. She was the woman he'd waited for, and soon he would finally finish what he'd started. As the minister said, *they become one flesh.*

His body trembled at the thought. It was a thought he had to momentarily dismiss. Becoming slightly uncomfortable, he shifted in the buggy seat.

As he pulled up to the hotel, a steward approached them. "Welcome to the Riverside," he said and took the reins from Douglas. "I'll see to your horse and buggy."

Douglas placed a coin in the man's palm. "Thank you." After the steward tucked the coin into his pocket and focused on the horse, Douglas helped Cora step down.

They walked into the common room of the motel and moved toward the inn keeper, who was standing behind the front desk. Douglas had to blink twice, not believing who he was seeing. She stood beside the desk as if she'd been waiting for them.

"Mrs. Peck?" he asked. "What are you doing here?"

She lifted her head and crossed her arms. "You didn't invite me to the wedding. I need to speak with you, Douglas."

Cora looked at him, wide-eyed with fear.

He patted her hand, then asked the inn keeper for their room key. Placing it into her palm, he told her to go there and wait for him, promising to be there soon.

"Douglas?" Cora whispered, and pulled him close.

He caressed her face. "I'll be right there. Don't worry. I'll see what she wants, then we'll have no further interruptions." He sealed his words with a tender kiss.

Cora looked at the key in her hand, then nodded slowly. "I'll be waitin'." She walked away and he returned his attention to Lena Peck.

She had turned her back on them while he spoke to Cora, and he assumed she was trying to be polite; giving them time. But now, she looked directly at him and took his arm.

"Why are you here?" he asked, trying not to be completely cold. He never should have trusted Elise to keep things from her mother and was angry with himself for believing he could.

"Douglas," she said, leading him across the room to a sitting area. "I'm worried about your mother."

"Mrs. Peck," he took a breath, wanting to remain calm. "Can't this wait? Today is my wedding day and I don't want to keep my bride waiting."

She motioned to a couple of wooden chairs. "Please, Douglas."

Her sad eyes softened his heart, so he complied and took a seat. "Why are you concerned about Mother?"

Lena looked around the room and was slow to respond. "She's very frail. You know that she's a nervous woman. Always stressed about one thing or another."

"You're not telling me anything I don't already know." He considered being rude. All he needed to do was stand and walk away. Cora's beautiful features filled his mind.

"Douglas," Lena scolded. "I'm trying to tell you something of importance and I can see that you're not interested in the least."

"Forgive me. But you must understand. Cora ..."

"Cora!" Lena snapped. "Can't you for one moment forget her? Isn't your mother more important?"

"My mother is important, but Cora is my wife. I will never forget her." He stood. He'd had enough.

She immediately calmed and tugged on his pant leg. "Sit down, Douglas. Please?"

He sat, though he didn't know why. He presumed it was because of all the years of being taught to respect his elders. "I'll listen."

She smiled a crooked smile and her upper lip twitched. "Mary, I believe, may need to see a doctor. Her mind is ..." She held her hand to her heart. "How do I say this?" Looking upward, she inhaled deeply. "Her mind is ... slipping. There are conditions in which the brain simply stops functioning." Tilting her head and furrowing her brow, she took his hand. "She may need to be hospitalized."

He jerked his hand away. "I don't believe you. Mother is fine. Yes, she's nervous and ... *edgy*, but I believe that *you* have something to do with that."

"Me?" Lena gasped. "Douglas, if she told you that, then she is *certainly* losing her mind."

He rose to his feet. "You may think me rude, but right now I honestly don't care. My wife is waiting for me and I don't have time for you." He took a step away from her. "I don't trust you and I wish you would stay away from my mother. She would fare much better with your ab-sence."

"Oh!" Lena grunted and stood. She placed her hands on her hips, then craned her neck and peered down the hallway.

He turned to see where she was looking, then when he faced her again, she was stomping her way out the door.

He glanced apologetically at the inn keeper, adjusted his collar, then walked down the hallway to their room.

Before entering, he placed his hand in front of his mouth and exhaled. Sniffing, he determined that his breath was fresh and that he wouldn't offend his wife. He closed his eyes and steadied his breathing as he turned the door knob. Fortunately, she had left it unlocked and he was able to enter.

The Riverside motel boasted of elaborately decorated rooms, and it was frequented by important guests that traveled the Mississippi. His main concern was that the bed was clean and comfortable. He had every intention of making this night the most memorable of all for both of them.

It was early evening and the sun was nowhere close to setting. Yet, the heavy draperies had been pulled, darken-ing the room.

"Cora?" he whispered. He opened the draperies enough to allow some light into the room.

"Mmm ... hmmm," she replied, followed by a very loud breath.

Turning to her voice, he realized that she was already sitting on the bed. He couldn't help but chuckle at her eagerness.

Her wedding gown was draped over the back of a chaise beside the bed.

She truly is anxious.

His eyebrows rose, seeing that she wore only a simple white chemise and ... *no undergarments?* Though a plain white sheet covered part of her lower body, she had one leg above it that revealed bare skin from the tips of her toes all the way up to her waist.

His heart thumped.

She covered her mouth and giggled, then tapped her hand against the bed.

Wasting no time, he unfastened the buttons of his shirt. He watched the expression on her face as she followed his every move. No woman had ever seen him bare, and yet he had no difficulty shedding his clothing for her. It seemed appropriate—not to mention *exhilarating*.

Pushing his pants to the floor, he stepped out of them, then watched her even more closely as he removed his under-drawers.

Her eyes widened as he stood there before her, wearing only that which God gave him. She bit her lip coyly and again, patted the bed and scooted to one side.

He took a step toward her, but then she pointed to the drapery while batting her eyes.

"Our room faces the water. No one will see in," he said, understanding her unspoken words.

Then he thought that perhaps she was nervous about him seeing *her* this way, but that idea was instantly squelched when she swirled her tongue around her lips, then took hold of the bottom of her chemise and lifted it up and over her head.

She tossed it to the floor, giggled, then beckoned him with her long, fluttering lashes.

He took another step closer, his eyes focused on her breasts.

Hmmm ... they don't seem as full as I remember.

And then, moving his eyes lower, he stared at her perfectly smooth, flat abdomen.

"Oh, God," he muttered and froze where he stood.

He had wondered why she hadn't let her hair down before getting into bed and now it all made sense. And Lena Peck was a part of it.

She hadn't spoken since he'd entered the room and she was much too eager. Yes, he knew Cora wanted him, but she was nervous about their union. The woman on his bed showed no trepidation.

"Why don't you let your hair down?" he asked as calmly as he could.

She slowly shook her head, *no*, and tried to grab him by the arm.

When he didn't comply, she pouted and batted her eyes.

"I'd like to see it down," he persisted, then knelt beside her on the bed, suddenly uncomfortable by his nakedness.

This time, he didn't wait for her to respond and took it upon himself to pull the pins from her hair. It fell just past her shoulders.

He ran his fingers through it. "You cut it?"

She nodded, then placed her hands around his neck and tried to pull him to her.

"Cora," he was about to lose his patience. "Talk to me."

She responded by moving her hand to his chest, then slowly slid it down his body. Before it reached between his legs, he grabbed it and held it firmly.

Her eyes flew open wide and her breasts moved up and down as her breathing intensified.

"Yer hurtin' me," she said, in what he thought was a terrible attempt to sound like her sister.

His heart pounded and his palms began to sweat. He laid her back against the bed, pinning her down. "Where is my *wife*?"

"What you talkin' 'bout?" Her eyes rapidly blinked.

"I'm done with the games, Elise! What have you done with Cora?"

"I'm Cora. Don't be silly, Douglas. How could you ever think I'm Elise?"

Her body trembled beneath him. "Because you don't sound like her and you don't look like her! If you're Cora, then where is your mark?"

"Mark?" Nervously, she licked her lips. "What mark?"

"Your birthmark." He placed his hand on her abdomen. "The one you didn't want me to see ..."

She stared at him, her breathing became panting. "You're ruining everything, Douglas!" She no longer feigned an accent. "I know it's me you want!"

He jerked away from her and grabbed his clothes; earnestly throwing them on his body.

"Don't ... please," she begged, crawling across the bed on her knees. "Just look at me. I ... I know you want me. Take me and you'll realize that I'm the one you should be with. I'll be much better than she ever would, because I know what I'm doing. I know how to please you. She's simple. She doesn't know anything!"

He raised his hand to run it over his head, which caused Elise to cower and cover her face.

She thought I was going to hit her. Even in anger, he would never hit a woman.

"I love her. She knows much more about loving than you ever will. You could learn a great deal from her, but I doubt you'll get the chance in prison."

"Prison?" She grabbed the sheet and wrapped it around her body.

"Yes, prison. And I swear, if anything has happened to her ..." His hands tightened into fists, and she cowered again. "Damn it, Elise! I'm not going to hit you. Just tell me where she is!"

"I don't know!" Her shoulders shook and her chin quivered. "He didn't tell me where he was taking her."

"He? Marcus Giles?"

She nodded rapidly. "He—he took me, thinking I was her. But all I had to do was talk and he believed my story." Tears came easily to her. "He said I had to bring her, or he'd hurt me." She lifted her hand to her face.

"That's where you got the bruise, isn't it?" He paced the room, trying to figure out what to do. With every step he took, his heart doubled its speed.

"Yes. And ... he ... he *had* me!" Covering her face, she began to sob.

He couldn't tolerate seeing her this way. She'd been a friend far too long. He sat beside her on the bed, draped the sheet over her body, and put his arm around her. "Why didn't you come to me and tell me what was happening? I could have helped."

"Be ... Because Mother said this would fix everything. She told me that once you had me, you'd stay with me." She lifted her eyes and looked into his. "I would have been a good wife, Douglas."

"Your mother knew about Giles?"

Elise nodded, then wiped her nose with the sheet.

He stood. "Get dressed. I'm going to the marshal. I have to find Cora before Giles harms her."

"But ... I don't want to go to prison!" She grabbed his arm.

"Then help me! My God, Elise. How could you let your mother influence you to do this?"

"Because ... she's my mother." She wouldn't look at him, but rather looked at her hands and grasped the sheet. "She promised it would all be made right. After Cameron died, she told me she was sorry and assured me that you would marry me."

He lifted her chin, making her look at him. "Why was she sorry?"

She swallowed hard. "Because ... Cameron wasn't supposed to die. He was supposed to marry *me* ..."

Lifting the wedding gown from the chaise, he handed it to her. "Put this on. As much as I don't want to see you in it, there's nothing else for you to wear."

He assumed that Cora must be wearing the clothes that Elise had worn, then anger returned as he imagined what she must be going through. Thankful that the sun had not set, he retrieved his horse and buggy from the steward, then he and Elise raced to the marshal's office.

At one point, he thought she might try to flee, but she seemed to have crumbled and had a difficult time simply sitting upright in the buggy.

"Your mother put the snake in the carriage, didn't she?" he asked, turning his head to see her reaction.

She looked away from him, but nodded her head.

"And," he continued. "She tampered with the wheel?"

Elise jerked her head around. "What do you mean, tampered with the wheel?"

She didn't know. "Someone loosened the bolts. That's what caused it to flip on the way to the hospital." He turned his attention to the road, not wanting to have an accident of his own.

"But ..." She sniffled and started crying again. "Mother said that it was the driver's fault. That he drove the horses too fast and went off the road."

"No. The wheel came loose." Seeing her devastation, he couldn't help but feel sorry for her. "You shouldn't trust your mother."

"Vivian was supposed to die, not Cameron."

Her words instantly erased his sympathy. "So, you condoned Vivian's murder, but you're upset because your mother orchestrated the death of my brother as well?"

She placed her hands over her face and sobbed.

Another thought occurred to him. "Was it your mother's idea or yours to give us Sophie?"

Gasping for air between sobs, she looked at him. "I'd never let a baby starve. I knew that Billy would need to be nursed—once Cora was gone."

With those words, his heart hardened completely against her. He stared forward, unable to look at her any longer. "Billy needs more than a breast to suckle. He needs his mother." His words were cold, feeling no warmth for the woman sitting next to him. He decided to leave her alone and let her cry, hoping that somewhere deep within her soul she would understand the horrible crime she'd been accomplice to.

Chapter 28

Cora's head pounded. She rubbed her hand over her hair, only to find a large goose-egg on the crown of her head. "Dang, it hurts," she muttered, then sat up on the bed and looked around the room.

As things became clear, her heart tripled its speed. The last thing she remembered was turning the key in the lock of her hotel room door. And now ...

Her eyes shifted from side-to-side and her breathing labored.

My old room?

It hadn't changed much since she'd left the *Bonny Lass,* with the exception that it smelled different. Lifting one of the pillows, she pressed it to her nose. It had a heavy, musky scent.

Some man's been in my bed ...

But then she noticed something that wasn't here before —something she recognized. Her head tipped to the side as she studied the object, not believing it to be real. She lifted it from the nightstand.

The smooth wood of the carved angel rested in her hand. Taking her finger, she moved it over the wings, then brushed it across the tiny features of its face.

I wonder if you look like my ma.

There was no mistaking. It was the angel her pa carved for her when she was a little girl. The one she'd kept in a box next to her bed. The one that was missing when she'd gone home.

Giles ...

As the reality of the situation struck her, she returned the angel gently to the nightstand, jumped from the bed and raced to the door, only to find it locked.

With wild, frantic fists, she hit it hard. "Let me out!"

Stopping, she listened and waited for the sound of footsteps. Someone to rescue her.

No one came.

She kicked the door, beating it even harder. "I said, let me out!" She refused to cry. She was too angry and scared to cry. "Open the door!"

When no one answered her plea, she went to the window. She tried to open it, but it was nailed shut. The sun was still high in the sky, so she couldn't have been unconscious for long. At least her mind was clear enough to know that she needed to escape.

Lifting a chair high over her head, she was about to smash it through the window when a key clicked in the door. She remembered that sound ...

"What do you think you're doin'?" Marcus yelled and lunged for her. He wrenched the chair from her arms, slapped her hard across the face, then threw her onto the bed.

"Don't touch me!" She scooted up against the wall and drew her legs close to her body.

He snarled and took a step closer.

"Ms. O'Brien?" Bessie stood in the doorway.

"Bessie!" Cora yelled, relieved to see a friendly face.

Marcus whipped around to face Bessie. "Get outta here, nigger!" He stomped across the room, pushed Bessie so hard that she tumbled backward, then slammed the door.

Cora closed her eyes. This wasn't happening. It had to be a nightmare. Obviously, she'd fallen asleep. All she had to do was open her eyes and Douglas would be here. It was their wedding night—the night she'd dreamed of.

"Did you miss me?" Marcus asked, breathing heavily.

No ... No ... His reality terrified her and her body trembled. "Why you doin' this?"

"Cuz I can. I'm only takin' what's mine. Your pa owed me, O'Brien owed me, and I reckon *you* owe me."

"What do I owe you?"

He grunted. "You watched when O'Brien threw me over the rail. You didn't try to stop him. You should a helped me."

Her jaw tightened. "You was tryin' to have your way with me. You deserved what he done to you."

Sitting down on the edge of the bed, he opened his eyes wide then moved them up and down, taking her in. Just as he did the first time he'd seen her.

Her stomach knotted and she covered herself with her hands.

"I aim to have you," he said. "I'm right curious 'bout you. After O'Brien had you, he stopped seein' Francine. I ain't stupid. Only reason I can figger, is that you was better than Francine."

She shuddered when his fingers brushed across her cheek. "I'm a married woman. I ain't like Francine. I don't let men have me the way she does."

He ran his tongue back and forth across his bottom lip and dragged his finger down the line of her neck. "Yep. I heard this here's your weddin' night." He sniggered, then continued moving his hand, until it reached her breast.

She wasn't about to have him touch her and smacked him hard across the face. "Get away from me!"

"All right." His eyes narrowed. "You wanna make this ugly, then I'll make it ugly."

She scanned the room for a weapon, then sprang from the bed toward the table and chairs. He grabbed at her, caught the back of her skirt, and tore the fabric. "Damn you!" He dove for her.

She ducked down behind one of the chairs, then pushed it toward him, making him stumble. Standing upright, he laughed heartily. "This is a fun game, Cora. I like frisky women. Your sister wasn't nearly as much fun."

"Elise? What did you do to my sister?" Her heart raced as she tried to catch her breath.

"Everythin' I wanted to."

"How could you?"

"She was easy. Like I said—not so much fun." He rubbed his chin, as if in deep thought. "I don't know why you care. She's with that husband of yours right now. I reckon they're havin' a *real* good time."

"Douglas? But ..." Her heart seemed to stop beating.

"Douglas. Such an uppity name. You don't belong with no *Douglas*. You're more *my* type. Feisty and ... a little dirty."

"I know you're lyin'. He'd never do that. He loves me."

"Loves you?" He let out a bellow and threw his head back. "He don't love you. All he wants is all this." He waved his hands around the room. "He knows it belongs to you ... bein' that you're O'Brien's widow."

"No! He don't care 'bout the money. He has plenty!"

Taking a step closer to her, he pierced her with his eyes. "But why would he want the likes of you? You ain't nothin'. That sister of yours talks better, looks better ..." He sniffed the air. "An she even smells better. He's got what he wants in his bed right now."

"If I'm nothin', then why do *you* want me?" With every word he spoke, a little more of her heart shattered. *No ... he hasta be lyin'.*

His tongue thrust out of his mouth, wetting his lips. "Like I said ... I'm curious."

He pushed aside the table and grabbed her arms with both of his large, strong hands. "You knee me like you did before and I'll hurt you."

Moving one hand to her hair, he clinched a fistful, jerked her head back and covered her mouth with his. When he stopped, he smacked his lips together. "You taste sweet. I like it."

He pulled her body tight against his and kissed her again. She struggled in his arms, but he was too strong for her.

"Please," she whispered. "Don't do this, Mr. Giles."

"Mister?" he laughed. "All formal now?" He moved his mouth to her ear. "You'll be *singin'* my name soon. I'm gonna do things to you O'Brien never dreamed of."

A familiar nausea crept into her belly. She closed her eyes. *Please God ... don't let this happen...*

Dragging her reluctant body across the room, he flung her onto the bed. "Don't look so sad, Cora," he rasped. "You might enjoy this."

Defensively, she curled into a ball. She wasn't about to willingly let him take her. He moved atop her, forcing her body to unfold as he lay down upon her. Before she could react, his mouth was on hers again, and she struggled for air as he intensified the kiss.

She thought of her life on the river—skipping stones and wading in the cool water. Then she envisioned Douglas and their first kiss at the cemetery in the rain. "Douglas ..." She mindlessly whispered his name.

Marcus lifted his head. "Call me whatever you want." He snickered, then bent down and ran his tongue along her neck.

His hands were on her just as they'd been so long ago when William had saved her. But William was dead and Douglas was with Elise.

"These are nicer than your sister's," he said, and slid his hand down the front of her dress.

"Don't touch me!" She squirmed beneath him. Though he had her pinned, one hand was free, so she hit him in the face as hard as she could.

His eyes blazed and he slapped her harder than ever. She wrestled with him—bit, scratched, and hit—anything she could do to save herself. In all the commotion, he'd paid no mind to the key clicking in the lock. Her heart fluttered, hoping that her prayer was answered.

"Marcus!"

He turned his head. Cora's heart leapt. *Francine ...*

"Get off of her!" Francine demanded and moved into the room.

Marcus scowled. "Get outta here, Francine!"

Bessie stood behind Francine, timidly peeking over her shoulder. *She must a brought her here.*

"No!" Francine yelled. She and Bessie were both standing just inside the door, now.

Marcus raised his body enough to look at Francine, but held Cora firmly. "I said, get outta here, you lousy whore!"

Francine's hand shook as she lifted it from her side. In her grasp was a pistol pointed at Marcus.

He laughed. "What you gonna do? Shoot me?"

"*Oui*," Francine replied, then placed her other hand on the gun, attempting to steady it with both hands together.

Marcus stood from the bed, but before he moved away from Cora he smacked her one more time. "Don't move," he snarled and pointed his finger in her face.

He returned his attention to Francine. "Put that thing away before you hurt yourself."

"No. I won't. I don't want you to hurt Cora. Come to my room—I'll give you what you want." Francine lifted her chin in the air, feigning confidence, but her quivering body gave her away.

As quiet as she could, Cora sat upright and swung her legs over the side of the bed.

"What I want?" Marcus asked, stepping closer to Francine and the shaking pistol. "What I want is layin' on that bed. I've had all I want a you."

Bessie cowered further away, stepping back out of the doorway.

Marcus pointed at her. "And that one, too. I'm sick a all a you."

Marcus had his way with her sister *and* her friends?

But where was everyone else? The passengers and the crew? Someone had to be running the boat.

"Get out and let me finish my business!" Marcus yelled at Francine.

Francine's face wrinkled into a frightened grimace.

She ain't gonna do it ...

This would end horribly if Cora didn't do something. So before Marcus had the opportunity to take the gun from Francine's hand, Cora jumped in front of him and took it herself.

She fell to the floor with the pistol secured in her palm. But before she could regain her composure and stand, he came down hard on her back and grabbed for it.

"Give me the gun!" He took a handful of her hair and yanked it with brutal force.

Ignoring the pain, she twisted beneath him and with every bit of strength she had, brought the gun around with her. The hard metal piece pressed against his chest and she pulled the trigger.

The shot rang through the air. Bessie screamed and dropped to her knees, covering her ears. Francine stood a short distance away, panting and crying with her hand clasped to her mouth. She watched with wide eyes as Cora pushed Marcus off of her, then dropped the gun on the floor. As dark, red blood drained from his body, it covered Cora and dampened the floor.

Horrified, Cora rested her hands across her body, then was unable to move any further. The undeniable scent of fresh blood filled her nose. She lay there trying to catch her breath, numbly staring at the carved angel perched beside the bed, until her eyes filled with tears.

When she finally managed to lift her hands, they trembled—soaked in foul, sticky blood. Francine and Bessie hovered over her, but she couldn't understand their words. Her head throbbed and her heart pounded.

I killed a man ...

* * *

When Douglas stepped through the door of Marshal Underwood's office, the man jumped to his feet. With only a few details out of his mouth, he persuaded the marshal to get help and return with him to the docks. Good fortune was on his side. Not only did they have several hours of daylight remaining, but the *Natchez* was docked and Captain Thomas Leathers was ready to take her downriver.

"How can you be sure he'd take her *down*river?" Marshal Underwood asked him.

"Because it's faster than going *up*river. He would want to get away as quickly as possible."

The marshal agreed with his logic and after explaining their ordeal to Captain Leathers, the *Natchez* was fired up and racing down the Mississippi.

She was about the same size as the *Bonny Lass*, but known to be one of the fastest vessels on the river.

"Yessir," Captain Leathers boasted. "She's fast." He puffed out his chest. "And helping you will get her noticed for something even greater. A deed like this will lend itself to an article in all of the papers."

"All I care about is getting to my wife as quickly as possible," Douglas said.

"Of course. But you can't fault me for wanting to do something that will get me more passengers." Leathers jiggled his brows and grinned.

Douglas chose to ignore the man. As long as his boat proved itself, that was all that mattered. Cora needed him.

Even though he despised what Elise had done to them, it bothered him having her taken into custody and left behind in a cell, tended to by Underwood's deputy. Though he knew she was guilty, he blamed her mother for misleading her. The marshal told him that he would see to it that formal charges were made upon their return, but he saw the need for rapidly following the *Bonny Lass*. They would confront Lena Peck later.

Still in his gray suit, Douglas felt completely out of place pacing the floor of the boat. Leathers had offered him a seat in the bow, near the wheel, but he couldn't sit. Pacing kept his nerves from getting the best of him. However, his mind was taking him to dark and horrible places. Visions of Marcus touching Cora—*hurting* her—drifted in and out of thought.

An hour passed, but it seemed like an eternity. The sun was lower on the horizon. They had to find her before it set.

"I see a boat!" the cub pilot yelled, pointing out the front window.

Douglas's breath caught, as he gazed anxiously to where he pointed.

"It could be the *Lass*," Captain Leathers said, craning his neck and firmly holding the wheel.

"It looks as if it's slowing down," Douglas said. He went out the side door and sprinted to the front of the boat. His heart raced. He recognized the bright red pad-dlewheel.

The *Natchez* was steered close to the side of the *Bonny Lass*.

Douglas rushed to the side facing her and gazed over the rail, looking for anyone who might be aboard.

"Mista Denton!" Bessie yelled, waving her arms franti-cally.

"Bessie?" There was still some distance between the two boats, but he could see and hear her plainly. "Is Cora on board?"

"Yessa!"

"Is she all right?" His heart thumped as he waited for the answer.

"Yessa! But they's been trouble!"

He needed to get on that boat. Frantically, he looked around, trying to come up with some sort of plan. They were nowhere near a dock and the shallows were dotted with sandbars and other dangers that could easily damage them.

"We can set the plank between the two boats," Captain Leathers said as he walked up to him. "I'll get my men on it."

True to his word, he was gone.

Marshal Underwood stood beside Douglas, gazing across the water at the *Bonny Lass*. "She's a beauty."

"No. The beauty is somewhere on board. I need to see my wife."

The marshal patted him on the back. "We'll get you there."

"Bessie says there's been trouble. You may need to go across with me."

"I aim to." He gazed upward. "Sun'll be settin' soon. I'd like to get back to Memphis." A group of men hoisted a plank from the side of the boat toward the *Bonny Lass*.

"Once we're on board, we can turn both boats around and head back," Douglas said. "I doubt that Cora will want to stay on the boat tonight."

The marshal shook his head. "I reckon you're right. No tellin' what she's been through."

Douglas's thoughts had already taken him there, but having someone else infer it wrenched his stomach. He had to prepare himself for the worst.

Once the plank was put in place and the boats were steady enough for the two men to cross, Douglas and Marshal Underwood crossed over.

What they found on the *Bonny Lass* was a trembling cub pilot and a very dead Marcus Giles.

* * *

"Cora!" Douglas screamed.

"Douglas!" She jumped to her feet and raced into his arms.

He covered her in kisses and held her firmly. "Did he hurt you?"

"Slapped me some, but I reckon I hurt him worse." She gripped him as tightly as she could, making certain he was real.

"Damn, him," he muttered, and cradled her even closer.

"God'll do that. I'm sure of it." She swallowed hard, tears filled her eyes, and she had to speak her mind. "I ain't never killed no one before. My pa learned me how to shoot. We had rats. I didn't wanna shoot a man, but I wasn't gonna let him have me. You're the only one I want touchin' me." Taking a deep breath, she nestled her head against his chest.

Marshal Underwood stepped into the room. "You had every right, ma'am. Killin' in self-defense is lawful."

Even so, she couldn't help but cry. "I had blood all over me. Francine lent me this dress. But—I can still smell him on me."

"Let's get out of this room," Douglas said, guiding her toward the door.

She nodded and looked one last time at Marcus. Francine had forced her to leave his body long enough to wash away the blood and put on clean clothing, but she'd returned to his side. She couldn't simply leave him there. She had to see it through.

"Wait," she said to Douglas, and crossed to the night stand. Her hand shook as she lifted the carved angel and

360 · JEANNE HARDT

held it to her breast. "My pa made this," she whispered through her tears.

Douglas placed his arm around her shoulder and took her from the room. Marshal Underwood lingered behind.

They walked to the steps and went down to the lower deck and stood at the railing. He told her horrible things about Elise, then she told him everything that had happened leading up to the shooting. Talking about it helped and she finally calmed enough to dry her tears.

"So, you saw her naked?" she asked with a frown.

"Yes, but it's what made me realize she wasn't you." He stroked her cheek with the back of his hand.

"Her small breasts?" She wrinkled her nose.

He chuckled. "Well, that and ..."

She sighed, afraid of what he might say.

"She had no mark." He moved his hand to her abdomen and rested it there.

"You mean my birthmark turned out to be a good thing?"

"A *very* good thing." He moistened his lips and bent down to kiss her.

Placing her hands behind his head, she kissed him back, deeper and stronger. When they stopped, she released a heavy sigh. "Douglas? What are we gonna do now?"

"We're going to have our wedding night. I'm going to hold you close and never let you go."

"That's all I want, but I reckon I'll never forget what I done." Even though the marshal told her she was in the right, she kept picturing Giles' face. She stared at the ground.

He lifted her chin. "You did what you had to do and I'm proud of you for fighting back. I hate that I wasn't here with you—that I couldn't protect you."

"But you *were* with me." She touched her hand to her heart. "In here."

"My God, I love you, Cora." A tear fell from the corner of his eye. He embraced her and kissed her again. "I love you so much. If anything had happened to you ..."

"I love you, too," she said, stroking his face. "I think I loved you 'fore I ever knew you. Don't be scared no more. We're together and Giles is dead. But ..." She turned her head and gazed out over the river.

"What?"

"I'm frettin' 'bout Bessie, and Francine, and the rest a the folks on board. Giles treated them sumthin' awful. And ..." She shook her head and lowered her eyes. "He done made a baby in Bessie."

Gripping the rail, his knuckles turned white as he grasped it tighter and tighter.

She lovingly placed her hand over his with a soothing touch. "He told her that when the baby came they was gonna throw it in the river." Her eyes filled with tears. "He was gonna kill it."

"Cora, we'll take her home with us. We can return to the estate. There's plenty of room there."

His words gave her hope. "And she can keep the baby?"

"Of course. It will give Billy someone to play with." His smile warmed her. "I promise you that she'll be treated well. If I'm going to return home, I'm going to have a talk with Father and let him know that some things will have to change."

"Will he listen?"

"I believe he will. Especially when everything comes to light about Cameron's death. He won't be able to blame me any longer."

For a short time, they stood there saying nothing, lost in the comfort of each other's embrace. A warm wind blew across the river and the sun sank lower and lower on the horizon. Wisps of lavender and orange painted the sky.

The boats traveled at a good pace. The *Bonny Lass* followed the *Natchez.* Manned by the cub pilot, Luke Waters, Cora told Douglas that they were in much better hands. Luke was quite able and had been a favorite of William's. And unlike the co-pilot, Marcus didn't throw Luke off the boat. For some reason, Marcus saw fit to trust Luke. Maybe because he was young and easily intimidated.

"Cora?"

They both turned to the soft, sweet voice of Francine. Her arms were folded across her chest and her hair flowed freely in the gentle breeze.

Cora moved from Douglas and took Francine's hands in her own. "Are you all right?"

Francine shook her head. "I could not do it." Her voice trembled as she spoke. "I could not pull the trigger."

"But you saved Cora," Douglas said. "If you hadn't come to the room ..." He stopped and his voice drifted away.

"He's right, Francine," Cora added. "You an Bessie came in time. I'll never be able to thank you enough."

Francine moved to the rail, facing away from them. When she turned back around, her cheeks were streaked with fresh tears. "What will I do now?"

Cora found it an odd question. She assumed Francine would continue doing what she always did. "Don't you wanna stay on the boat?"

"I don't know. How can I? The *Bonny Lass* belongs to you. Why would you want me to stay?"

Cora smiled at Douglas, who nodded as if he knew what she was thinking. "Giles tried to ruin this boat. She needs someone takin' care of her who loves her. Someone who cares as much as William did."

Francine ran her hand over the rail. "I love her. She's been good to me."

"Then stay." She moved beside her. "Luke can handle her and we can find someone to be a co-pilot. Most a the crew's still on board. They was scared a Giles, but they trust you. If you mind your manners, I reckon you can get business goin' strong again." She placed her hand on Francine's shoulder. "You just gotta remember to leave the married men alone. Let their *wives* make them happy."

Francine wrapped her arms around her and squeezed. "*Merci*, Cora. You are too kind." She sniffled and raised her eyes, looking at Douglas who stood over Cora's shoulder. After releasing her, Francine stepped back and smoothed her dress. She pulled her shoulders back and once again looked like the confident woman Cora remembered her being. "Douglas? I hope I'm not being too bold, but please tell me. How is your brother? I've thought of him often."

Cora turned her head, looking to Douglas for help. The night she heard Francine and Cameron in the hallway seemed like another lifetime ago.

"I'm very sorry, Francine, but my brother died," Douglas said, gently. "A carriage accident last month."

Francine covered her mouth. "Oh ... I am so sorry." The smile that had been there briefly, disappeared.

"He spoke well of you," Douglas said. "You made an impression on him."

"He was good to me," Francine said, holding her hand to her breast. "Men like Marcus enjoy hitting women, but Cameron was different. He was gentle."

Cora looked into Douglas's eyes, searching his reaction to Francine's comment. From everything he'd told her about his brother, few had been positive. If any.

"I appreciate knowing that, Francine," Douglas said. "That was a side of my brother I was unaware of."

Francine stepped forward, reached up, and placed her hands on the sides of Douglas's face, then stood on her tip-toes to kiss his cheek. Then she walked slowly away, leaving them alone again.

Cora rubbed his back, while they peered out across the water, lost in their own thoughts. Time couldn't pass quickly enough for her. She wanted to set foot on land again and to change the events of the day. It had started perfectly and she prayed it would end the same.

She was surprised to see both Mary and Arthur Wellesley waiting for them to dock in Memphis. But then Marshal Underwood explained that he'd had his deputy send a messenger to the Wellesley estate to tell them about what had taken place, and let them know they'd gone after the *Bonny Lass.*

The relief in Mary's eyes was all Cora needed to see to assure her how much she loved her only son. She understood. She felt the same way about Billy.

They all gathered on the dock as the marshal stated plainly what was going to take place. "The *Bonny Lass* will remain docked until all matters are settled," he began, looking sternly at Luke Waters.

Luke nodded and so did Francine, who stood to his left.

The marshal looked upward. "It's pert near dark. I'll need to hurry if I'm gonna reach the Peck's 'fore it's too late."

"I'm going with you," Douglas said.

Arthur puffed out his chest. "As am I. I intend to get to the bottom of this."

"Well you ain't goin' 'thout me," Cora added.

"Or me," Mary said timidly. "There's much that needs to be settled."

Marshal Underwood scratched his head. "Y'all ain't makin' this easy, but I reckon we'll all go."

"I *need* to be there, Marshal," Mary said, then glanced at her husband. "Lena and I need to clear the air."

It was an odd thing for her to say, but then again, Mary and Lena had a very long history. Cora found it even stranger that when Mary made her remark, Arthur looked away as if he was ashamed.

Had it not been for the three-quarter moon, it would have been difficult to see the Peck home. By the time they arrived, it was well past eight o'clock.

Cora clutched her breasts, leaned in, and whispered in Douglas's ear. "I can tell it's time to feed Billy. Reckon we can stop by the boardin' house 'fore we go back to the hotel?"

He smiled at her and nodded. "And if Sophie has already fed him?"

She wrinkled her nose. "I'll figger sumthin' else out." She grinned as he bent and kissed her on the forehead.

Marshal Underwood knocked on the door. Pulsing light shined through the front window, growing brighter as it neared the door.

"Who's there?" Edward Peck cried out.

"Marshal Underwood. I need to have a word with Mrs. Peck."

The door opened, one slow inch at a time. Edward stood there gaping, wearing a long robe that brushed the wood floor.

"Where's your wife?" the marshal asked, peering into the house.

Edward cleared his throat and coughed. "In bed. Said her head was aching."

Mary pushed past the marshal and entered the house. "Lena!"

The marshal tried to stop her and insisted it was his job to handle Mrs. Peck. But Mary ignored him and went further into the house.

"Lena!" Mary cried again.

"Mother," Douglas said, "you need to let Marshal Underwood do his job."

"No," Mary said, firmly. "I should have done this years ago." Looking around the room at each one of them, she began to cry. "Lena!"

"What's going on here?" Lena asked as she entered the room, rubbing her temples. "Mary? Have you completely lost your mind?"

When Lena saw Cora and Douglas standing behind Mary, her eyes drew open wide and her upper lip twitched out of control. Even in her nightgown and robe, she was well put together, but her expression showed that at any moment she might crumble.

"Douglas? Cora?" Lena clasped her hand to her breast. "Why are you here? The two of you should be wrapped up in a lover's knot in your hotel room."

Marshal Underwood stepped between them and Mrs. Peck. "Lena Peck," he said formally, "I have evidence that you conspired with your daughter to deceive Mr. Denton and pass her off as her sister, Cora."

Lena released an obnoxious laugh. "Me? A conspirator?"

"I'm also led to believe," he continued, "that you played a part in the death of Cameron Wellesley and his fiancée, Vivian Stamford."

Lena waved her hand at him as if to dismiss him. "You're all mad."

Arthur stepped forward. "Lena," he said with a quivering voice. "Is this true?"

Lena shifted her gaze to meet Arthur's. Cora recognized something. The two of them were very *familiar*.

This was more exciting than any book she'd read. She'd never dreamed that her life would take such an incredible turn. This was as amazing as Jane Eyre discovering the hidden wife.

"Arthur," Lena replied, "I would never hurt Cameron. You know I cared for him like I would my own son."

"And what about Miss Stamford?" the marshal persisted.

"What about her?" Lena sneered.

"Your daughter claims that you placed the box holdin' the snake inside the carriage." Marshal Underwood stepped closer to her and she backed away.

"My daughter?" Lena feigned surprise. "Oh, you must mean, Elise. Where is Elise by the way?"

"Locked in a cell," Marshal Underwood said, crossing his arms over his chest. "Seems she can't stop talkin'."

His words sunk deep and the expression on Lena's face made Cora realize that everything Elise had said was true. But she knew there was more. Her heart thumped as she waited with anticipation.

"Tell him about Cameron's mother!" Mary shouted, moving across the floor as fast as her small frame would carry her. "Tell him what you did to Annie!"

Mrs. Peck did sumthin' to Cameron's ma?

Cora's head spun. But the more that was said, the more she became engrossed in the tale. Her eyes moved from person to person as they spoke, and in her mind she tried to keep their stories straight and piece together this confusing puzzle.

Lena scowled at Mary. "Be quiet!" She eyed the marshal. "Mary is not in her right mind. As I told Douglas, just this afternoon, she should be hospitalized!"

Mary faced Lena squarely, shaking her finger in her face. "No more lies, Lena! You know I'm as sane as you are. Though I'm not certain that speaks well of me."

Lena crossed her arms, sat in a chair, and pursed her lips.

Mary whipped around, facing the marshal. "She killed her!"

"Vivian?" the marshal asked.

"No." Mary's voice fell to a whisper. "Annie. She killed Annie."

Cora gasped and clutched Douglas's arm. He looked down at her with as much sorrow and confusion in his eyes as she felt. But he, too, remained silent, obviously trying to sort out the details just as she was.

Arthur breathed heavily. "My Annie? But ... it was an accident ... her carriage ..." His voice fell away as his face revealed an understanding of the truth.

"Another carriage *accident*?" the marshal asked.

Mary nodded, then looked at Arthur with pity. "Lena was in love with Arthur, but he was married. I knew they'd been meeting secretly. She was my best friend and I kept her confidence. When she came to me and told me that she'd planned a way for them to be together, I told her—I *begged* her—not to do it."

All eyes shifted to Lena, who was folding into herself; defeated.

"She wouldn't listen to me," Mary continued. "I followed her to the livery and tried to convince her to change her mind. She knew Annie would be going home to visit her parents. Lena thought that all she'd have to do was loosen the carriage wheels and that would take care of everything. I couldn't watch her do it. I stood outside the stable. And even though I didn't see her loosen them, I knew she'd done it when she came out with her smug smile. She clapped her hands together and said that it was all taken care of. I should have gone for help, but I was young and scared. I prayed it wouldn't work, but when it did, she went to Arthur to give him comfort. She asked me to accompany her so that no one would suspect her. So ... I did."

Arthur paced the floor and said nothing.

"I'd never met him before." Mary's voice fell to a whisper. "I felt compassion for him. He loved Annie, and he and I shared a common grief. We knew what it was like to lose a spouse and we both had children who needed a parent."

"You took him from me!" Lena yelled. "You knew I loved him and you wormed your way into his bed!"

Mary shook her head. "No, that's not how it was. We fell in love."

"Please!" Arthur yelled. "I can't take any more!" He strode across the room and glared down at Lena. "Why? Why did you take my wife and my son?"

Lena grasped his arm. "You said you loved me. I was to be the woman of your estate. The one to raise your son as my own. Instead, I had to settle for him!" She pointed an angry finger at Edward. "He couldn't even give me a child, so I had to take one. And I was determined to see to it that she would get what I never did. It was all supposed to be mine!"

"Lena?" Edward's meek voice filled the large room. "I ... I loved you ..."

"You made a very big mistake," she snarled.

Marshal Underwood took her arm and snapped a cuff on her wrist. "I've heard enough." He looked around the room at all the stunned faces. "Everyone here has heard more than enough."

He was right. Anger turned to sadness on almost every face in the room. For a day that was supposed to be happy, today would be one Cora would never forget. At least it was all out in the open now, and folks could get on with their lives. Including her and Douglas.

Douglas placed his arm around Mary. "Let's go home, Mother."

"Mary?" Arthur was calm now. "You could have told me. I never understood why you were always so guarded. Why didn't you tell me?"

Mary took a deep breath before answering him. "I was ashamed. I should have stopped her."

Arthur pulled Mary close and whispered words that Cora couldn't hear. Then he raised his voice, "Let me take you home. Our son has a bride to tend to."

Cora shook her head. "I'd understand if you need Douglas to come home. My head's spinnin' and I reckon it's far worse for y'all."

Mary moved away from Arthur, then kissed Cora's cheek. "No. He belongs with you. Thank you, Cora."

"What for?"

Mary smiled and stood taller than Cora had ever seen her. "For helping my family heal."

Arthur took Mary's hand and led her out the door to their waiting buggy. The driver hopped down and helped them in and in no time they were out of sight.

Marshal Underwood escorted Lena from the house and with the help of Cora and Douglas, returned with her to the jail, where she joined Elise.

"I reckon it's gonna be a very long night," the marshal said, scratching his head.

Cora and Douglas looked into each other's eyes. With a smile, they silently agreed ...

Chapter 29

The boarding house was a welcome sight after Cora's horrific experience on the *Bonny Lass*. Though she looked forward to returning to the hotel with Douglas, she needed to see Billy. Simply to hold him. Douglas took a seat on the sofa, while she crept away to her room and lifted Billy from his crib.

Sophie was snoring loudly and didn't stir.

Cora sat down, placed Billy into the crook of her arm, and opened her dress. He immediately latched onto her and she watched as his tiny hands opened and closed atop her breast. Sighing with contentment, she finally relaxed.

Once Billy ate his fill and drifted off to sleep, she placed him back in his crib, then returned to Douglas. He'd been joined by Mrs. Moss and Daisy, and she could hear Rosie bustling around in the kitchen.

"Come here, my dear," Mrs. Moss said. How it was that she recognized her footsteps, Cora would never know. She went to her and was pulled into a loving embrace. Mrs. Moss kissed her cheek and began to cry.

"Don't cry, Mrs. Moss. I'm fine," she said, and offered her a handkerchief. "It's clean."

Mrs. Moss laughed through her tears. "Douglas told us what happened. I don't want to think about what *could have* happened to you."

"Then *don't* think 'bout it." Cora knelt down in front of her and rested her head in her lap. "He ain't gonna hurt no one ever again."

Mrs. Moss stroked her hair. Cora sat up and took her trembling hand, then pulled it to her cheek. "I love you, Mrs. Moss. I don't want you to worry 'bout me ever again. Douglas is gonna take good care a me."

"Mothers never stop worrying about their children. You'll understand that soon enough."

"It's a very good thing your daddy taught you how to use a gun," Daisy chimed in. "I had no idea when you came to live with me that you'd bring such an adventure into my home."

"Me neither," Cora said, wishing that Daisy hadn't mentioned the shooting.

Daisy clasped her hands together. "It's all been quite exciting. However, I prefer things simple. I don't like trouble."

"Cora won't trouble you any longer, Miss Daisy," Douglas said, lifting Cora to her feet. "My parents have asked that we return to the estate. I believe they need us."

Daisy's eyes widened. "You'll be leaving?"

"'Fraid so," Cora said, encircling Douglas's waist with her arm. "But I reckon you won't have any trouble gettin' boarders. Once folks know what happened, they'll be comin' 'round askin' questions. Could be good for business." She noticed that Mrs. Moss was still crying. "Mrs. Moss, everythin's fine. Please stop cryin'."

"But what will I do when you leave?"

This time it was Douglas who knelt in front of her. "Have you already forgotten? You're coming with us. We wouldn't want it any other way."

Muffin's bell jingled and she jumped past him into Mrs. Moss's lap.

"And Muffin, too, of course," he added.

Rosie entered the room, wiping her hands on a towel. "What you two still doin' here? Thought you was havin' a weddin' night. Hard to do with so many folks 'round."

A familiar heat rose in Cora's cheeks.

"You're right, Rosie," Douglas said. "We should be going."

Cora took his hand, and leaned into his shoulder. "I'm ready whenever you are."

"Then let's go." The look in his eyes sped the beat of her heart.

* * *

Douglas hesitated before returning to the hotel. He paid the inn keeper for a different room. One that didn't face the river ...

By special request—and an additional stipend—a steward brought in several buckets of hot water and poured them into a large tub. Though it wasn't enough to fully bathe, it was enough for them to wash away the memories of their tumultuous day.

As Douglas moved a washcloth across his face, he thought about everything he'd learned in a very short period of time. Now he understood why his mother was always so nervous. She'd guarded a secret which taunted her and tore at her soul. Fearing she'd lose her husband and everything she had, she'd kept it hidden deep within her. It came out in the form of nervous gestures and insecurity, always intensifying when Lena was around.

"What are you thinkin' 'bout?" Cora asked, reaching her hand to his face.

He sighed. "Forgive me. I keep thinking about Mother. I hope that Father will be good to her."

She brushed his cheek with her fingertips and smiled. "Least he knows what happened. I reckon she'll feel better now that she told him everythin'."

"I'll always be honest with you, Cora." He kissed her forehead, then pulled her against his chest. "Always."

She nuzzled into him. "Me, too."

They stood, locked in an embrace and didn't say a word. They simply relished the pleasure of being together. After moments passed, she moved away from him and gazed out the window.

"Look, Douglas." She pointed at the glittering stars. "Ain't it beautiful?"

Coming up behind her, he ran his fingers through her long hair, which cascaded all the way to the middle of her back. "Yes, it is," he whispered, with his mouth close to her ear.

With gentle fingers, he moved the fabric from her shoulders and kissed her bare skin.

She turned in his arms. "Everything's gonna be all right now, ain't it?"

"Oh, yes." He pushed her hair back from her face. "Perfect." He no longer wanted to talk about the events of the day or the surprise revelations from his mother and Lena Peck. He wanted to concentrate on his beautiful wife. "You're the most incredible woman I've ever known."

She lowered her head. "I don't understand what you see in me."

"How many times will I have to tell you?" He lifted her chin. "I love you."

"I love you, too."

Taking her face in his hands, he inched closer to her. He placed a tender kiss on her forehead, then a tiny peck on the tip of her nose, then brushed his lips across hers, until he couldn't hold back any longer, and kissed her fully.

Sliding his hands down her body, he explored every curve. His palms glided across the fabric of her dress and he wanted desperately to feel her skin.

"Cora," he breathed her name as his lips moved down toward the nape of her neck.

Her body quivered against his and her breathing was heavy and staggered. She helped him unfasten the buttons on her dress, then he easily pushed it to the floor.

She stood before him in her undergarments—ones which Francine gave her to replace the blood-soaked garments she'd been wearing. Her chemise was made of soft silk, and he slid his hands over the smooth fabric, instantly receiving a response from her full breasts.

Coyly, she looked up into his eyes. Then biting her lower lip, she crossed to the bed. She lay back and perched herself on the edge.

He cocked his head. Her behavior seemed a little odd.

As he crossed to her, she inched down even further, then removed her undergarment and opened her legs.

He didn't want to embarrass her. Assuming this must have been how William had her, she knew nothing else. The only reason *he* had an idea of what should be done with a woman was from countless recanted tales from Cameron. Stories which he would have preferred not to hear. But something deep within him screamed that there was more to making love than the physical act, even though his body begged for it.

He would take things slowly ... They would learn together.

Placing his hand on her bare thigh, he moved it up and down in a tender caress. Her skin was soft against his heavy hand and the hunger in his body grew. He thought his heart would most certainly beat out of his chest. He could scarcely breathe. His senses were attuned to every part of her; the scent of erotic perfume that Francine misted onto the chemise, the rise and fall of her breasts as her breathing became rapid, and the tiny whimpers coming from deep within her telling him that she was ready for him.

Her legs parted even further.

His heart pounded—seeing her this way—and his mouth dried like an empty riverbed. He undressed as quickly as he could, bursting with more love for her than he knew he possessed.

Moving to the side of the bed, he reached beneath her body and lifted her.

"What are you doin', Douglas?" she asked, with wide eyes. Tenderly, he laid her down against the pillows.

"I'm going to make love to you," he whispered and brushed his hand down her side. He positioned himself beside her and began to trace every inch of her with the tips of his fingers.

She trembled and closed her eyes to his touch. "I figgered you'd wanna put it in me."

"Oh ... I do ..." He was endeared by her simple honesty.

"Well ... I don't understand. Why didn't you?"

He rose up on one elbow and with his other hand cupped her cheek. "Give me time." Bending down, he kissed her with all the love he held. His lips surrounded hers and without words spoke volumes.

She responded as he'd hoped and kissed him back with fervor and eagerness.

He tugged at the ribbons tying the front of her chemise. The fabric opened just enough to reveal her breasts. They were as he remembered; full and firm. The breasts of a loving mother and passionate wife. No longer fearful, he touched them as he'd longed to do and circled them with his fingertips. He then followed his fingers with gentle kisses and received a low moan from her in response. Her entire body quivered.

Moving his hand further down, he touched the area where she indicated *it* lay and circled it with the pads of his fingers. "I'll be forever grateful for your mark."

She sat upright and tentatively lifted the chemise. Then with a deep breath, she pulled it up and over her head and tossed it onto the floor.

As she lay back down, he smiled and showed his affection by running his hand over the raised skin. "No matter how many lives Madame Beaumont told you that you lived before this one, all I care about is that you're here with me now. When you told me about her and what she said about your mark, *and* about Billy ... you were very afraid." He continued his caress and followed his touch with gentle kisses.

"I'm not scared anymore, Douglas. I want you to see all a me."

"I *want* all of you," he rasped, then rolled over onto her.

* * *

Cora gasped. How could someone else's flesh against hers feel so wonderful? She finally understood. This was how it was supposed to be.

They shall become one flesh ...

Her eyes couldn't get enough of him. She was finally close enough to see each line of his handsome face and every rippling muscle in his arms and chest. Running her hands along his back, she felt each perfect part of him. Then she became bold and moved her hands lower, passing over his firm buttocks, then back up again to his waist. A piece of heaven was at her fingertips.

He moaned as her fingers wandered and her heart beat stronger and faster in anticipation of their union. This wasn't like any of the times with William. It wasn't a daily task or something she had to do. She wanted this. She wanted *him*.

Her legs inched slowly apart, and as his mouth covered hers in a deep, penetrating kiss, he moved into her in a firm, slow steady thrust. "Yes, Douglas," she rasped, and raised her hips to welcome him.

She wanted to cry out with joy, understanding what it meant to make love. The movement came naturally to her. Their bodies rose and fell together, completely in tune to each other and perfectly joined. He filled her body with his own and all the while he caressed her and whispered soft, reassuring words of love.

Warmth permeated every part of her, then it happened. A strange, but intoxicating sensation swept over her, beginning at the point of their union and bursting out all the way to the tips of her fingers and toes. She panted and pulled him tightly to her. Their movement became frantic and intense as she held on, continuing on to a place she'd never been before. A feeling unlike anything else that bound her to him forever.

"Douglas!" She arched her back, and when she pulled back down, she brought him with her. He moaned and cried out, then clung to her with a final thrust.

Damp with sweat, and quivering with unexplained satisfaction, they eased to a halt. He buried his face in her hair, then rose and gave her a feather-soft kiss. Though their bodies were no longer moving, he continued to pulse deep within her.

"Oh ..." she rasped. She didn't want it to be over.

Licking his lips, he nodded slowly, and his breathing steadied. All the while, his eyes remained affixed to hers.

"Ain't you got nothin' to say?" she asked. Unable to keep her hands still, she moved her fingers into his hair with hopes for more to come.

He took a deep breath and grinned. "*Dang* ..."

She giggled and pulled him down, ready to start again.

Acknowledgements

There are so many people to thank for making the publication of "Marked" possible. But first and foremost, I thank God for His many blessings in my life and for surrounding me with people who love and care about me. It's easy to write about love when my heart is filled with His.

My husband, Rick, is my never-ending source of encouragement and ideas. Without his support I wouldn't have been able to devote my time to do this. He is the love of my life and I believe there's a little part of him in every hero I write.

Thank you to Julia Jones for listening to my idea for this book and giving me the nudge to put it on paper. And to my former coworkers, Kim Gray, Bobbie Bauer, and Darlene Elmore, thank you for listening to my non-stop chatter about my characters and for reading what I wrote. Kim was the first one to ever read a completed chapter, and if she'd said it was horrible, I probably would have quit right then. I'm glad she liked it. And Bobbie was kind enough to read this book more than once to help me find those annoying typos!

Thank you to my local chapter of RWA, Music City Romance Writers. I've learned a vast amount about writing from this talented group of women. I want to give special thanks to Tina Reid for doing my first round of edits when this book was in its infancy, and to Cindy Brannam for doing the final edit and getting me off my tail to get it published. She definitely went above and beyond, helping me. And somewhere in the middle, Kristin Anders did a read through and gave me her honest opinion on areas that needed polishing. That was a great help, Kristin! Thank you to Joy Dent for doing a final read through, and also for suggesting Rae Monet as a cover artist, and Jesse Gordon for formatting. They are both awesome and gave my book the professional touches it needed. Also, thank you to Dana Sieders for her great notes and read through prior to the final edit. They helped me put on that last coat of polish before sending it on.

Thank you to all of my Beta readers who helped find errors, and told me when something didn't sound quite right or maybe needed to be expanded on. But mostly, they gave me their honest opinions and pushed me forward. I especially want to thank Diane Gardner who not only found those pesky typos, but also sent me great resources on publishing and marketing. Thank you to all my other Beta readers: Birgit Barnes, Delana Cart, Shawn d'rae Johnston, James McCormick, Stacy O'Brien, Lisa Rehl, Judy Reynolds, Lateia Sandifer, Diana Steele, Judy

Story, and Susan Tucker. You all are wonderful and keep me smiling!

Thank you to Laura Sable and Bill Wiemuth for their professional insights on steamboats, and for taking me and Rick on a tour of the American Queen and arranging the tour of the Delta Queen. I'm so happy that you both enjoyed the book and that I was able to give it the historic, majestic feel that these magnificent boats hold within them.

Thank you to Hugh and Marie Nichols who gave their unending support. And Hugh…sorry that Marie's reading took precedence over other things for a while!

I want to give a special thank you to my sister, Julie Wieringa, and my son, Nathan. They don't read romance but have never stopped encouraging me to write it. Thank you for always believing that I could do whatever I set my mind to.

Thank you to my dad, Bob Launhardt, for introducing me to Gregg Olsen, the first published author I'd ever met. And thank you, Gregg, for encouraging me to write what was in my heart, for answering all of my endless questions, and for steering me in the direction of Romance Writers of America.

And last, but by no means least, I want to thank my mom, Janet Launhardt, who has always been my biggest fan in whatever I've attempted to do with my creativity. She's read every book I've written and loves to share them with her friends. I'm glad she can finally hold a real, published novel in her hands with my name on it.

You can stop holding your breath now, Mom. :)

COMING IN THE FALL OF 2014

Tainted
River Romance, Book 2

Despite her new position as manager of the *Bonny Lass*, Francine DuBois doubts her abilities. After all, the only skill she's ever been recognized for is entertaining men and giving them pleasure. But she'll never let her insecurities show in the presence of the new captain. In her opinion, he's not old enough to be a pilot and will never measure up to his predecessor.

Luke Waters may be young, but he's determined to prove that he's more than capable. He'll show everyone that he's the best pilot the Mississippi River has to offer. His only problem is the new crew manager. His religious upbringing taught him to frown on women of her profession, so how can he bring himself to overlook her way of life and work beside her?

Which is worse? A tainted past, or a tainted opinion?

* * *

To find out all about upcoming releases, be sure to follow Jeanne Hardt on Facebook: facebook.com/JEAN NEHARDTAUTHOR

And on her website: jeannehardt.com

Made in the USA
San Bernardino, CA
17 September 2014